ALL THINGS
BEAUTIFUL

What Reviewers Say About Alaina Erdell's Work

Off the Menu

"In terms of the actual writing, Erdell has an easy-to-read writing style. She excels at creating chemistry between the main characters and she is not afraid to have the characters do things that are not necessarily in line with expectations around romance novels. ...I like the way Erdell writes chemistry. I loved the restaurant setting and how awesome it was to have such a realistic feel for it. ...Erdell's books explore genuine character flaws rather than romanticised ones and I am here for it."
—*Lesbian Review*

Fire, Water, and Rock

"Erdell's love for the desert flowed out of the story like a love poem. One of my highlights of the book was getting to discover the setting through the author's words."—*Lesbian Review*

"When I read a book with themes that I know next to nothing about and the narrative makes me want to go investigate. ...Well, credit must go to that writer. This is Erdell's first published novel and one can easily see the passion she has for storytelling. Using colorful language and vivid detail, she immerses her readers in an impressive story world. Erdell's debut is a compelling and read-worthy tale; it's definitely a sign of exciting things to come."—*Women Loving Words*

Visit us at www.boldstrokesbooks.com

By the Author

Fire, Water, and Rock

Off the Menu

All Things Beautiful

ALL THINGS BEAUTIFUL

by

Alaina Erdell

2024

ALL THINGS BEAUTIFUL

ISBN 13: 978-1-63679-479-2

This Trade Paperback Original Is Published By
Bold Strokes Books, Inc.
P.O. Box 249
Valley Falls, NY 12185

First Edition: January 2024

Credits
Editor: Cindy Cresap
Production Design: Susan Ramundo
Cover Design By Ink Spiral Design

Acknowledgments

Rad and Sandy, thank you for giving me this third opportunity to tell a story. To all those at Bold Strokes who work hard to get our books into the world, I'm so grateful. I'm looking at you, Ruth, Cindy, Toni, Stacia, and the rest of the proofreaders and behind-the-scenes magicians.

I'm grateful to have Cindy Cresap as my editor. She unequivocally makes every manuscript of mine better. We had some hurdles this time, Cindy, but we made it through! Let's hope the next journey is a bit smoother. Thank you for all you do for me.

Thanks to my writing group friends for being so supportive and passing along knowledge of the craft to make this a better book.

I'd like to thank KC for suggesting a great name for a main character. I hope your Leighton gets a kick out of it. To my readers who've enjoyed my books and have given me inspiration through your kind words, I'm so fortunate and appreciative. You inspire me to make the next book even better.

I'd like to express my gratitude to the group of people—dare I say friends—who are willing to read early drafts. Your eagle-eyes, suggestions, and support mean the world. Special thanks to Win, Anne-Sophie, Casper, and Jayne. Thank you also to the many ARC readers who volunteer their precious time to read my book and write a review.

Many thanks to the early readers of the first version of this story who encouraged me to get it published. You embraced a romance that involved alcoholism and domestic violence and the lingering effects those things have, and I'll never forget that.

Thank you to Callie and Caleb for answering all my medical questions and making sure the injuries and treatment were accurate.

A posthumous thank you goes to Leonardo da Vinci and Petrarch for the title. Scholars once believed Leonardo wrote, "*Cosa bella mortal passa e non darte,*" on the sketch of an old woman. They loosely translated Leonard's mirrored handwriting as, "All things beautiful and mortal pass, but not art." Years later, they realized he'd instead written a line from one of Petrarch's sonnets. "*Cosa bella mortal passa e non dura.*" This changed the meaning. "All beautiful mortal things pass and do not endure." By then, I'd already titled my manuscript and wanted to keep the title. Sadly, mortal beauty does not last, but I'd like to think that art does, especially in this digital age.

So many wonderful people gave me feedback and helped me tell this story, and I'm thankful. I wanted to write a story about what happens when we fall in love in a less-than-ideal situation. The reality of the characters' poor decisions and the consequences that resulted needed to be handled in a delicate manner to be believable. We might not be able to help with whom we fall in love, but we have to take responsibility for acting upon those feelings. Your contributions, suggestions, and input were invaluable. I hope readers enjoy Casey and Leighton's journey.

Lastly, thank you to my loving partner for reading another incarnation of this story for the umpteenth time, for your unwavering support, for always being up for a writing date at a café or brewery, and for your willingness to bounce ideas around. I don't take for granted how you walk into a room on a random Tuesday and tell me you're proud of me.

Dedication

For the brave who left and for those who
need to hear that leaving is possible.

CHAPTER ONE

Casey tightened her grip on the pole as the train lurched beneath her. Beside her, Mark shuffled his feet, presumably for balance, but knocked into her anyway, threatening her already precarious mood. She clenched her jaw at the squealing brakes and blast of the overhead speaker announcing their arrival in Queens.

A sleepless night had left her feeling out of sorts, but insomnia plagued her during times like this. She fluffed the hair at her neck still damp from her shower and tried to blink away her weariness. The woman beside her shot her an irritated glance as the train rumbled into the station, so Casey stilled her jiggling leg and inched away.

Mark yawned and gave her a sheepish smile. "I'm glad you set a backup alarm. Leave it to me to set mine for six in the evening instead of the morning."

His sandy hair covered his eyebrows, and she envied his long eyelashes. Add in his flawless complexion, and Casey couldn't help but admire his looks. She'd never been interested in dating him, though. Their friendship and arrangement as roommates suited them.

"We're going to need to buy a coffeemaker if we're getting up this early every day." Casey rubbed her eye.

"Not quite this early. I asked you to set it for six to make sure we weren't late today."

The train came to a stop. Casey exited the car onto the platform, and her swollen backpack bumped into commuters hurrying to board. As she and Mark ascended the stairs at the Vernon Boulevard-Jackson Avenue station, she squinted into the bright sunlight warming the neighborhood. The temperature never dipped too low in August, even overnight.

Mark motioned to a nearby café. "Erica says the food here is good." He checked his phone. "We still have forty-five minutes. Want to grab breakfast?" When she hesitated, he elbowed her. "My treat, to celebrate our first day as students of the great Leighton Vaughn. I know you don't get paid until Friday."

Casey appreciated his thoughtfulness. While the art store paid her every other week, the coffeehouse wouldn't deposit her next check until the end of the month. At least she'd have her tips until then, but she'd need them for groceries and her half of the utility bills. Her checking account balance depressed her, and she didn't want to think about her credit card. "Sure, thanks." A proper breakfast sounded more appetizing than the granola bar in her backpack, and Mark wouldn't have offered if he hadn't meant it.

When they entered the café, the inviting smell of bacon and maple syrup greeted them. Cracked floor tiles and faded framed prints on the walls made the place seem quaint rather than old. So did the way they touted their diner-style fare on the front windows in chipped yellow paint. Customers occupied all of the tables, but she and Mark snagged a couple of stools at the counter and two hot cups of coffee from a waitress passing by with a pot.

Mark studied the sticky menu they shared and ordered pancakes, three types of meat, and eggs over easy. "Hash browns and toast, too. Wheat, please."

Casey ordered an apple turnover, one of the least expensive side items. With her nervous stomach, she wasn't sure how much she could eat, anyway.

The server lifted an eyebrow over her red cat's-eye glasses. "That's it, hon?"

"You better get an order of bacon, so you don't steal mine." Mark stirred some creamer into his coffee.

"Yes, bacon, please." She'd planned on snatching a strip. He knew her well.

The server slid her pencil behind her ear and slapped their ticket beside the short-order cook.

While they waited for their food, Mark texted someone, and Casey distracted herself by watching the cook crack eggs one-handed onto the flat-top grill. She took a large swallow of her coffee, and her mind wandered to the thoughts nagging at her—more time demands, fewer hours to work, and less money. And what about Andy? Was she being selfish? When a plate slid in front of her, and the warm, sweet cinnamon scent rose from the steaming apple turnover, she sighed. Sugar and caffeine. Just what she needed, if only for now. And within minutes, the rest of their food arrived.

"Why didn't Erica come with us?" She didn't live with them, but she had a place nearby.

Mark, lean and muscular in his navy T-shirt, swirled a bite of pancake through maple syrup. How he ate like he did and stayed so fit astounded Casey.

"She wanted to be there early to help get everything ready." He poured more syrup.

Casey looked away to keep from rolling her eyes. She peeled the flaky layers of her pastry apart. "Is she excited?"

"Mostly because she gets to boss me around in an official capacity." He didn't sound thrilled at the prospect.

Mark and his cousin Erica shared an almost sibling-like relationship within their close family, with all the squabbling and competitiveness that entailed. One of the second-year students, Erica would be a teaching assistant in some of their art classes, at least for the first of their two years at the atelier, so she'd have ample opportunity to lord power over him.

Despite her queasy stomach, Casey ate a strip of bacon and a few bites of the turnover. The rest she'd save for later. Mark finished his breakfast while Casey stared into her coffee and wondered if she'd made the right decision.

After paying for their meals and leaving the café, Mark took off down the sidewalk, and Casey struggled to match his long strides. He glanced back and slowed his pace. "Why so quiet? You're not nervous, are you?"

Nervous didn't come close. She had so much riding on her acceptance to Atelier Vaughn. "Some. It feels more real today than it has the past few weeks. Now that we're starting classes, I wonder if I should've chosen to work full-time instead. At least I'd have money to pay my bills and debt." She stepped over a chalk drawing on the sidewalk.

"Your dream isn't to slave away at two minimum wage jobs the rest of your life to make ends meet. *This* is your dream, isn't it?"

She ran her hand through her hair. "Yeah, it is." The magnitude of how much she wanted this opportunity embarrassed her. She'd even had dreams in which she worked in Atelier Vaughn's studio, but she never seemed to complete her painting before the dream ended. She wouldn't be sharing that with Mark. "I've wanted to become an oil painter since the first time I stepped inside the Met. As a kid, I hoped one day to create a piece worthy of hanging in a museum. High aspirations for a third grader, weren't they?"

He laughed. "I never realized you were that young."

"I knew early." She gave him a wry grin.

He nudged her. "Do you know another reason you shouldn't be having second thoughts? No other students arriving today received a full-ride scholarship to go to one of the best art schools in New York, if not the country, me included. That alone should tell you that you're doing the right thing. Who'd turn that down?"

"Sorry. I'm grateful, I am. It must be first-day jitters getting to me. You know I worry about money, and attending classes will cut my work hours in half."

He stopped and took her by the shoulders. "Hey, I'm doing this alongside you. We'll help one another out, and together we'll make it work."

He always knew what she needed to hear, and his generosity in giving it touched her. She one-arm hugged him, then pulled him back into step beside her to keep him from noticing the sheen of tears stinging her eyes.

They'd met at the community college where they'd earned their art degrees, but their education had lacked in expertise and left them in debt. It took them an extra year to graduate while working multiple jobs to afford luxuries like their shared walk-up and food. And through it all, he'd been right with her.

Then, last year, Erica had gotten accepted into Atelier Vaughn, and from what she'd told them, the school appeared to offer everything they wanted. The elite atelier only took the most serious students interested in classical realism and ranked personal referrals high when considering new applicants. Casey and Mark had crossed their fingers and hoped their portfolios, coupled with Erica's letters of recommendation, would be enough to get them in.

It had.

They stopped at the corner and waited for the light to change. This area of Long Island City looked forlorn, with concrete or brick comprising almost everything. Only a few scraggly trees dotted the street. It screamed utilitarian, its purpose pragmatic rather than aesthetic. It was an unusual place for an artistic atelier.

"We could look for better-paying jobs," Mark hadn't dropped the conversation, "or find a less expensive, one-bedroom apartment. I'd be fine sleeping on the couch. Let's not worry just yet. Try to enjoy what we're embarking on, what *you're* embarking on today. You've been given a gift, Casey, and I'm not talking about your talent."

She nodded, and they stepped off the curb in tandem. He was right, as usual, and saw hope where she found worry. It was part of what drew her to him as a friend.

"I'm just as jealous of you as I'm proud of you." He gave her a smile but rolled his eyes.

Her face warmed at his words. When was the last time someone had been proud of her? She'd never admit it out loud, but she was a bit proud of herself, too. This was important. She'd wanted it, and she'd done everything in her power to get it, painting like a madwoman for a month to fill her portfolio with works she deemed worthy of submitting to the famous artist and atelier owner, Leighton Vaughn.

In the distance, the four red-and-white smokestacks of the Ravenswood Generating Station stood tall along the East River, transporting her back in time to the trips she and her parents made to visit her grandmother in Islip.

That was long ago, she recalled with equal parts fondness and melancholy. Her grandmother died when she was seven. Casey's life might be different if the compassionate matriarch of her family still lived, but that didn't matter now. The past was the past.

Over time, she'd learned she needed to be strong and pursue her goals. Her independent spirit and reliance upon herself were two of the few constants in her life. After all, it wasn't like she had anyone to help her financially. Mark provided emotional support and pitched in more monetarily when he could, but he also struggled to make ends meet, and now he had tuition to pay.

Casey took a deep breath, then exhaled slowly to regroup. Despite her misgivings and second thoughts, she'd make this work. That's what she did. Failing wasn't an option.

CHAPTER TWO

L eighton glanced from the large monitor to see her godmother's name on her vibrating phone. She answered on speaker. "Good morning, Maxine."

"Hello, dear. I won't keep you but a minute. My driver is waiting. How are you feeling about today?"

Leighton clicked her mouse. The thirty-two-inch flat-screen television showed the feeds from each of the atelier's eighteen high-definition surveillance cameras. She'd tweaked their angles until they covered every inch of her art school. Not a single door, window, fire escape, or elevator eluded her electronic eyes. "Confident. I'm rechecking all the cameras now."

The system had been expensive, but it was worth it. It allowed her to sleep at night. Between the cameras, motion and glass-break sensors, and the elevator and doors that required an entry code or key card, her atelier might be more secure than the Pentagon or Fort Knox.

Maxine cleared her throat. "I doubt they've moved since you last adjusted them. And I'll be downstairs the entire time monitoring the front door, so don't fret about that."

"I appreciate it." Leighton rolled her shoulders, releasing the tension. She had enough to worry about today.

Content that all her security systems were working, she smoothed her blouse and skirt. On a normal school day, she'd never wear expensive clothing. No paint would leave its tube today, though, so she wouldn't ruin her new suit, and she wanted to look professional. She slipped into her jacket and checked for lint. First impressions were everything.

Maxine sighed. "Seeing the new students, their faces bright with unbridled energy, excites me. I'm heading out in a few minutes. See you soon."

"All right. Thanks, Max." Leighton was about to add drive safely when the call disconnected. No need. Maxine hadn't driven herself in decades.

Eager to turn her attention from the minutiae of security matters and clothing to her classes and students, she began rehearsing what she planned to say as she zipped her boots. Strange, she'd winged her introductory speech last year. After all, the material came as naturally to her as the exact ratio of ultramarine blue to azo yellow to create the perfect shade of green for wild grasses. Yet her entire being vibrated with anticipation.

This year came with higher stakes. She understood the importance of the incoming class. Her atelier was shedding its fledgling status and beginning to prove her talent extended beyond her artistic skills into teaching. Her students had made names for themselves, winning awards and receiving high praise from esteemed judges. Since early spring, galleries and collectors had paid attention to what was happening at Atelier Vaughn.

She'd always dreamed of continuing the long-held tradition of teaching fine art painting. With the public's obsession with impressionism and modern art, few places taught classical realism, and even fewer did it well. Personal tastes and trends were fine, but classical realism shouldn't become extinct. After all, artists like Rembrandt van Rijn and Leonardo da Vinci deemed it worthy enough.

Now that she'd gotten the atelier running smoothly and garnering attention from potential applicants and respected figures in the art world alike, it was time to move forward with her goals. She'd hired her friend Stefan as a second instructor and asked Erica, her top student, to be her teaching assistant.

This year would put Atelier Vaughn on the map. In the future, they'd attract the best students and produce the top talents of artists painting in this style. Her school's name would be whispered at Sotheby's and Christie's auctions, for good reason. Why shouldn't it? *Her* artistic lineage extended back over two centuries.

The memory of her mentor, Caulfield Canton, rushed in on her. He'd been gone for almost five years, yet, the weight of her grief and her responsibility to him still frequented her. After everything he'd been to her and all he'd taught her, she had a duty to continue his legacy. At least his kidneys had given out before he saw the mess her personal life had become.

Truth be told, the course of events that had taken place still stunned *her*. She hadn't seen it coming. Of course, no one ever thinks it will happen to them, but she'd learned from it and vowed she'd never trust her heart to someone like that again. It wasn't worth the risk.

Her phone vibrated.

She smiled as she answered. "Hi, Stefan."

"Hey, Leighton. Just wanted to tell you I'll meet everyone in the studio. I'm bringing doughnuts, and I'll get the coffee started."

Again, she put the phone on speaker and slipped the manila envelope into her bag. "That's great. I haven't had coffee yet, and I need some. I'll meet the students in the gallery and bring them up. Are you still willing to give everyone a crash course on the layout of the place?"

"Of course. And, Leighton? I'm thrilled we're working together. The small class sizes will be a pleasant change from what I'm used to. I know you had your pick from a lot of great instructors, so thanks for giving me a chance." His voice cracked a little.

She'd never known Stefan to be emotional. He let events roll off him, even back when they were in school. Having him in her daily life again pleased her.

"You were top of my list, and I can't believe you'd think any different. The pleasure is mine. Our students will be better artists, and people, for knowing you. Now, don't be a tease. Go start that coffee. You won't want to associate with me today if I don't drink a cup or two."

He laughed. "Thanks, Vaughn. I'll see you soon."

She dropped her phone into her bag, aware of how much of her confidence today came from having Stefan and Maxine beside her. Granted, she made the make-or-break decisions, but they had her back.

Her mind drifted to the most important of those choices she'd made concerning this year's new class. While Stefan and Maxine helped read through the applications and analyze the portfolios, Leighton had the final say. The second she'd glimpsed Casey Norford's stunning work, a shiver had run the length of her spine. Casey had a natural talent only seen on rare occasions. Critics had once called Leighton a savant, an artistic genius, and *a talent that burst onto the scene once in a hundred years.* She had the newspaper clippings to prove it. Still, had Leighton's own prowess been so pronounced at such a young age?

Casey wasn't *that* young. At twenty-five, she was a few years older than some of the other students. How had her past instructors missed or ignored her gifts? No wonder her essay had expressed regret over her thus far poor experience in art education. Leighton wasn't being hyperbolic. As raw as her skills seemed now, Casey might be the most gifted artist Leighton had encountered, student or professional. Hers had been the first name added to the acceptance list.

Leighton held in her grasp the piece of the puzzle she'd been missing. She planned to refine Casey's talent until the art world knew her name, and by extension, the name of the preeminent atelier that discovered and trained her.

CHAPTER THREE

Casey never would've guessed what the three-story, rectangular brick building housed had she not already known. It looked like an old warehouse with large windows dotting the unimpressive facade, HVAC units protruding from the roof, and a small green awning marking the entrance.

She rang the buzzer beside the wrought iron and glass door stenciled with the school's name. Inside, an older woman at a desk acknowledged them with a sparkle in her eyes and a nod, then released the lock with the push of a button.

Casey held the door open for Mark to enter ahead of her, a little intimidated all of a sudden. But once inside, she inhaled and relaxed. If a scent could make her feel at home, the smell of Atelier Vaughn came close. Her lungs filled with cool air redolent of a mixture of floor wax, jasmine, and coffee. She smiled at the familiar and welcoming scents in what would be her home for the next two years.

The interior of the building looked stunning in contrast to the exterior. What economy had forsaken outside received just attention in here. Casey's rubber-soled sneakers squeaked on the immaculately polished hardwood floor in the art gallery, and she stared at the framed sketches on the walls in awe.

"Welcome." The woman came around her desk to greet them. "I'm Maxine Shipton."

Casey blinked. She should've worn something besides jeans and a SummerStage T-shirt she'd had for years. "Mrs. Shipton?" The woman was the epitome of class. She wore a tailored skirt and jacket with a white silk blouse, and her pumps matched the fabric of her suit. Her jet-black hair fell to her chin and looked like it cost her a fortune in the salon each week.

Casey struggled to recover from her surprise. "I...um...I'm Casey Norford. Thank you so much for my scholarship. I didn't realize you'd be here today."

"Oh, so you're Casey. Please, call me Maxine." She extended her hand. "And, yes, I run the gallery for Leighton."

Maxine's delicate skin reminded Casey of the same baby softness of her grandmother's. "It's nice to meet you."

"I looked forward to putting a face with your name today. Your art impressed me. I think you have much to offer with a bit of guidance." She leaned in and touched Casey's forearm as if revealing a secret. "I think Leighton is the perfect instructor to give you just that."

"Thank you." Casey wasn't sure how to express the enormity of her gratitude. She pressed her hand to her chest. "Your generosity means so much to me. I wouldn't be here without it."

Maxine studied her. "Something tells me you would've found your way." She turned toward Mark and grasped his hand. "And you must be Mark. I see the familial resemblance to Erica around your eyes."

"Yes, ma'am." He shuffled from foot to foot.

"Please, call me Maxine or Mrs. Shipton, if you must. Anything but ma'am. It makes me sound old."

"Maxine." He gave her a boyish grin.

"It's nice to meet both of you." She motioned to the rooms behind her. "Why don't you wander through the gallery? Once everyone arrives, the group will head upstairs together." With that, she returned to her desk and left them to explore.

The gallery comprised three rooms, one opening into the next in shotgun style. Casey and Mark circled the first. In addition to the reception desk, it held small works of what appeared to be students' drawings. A printed sign near the front explained how students earned ninety percent of the proceeds when their artwork sold through the gallery.

"Did you know this?" Casey motioned to it as she marveled at an exquisite figure drawing done in charcoal on blue-toned paper and highlighted with white chalk. It featured a woman facing away, and the likelihood a student had drawn it from life was high.

"Yeah, Erica sold a couple of pieces here last year." Mark moved to the next display. "The gallery has a small but loyal following. Collectors like to get in early on artists they perceive as up and coming. Erica sold a few pieces for other students, too, and even one of Leighton's paintings."

"Erica works here?" Casey turned. "I didn't know that."

"Nah, it's like volunteering, but sort of mandatory. Everybody does it. The upside is you get a commission if you sell something. They have it set up so everyone gets a cut. What's good for one is good for all. Erica said it encourages students to promote the sale of all the artists. I'm sure they'll explain." He walked through the large open doorway into the next gallery.

Casey followed, pondering the ramifications of the revelation. "This might be the best news I've heard all week. I've wanted to quit the coffeehouse for a while now." She twirled her finger in a circle. "It'll be nice having my classes and a source of income in one place, as long as I make enough money doing it."

"I guarantee your drawings and paintings will sell. Erica gets a check every month." He lowered his voice. "And you're a better artist than she is."

Shocked, Casey jerked her head to look at him. Erica was his family. He'd said nothing of that nature to her before. "Thanks." The one-word response was all she could manage.

The second gallery, which appeared to be the largest of the three, held paintings. Were they, too, done by students like the drawings in the previous room? The works were masterful and nuanced, museum quality. Her doubts from earlier about whether she'd made the right decision by applying for acceptance at Atelier Vaughn instead of working to pay off her debt took flight like freed doves at a wedding. The digital renditions of the art produced at the atelier on their website didn't do them justice. If she graduated having gained these skills, the sacrifices she'd have to make over the next two years wouldn't matter. She'd live on beans and rice if it meant learning to paint like this.

Mark pointed to a canvas. "This one's Erica's."

The buzzer at the front door sounded, and Mrs. Shipton welcomed someone new, but Casey's attention remained riveted on the beauty and technique around her. She stopped beside Mark, and they studied Erica's piece.

Bold brush strokes sometimes extended into surrounding areas with a flourish. They gave it an energy, an electricity.

Casey liked it, although she couldn't imagine painting in that style. She'd never been that flamboyant. "Will it be strange to learn from your cousin?"

"I don't think so. She's been teaching me all my life. Erica watched me when Mom had to work, so she got stuck entertaining me. She relied on crayons and markers to keep me out of trouble."

They continued to wander around the room.

Voices from the reception area, now perhaps four or five, grew louder. Casey tensed, listening more closely. Was one Devin's? As casually as she could, she glanced behind her. No. Not yet, at least. Being in the same class as her ex-boyfriend was the only drawback to starting at the school this year, but she'd decided not to let her past hinder her future.

Mark smiled astutely. "Will it be awkward being in class with Devin?"

She hated it when he read her mind, and he did it often. Before she could speak, a painting caught her eye and stole her breath. All she could do was point.

"What?" Mark turned in the direction.

"Look at that." Her voice came out a degree above a whisper. She couldn't have torn her gaze from the canvas if the building were on fire. "It's magnificent."

She inched closer and stared at the captivating nude lying half on her side, half on her stomach, her breasts pressed into the bed. Sunlight streamed in from an unseen window, illuminating her curves and the folds of the sheet.

Casey's breath quickened, and a strong temptation to reach out and run her hand along the woman's body, to explore each hill and valley, almost overcame her.

The painting drew her to it with a magnetism she'd never experienced from a work of art. She wanted to feel the thickness of the sheets between her fingers and touch the draped creases of the fabric. The material looked smooth like percale and translucent where the sunlight hit it. Despite the warm invitation of the painted room, the tableau portrayed a solemn mood, as if she'd intruded on a private moment. Her heart pounded.

Beside her, Mark leaned in. "God, that's beautiful." He gestured to the placard. "It's Leighton's."

"Leighton's." Casey's tone sounded reverent, even to her. Tears stung her eyes, and she tried to blink them away.

Mark turned in a circle, scanning the room. "Oh, I just realized. Our instructors painted all the art in this gallery. The pieces on this wall are Leighton's, and those over there are Stefan's." When she didn't answer, he studied her. "You're pale. Are you all right? You should've eaten more for breakfast."

She continued to stare at the painting.

"You're not going all Stendhal on me, are you?"

More people entered the room as he poked fun at her. His quip broke her trance. She laughed and took a step back. "Of course not. I don't believe in that sort of thing. I just like it."

Mark exhaled a low, even breath. "I'd give my non-brush hand to paint like that." He glanced at his phone. "I wonder how much longer we have. I'm going to find a bathroom." He headed toward the front.

A ding sounded. Someone else arriving? No, it wasn't the buzzer at the front door. But neither the thought nor the noise distracted her from admiring the stunning image in front of her some more.

She leaned closer to view the brushwork. At this distance, her nose inches away, she often found herself in trouble in museums by either setting off alarms or receiving verbal warnings from the gallery attendants. However, she couldn't become the artist she yearned to be if she couldn't examine the brush strokes. The accent light mounted on the ceiling highlighted the exquisite, intricate details of the work, but when Casey tilted her head for an even better look, instead of finding the individual strands of the woman's hair depicted, as she'd expected, masses of tone comprised it. What appeared as blocks of light and dark up close became lustrous waves when Casey stepped back.

And when she did, she smacked into someone.

"Oh! I'm so sorry." She tried to regain her balance, and the firm hands on her shoulders helped. "I didn't know anyone was behind me."

Those same hands, strong and steadying, turned her.

Casey stood face-to-face with Leighton Vaughn. If the painting had captivated her, the woman who'd painted it put her awe into perspective.

When she'd imagined this day, she'd envisioned Leighton in artist's garb, like paint-splattered coveralls and a bandana, but she wore an impeccable gray skirt and matching jacket, crisp white shirt, and knee-high black boots that hugged her calves. Her glossy, light brown hair brushed her shoulders. More than all that, though, she had a regal presence with her straight back and confident air.

One single thought occupied Casey's mind. *Damn.* Leighton's Wikipedia photos hadn't affected her like this. Nor had her reputation or the acceptance letter to Atelier Vaughn she'd received. Or even the full-ride scholarship. What *was* this?

Leighton's intense brown eyes enthralled her the most. Like a shot of espresso, they possessed a richness and depth. Casey had a sense she knew her, although she was certain they hadn't met before. She'd have remembered. They stared at one another a beat before Leighton squeezed Casey's shoulders, then released her.

"Steady now?"

Casey's mouth went dry. "I am, thanks. And sorry, I didn't know you were there."

"You mentioned that." A gleam of amusement flashed in Leighton's eyes.

What a lousy first impression. Maybe if Casey didn't mention her name, Leighton might forget who almost bowled her over. But what could she say? "Did I hurt you?" It was the only thing that came to her.

Leighton executed a graceful wave down the length of her torso as though advertising a Murano glass vase on the Home Shopping Network. "Do I appear injured, Casey?"

So much for going incognito.

"No. You look great." Oh, no. Had her voice lowered? Had her eyes lingered anywhere too long? Heat climbed up her neck and face, all the way to the tips of her ears. "I mean—" She cleared her throat. "No, you don't look injured." She swallowed and motioned like Leighton had done, but her movement looked clumsy, like she had a broken wrist. "You look…normal." She wanted to bolt outside and throw herself into traffic. It'd be less painful than this conversation.

"Normal?" Leighton arched her eyebrow. "No one's ever given me a compliment quite like that before."

Casey winced. *Kill me now.* She rubbed her eyes. "Can I start again?" She indicated the painting. "This did something to me, so I blame you. From the moment I saw it, I've been a bumbling, babbling mess."

"You blame me?" Leighton appeared to be holding back a smile.

The tiny lines near the corners of her mouth that Casey hadn't noticed before now captured her attention. Staring. She was staring. She spun around, fixating on the painting. Its allure bewitched her again. "This is one of the most beautiful things I've seen in my entire life."

Leighton remained silent until Casey faced her again. Then she smiled.

"Now that's a compliment," she said, her voice low and melodic. She squeezed Casey's elbow. "Come. It's time."

At Leighton's touch, Casey warmed all over. She inhaled, then exhaled, and didn't choke. No stumbling or tripping, either. Whatever effect Leighton's painting had on her seemed to have passed, and she relaxed. Maybe she'd survive her first day after all.

Apart from her stunning looks, what impressed Casey most about Leighton was the magnetic effect she had on everyone. By the time she'd called for the other students to join her in front of the elevator, they'd already drawn close, like tourists viewing *The Starry Night* over at MOMA.

"I'm Leighton. Welcome to Atelier Vaughn." She did a head count. "This is a small compartment, so we'll do this in two groups." She held the doors open. "Second-year students, your codes and key cards are the same as last year. You'll go first."

Mark and Casey waited as the others filed by.

Erica tousled Mark's hair as she passed him.

He leaned away from her touch, his cheeks reddening. "Hey. I didn't see you come in."

Her brown hair was a shade darker than his, but her legs were just as long, bringing her almost to his height. Where his shaggy bangs almost obscured his vision, she kept hers stylishly short.

Someone bumped into Casey. "Hey." It was Devin.

She hadn't seen him in months. He wore his blond hair longer now, and it looked like he'd started working out. She caught a whiff of his favorite cologne, one she'd never cared for. "Devin." She tried to hide her annoyance in her quiet reply, but from the corner of her eye, she caught a glimpse of Leighton watching them, which made her uneasy.

Erica inserted a card into a slot, and the doors slid shut.

As soon as the elevator began its ascent, Leighton pressed the button on the wall to summon it again. She faced them as they waited.

Not wanting her to think she was with Devin somehow, Casey stepped away from him to stand closer to Mark. She'd stood between them many times, but now it seemed strange.

Devin and Mark had been friends their freshman year. They played on the same intramural basketball team and had a handful of art classes together. It'd been a convenient friendship, born of proximity more than anything, and it'd fizzled when Casey and Devin's romantic relationship had come to its disappointing end. While they all remained civil, Casey and Mark no longer interacted with Devin in social settings, even though Mark still saw him at work. Devin had gotten him a job at his family's framing store.

Through Mark, Erica had become friends with Devin and had helped him get into Atelier Vaughn, too. Kismet? Maybe he'd remember to return Casey's precious copy of *The Art of Still Life.*

Casey didn't know the fourth student in their class, a young woman with curly hair and glasses.

"So, my first years." Leighton crossed her arms and assessed them.

Everyone gave her their attention. Heat rushed to Casey's cheeks when Leighton's gaze lingered on her. Self-conscious, she shrugged out of her backpack for something to do, just in case the elevator's small compartment required it for five of them to squeeze inside when it returned.

Mark did the same.

Casey expected some formal introductions to follow, but the lack thereof hung heavy in the air. It appeared Leighton's confidence extended into silences. No one said anything until the elevator dinged its arrival, and they filed inside.

Casey entered last and jumped at the brush of Leighton's hand across her lower back. Her flinch had to have been apparent, but when she turned, Leighton faced the panel of buttons like nothing had happened. Maybe she'd guided her to make sure everyone fit. If only the heat in Casey's cheeks would cool before the crowded compartment came to a stop and she had to face everyone again. Her awareness of the warmth of Leighton's body and the millimeters separating them consumed her attention.

Then the faint scent of a sweet perfume, light yet heady, drifted over her, caressing her senses. Before she could stop herself, she closed her eyes and breathed it in. It might not even have been Leighton's—it could've been wafting off the woman with curly hair—but in that moment, if for Casey only, it was Leighton's. She allowed herself to enjoy it as she faced forward until the doors opened and freed her from the claustrophobic confines and the scent that tempted her to think things she shouldn't.

What greeted her when she exited the elevator made her heart beat faster. If she could fall in love at first sight with a room, she had. With its gleaming maple underfoot and perfect lighting, the grand floor plan extended before her. She glanced up at the high ceilings, the exposed ductwork, and the complex grid of lights hanging above the array of easels in the airy space and grinned, knowing this was where she'd spend most of her time over the next few years.

As Leighton rounded to address the group, she smiled at Casey as if she could read her thoughts. "Now that everyone's together, let's do some introductions. Come." She strode away, the heels of her boots tapping against the floor.

She walked past a small kitchenette toward a cluster of older but comfortable-looking sofas and chairs that formed a ring around a large coffee table strewn with art books and magazines. Shelving filled with more of the same occupied the wall between two windows behind the furniture grouping, creating a tiny library.

A man who'd been sitting at the kitchen table eating a doughnut joined them. He was a couple inches shorter than Leighton, and definitely didn't have her fashion sense. His baggy jeans and threadbare T-shirt looked straight from his hamper.

"Make yourselves at home." Leighton leaned her hip against the end of a sofa, half-sitting and half-standing as she waited for everyone to settle.

Casey sank into a gray sofa, and Mark sat next to her with the curly-haired woman on her other side. A few people lowered themselves cross-legged onto the area rug with their backs resting against the plush furniture.

After Casey's bizarre reactions to Leighton downstairs and in the elevator, being sandwiched between Mark and the woman beside her gave her some solace. But Leighton surveyed the group until she found her, and a fresh wave of uneasiness washed over her. What was going on? Casey studied her fingernails and attempted to brush off the unnerving feeling as jitters.

"I assume you all know who I am." Leighton flashed a smile that held a hint of amusement. "So, I'd like to introduce you to your other instructor." She extended her hand toward the man still munching on his doughnut. "This is Stefan Jovic. He graduated from Rhode Island School of Design, and he's taught at various colleges and universities for more time than he'd like to admit. He'll be sharing teaching duties with me. If I'm not in your class with you, Stefan will be. Be aware, you can bribe him with sweets."

He nodded and stuffed the last bite in his mouth in agreement.

"To his right," Leighton pointed, "is Erica Fitzgerald, our new teaching assistant."

Casey could tell Erica was uncomfortable beneath the bright smile she gave everyone, but even Erica's discomfort couldn't dampen her elation at earning the position. She'd been talking about it for months.

"Erica completed her first year at the atelier and will help run the classes this year while she also continues her own studies. I don't recommend trying her protein bites if she offers. They're terrible."

Erica chuckled and gave a little wave. "Hi, everyone. They're healthy, not terrible. Leighton's not a fan of flaxseed."

"Flax is fine if it's involved in making linen or linseed oil, but I draw the line at having it in my food."

To Casey's delight, Leighton looked haughtier than anyone had a right.

"We're thrilled to have her assisting us, and I think you'll learn a lot from her, even if she's related to you." Leighton winked at Mark.

The football player Casey hadn't known lived inside her wanted to leap in front of him, body sprawled out, to intercept it. She wanted to clutch it to her chest and claim it as hers. For reasons she didn't comprehend, she wished Leighton had winked at *her*. The realization bothered her, almost as much as her other reactions to Leighton did.

Her pulse pounded in her ears. First-day nerves, seeing Devin again, and her uneasiness since meeting Leighton caused her insides to surge. She tried to calm herself with a few deep breaths.

"Let's start with you." Leighton looked at the young man sitting on the floor beside Erica. "Please introduce yourself and tell us something about you unrelated to art."

He wore a Rage Against the Machine hoodie that looked new and a Yankees hat that looked like it might have witnessed Babe Ruth call his shot. He gave her a crooked grin. "You always make me go first. For those who don't know me, my name is Jaiden Delgado, and I'm the fourth of five kids and the only male."

Great. Casey increased her focus on her breathing as her apprehension rose. What was *she* going to share? Something else to freak out about.

"Thank you, Jaiden. I can't imagine what having four sisters is like. I often wondered last year if that's why you spent so many hours in the studio." Leighton laughed softly and looked to the guy sitting beside him. She raised her eyebrows in evident expectation.

In contrast to Casey, Leighton appeared calm and self-assured. With a hand on the back of the sofa to support herself, she'd crossed one booted leg over the other and ran her fingers through her wavy hair. Meanwhile, Casey's anxiety bloomed. She'd never had a panic attack. Was this what it felt like? But what was she panicking over?

"Phoenix Murray," the guy said.

His gentle voice seemed incongruous with his large, athletic body.

"My pronouns are he/him or they/them."

Casey didn't catch all he said.

"…played lacrosse at St. John's."

"Remind me. What position did you play?" Leighton looked to the ceiling as if trying to recall.

"Attacker." When Leighton furrowed her brow, he explained. "I like to score."

Jaiden snickered and flashed the room his perfect grin. Phoenix's jab to Jaiden's leg told them more about Phoenix than his lacrosse tidbit ever could.

Leighton failed to hold back her smile as she looked at Devin. "And you?"

"My name's Devin Glasco. My family owns a framing business, and three generations of us work there."

Casey already knew this. And didn't a framing business have to do with art? Beyond a nostalgic moment of missing his grandfather's homemade hot chocolate, dry humor, and cigar scent, Devin's voice swept past as she battled her nerves.

"That's wonderful, Devin. I'm sure you can enlighten us when it comes time to frame our works." Leighton turned toward the woman with curly hair sitting beside Casey. "And you?"

Casey watched her lips move but missed what she said. Her smile appeared sincere and innocent, though.

"How long have you volunteered there, Jenna?"

"About three years."

Casey tried to focus on the conversation while remembering to breathe. She'd missed whatever had started as a volunteer requirement for Jenna.

"Good for you, Jenna. And you?" Leighton directed the question to the brunette sitting on the floor in front of her, but her glance landed on Casey for a second or two.

Why did she keep doing that? Casey shifted nervously.

"I'm Mikala Ng. I'm a weekend warrior, National Guard, that is." Her pride was as clear as her well-developed biceps in her gray camouflage T-shirt.

"If she needs them, Mikala will have extended deadlines following the weekend each month she trains, but her service is important." Leighton gave Mikala a nod before turning toward Mark.

She grinned at him. "Now that you're here, I'm hoping you'll regale us with embarrassing stories or photos from Erica's childhood."

Mark chuckled. "Hey, I'm Mark. Erica's my cousin if you hadn't picked up on that. Uh, what can I tell you about me?" He scratched his head. "I enjoy playing *NBA 2K23*, if anyone's into that."

Jaiden held out his fist for a bump. "Oh, yeah."

It was time, the moment Casey had been dreading.

Leighton turned to her and smiled. "I wanted to introduce you last." She addressed the others but gestured in Casey's direction. "I'd like to congratulate the recipient of the Shipton Endowment for the Arts Scholarship, Casey Norford." She clapped, and everyone else joined in.

In an instant, Casey's anxiety disappeared. Her hands no longer trembled, and she could breathe. Leighton's smile and congratulations left her more euphoric than when she'd received the scholarship months ago.

The applause dwindled, and Leighton nodded at her.

"Thank you. Hi, I'm Casey."

"Well, Casey. Tell us something about yourself."

Casey had never liked her plain name, but she did when Leighton said it. The way she drew out the syllables in such a languid way made it sound beautiful. That didn't help Casey in her quest for something interesting to say, though.

She didn't have siblings or play video games. Where she'd earned her degree was boring. Besides, her education had fallen short of her expectations, so why draw attention to it? She didn't have hobbies outside of art. Her life held no time for that. And, Leighton had asked for something non art-related. That eliminated her job at the art supply store.

So, with everyone's focus on her, including Leighton's, she chose. After all, the decision had been the most important she'd ever made. She included nothing about it in her application because she didn't want it to influence her acceptance or rejection. It wasn't something she could hide for long, though, nor would she want to. She chose the one thing that guided her every step. She inhaled and looked at Leighton.

"I have a two-year-old son. His name is Andy."

CHAPTER FOUR

L eighton wished she could skip the housekeeping tasks the first day involved now that the introductions lay behind them. These mundane necessities impeded the way to an exciting destination like annoying speed bumps that had to be traversed. She would've preferred an introductory drawing lesson, but she pushed aside her impatience and assessed the semicircle of students.

She surveyed this year's offerings. Devin appeared to be bonding with Phoenix and Jaiden, laughing over some private joke. Jenna, her wide eyes taking in everything from behind her glasses, seemed a bit shellshocked. Casey stood near Mark with her hands in her pockets. Her forest-green shirt complemented her chin-length, dark brown hair and brightened her hazel eyes Leighton had noticed when Casey bumped into her in the gallery.

Casey gave Leighton a tentative smile that showed her dimples.

Casey's revelation she was a mother had surprised Leighton, though she'd tried to appear unfazed by it. Her application hadn't mentioned it, and Leighton would know. She'd read over it at least a dozen times. A toddler, too, by age twenty-five. She couldn't fathom why Casey excluded that. She'd ponder it later. Casey fascinated her, but she needed to get back to the business of the day.

"As I'm sure you've noticed, this is a secure building, but I want you to have twenty-four-hour access to the studio and your work." She opened the large manila envelope she'd left on the coffee table earlier. "Both the building and elevator require an electronic key card that you'll find in here." She handed each new student the smaller envelopes with their names on them. "There's also a four-digit code inside. Should you forget your card or choose not to use it, you can enter your code on the keypads. Please, don't share it with anyone. Second-year students, like I said, yours are the same as last year. I'm sorry you have to sit through this, but I've made some upgrades I want to share with you."

Some of them shrugged, but no one seemed bothered.

"The lights are motion-activated. If you arrive and they're off, you're the first one here. You have one job, and that's making coffee."

Stefan shouted an emphatic "Yes!" from the back of the room. Most of the group grinned and nodded in agreement.

"The ventilation system is also motion-activated." She pointed to the array of ductwork hanging from the rafters high above the easels.

"All this new stuff is great, but are you sure you won't spring for a coffeemaker with a motion sensor?" Jaiden elbowed Phoenix and laughed.

"I looked. They don't make one yet. We'll have to stick with the caveman way." Leighton enjoyed the jokes and banter, but she intended to stay on track.

"These windows face north. As artists, I'm sure you know natural northern light is preferable when painting because it changes little throughout the day. You'll notice that all the southern windows have blackout drapes on them. It'll be a rare day you'll see them open." She crossed the room. "That's why we reserve this side for other uses. Go ahead, help yourself to coffee and a doughnut, and look around."

The group spread out, but Casey held Leighton's attention. Casey wandered toward the bookshelf, but watching her wasn't necessary. It was like Leighton sensed her presence wherever she was in the room.

Casey bent to read the spines of the books.

Curious, Leighton moved behind her to see which title in particular had caught her eye. Ah, a book of masterpieces by Artemisia Gentileschi. When Casey stood, Leighton rested her fingers on her arm. "It's a great place to curl up with a *catalogue raisonné* when you need a break from painting."

Casey looked at Leighton's hand. "I can see myself doing that."

"Yes, so can I." Leighton removed her touch and turned back to the group. "A few final things. I have security cameras installed both here and in the gallery," she pointed to the corner, "and the ventilation system I mentioned is state-of-the-art. One downside of oil paint is that we'll be working with solvents that are hazardous to our health. My goal is to have as few fumes in here as possible, so I've installed this to ensure we're breathing the highest quality air. If the system senses motion in the studio, it's on." She paused for effect.

"Now, I have some non-negotiable rules. The windows are to remain locked at all times. Keep the door to the fire escape closed except in the instance of a fire. Don't prop open any stairwell door or the elevator doors. With the ventilation system we have, it's unnecessary. Breaking these will be grounds for dismissal. Am I understood?"

The joking, jovial atmosphere disappeared. The second-years already knew this, and Leighton's tone and demeanor seemed to have made her point to the first-years. They *all* nodded like bobbleheads.

Good. She was serious.

Slowly, Jenna raised her hand, her eyes again wide behind the rims of her glasses.

"You don't have to raise your hand. Just speak."

"Dismissal? Like, for the day?"

Leighton folded her arms across her chest. "Dismissal, expulsion. Call it what you will. I won't tolerate non-compliance, not on these issues."

Casey straightened like someone had electrocuted her. No one else moved or said a word. Leighton wasn't sure they still breathed.

For a second, Leighton considered her harsh words, but she didn't regret them, or her policies. She had to illustrate the seriousness of the issue, even if she frightened them. She'd put on her friendly face later. First, they needed to understand her rules, even if they didn't know the reasons behind them. Based on their wide eyes and grim faces, she'd gotten her point across.

CHAPTER FIVE

Stunned, Casey stared at Leighton. The reactions of the other first-year students around the studio seemed to be the same. Stunned might be an understatement. Leighton had announced her strange rules so matter-of-factly, like she hadn't just promised the worst repercussion imaginable for the most minor of infractions. And on top of that, she seemed almost pleased by their reactions. Casey didn't understand.

"Let's talk about some of the atelier's other features."

As Leighton passed, Casey felt her presence in the charged air between them. A chill shot through her, and she took a step back, giving Leighton far more room than necessary. She hadn't meant to be so obvious, but moving away had been instinctual, like something warned her to keep her distance. Yet she wanted to be close to Leighton, although perhaps not while she was threatening expulsion. There was something enthralling about her. Casey regretted drawing attention to herself, attention that made her uncomfortable. Whatever Leighton harnessed had power, but Casey hadn't decided if she liked or feared it.

"While natural light is preferable, it isn't always sufficient, and it's not available if you prefer to work at night." Leighton pointed upward. "Each station has a set of bulbs above it. They're tungsten, 3500-5000 Kelvin, white-balanced to mimic natural daylight."

"Are they motion activated?"

Devin proved to be as annoying as ever, interrupting Leighton.

"No. You can turn them on to suit your needs. Each station has a single-mast oak easel." She trailed her fingers along one before turning and resting her hand atop a waist-high cabinet. "You each have a taboret for holding your palette and storing your paints and brushes. These dark boxes are shadow boxes we'll use when we study still life painting." She adjusted the black fabric draped over the top of one.

Leighton seemed bored, like she'd rather be doing something else, and she probably would. Casey understood. She'd fought the duty versus desire battle before.

"We set up each station on a rug with a foam mat underneath." Leighton poked at the edge with her black-booted toe. "It serves a dual purpose: it's easier on your feet, and it keeps paint off the floor."

"Do we need to bring stools?" Mikala surveyed the room.

Casey glanced around, too. Strange. No stools anywhere.

"No, we won't be using them, at least not in the beginning." Leighton leaned on the taboret.

Someone groaned.

"We didn't do this last year." Phoenix's scowl emphasized his opinion on the matter.

Leighton blinked. "No, we didn't."

"So, we'll be using the sight-size method?"

Of course, Devin had to flaunt his knowledge. Casey held in a sigh, remembering why she'd avoided being in the same spaces with him since their breakup. And this was only the beginning.

"That's part of it." Leighton straightened. "More importantly though, I want you to learn to distance yourself from your work and assess it. Standing is the best way to remember to step back once in a while. I grew tired of reminding last year's students," she smiled at Phoenix, "so I'm trying a new tactic."

Casey cringed, thinking how her feet would feel after a day of standing at an easel, then working a shift on the hard floors of the art store. She made a mental note to save for a pair of comfortable shoes.

Leighton must have noticed the disgruntled looks around her. "It's only temporary. Once you're in the habit of stepping back and assessing your work, I'll let you sit if you still want to, but by then, many of you won't."

Stefan laughed. "Look at their faces. I told you they'd balk when you made me haul the stools to the third floor." He unwrapped a Starburst and popped it in his mouth.

Leighton shot him a look. "Haul? It took you one trip up the elevator. And don't pretend you don't agree with me."

Casey caught a hint of teasing by the way Leighton's mouth twitched. They must be friends. It'd be nice to have a place to learn where she knew everyone and felt like she belonged. She wanted to connect with these people, both the other students and her instructors. They had much in common, including their love of an artistic practice that had fallen by the wayside. She saw herself laughing, joking, and feeling at home while in the studio.

Leighton tilted her head toward Stefan. "Would you like to take it from here?"

He stepped forward. "Sure. You're welcome to use the kitchen, just please clean up after yourselves. If you need to keep any food items frozen, put them in the refrigerator's freezer. The chest freezer is for palettes and brushes only."

"The freezer?" Devin chuckled.

Casey caught herself tapping her heel with the toe of her other shoe and stopped. Devin would be in her life again, and she'd have to adjust. She needed to cease her annoyance with him. He wasn't a bad guy, and she'd liked him well enough. They'd enjoyed some good times together until she'd brought up having a baby.

"Oil paint doesn't dry," Stefan met Devin's questioning gaze, "it oxidizes. Freezing temperatures retard the process. So, you can keep any unused paint on your palette and use it over days or even weeks." He laughed. "Or if you're like me and hate cleaning brushes, you can wrap them in aluminum foil, throw them in the freezer, and use them the next day. Just keep food away from paint and vice versa. We'll talk more about the toxicity of certain pigments when it comes up."

Casey couldn't wait to attend class with Leighton. She was a sponge, ready to absorb all the knowledge from her she could. It still seemed surreal that Mrs. Shipton had given her a full scholarship to study at Atelier Vaughn.

It'd been one thing to admire Leighton's talent, but Casey had wondered if she'd like her as a person. So far, she liked everything she'd seen, and her surreptitious glances had seen loads. Leighton's suit and boot combination should be illegal.

"Along the same line, *this* sink is for dishes." Stefan bumped his fist against the edge of the one in the kitchenette.

Casey curbed her daydreaming.

"That's for cleaning brushes." He walked toward a paint-splattered concrete utility sink in the far corner of the studio near the large workbench.

Everyone followed. Everyone except Leighton.

A few feet from them, she leaned against the back of a sofa and crossed her arms over her chest. The stance pressed her breasts together, giving Casey a glimpse of her cleavage. She looked away before Leighton caught her. Ogling her instructor on the first day wasn't a good idea. Casey had been memorable enough by running into her downstairs.

Leighton had painted the voluptuous nude in the gallery, and she'd be teaching Casey how to do the same. Had Leighton been lovers with the woman? Casey had read enough about her online to know she was openly bisexual, and she recalled how glimpsing the intimate scene Leighton had painted with such a tender touch felt intrusive. Had Leighton run her hands over the woman's body before she dragged her brush over canvas to create those soft undulations of flesh that made Casey want to stroke them? She trembled at the wave of unexpected arousal.

"This is the supply area."

Stefan's voice jolted Casey back to the present. Her pulse pounded as she checked to see if somehow anyone—specifically Leighton—had seen where her mind had been. How ridiculous.

"You're responsible for purchasing your paints and brushes, as your welcome letter stated, but you'll find the other supplies you'll need in these cabinets. They're here for you to use for class projects. The workbench area is for preparing canvases, varnishing, framing, or anything else where you'll need a horizontal surface."

Phoenix elbowed Jaiden, and they laughed so hard they couldn't stop. Leighton raised her chin.

Stefan gave them a wry look and rubbed the top of his head, making his thinning hair stick up. Once they'd calmed down, he motioned toward the end of the room. "Those two glass boxes are our offices. If our doors are open, you're welcome to come in."

Casey craned her neck to see Leighton's. She assumed the corner one with a small bouquet on the desk belonged to her. Diplomas and certificates graced the walls, as well as small oil paintings. The desk held little more than a laptop, a sparse and stark contrast to most of the artist spaces she'd seen in her lifetime.

Clutter filled the second office, and half-unpacked boxes littered the floor. An open bag of popcorn had tipped over on the desk. Nothing hung on the walls.

When she turned back toward Stefan, Leighton watched her. Casey shivered. What was it about Leighton that unsettled her? It could be infatuation. She was one of the biggest names in realism, and Casey had admired her for years. If only the articles and websites had posted better pictures of her instead of the candid shots where she was talking or gesturing. Casey had been able to tell she was good-looking, but the photos didn't portray how attractive she was in person. Leighton was gorgeous. Would Casey stumble under the gaze of another woman of equal beauty? She wasn't sure since she couldn't ever recall being in the presence of someone so stunning.

Casey shook her head. It wasn't professional to objectify her teacher. Leighton's painting had affected her. Was her unease because of that? A greater question lingered. Was she more drawn to Leighton as an artist or as a woman? She rubbed her forehead and chastised herself for having such thoughts. Leighton was her teacher and at least a decade older.

Stefan stopped near the center of the easel stations beside a model stand. "Let's talk about music."

That subject seemed to grab everyone's interest. Everyone except Casey's. Why couldn't she focus on anything besides Leighton? The first day featured explanations and introductions, and she should pay attention. If Leighton quizzed them, she'd certainly fail.

"We divide your time here into class and open studio time, the latter being whenever class is not being held."

Mark slung his arm over Casey's shoulders, a common move for him. She was shorter, and he liked to lean on her. Normally, it didn't bother her, but when Leighton's eyes slightly widened, her lips parted, and one of her eyebrows went askew, she wanted to squirm. She didn't want Leighton to assume she and Mark were anything but friends. Casey barely knew her, but Leighton's image of her mattered for reasons yet unclear.

She shrugged from beneath Mark's arm. "Sorry." She bent to retie her shoelace that didn't need retying, and when she stood, Mark had propped his forearms on the taboret instead.

Leighton turned her attention to Stefan.

He'd moved on to AirPods and headphones being allowed during open studio times but not class, and Casey half listened, catching the highlights of there being opportunities to learn from feedback given to another student or spontaneous demonstration techniques.

Stefan stopped in front of a Belgian art horse, a simple wooden bench with a raised end on which a drawing board could be supported. He straddled the seat and looked at Leighton. "That's all I have."

"Thank you, Stefan." Leighton uncrossed her arms and stood, directing her attention to the students. "Okay. We've given you pertinent information this morning about the building, the studio, and some of the rules. Now, everyone sit, and let's talk about what's really important." She flashed a wide grin like she'd found a clue to the whereabouts of the artwork stolen from the Isabella Stewart Gardner Museum.

Casey grinned back as she scurried to a couch, and when Leighton sauntered to a spot in her line of vision just outside the furniture grouping, Casey's blood pounded so loudly she could hear it.

"You're all here for one reason. Each of your applications expressed a desire to learn classical painting methods that have been around for centuries. Despite some of you holding art degrees, you felt that your prior education has been lacking in these practices." She turned and began a slow stroll, following the curve of the circle. As she passed the first chair, she grazed her fingertips along the top of the plush backrest, almost trailing them through Erica's hair.

What would *that* feel like? Casey stiffened against a light flurry in her belly.

"Part of that's because the material covered in undergraduate degree programs is an inch deep and a mile wide. However, the revolutionary art movements that came about during the twentieth century that shifted focus toward modern art are also to blame. Unfortunately, the time-honored practice of teaching classical realism fell by the wayside for over fifty years."

As Leighton's path brought her gradually closer, Casey turned her head to keep her concentration on Leighton's face and words. The movement of her touch from one backrest to the next and the way she seemed to caress the fabric as she passed created a challenging distraction, though.

"We've seen a return to realism," Leighton continued, "at least in some areas. We'll teach you the methods they've taught in the ateliers and academies of Europe since the Renaissance. Those ateliers were studios where apprentices learned from and worked with masters." She smiled a coy smile. "That said, neither Stefan nor I proclaim to be masters at our craft, nor do we want to teach you to paint in our styles. Our goal is to give you the knowledge needed to paint realism while finding your own."

Casey's heart fluttered in her chest, likely due to the potential the year held. Well, mostly. But neither her fascination with Leighton nor her nerves could dampen her enthusiasm, and she planned to learn everything she could at Atelier Vaughn. It was the fulfillment of her dream, a step toward becoming an accomplished and successful painter to support herself and Andy, to give him the life he deserved. How had she been wondering just hours ago if she'd made the correct decision?

"Your application asked for a written recommendation, preferably from one of my former students."

Leighton now stood at the end of the couch on which Casey sat, only one person away. So close Casey had to crane her neck to continue looking at her.

"We do this for several reasons. It's our first step toward filtering potential applicants to find those who are sincere about wanting to learn classical methods. Our students know which of their classmates, friends, or family members are serious and will be a good fit. While not everyone accepted has had a former student's recommendation, most have, so some of you may know one another."

Casey glanced at Devin to find him staring at her. She'd get used to seeing him every day again, wouldn't she? She looked away.

"It also serves to foster a pleasant atmosphere. By providing you with a letter of recommendation, those former students have vouched for you. Look around this circle."

Casey did, finding Mark first, right beside her as always, then Mikala, who smiled at her.

Before she could look at the others, Leighton moved behind her.

Casey stilled. She remembered the nearness of Leighton's fingers to Erica's hair earlier. Where were they now?

"These are the people with whom you're going to be spending a lot of time."

The brush of Leighton's touch on the worn upholstery of the sofa sounded close to Casey's ear, making it difficult to keep her mind on Leighton's voice.

"Our atelier family," something, probably her hand, lifted from the top of the backrest then pressed down again, even closer, "scrutinized your portfolios for talent and work ethic."

Casey leaned her head back, then caught herself. What was she doing? She sat straighter and adjusted her position.

"We also looked to accept students we'd enjoy getting to know. I hope we'll become your second family and the studio your second home for this next year." Leighton moved further around the circle.

Casey breathed a sigh of relief. How stupid could she be? Hadn't she embarrassed herself enough already today?

Mark poked her in the side and gave her a WTF look.

She ignored him.

"We also believe in learning from those around us," Leighton was still speaking from where she now stood behind Jaiden, "regardless of education, age, or experience. Stefan and I may be your instructors, but you'll also benefit from Erica's knowledge and by observing and talking to one another."

Her eyes shone with an optimism Casey found enchanting.

"Our goal is for everyone to succeed, and to that end, besides attending classes and practicing your craft in the studio, I also expect you to volunteer four hours a week downstairs in the gallery."

Casey smiled, remembering what Mark had said about Erica earning extra money from her sales.

"We think four hours is a fair amount of time, and it has a purpose. You'll gain valuable experience talking with the public about your art and that of your peers'. You'll learn ways to market and promote yourself and how to handle the financial aspects of selling paintings and running a gallery. It's as much a learning experience as your formal classes."

Andy flashed through Casey's mind. While her time spent in the gallery could mean more money, it entailed four more hours away from him each week. But then, there was the possibility of being able to quit her job at the coffeehouse.

Leighton came full circle and stopped directly across from Casey again, then lowered herself to sit, balanced on the arm of Erica's chair. "You aren't required to put your work in the gallery, but we encourage it." She went on to cover how they could receive up to ninety-five percent from the sale of any of their pieces if they were the seller. "We believe the five percent the gallery gets to be more than fair. Most galleries take fifty, and often the artist has to pay for advertising and promotional materials."

Casey had to admit having a roomful of people promoting her artwork was a nice perk. Plus, she welcomed any additional income from her sales of theirs. She froze as she recalled the price of some of Leighton's and Stefan's works. They ranged into five-figure territory. Five percent of that would make a major difference in her life. The realization must have brought a smile to her face because when she looked up and locked eyes with Leighton across the circle, *she* was smiling, too. Casey tried not to fidget under her evident amusement.

"I believe you all met Maxine Shipton downstairs." Leighton sent a glance to each of the first-years before continuing. "She runs the gallery and manages most of its operations, so you'll schedule your hours with her, and she'll cover the times when one of you can't be present. In addition, she'll work with each of you to price your art. She donates her time here as well as generously dividing her five percent commission on any sales *she* makes between all of you. Students have received checks every month since the atelier's start, even if the sums weren't always significant." Leighton paused, her expression becoming serious. "Maxine is so giving of her time because she enjoys being a part of what we do here. She's an ardent supporter of the arts, and she believes in me, my school, and *your* potential. I don't take her for granted, and neither should you."

Leighton's demeanor made her point far better than her words.

With that, her smile returned, and she stood. "Erica, do you have the syllabi?" She held out her hand expectantly.

Erica pulled a stack of papers from between her hip and the arm of her chair and gave them to Leighton.

She took one and passed the rest to Jenna, who occupied the seat on her other side. When everyone was ready, she raised hers. "You're holding your syllabus for the semester. It's also online. It spells out what we expect to cover and in what order. Your homework is to read through it tonight and bring any questions you might have tomorrow." Her warm smile returned as she looked around the circle, this time with a glint of something in her eyes.

Happiness? Pride? Casey wasn't sure.

"That's all I have for you today. You're welcome to choose a station and put your belongings in your taboret. Familiarize yourself with the studio, open cupboards and see where we store things, check out the still-life objects on the shelves, and try out your access cards and codes. Be sure to introduce yourself to Maxine before you leave, if you haven't already. Questions?"

Jenna raised her hand.

"Just speak, remember, Jenna?"

She lowered it with a sheepish expression. "What's your policy on absences or tardiness?"

Leighton took a deep breath. "We expect you to be in class. Stefan, Erica, and I make the effort to be here, and I hope you respect us enough to do the same. I'm not wasting my time taking attendance, however, when you're late, it disrupts the class, so please try to be here before it begins. You'll notice we never start especially early, so plan to arrive beforehand and put in some open studio time if running behind is a problem for you. That said, you'll get out of this what you put into it. It's all about brush miles." Her tone was frank. "If you want to be a great artist, you need to practice your craft. Any more questions?"

When no one spoke, Leighton's expression softened, like a proud mother pleased to have her family together for the holidays. With a wave, she set them free. "We'll be around another hour, if anyone needs anything, but you're welcome to stay as long as you like."

Casey rose and turned in a circle, taking in the room and the people in it. She couldn't wait to spend hours here, lost in her art. She liked everyone she'd met, and she could tolerate Devin. Yes, Atelier Vaughn already felt like home.

If only what she felt in Leighton's presence were as clear. She pushed the thought aside, retrieved her backpack from the floor, and headed to the stations.

Three easels held canvases, two of them larger than the rest. Casey assumed the latter were the instructors'. Half-finished paintings showed a female figure's outline, one on a white canvas, the other against a stained ground that looked like raw umber. While both depicted the same model, the artists had taken much different approaches. She studied them but couldn't be sure which one was Leighton's.

Just like she never won at musical chairs, Casey ended up with the last easel. It stood beside one of the bigger ones and was closest to Leighton's office. Mikala had chosen the next station and Mark the one beyond that.

After running her hands along her taboret's lacquered top and opening the drawers and cupboard below, Casey unzipped her backpack. An excited hum filled the room as everyone started putting away their supplies. It reminded her of being a kid. The first day of school had always thrilled her. She recalled the unmistakable scent of a fresh box of Crayola Crayons, the tip of each colored stick flawless, but their perfection so fleeting.

Instead of crayons, Casey removed a gallon-sized plastic bag of paints from her backpack and organized the tubes of artist-grade pigments Leighton had instructed them to purchase in a row inside a shallow drawer. Even their names brought her joy, colors like ultramarine blue, dioxazine purple, and alizarin crimson.

She unrolled her new bristle brushes and laid them on top of the taboret, then arranged a smaller group of soft, sable brushes alongside them. Two wooden-handled palette knives and a couple of lidded palette cups came next, and finally, she pulled a jar of brush soap from the bottom of her backpack.

"So, is it Andrew?"

She turned to find Leighton holding a bag of paper towels.

"Andrew?" Casey tilted her head, a little confused.

"Your son. Is Andy short for Andrew?"

"Oh, no. Anders, actually." No one ever asked her that. They assumed his full name was Andrew without question. Was Leighton really curious, or had she simply wanted to talk to her?

"Is it a family name?" Whatever her initial reason for asking, Leighton seemed interested now.

"No." Casey couldn't imagine naming him after anyone in her family. "He's named after his father's favorite artist."

Leighton opened her mouth, then closed it, as though Casey's answer had flustered her, but she recovered quickly. "How original." She moved beside Casey and dropped the bag. She attached the roll of paper towels she'd had under her arm to a chain on the side of the taboret. "There." She stood close, as if waiting for something.

Casey inhaled her perfume, the same evocative scent that had clouded her mind in the elevator. It's effect was no different now. "Thank you." She fiddled with the jar of brush soap.

"Excellent choices." Leighton perused the supplies Casey had laid out. She touched the hairs of one of the sable brushes. "These are some of my favorites. It's difficult to put a price on quality."

How was Casey supposed to respond when Leighton complimented her brushes? She'd recommended the brand in the welcome packet. At first, Casey had thought ordering paintbrushes from England was a little much. She never spent money on herself, not since her parents cut her off. But as soon as she opened the package and snapped the hog hair bristles against her palm and felt the silky sable between her fingers, she envisioned how wonderful it'd feel to drag them across a canvas.

And now, seeing Leighton's reaction, she was even happier with her choice. "Thank you." She couldn't devise a better response.

Leighton smiled and picked up the remaining paper towels.

"Oh!" Leighton swung around, coming face-to-face with Casey, who'd taken a step forward. She grabbed Casey's shoulder to avoid a collision.

Startled, Casey froze.

Leighton let go of her but remained in her personal space. "You're welcome to bring Andy when you do your volunteer hours in the gallery. I don't want you to be away from him any more than necessary."

Casey could feel where Leighton's fingers had warmed her skin through her shirt. Leighton's voice had become much softer than when she'd spoken to the group.

"He'll have a ball in the enormous space and, I'm sure, charm potential customers."

Then Casey received a wink of her own from Leighton, and she thought she might burst. "Thank you. He'd like that. *I'd* like that."

"Good." Leighton seemed pleased. She moved on to Mikala's station with the paper towels.

Casey watched as Leighton walked away, her shoulder still tingling. She never would've even thought to ask if she could bring Andy to the atelier for any reason, never mind when she'd be in the gallery. Leighton's thoughtful gesture meant a lot. Most people wouldn't want toddlers, with their sticky fingers and runny noses, around art, but Leighton seemed to prioritize a child's time with his mother. Her considerate offer made Casey's heart give a little squeeze. Had Leighton any idea the gift she'd given her?

Chapter Six

Leighton stepped off the elevator into the reception area of the gallery after Casey had left. She checked herself. After *all* the students had left.

Maxine worked at her desk, her posture poised and erect, like she waited to receive marks on sitting like an elegant lady in an etiquette class. No doubt she could teach it. She could probably walk the entire length of the gallery with three of the Met's exhibition catalogs balanced on her head.

Even this late in the afternoon, her raven hair looked coiffed, not a single gray showing, unlike Leighton's, where they seemed to appear every other day. Yet, Leighton would resent the time-consuming and expensive upkeep, not that expense mattered to Maxine.

Maxine turned. "Are you finished for the day, dear?"

"Yes, and I thought it went well." Leighton sat on the corner of the desk.

Maxine flicked Leighton's hip. "Don't be a neanderthal." She removed some catalogs from a chair and pushed it toward her.

Maxine had been her mother's best friend since before Leighton had been born. They'd met as roommates at Bryn Mawr, and their friendship had thrived for decades before Leighton's mother passed away. Maxine had been as devastated by the loss as she'd been. Whenever Maxine brought up stories about Leighton's mom from times Leighton hadn't been privy to, it brought equal parts fondness and sadness.

Now bored with her retired husband and having no children of her own, Maxine devoted her time to the atelier; Leighton, whom she loved like a daughter; and Kalyssa, who'd fulfilled her broken dream of being a grandmother. Well, the type of grandmother who took a four-year-old to tea rooms and Christmas dinner at the Ritz, not so much the kind to whip up a batch of cookies or opine whether Anna's or Elsa's dress would make a better choice for Halloween.

Speaking of which, Leighton needed to get Kalyssa to pare down her costume shortlist from Anna, Elsa, Olaf, Puss in Boots, and the entire cast of *Gabby's Dollhouse* to a more manageable size. Halloween would be here before she knew it.

Leighton settled into the chair Maxine had provided and crossed her legs. "Did you enjoy meeting the new students?"

"Yes, I liked them, and I reconnected with last year's." Maxine stroked her blood-red fingernails through her temples. "I dare say, I think Phoenix may have developed a thing for older women over the summer. He complimented my cosmetics and asked where I purchased them."

Maxine appeared to have applied her impeccable crimson lipstick seconds ago, though Leighton doubted it. In contrast, her own always rubbed off on her coffee mug or Kalyssa long before now. Part of her wanted to tell Maxine that Phoenix's interest in her beauty products was more likely a result of him discovering his true self rather than his attraction to someone mature enough to collect Social Security. "That was nice of them." Leighton wanted to practice using Phoenix's preferred pronouns after what he'd shared upstairs, even if he wasn't around. She kept her mouth closed about the rest.

"Will you and Kalyssa be too busy for brunch on Sunday?" Maxine switched off her laptop. "I can cancel the reservation. It's a hectic week for you."

The mention of the mid-day meal called to mind another Leighton didn't like to think about and hadn't in some time, one she hadn't even attended. Messy and lengthy divorce proceedings had followed, but she'd gotten the only three things she cared about: her daughter, her freedom, and the old brick building that housed her atelier. "We'd love to have brunch with you." She squeezed Maxine's arm. "I hope George can make it this time."

Maxine gave a dainty cough. "As you know, I allow him to skip brunch to play golf once a month. Since he used his free pass last week, he'll be there."

They couldn't be more different as godparents. As involved in her life as Maxine was, George was the polar opposite. Years ago, before his retirement, he'd been even busier. It always seemed to be something.

Manufacturing, silver, stocks. He must have known what he was doing because they weren't hurting for money.

"Tell Kalyssa she can drink a Shirley Temple and have as much whipped cream on her Belgian waffle as she wants. I haven't spoiled her in a long time, and a bit of sugar won't hurt. You made her order scrambled eggs last week, if I recall. I need to make sure I remain her favorite gallery volunteer." Maxine gave her a little pinch on her cheek, something she'd learned was Maxine's love language.

Leighton tilted her head. "What do you mean *remain* her favorite volunteer?"

Maxine pulled her purse from a lower drawer. "Casey, of course. Didn't you notice her effervescence? Her adorable personality? Her smile? And those dimples. Kalyssa's going to love her."

Leighton tried to hide her shiver. Great. That was all she needed. What she *really* needed was a glass of wine.

Maxine glanced at her. "You look tired. Why don't I pick up Kalyssa from preschool? Go rest."

Leighton sighed. "She has ballet."

"Perfect. I need to run an errand near there. I'll be back long before she's finished."

Leighton dreaded fighting traffic. At least Maxine wouldn't have to either. She paid her driver to do it. "You don't mind?"

"Not at all."

Less than twenty minutes later, Leighton poured two glasses of wine as Stefan rummaged through her pantry for snacks. She relaxed into her sofa with her chardonnay and struggled to forget about Casey's smile and her dimples, but both lingered at the forefront of her mind. So, what if she'd indulged in a fleeting, pleasant interaction? Leighton had felt a strange connection as she listened to Casey explain her reaction to her painting.

Regardless, nothing could happen between them. Leighton had allowed herself to appreciate a few moments with her today. Tomorrow, she'd be all business. Her days of indulging in an enjoyable interaction with someone striking, let alone dating or having a romantic relationship, lay in her past. Marriage had taught her a hard lesson. She breathed out a sigh and took a sip.

"Those two knuckleheads are going to be a handful." Stefan assessed a box of graham crackers before returning it to the shelf.

"Phoenix and Jaiden?" She chuckled and swirled her wine. "I agree. I don't remember them being this bad last year, but they started rooming together at the beginning of the summer. Maybe that has something to do with it. They're going to drive us nuts with their innuendo, but they amuse me."

He joined her in the living room and dropped into her green wingback chair. "What's your impression of the new students?" He ripped open a bag of pretzels.

"What do you mean?" Leighton set her glass on the coffee table.

"What do you think I mean? It's not a trick question." Humor and annoyance mingled in his voice. "Did you like them? Their personalities?"

"Of course. Didn't you?" Her response came out forced. She unbuttoned her cuffs and rolled up her sleeves.

He laughed. "This isn't an interrogation. I'm just making conversation. So far, I like everyone."

"Yes, they're an exceptional bunch." When she'd gotten comfortable, she retrieved her glass. "Still, everything has to go well. I have a lot riding on it." She'd doubled her number of students and teaching staff from the previous year. And while last year's students had drawn attention with the paintings they produced, even more eyes would be on the atelier and gallery this year. She tucked her legs beneath her. She'd discarded her boots seconds after entering her apartment.

Stefan studied her. "It will. I'm certain of it. We vetted everyone as much as we could, we planned the curriculum down to meticulous detail, you know what worked and didn't work last year, and we have Erica to help." He downed a gulp of wine.

"Sure, we vetted everyone, but one of our first-years has a toddler we didn't know existed." It wasn't a question of how it'd happened. Casey hadn't wanted them to know. Why?

He shrugged. "That doesn't change her talent or her goals. Are you worried about her focus? Her commitment?"

Leighton considered his question. "No, she seems more committed than most. Having a son might make her *more* dedicated. You read her essay. She seems to want this more than any of them, Erica included." Leighton was no stranger to aiming high. She admired that facet of Casey.

"So, what is it then?"

"I'm just worried. Everything has gone into this dream of mine." After her divorce, she'd poured all her energy into Kalyssa and the atelier. Her personal life had come to a thundering halt, but Kalyssa was doing great, and her school looked to flourish. Unless something unexpected happened.

"So, what's worrying you?" He popped a pretzel into his mouth and crunched loudly.

Leighton remained quiet. It sounded silly, being knocked off balance by one little encounter. She debated whether to admit it or say nothing, but their long friendship and mutual trust won out.

"I got thrown a curveball. Of all the things I thought might happen today, it was most unexpected." She instantly regretted the confession, but it was too late to turn back.

He chewed and swallowed. "Casey?"

"Yes. Casey." She enjoyed saying her name aloud despite being stunned he'd guessed. "How did you know?"

He cleared his throat. "Well, she's the most talented student we have, and that's counting the second-years. I know that captured your attention even before you met her. She's also the most attractive, and I'm not even into women. But, Leighton...Well, I'm not sure it's my place to mention it—"

"I'm her teacher, and she's my student? Yes, Stefan, I'm aware." Too aware. That reminder had surfaced so many times throughout the day she wondered how she'd managed to talk about motion sensors and tardiness.

"Okay, good, because that could complicate things." He raised his eyebrows. "However, for what it's worth, I think you may have also thrown her a curveball. I saw how she looked at you. She's not very good at hiding her appreciation."

Leighton laughed. "You should've seen her in the gallery." She also thought she'd caught a glimpse of Casey's admiration but wondered if she'd imagined it. Still, Stefan's words rattled her and confused her more. "We might be misreading things. She could be straight. After all, she has a child." Minimizing her interest in Casey had become more difficult with the knowledge Casey might also feel whatever this was between them.

He rolled his eyes. "You're queer, and you have a child. I'm sure you noticed how she responds to you. I'd bet on her being about as straight as I am. She jumped away from you like you might burn her if she got too close."

Leighton shook her head. "Why would she do that? It makes little sense." Casey's reaction seemed out of place. It'd thrown her so much she'd fumbled to regain her train of thought.

"I think you scare her."

"Scare her?" Leighton twirled the bracelet on her wrist. "Scare her how?"

He shrugged. "Perhaps the idea of you is frightening. She might have a bit of an infatuation with you as an artist, then she meets you and, well, you're you." He traced her outline in the air. "Now she's about to spend a lot of time in close quarters with a beautiful woman she admires and finds attractive. Despite taking longer to graduate from college, she's still young and impressionable. I'm sure it's a lot to manage."

"You sound like you may have some experience in this area. Don't tell me young Stefan Jovic had a crush on a teacher." She shot him a wry grin.

He dug another pretzel from the bag. "Too many to count."

His admission sank into her heart and the realization of how serious the situation could get shifted her mood. "Look, it's fine for us to joke about this now, but she's my student, and that's not going to change. Having a successful atelier is my dream, and I'm not about to jeopardize it. Let's also remember Casey is Maxine's scholarship recipient, so this discussion needs to stay between us. Maxine would have a coronary if she heard even a whisper about this. I could lose her funding, not to mention her respect."

"I've spent little time with Maxine so far, but from what I've gathered, she does seem a bit conservative. Still, it's not like we use grades, or you could use your position of authority to advance or impede Casey's status here. You were careful to design your atelier in a way that doesn't create an atmosphere of competition." He stood and tipped his empty glass toward her.

She extended hers to accept his offer of more wine. "True, I intend for them to compete against themselves to become the best artist they can be. Even so, it's impossible. It'd be scandalous if I had a relationship with one of my students."

Stefan nodded and walked to the kitchen.

"Maxine might be my biggest funder, but the smaller investors are just as important. I have to consider optics. Plus, I wouldn't want to jeopardize Casey's scholarship." She shook her head. "I can't believe I'm even talking about this in the hypothetical sense."

He returned to the living room with their wine and a sleeve of crackers. "Jesus, Leighton, I'm not advocating for it. I'm merely pointing out that if something happened, it'd be between two consenting adults.

It's not like she's seventeen. She graduated from college and has a child. Although, I admit it surprised me when she said she had a two-year-old."

Leighton replayed her encounter with Casey in her mind. "His real name is Anders. Her son. I asked."

His forehead creased. "That's a strange name."

"She said she named him after his father's favorite artist." Leighton gave him a knowing look.

"Anders? As in Sweden's famous Anders Zorn?" His eyes narrowed. "Who's the kid's father?" He scooted to the edge of his seat.

She shrugged. "I didn't ask."

"So, daddy likes realism, too. I wonder if any other famous artists are named Anders." He leaned forward, his elbows on his knees. "Shall I google it?"

"All she said was that she'd named him after his dad's favorite artist." Leighton wished she'd never brought it up. It felt like a betrayal.

"She might have met his father in art school."

He didn't abandon the subject even as she retreated into thought. She needed to end this tangent since Andy's father had nothing to do with her. With a groan, she unfolded her legs and took her glass to the kitchen. "Kalyssa will be home soon. I don't want to be having this conversation when Maxine drops her off. When it comes down to it, it's not ethical for me to have feelings for a student. Besides, the last time I fell for someone, look where it left me." She paused for effect. "I'd rather be alone the rest of my life than risk going through that again."

He winced and stood. "I get it. Let's chalk this up to meaningless chitchat over a glass of wine. You won't hear any more from me unless you bring it up." He held out his arms.

She gave him a rueful smile and stepped into the embrace. "Thanks. I'm grateful you accepted the position. I know it's going to be an amazing year." It had to be. She'd worked so hard to get to this point.

"Yes, it is." He hugged her tightly. "Thanks for the wine. Since you're kicking me out, I'm taking the crackers."

When he left, only silence remained. And in that space, void of sound or distraction, her mind wandered again to Casey's hazel eyes. This couldn't be happening. Her expectations for the day had been so high. And now this.

CHAPTER SEVEN

Casey ignored the pile of dirty dishes in her kitchen sink, opting instead to spend a few minutes with Andy while he ate his snack. She glanced around her. In truth, the apartment could use a good cleaning before she and Mark got busier with the addition of classes and studio time at the atelier. But then, it wasn't like the place ever appeared much cleaner after a thorough scrubbing. The marred linoleum that looked like it was from the eighties and might once have been white stayed a grayish beige, and the brown splotch in the center of the green Formica-topped table never got any better no matter what they used on it.

When they'd first moved in, she'd quickly grown tired of balancing her meals on her knees, so she'd been grateful when they'd found the discarded table on the sidewalk with a *FREE* sign taped to it. It served their purposes nicely as long as they kept the folded matchbox under one leg and the back edge shoved against the wall.

"Here, let me cut that for you." She tried to take the half-banana from Andy's grasp.

"No." He leaned away and dug his fingers deeper into the soft yellow flesh.

She gave in, worried he might tip over the chair on which she'd strapped him and his new booster seat. Well, not new, but new to them. Erica's friend had offered it to Casey when his daughter outgrew it.

"Do you want orange juice?" She finger-combed his unruly hair that showed evidence of his nap. His cowlicks curled when wet or sweaty, and she hoped that wouldn't change as he got older.

"No." He gnawed on the gooey piece of fruit.

From the safety of the far corner of the table, the syllabus Leighton had handed out earlier taunted her. She yearned to read it, but she wanted to save it for when she had uninterrupted time. It outlined the curriculum for the semester, but it contained far more. It'd give her a much-desired glimpse into Leighton. With all the strength she had in her, she returned her attention to Andy.

"When you're done, we'll read a book." She picked up a sticky bit of banana from the floor, then squished it into a napkin.

"No."

"What? You like books." This argumentative streak better be a phase.

He shook his head with vigor. "No."

"Yes, you do, funny boy." She tickled his side.

As much as she tired of hearing no, it was part of his language development, and she enjoyed watching him learn how to express his thoughts as his vocabulary expanded and he began stringing together two or three words.

"Milk, please."

Right on cue. She smiled, adoring everything about him. He might have inherited her coloring and bone structure, but his dark eyes and lashes were his daddy's. She kissed him on the forehead. "You got it."

As she rose, the syllabus beckoned her again. Waiting to read it ate at her. She filled Andy's sippy cup, then returned to the table. If Mark hadn't been with her when she'd left the atelier, she'd have pored over it on the train ride home. She handed Andy his milk.

He grabbed it with one hand, waving his mangled banana in the other.

What the hell. She snatched up the syllabus.

As she read, she heard Leighton's voice in her head. Her speech patterns, and somehow even her tone, came through in her writing, but the content impressed Casey even more.

In particular, the section that detailed Atelier Vaughn's evaluation system stood out. Above all, Leighton deemed critiques the most valuable part of the learning process. The lack of any formal grading system surprised Casey. Leighton envisioned success for every student, so she'd structured her school to avoid comparing the progress of one against another. Both instructors would critique each work, and the artist could anticipate acclaim as well as constructive criticism.

In addition, Leighton expected students to turn in every assignment, but the atelier operated under the presumption they were adults and, therefore, would take responsibility for their learning. Casey almost chuckled as she translated what Leighton hadn't written. It was their money. If they paid to attend Atelier Vaughn and wasted the opportunity, that was on them.

Wasting money wasn't a problem in Casey's case since she had none. However, as a scholarship recipient, she didn't intend to squander the opportunity Maxine had given her, the best chance to give Andy a better life.

As she continued through the syllabus, Casey almost bounced in her seat when she read what she'd be studying. If they had a Make-A-Wish foundation for artists like herself, the syllabus read like a fairytale dream come true. Plus, she'd be doing it alongside Leighton.

"Done." Andy splayed his glistening hands, banana smeared all over his face, in his hair, down his shirt, and across the table in front of him.

Casey blinked. Was that all from half of a banana? The sippy cup lay in a puddle of milk on the floor, the lid beside it. So much for spill-proof. But it was worth every second she'd been able to spend devouring her course curriculum.

"Okay, I guess you need a bath instead of a book." She laughed.

"Bath!" Andy's squeal matched the enthusiastic smile that lit his face.

Finally, something other than a no.

In the bathroom, Casey's thoughts wandered as she tested the water temperature. What was it about Leighton? Why was she so captivated by her? She tried to distinguish whether her fascination stemmed from the sheer talent Leighton possessed, or Casey's admiration of her as a person. It was difficult to untangle the two.

She'd known about Leighton as an artist through her works and websites, as well as the articles Casey had read. Now that she'd met her, Leighton seemed just as impressive as a woman without factoring art into the equation at all. She'd understood the struggles in Casey's life and had shown her acceptance and kindness by welcoming Andy to the gallery while Casey volunteered.

Beautiful, thoughtful, funny—what wasn't there to like?

❖

The next morning, excited about her first actual class, Casey stepped out of the elevator on the second floor. Since she'd left early, she assumed she'd be the first to arrive, but light flooded the studio. Movement in the kitchen caught her attention, and Devin looked up from a stack of coffee filters he struggled to separate. Beside him, Stefan read a paper at the table. Who read real newspapers anymore?

"Good morning!"

Devin's cheeriness grated on her. She wished she could ignore him, but maintaining a level of civility would make things easier while they were students together. Leighton wanted a familial atmosphere, so Casey would do her best to oblige. Even after only a day, she yearned to make Leighton happy. If difficulties arose between her and Devin, it wouldn't be because of any attitude on her part.

"Hi. You're here early." When she extended her hand, he gave her the filters. They were difficult to separate with her short nails, but she managed.

"I wanted to get a start on my sketchbook assignments, and I figured it'd be quiet here. It never is at my house, as you know." He flashed her a wry smile.

Casey remembered his large, jovial family. The laughter, jokes, banter, and decibel level never subsided.

"Want some coffee?" He dropped the filter she gave him into its holder and scooped some grounds into it.

"Sure, thanks." She headed for her easel. No sooner had she hung up her jacket than the elevator ding signaled a new arrival.

"Good morning." Leighton greeted Devin as she breezed in wearing dark blue jeans and a tan blouse, her shirt untucked. "Stefan." As she crossed the open room, she ran her fingers through her damp hair.

Casey couldn't distinguish their murmured responses.

"Hello, Casey." She smiled and continued toward her office.

In Leighton's wake, Casey caught the sweet scent of her hair products. "Good morning." She tried to focus on selecting the perfect length of vine charcoal, but it didn't help. All she could think of was Leighton in either the bath or shower. She dismissed the unbidden images.

As she started her drawing, her thoughts continued to stray until a movement beside her brought her back. Devin stood at her elbow with a mug of coffee.

"A splash of milk, just how you like it." He beamed.

Based on the dip of Leighton's eyebrow as she exited her office, she'd heard his statement.

Casey inwardly winced.

"And here's your book." He brought it out from behind his back with a flourish and a sheepish grin. "Sorry I kept it so long."

Was he trying to be cute? At any other time, she'd be ecstatic to get it back, but not in front of Leighton.

"Oh, and here." He pulled something from his pocket.

Good God. Was that her retainer? It'd been missing for months.

"I found it behind my nightstand."

Casey noticed the little piece of fuzz clinging to it just as Leighton walked by. Eww. Silly her, thinking the situation couldn't get any worse. She avoided eye contact.

She glared at Devin and snatched the retainer from him. "Thanks. You can set the coffee down."

"How's Andy?" Unaware of her discomfort, he tried for small talk.

"Not. Now. Devin." Her terse words came out through clenched teeth. In an instant, she regretted them. "Sorry, I'm not a morning person."

With a downcast expression, he returned to the kitchen, passing Leighton with her own steaming coffee.

As she neared Casey, she slowed. "Is everything all right?"

The damp ends of her hair had created translucent spots on the fabric of her shirt near her collarbone, causing it to stick to her skin. Casey found herself staring and snapped out of it. She raised her chin. "It will be." Her voice held conviction. There was no way she'd let her past with Devin interfere with her learning, or with Leighton's opinion of her.

"Okay." Leighton entered her office and closed the door.

Casey shoved the book into her taboret, dropped the retainer into her garbage, and moved the coffee she no longer wanted aside.

Mark exited the elevator with his bicycle balanced on one wheel. He lowered it with a bounce and pushed it into the studio. "Hey, Stefan?"

Stefan straightened from where he'd been digging in the refrigerator for something. "Yep."

"Is it okay if I store my bike inside? I've had two stolen in the last year, so I'd rather not lock it up out back." He peeled off his fingerless gloves.

He loved his bike and used it as his main form of transportation, and he didn't have money to replace it yet again.

"Yeah. No problem." Stefan pulled a glass from a cupboard.

"Should I leave it in here, or is it better to put it up with the stools on the third floor?" Mark hadn't moved.

"What?" Stefan's forehead creased with his obvious confusion. "Oh." He gave a slight headshake. "No, leave it against that wall." He pointed to a space under the northern windows near Casey's station.

Mark leaned his bike against the bricks and hung his helmet on the handlebars. "Morning, Case. You're up early."

"Hey, Mark."

Jenna had arrived behind him and wandered over. "Nice bike." She lowered her voice. "I don't think they want us up in the storage area. The third floor lights were on when I came back last night to get my wallet. I tried to go up to turn them off, but the elevator wouldn't let me."

"I did, too." Mark tucked his gloves inside his helmet. "Not because of the lights but out of curiosity." He shrugged. "Neither my card nor code worked."

Casey gave a short laugh. "I feel left out. Am I the only one who hasn't tried?"

Jenna shuddered. "Storage rooms and attics tend to be haunted and full of spiders. I was secretly glad I couldn't get up there."

"I don't care." Mark patted his bike's cushioned seat. "I'd rather have my baby where I can see her, anyway."

Locks and sensors, more cameras than Casey could count, and doors and windows they couldn't open. Why was Leighton so paranoid? Casey could understand wanting it in the gallery since Leighton's pieces sold for the prices they did. However, wouldn't she carry insurance in case of theft? Why was the entire building so secure? It seemed a bit much.

After only a few days, Casey had determined her classes were the best she'd ever attended. She filed her drawing from Stefan's lesson on perspective into her portfolio bag and tidied her station. Already, twenty-four pages of her sketchbook contained notes and diagrams. Sometimes she used her laptop, but she liked how her combination of techniques, sketches, quotes, and ideas looked together. It motivated her.

Leighton, on her own, possessed more talent and knowledge than all of Casey's previous professors combined. Stefan was a proficient instructor, too, and quite skilled in his own right, but in Casey's opinion, Leighton's teaching style parted the clouds and made the sun shimmer through. She taught in a way that cultivated the seeds of inspiration alongside the fundamentals and turned pigments suspended in oil and brushed onto canvas into something magical.

In addition to being mesmerized by her intellectual and artistic abilities, watching Leighton demonstrate techniques or write words like *penumbra* or *esquisse* on the whiteboard in her elegant handwriting captivated Casey. Without intending to, she'd memorized Leighton's curves and the sculpted shape of her legs. If she remained this distracted, she'd have to work twice as hard as everyone else to keep up. She tried to convince herself that being consumed by the beauty of the female form, especially in an art class, was normal. At any rate, if her concentration faltered any further, she might require a prescription for her focus issues.

She needed to suppress her admiration for Leighton so she didn't attract attention, but how could she refrain from looking? It reminded her of when she'd been told not to stare at the sun as a child.

Physical attributes aside, she'd enjoyed getting to know Leighton during her classes. The more she learned about her, the more she longed to discover. Casey had enjoyed almost every minute of her time at Atelier Vaughn, and the semester had just begun. It filled her with joy thinking about the future. She hadn't felt so energized and inspired in years.

She had an hour before her next class, so she fished in her backpack for her wallet. Almost everyone had cleared out for the noon hour except Mikala and Leighton, who readied the room for her afternoon lesson.

Mikala stopped at Casey's station. "Hey, I know a great deli nearby. Want to grab lunch?" She ran a hand over her short, dark hair.

Casey checked to make sure she had enough tips left from her final shift at the coffeehouse to buy a sandwich. "Sure. I'm starving."

Leighton passed them.

"Do you want to join us for lunch, Leighton?" Mikala stretched her neck, like she needed to work out a kink.

Casey wished she had Mikala's easygoing manner. Asking Leighton to lunch would be so much more than lunch in her mind. Even now, she wasn't sure she wanted Leighton to accept or decline.

Leighton gave an apologetic smile. "I'd love to, however, I have a standing lunch date on Fridays." Her eyes lit with anticipation.

Casey stomach pitched, and she busied herself with her wallet to appear disinterested. A date? And not just one, but a standing date? She'd surely dwell on that for the rest of the day.

"Next time then." Mikala turned to Casey. "Ready?"

They headed for the elevator. When the doors slid open, Jaiden edged past them with a half-eaten falafel. "Oops, sorry." He waved his sandwich in front of Casey. The scent of the tahini filled the alcove. "Hey, Case. Want a bite? It'll cancel my garlic breath, so we can do some sweet, sweet kissin' later."

She laughed. "Aw, Jai. As inviting as you make that sound, I'm busy all day." Her lack of desire to do any sort of kissing equaled his, but somehow they'd naturally fallen into teasing one another. His girlfriend attended Montclair and was studying to be a kindergarten teacher, and Jaiden was crazy about her. If they weren't engaged by the end of the year, he could name Casey's next child.

Leighton didn't follow them into the elevator. "You two go ahead. I want the exercise." She entered the stairwell.

Casey sniffed again. Had the strong scent forced Leighton to take the stairs? It *was* potent, but it smelled good. Maybe she didn't like garlic. Casey chewed on her thumbnail. Did Leighton want to avoid riding with them, or worse, with her?

Had Casey done something to offend her? How could she have? She'd only been with her for a minute other than class time. Leighton simply had other lunch plans, and she wanted some exercise.

No. She had a date. God, Casey had to stop internalizing everything where Leighton was concerned, or she'd make herself insane. If she hadn't already.

CHAPTER EIGHT

L eighton looked up with a start as Stefan barged into her office. He kicked the door closed, plopped a croissant on the desk in front of her, then dropped into a chair and took a bite of a filled doughnut. "I was right." His eyes twinkled. "That gorgeous redhead at the bakery told me he works Monday through Friday. So, I bought a dozen of his pastries, and he threw in a few extra for me." He wiped a smear of cream from his lower lip.

"Mmm, thank you." Leighton took a delicate bite from one end, trying to keep the falling crumbs on the napkin. "Did you ask him out?"

"Not yet. That would be too obvious. I'm still feeling my way and want to try his snickerdoodles first. They might be a deal-breaker."

His serious expression had her wondering about the truth of his statement. "You're awful." She sipped her coffee.

"What? I like my sweets." He patted his belly.

That was an understatement, and she'd have to show some self-control if he continued to bring her baked goods each morning.

"You should ask him. Buy your snickerdoodles elsewhere if his aren't to your liking." She brushed a few flaky crumbs from her chest.

"Why buy the cow when you can—"

"Stefan Jovic! Don't you dare." She glared at him. "Besides, that saying isn't meant as a reference to a few free pastries."

He grinned as he finished the last bite of his doughnut. "Relax, I'm just joking. You know I'd like the complete package. I'm not twenty-nine anymore." With a napkin, he swiped at his mouth. "Speaking of milk, now I want some."

"I have oat milk in the fridge. Help yourself, but before you go, I have some information that might interest you, Sherlock." It'd intrigued her.

"Do tell." He tossed his crumpled napkin at the trash can. It missed.

Leighton retrieved it and discarded it. "While you were in the kitchen this morning, Devin returned a book he'd borrowed from Casey."

Stefan rested an ankle on his knee. "So? We knew they'd all gone to college together."

"He also returned her retainer that he found behind his nightstand." She waited a beat for his reaction.

"*In*-teresting." He leaned back in his chair and glanced at the ceiling. "And gross. What did she do?"

"She didn't seem too happy with him, especially when he asked about her son." Leighton threw her napkin away, sinking it like a free throw.

"How so?" He rubbed his hands together.

"His question seemed to irritate her. She hissed at him to let it go, and he dropped the subject." Leighton never wanted to be the recipient of the look Casey had given Devin.

"Hmm." Stefan tapped his upper lip, then stood and clasped his hands behind his back. "Thank you for the informative morning briefing. I will consider the recent evidence while I further explore my theory. However, to work now, I must go." With a twinkle in his eye and a mock salute, he left her office.

His words lingered long after he'd gone. Why had she told him about the exchange between Casey and Devin? He was sure to dive into the middle of it. He was a gossip and a pot stirrer by virtue of his nature. He always had been. At least he was excellent at his job, and most of the time he amused her. She supposed it was better Stefan dug for information rather than her, because as much as she didn't want to admit it, she wouldn't mind knowing who Andy's father was. It could shine a light on what made Casey choose to have a baby while in college, if having a child had been a decision. Even though not all babies were planned, it was a decision to keep it.

Her desire to know personal details about Casey bothered her, but she couldn't quash it. After all, Leighton didn't think she'd imagined all the appreciative looks Casey continued to give her. Was it possible she'd misinterpreted what felt like a connection between them? She wasn't about to call it chemistry, not with a woman she wasn't sure liked women.

Regardless, her instinct led her to believe something existed between them, something she couldn't name. Her eagerness to scan the studio each morning to see if Casey had arrived made the elevator doors seem to work in slow motion, and that sense she got during a lecture that Casey grasped the concept she was teaching before anyone else made her want to break out in a grin. Whatever it was, it made her hold back when she saw Casey working in the studio late at night rather than inquire if she'd eaten or was getting enough sleep. Leighton cared about all her students, but it didn't occur to her to ask the others these questions.

With a sense of dread, she concluded these little things added up to one big problem.

❖

A week later, Leighton settled into her favorite spot on the small sofa near the bookshelves with a fresh coffee and the latest copy of *PleinAir* magazine. The students had an hour of open studio before their next class, and she wanted to make herself available. She'd learned last year that some of them appeared uncomfortable disturbing her in her office.

Stefan passed her. He formed a V with his fingers, then wiggled it near his eyes, a signal for her to watch him.

She glanced around, unsure what was happening.

He tiptoed across the floor with exaggerated steps, as though mimicking a cartoon burglar. Leighton could almost hear the *Mission: Impossible* theme song and tried not to laugh. He stopped behind Devin, who had his head in the supply cabinet, and arranged himself against the workbench. His antics looked ridiculous.

"Hey, Devin. How's it going?"

Devin leaned to see past the open door. "Fine. I'm just looking for a razor blade to sharpen my pencil." He resumed his search.

"I mean, how are things working out?" Stefan struck a pose like a model half sprawled over the surface, hip jutted out and chin in hand. "Are you liking the classes so far?"

Leighton shook her head and gave Stefan a knowing look.

"Yeah. Where are the razor blades?"

Leighton strained to hear Devin from his location halfway inside the cupboard. She glanced across the room to find Casey clearly engrossed in her drawing and unaware of the conversation.

"Third shelf down." Stefan rolled his eyes, seemingly annoyed he didn't have Devin's full attention. "So, are you hoping to learn to paint in the style of another artist while you're here?"

Leighton mouthed the word *smooth* at him.

"Nah, I just want to be good."

A rattle and clang sounded from inside the cabinet, like a stack of supplies had been knocked over. Leighton tensed but forced herself to remain seated.

Stefan peeked at her, grimaced, then turned back to Devin. "But isn't there an artist who inspires you, whose style you wish to emulate?"

"I guess if I had to, I'd pick—Shit! I cut myself." Devin withdrew from the cabinet and studied his hand.

Leighton sprung from the couch and rushed to him. A bright line of crimson oozed from his index finger. She examined it. The cut was shallow but still needed tending.

"You won't need stitches." Her breathing steadied as the fear of one of her students suffering a serious injury ebbed. "You'll find bandages in the first aid kit in the bathroom. Do you want help?"

"No, thanks." He headed that way, his good hand cupped under his damaged one.

Leighton turned to Stefan. "You're incorrigible."

He snapped his fingers in mock frustration. "So close! No, I'm dedicated. Unlike some people who will let a good mystery pass them by, I'm trying to solve it."

"That's just it." She kept her voice low. "I don't think it needs solving. It's irrelevant." If only she truly felt that way.

"Oh, honey. You're dying to know as much as I am." He pointed at her. "I know you, Leighton Raphaela Vaughn."

She closed her eyes. "That's not even my middle name."

Hiring Stefan had been a simple decision. His paintings were gorgeous, and he was a natural teacher. She'd already learned several helpful pedagogical techniques from him, and the students already seemed to like and respect him.

His antics, which had been silly and comical for as long as she'd known him, left her a little uneasy when it involved Casey. He could be impetuous while being funny. He'd always known where to draw the line, but this was different. She trusted him, but if he inadvertently slipped up, the stakes were high.

What if Casey hadn't been so absorbed in her drawing, if she'd seen or heard Stefan's shenanigans? What if somehow she figured out they were snooping into her private life? Casey and her talent were Leighton's best chance at launching Atelier Vaughn into the spotlight. She couldn't afford to let her, if not cause her, to walk out the door.

Yes, Leighton had a crush on her, something she would've thought she'd outgrown years ago, and that made her curious about Casey's personal business, but that could and needed to be squelched. And as much as Leighton hated to admit it, Stefan's interest in the matter was her own fault. She knew him well enough to be sure that if she mentioned the scene between Casey and Devin, along with having told him about Casey's son being named after his father's favorite artist, he'd immediately want the scoop and do anything to get it.

She had to get him—and herself—under control.

CHAPTER NINE

Casey hiked Andy higher on her hip and punched her code into the keypad beside the atelier's entrance. She'd vetoed digging her access card from her wallet in the bottom of her bag while wrestling a toddler. The door unlocked, and she stepped inside.

"Ah, Casey." Maxine glided across the room.

Every time Casey had seen her, she'd been stunning, and today was no exception. A designer skirt suit with CHANEL or Donna Karan vibes, immaculate makeup and manicure, and hair just as perfect as always. Did she have a live-in stylist?

"This must be Andy." Maxine tipped her head to look at him. "Such a handsome boy. And those eyelashes."

"Can you say hi?" Casey gave him a tiny jostle.

He buried his face in her neck.

"He's shy." She patted his back. "Thanks for letting me bring him when I'm in the gallery. I appreciate the time with him." She'd been grateful the volunteer requirement hadn't gone into effect before now. Instead, Leighton had encouraged them to take the first few weeks to get into a routine and focus on their classes. Casey had managed both, in addition to spending a little time with Andy at home.

"Nonsense." Maxine dismissed the notion with a flick of her head. "There's no reason he can't be with you. I assume you'd tell us if he had behavior issues. Volunteering here isn't rocket science, and Leighton insisted."

Casey lowered him to his feet, and he wrapped an arm around her knee. She pulled his plush ball from her shoulder bag and dropped it. One side flattened where it hit the polished wood floor. That was the reason she'd brought it. It didn't roll or bounce, only slid.

And Andy knew not to throw it indoors.

He kicked it, then looked at her and grinned. He let go of her leg, ran the short distance to the ball, and repeated the process.

It would be perfect if he needed to burn off energy here.

With him occupied, they moved to the reception desk.

Maxine motioned toward a simple love seat and coffee table in the corner. "This is a good place if you brought additional toys. There's little traffic, and you can see him."

"This will be great." Casey pulled out a few books and cars and set them near the low table.

When she stood, Maxine touched her arm. "Your thank-you card was lovely. It even impressed my husband, and nothing impresses him. We're fortunate to have you."

Casey smiled. She'd put everything she had into conveying her immense gratitude from her heart and was happy to learn she'd succeeded. "I'm the lucky one. I'm ecstatic to be here." Her scholarship was the most important gift anyone had given her—aside from Andy—and she'd said as much.

Maxine peered at her through her designer frames. "Did you know that four hundred and sixty-one people applied for your scholarship? Artists from all over the world?"

Dumbfounded, she shook her head. She hadn't known the fierceness of the competition. How had she been chosen over that many other candidates?

"I spent two solid months alongside Leighton and Stefan reviewing applications. Once we'd narrowed that down, my husband and I reviewed those who'd applied for the scholarship." Maxine swiped a fingertip along a floating shelf and inspected it as though for dust. "Atelier Vaughn looks for certain things in its students, and my husband and I have our set of criteria. George likes to peruse the applications, but he's content to give me the final say. It can be a life-changing opportunity, so we make sure we award it to a deserving recipient."

Was there an edge in Maxine's tone, or had Casey imagined it? Unease rippled through her. "Well," she hesitated, choosing her words, "I hope that if you have any concerns, my dedication and progress during my time here will assure you that you made the right decision."

What *were* their criteria that made one deserving? If it was financial, Casey certainly qualified. Even with the scholarship, peanut butter and jelly sandwiches would likely be a staple for her and Andy over the next two years.

Thankfully, when he was born, her friends had put her in touch with their friends and relatives who had little boys. The stream of hand-me-down clothing, toys, and equipment seemed never-ending. She shuddered to think how they'd manage entirely on their own. There'd been a time she could count on her parents for her tuition, but now—

"Your application omitted something important." Maxine threw a pointed look at Andy, lying on his stomach on the love seat, engrossed in a picture book.

Casey snapped out of her thoughts. "Yes." She cleared her throat. "I apologize for that, but I had my reasons. I needed to succeed or fail on my own, independent of him. If I hadn't been accepted, I'd wonder if you thought I couldn't handle it because I have a child. If I had been, I'd wonder if you gave me the opportunity because you took pity on a broke, single mother who wanted to learn to paint like the old masters."

Maxine scowled and adjusted her glasses. "First, I don't award my scholarship based on pity. Secondly, I don't understand your thinking. He's your son and a big part of your life. Whether or not you want to admit it, you *aren't* independent any longer. Everything you do affects him."

Casey bristled. Like she didn't know that. Andy was the one reason she hadn't plunged headlong into the application process for Atelier Vaughn the second she'd heard about it. And being able to give him a better life was also why she'd ultimately decided to go for it. "I understand that," she studied her scuffed shoes, "but this meant something to me. I needed to get here on my merit." When Maxine remained silent, she looked up.

Maxine stared at the blank wall beside them. "I wanted a child, long ago." Her tone was wistful. "We tried, but for whatever reason..." She waved her hand like she was dismissing memories she'd prefer not to recall. "Then," her demeanor brightened, "my best friend had a baby girl, the most beautiful baby I'd ever seen. I wanted a child even more after that, so badly I ached." She gave a short laugh. "Despite that, having her around helped. She was the sweetest thing, her love so pure, so unending. No, she wasn't mine, but I loved her as though she were. I'd have given my life for her. I still would." Maxine blinked rapidly and picked up a folder, like she'd realized she'd gone off on a tangent. "Suffice it to say, I don't have any concerns about awarding you the scholarship. You were, and are, the perfect choice, with or without your beautiful little boy. Now, we should get started. I'll show you what to do if you make a sale."

"Wait." Casey didn't want to be rude, but Maxine had piqued her interest. "What happened to her?"

"Happened? Well, that's a long story, but in short, her mother died. About a decade ago. It was a difficult time for everyone." Her eyes glistened with a sheen of tears. "I've tried to do my best to be there for her. After all, I love her like a daughter."

It clicked. "You mean Leighton." Casey suppressed a smile that threatened to emerge simply by saying her name.

"Of course, Leighton. Who did you think I was talking about?" With a soft laugh, Maxine opened the folder. "Let's get you trained. You seem to have a way of sidetracking me, dear girl."

Casey considered Maxine's story as they worked. How tragic to want children when fate had other plans. She tried to imagine her life without Andy and couldn't. She'd known she'd wanted him like he already existed somewhere out there, and all she needed to do was bring him into her life. So, she had, and she didn't have an ounce of regret.

❖

The next morning, Casey attended Leighton's class. With their easels beside one another, Leighton often worked only a few paces away during open studio hours. Each time Casey turned to her palette, she cast furtive glances her way.

Similarly, Casey remained conscious of her when Leighton spent time in her office. Was it the same for Leighton with Casey just outside her door? Whenever she checked, Leighton appeared engrossed in her laptop's screen, but she supposed it was possible. It'd explain the unexpected shivers that came out of nowhere and ran up Casey's spine. She hadn't chosen her station's location. It'd been the last easel available. Fate gave little thought to the feng shui of her growing attraction.

Casey focused on making her color charts. According to Leighton, one of the best ways to learn color mixing was to know how the colors on their palettes interacted. Cadmium yellow was her first chart, but she'd already learned so much. She mixed it with olive green and tinted it with increasing amounts of titanium white. Leighton had instructed them to make a grid on canvas paper with thin lines of masking tape, and once Casey had the correct blend, she painted the first little square.

She found the process enjoyable but time-consuming. Her eagerness to peel the lines of tape away to reveal the sharp, clean squares of color motivated her. Maybe she'd make a TikTok video when she got to that gratifying stage. People were into that kind of thing.

"Let me show you a trick."

Casey froze at the closeness of Leighton's voice and her gentle grasp of Casey's waist as she moved her aside.

Leighton took her offset palette knife and added more white to the mixture. When it was one homogenous color, she loaded some onto the blade, and in a single, confident stroke, she swiped the mixture in the next square and turned to her. "It's a bit faster this way."

"I didn't think to use the knife." Casey hadn't moved away, and neither had Leighton.

"Why should you? I forgot to tell everyone." Leighton gave her a playful smile and flipped the knife around to offer Casey the lacquered handle.

She took it, and Leighton exchanged places with her but stayed close. Uncomfortable under the scrutiny, Casey used the tip to lift more white paint. She mixed it into the avocado-colored pile, lowering both its value and chroma. Nervously, she glanced up.

Leighton nodded.

Casey loaded the knife and lifted it toward the next square.

Leighton caught her wrist. "Like this." With Casey's hand in hers, she returned the glob to the palette, then pushed the knife into the paint, creating a ridge on its underside. "Use the bottom. It's easier to make your mark."

With Leighton's warm, smooth hand enveloping hers, and Leighton's body nearly pressed against her back, they made a bold, downward stroke that left a smear of light green on the grid and an indelible mark on Casey.

Leighton stepped to the side, but her fingers lingered on Casey's wrist. "Better?" A catch in her voice kept the word at only a whisper.

Casey swallowed. "Yes, thank you. I like that." *I like that?* She mentally kicked herself.

Leighton stepped away, not looking at Casey. "Glad I could help."

While Leighton gathered the others around Mikala's station to show them the new technique, Casey tried to mix the next color, but her hand shook. She laid down the knife and wiggled her arm. Leighton's demonstration had rattled her. Who was she kidding? It hadn't been the demonstration. It'd been her closeness. Her touch. That whisper.

It was rare for Casey to be so close to someone, almost enveloped by them. Sure, Mark hugged her now and then, and her parents had years ago. Girlfriends and boyfriends had been affectionate, even Devin occasionally, though their relationship on the whole hadn't been that physical. Andy cuddled with her every day, but he was her little peanut.

This felt different, nice, even inviting. She'd missed that.

She spent the remainder of the class finishing her chart and intermittently shaking out her arm until the trembling finally subsided. Leighton had also disappeared. Coincidence?

Casey hadn't spoken with her after the knife episode, which was for the best. If she hadn't gotten her tremor under control, she'd be googling signs of a stroke or other sudden medical conditions.

Her stomach rumbled as she bent over the utility sink and cleaned her brushes. Her egg salad sandwich called to her from her lunch bag.

Beside her, Stefan lifted a large canvas onto the workbench, the vibrant colors bouncing off his white T-shirt. After choosing a frame molding from the wall, he pushed it flush with the corners of the stretcher bars, then stood back and assessed the pairing.

Casey massaged soap into the bristles. "You're framing today?"

He glanced up. "Yep. It's important to choose the right one. Nothing less than perfection will satisfy Leighton with this piece. She plans to hang it where she'll see it every day."

"That sounds like a tall order." She rinsed the brush under cool water as he chose another molding.

"What's this?" Phoenix sidled up beside him.

Stefan took a step away like he was re-establishing his personal space. "It's a painting."

Casey noted his curt answer. She wasn't sure if Phoenix was in Stefan's way or if his irritation stemmed from Phoenix's apparent lack of something to do.

"Dope. Abstract art's fun to look at, even if I don't care to paint that way." He appeared oblivious to Stefan's vexation. "Although when I think about how loose and free artists like Pollock, Picasso, and Kiefer painted, I consider changing my style for a hot second. It'd be way less stressful, you know? But if I did, I'd be throwing my money away here, wouldn't I?" His rambling went unanswered.

Casey worked the soap in the next brush's bristles into a lather.

Stefan retrieved a wooden, floater-style frame from the wall and pushed it against the corner of the piece. "Ah-ha. This might be the one."

Casey stared at the energetic array of shapes, swirls, drips, and splashes on the canvas in awe. Stefan was right. That particular frame set off the character of the piece beautifully.

Phoenix tilted his head and squinted. "Wouldn't it be fun to throw a gigantic sheet of canvas on the ground and fling colors at it?" He rested his forearms on the workbench, his posture suggesting he'd gotten comfortable for the long haul. "Stand on a ladder, drip paint on it from high above. Smear it around, step on it. You could take out your aggression. How awesome would that be?"

Stefan met Casey's gaze behind Phoenix's back and rolled his eyes. She could guess where he wanted to work out his aggression.

"Wait!" Phoenix straightened with a jolt, his jaw dropping open. "Is this a famous painting?" His boyish enthusiasm transformed into wonder.

Casey stifled a laugh.

Stefan still said nothing as he measured the piece, letting Phoenix's question linger in the air.

"For real?" Phoenix seemed to run with it. His eyebrows shot up. "You're kidding, right?" His hushed, conspiratorial tone was still loud enough for Casey to overhear. "Where'd she get it? At an auction, right? Yeah, she'd buy it legit, at Sotheby's or something." Words poured from him. "It must have cost her a ton of dough. I heard she made bank in her divorce, so it could be chump change for her. Still, hot paintings like that go for millions."

Stefan's disinterested expression sharpened to a glare, making him look uncharacteristically angry. He straightened to his full height and faced Phoenix squarely. "Your pseudo-knowledge of Leighton's private life is based on assumptions. Ensure everything you say here is something you'd say to Leighton." He pointed to the camera in the corner.

Phoenix followed his gesture and swallowed.

"What's the status of your cast painting? You're doing the *Belvedere Torso,* correct? Or have you decided to become an abstract artist?"

Phoenix shrank. "Yeah, I'm working on the *Belvedere.* So far, I've transferred my drawing. I'm just joking about the abstract stuff." He puffed out his chest and gave a cocky lift of his chin. "I'm going to be the next Sargent."

Casey held back a grin as Stefan closed his eyes and sighed. It sounded like he muttered, "God, help us all."

"Well," Stefan gestured at Phoenix's Bermuda shorts and flip-flops, "Sargent would've been wearing a three-piece suit while attacking his painting like a fencer instead of standing here talking to me."

Obviously, Phoenix's attire was fine to wear in the studio, but Casey assumed Stefan was trying to make a point.

Phoenix looked at his clothes. "You're right. I should start my underpainting."

"That would be a good idea."

With a grin, Phoenix turned and stage-whispered over his shoulder. "Don't worry, its provenance is safe with me." He ran his finger along the edge of the canvas-covered stretcher bar. "Now I can tell my fam I got to touch it." His fist pump bought him another glare from Stefan.

Casey didn't recognize the artist who painted it, and she'd taken plenty of art history classes. That said, she didn't consider herself well-versed in modern art. The fact that Leighton liked it surprised her since it resembled nothing else inside the atelier or gallery. Perhaps Leighton had eclectic taste.

She was such an enigma. And one Casey wouldn't mind solving.

CHAPTER TEN

Leighton took one last bite of her butternut squash soup and glanced around the restaurant. The owners had decorated the windowsills with fall leaves and dotted the shelves with miniature pumpkins. It gave the place a cozy, rustic feel that, combined with the delicious meal she'd enjoyed and the essence of autumn itself, made her sigh with contentment.

Stefan plucked a blueberry from her half-empty fruit cup and tossed it into his mouth.

"Eat all you want. I'm finished." She pushed the bowl closer to him. They'd gone to lunch at her favorite spot near the atelier. With some effort, she'd convinced him she had no desire to eat at the bakery, and he'd survive giving his crush on the redheaded baker a day off.

"My club sandwich was huge. I'm stuffed, but your blueberry called my name like a post-meal mint." He leaned back against the booth.

Without a word, a busser cleared their dirty dishes. Stefan's class didn't start for another fifteen minutes, so they sipped their coffees in a moment of comfortable silence.

"She's talented."

He threw it out there with no preamble, but Leighton needed none. She'd already been thinking about Casey. "Yes, she's a very gifted *student*." Her emphasis would've deterred most people, but not him.

He seemed to consider his next words. "That's not where I was going. She's *extremely* talented. If you want the truth, the last time I met a student who had natural skills like hers was the first day of our figure drawing class together in Florence." His knowing look punctuated his statement.

"She's good." Leighton brushed off the last part by tossing her napkin onto the table. "Her portfolio showed that, but the way she approaches her craft, and the decisions she makes—you can't teach that. Include the depth to which she listens, asks questions, and comprehends, and she could be something special."

Casey was looking more like a prodigy each day, like the artist Leighton had hoped she'd be. While Casey's success would reflect well on the atelier in the coming years, that didn't concern Leighton as much as it had only weeks before.

Lately, thoughts of Casey left her with a pleasant warmth, and only a small percentage of those thoughts had to do with Casey's talent. Leighton had caught her sweet scent when she'd shown her the palette knife trick, and the memory flooded back.

She'd believed she could snuff out any sparks of interest after the divorce, but the heat that burned within her when Casey was near suggested embers still smoldered, perhaps covered in ash, but not yet extinguished. All it'd take was one healthy dose of oxygen to start them aglow, and perhaps they'd alight when the time was right. However, for that to occur, Casey couldn't be her student, and Leighton would need to change her stance on dating, which wasn't happening. She never wanted to experience physical or emotional pain of that magnitude again. She'd be fine, just her and Kalyssa. This attraction to Casey would pass.

"I framed the painting, and I think you'll like it." Stefan took a drink.

Leighton found the abrupt change of subject startling, while at the same time, the news exciting. "You did?" She couldn't wait to see it. "Where is it? You didn't leave it on the workbench, did you?" Leighton failed to conceal the worry in her tone. What if it'd been damaged? The security cameras would show her. She grabbed her phone and tapped the app.

Stefan covered her hand with his, stopping her. "No, I hung it on the south wall to keep it safe."

She exhaled slowly, relieved. "You've always been excellent at framing. Thank you for doing that for me. I'll clean your brushes some night to repay you." She motioned with her chin. "Now finish your coffee so I can see how it looks."

A short time later, they arrived at the atelier and Leighton insisted they take the stairs, despite Stefan's grumbling. She liked eating out, but not necessarily the calories that came with it. Plus, the stairs kept her calves firm, and she'd caught Casey appreciating them. Just because she didn't want any kind of involvement didn't mean she didn't enjoy being noticed.

She used her card to badge them into the studio. While the elevator announced newcomers with a ding, the stairwell door did not. She put a hand across Stefan's chest to stop him. With a finger to her lips, she pulled him back into the small alcove, then peered around the corner. A few students gathered in front of the newly framed painting hanging between two of the southern windows.

"I'd hate to own something that expensive." Jenna stared at it, her hand on her hip. "I'd spend all my time worrying someone would steal it."

Devin stood beside her, assessing it. "Maybe that's why Leighton installed the cameras."

"I'd get some, too." Phoenix moved closer. "Stefan wouldn't confirm if she'd bought it at auction. He was being super secretive."

Leighton glanced at Stefan. He held up his hands in a don't-ask-me pose.

Phoenix scratched his chin. "What if she got it off the black market? I'd want a high-tech security system with cameras if I was dealing with unscrupulous characters."

Despite their absurdity, Leighton admired the piece. With the blackout drapes closed, the small picture light above illuminated the canvas, and the floater frame Stefan had chosen accentuated it without detracting from it. Leighton approved. It looked perfect.

"Where are you getting these crazy ideas?" Casey glanced over from where she worked at her station. "That sounds nothing like Leighton. Even if she did buy stolen art, why would she hang it where everyone can see it? It's ridiculous."

Leighton melted a little witnessing Casey stand up for her.

"I don't understand why someone would pay monstrous amounts of money for something like that." Mikala turned back to her easel. "It doesn't appeal to me."

Leighton gave a little scoff, making Stefan elbow her.

Jenna tilted her head. "Who do you think painted it? The dots and funny little animal things make me think it's a Miró, but I've never seen swirls and splatters like this in his works. They're almost reminiscent of Kandinsky."

Are they serious? Leighton looked at Stefan, and he raised one finger in a clear gesture for her to wait.

"I don't see a signature on it anywhere." Devin's nose almost touched the canvas.

Jaiden waggled his finger. "I think it's a Pollock based on these drips and splashes."

Phoenix put his hands on his hips. "Nah, but it's weird enough to be a Picasso."

"No way." Jenna's voice rose. "Not a chance. Have you ever seen a Picasso in person? Picasso was tighter than this, even when painting abstract, and this doesn't have the geometrical elements that he employed."

Clearly, Jenna had strong feelings about Picasso.

"Not all of his do." Phoenix jutted out his chin. "Google it."

Leighton held back a laugh.

"Hey, folks, don't you have something better to do?" Erica didn't look up, instead erasing something on her drawing.

Leighton appreciated her attempt to refocus them, especially since she wasn't getting paid as a TA for this hour.

"These sort of look like faces." Jenna pointed to a corner. "It could be a Picabia."

"It's not a Picabia." Erica and Mark spoke in unison.

Devin swung the bottom of the canvas away from the wall. "I wonder if Stefan installed a dust cover on the back."

"Careful, bruh. Cameras." Jaiden's sing-song warning suggested it was a bad idea.

"I'm just taking a peek. If I can spot a signature, we can find out how much it sold for at auction." Devin lifted the painting off its mount.

Jaiden stepped forward to help him.

Leighton had seen enough. "What the hell do you think you're doing?" She strode out of the alcove and over to where they stood.

Stefan hung back and leaned against a column.

With a nod from Devin, Jaiden helped rehang the painting.

"Sorry, Leighton." Devin seemed to shrink two inches in height.

"We were just curious." Phoenix straightened the frame and shoved his hands in his pockets.

"What're you so curious about that you couldn't simply wait to ask me?" She directed her question to Phoenix.

"Well, we all were—"

"Not all of us." From her station, Mikala interrupted him.

As Leighton surveyed the room, she lingered on Casey a moment longer than necessary, but she couldn't help herself.

Phoenix swallowed. "Okay, *some* of us were wondering how much it cost. We thought if we spotted a signature, we could figure it out. After all, we don't get the opportunity to see art like this often."

His feeble attempt to justify their actions made her want to roll her eyes. She frowned instead until a noise from Stefan made her turn. She planted her fist on her hip. "Is something funny?"

"Oh, yes." He gasped for air. "This has snowballed beyond my imagination."

"Care to share?" Leighton could hardly wait to hear what he had to say. Knowing Stefan as she did, it was bound to be good.

He wiped tears from the corners of his eyes with a paper towel he snagged from Erica's roll as he passed by. "Phoenix became interested in your new acquisition while I was framing it. He made some assumptions and theorized a bit." He stopped beside her. "I didn't correct him because it's not my story to tell."

She turned to Phoenix. "Tell me, please."

With slumped shoulders and a meek expression, he shrugged. "We knew it was a famous painting, but we wanted to confirm our guesses on the artist." He shifted from foot to foot, his flip-flops clacking.

"Is that so?" She stared at him. "And what conclusion did you arrive at?" Is this nonsense what they did when she wasn't around?

"Um, we weren't sure. We guessed Pollock or Miró, among others." His volume tapered as he deflated.

"How did you think I came into possession of a famous piece of art?" Leighton looked at them.

Devin took the bait. "We assumed an auction house. I was only joking about you buying it on the black market."

His earnest demeanor was too much.

"The black market!" Stefan bent over and grabbed Leighton's arm for support.

She couldn't help but let her facade slip, and a laugh escaped her. She sneaked a peek at Casey, who returned her smile. Leighton returned her attention to the group before her. "How much money do you think I earn with this school? The cost of tuition is transparent. It's fair and not inflated in the least."

Phoenix barely spoke above a whisper. "We thought you...um, well...made a lot of money in your divorce."

She looked at Stefan, and his eyes sparked with glee.

"So, who is the artist? Is he at least kind of famous?" Jenna hadn't joined in the laughter. Nor had Jaiden, Devin, or Phoenix.

Leighton tilted her head. "Jenna, I'd expect you'd be open-minded to the possibility it was a female, yet you only listed male artists."

They all exchanged glances.

Leighton exhaled, only half feigning her dismay at their manner of conducting themselves in her absence. "My four-year-old daughter Kalyssa painted this. She titled it, *Ants Eating a Picnic.*"

Her revelation sank in, and their eyes flicked between her and the canvas. Everyone's except Casey's.

Casey's attention remained on her.

Leighton's heart did a little jump. "Its value is inestimable to me, so leave it on the wall, please."

"Remind me not to entrust you with any secrets, buddy!" Stefan gave Phoenix a playful bump. "You fold like a bad poker hand."

Leighton stole a glance at Casey as she walked to her office. Casey's surprise had transformed into a grin. She shut her office door, leaned against it, and closed her eyes.

Now that Casey knew she had a child, would she view Leighton differently? It could go two ways. Casey might get over her little infatuation with her, if one existed to begin with. Or being mothers could give them more common ground on which to connect.

Leighton dreaded the consequences of either option.

CHAPTER ELEVEN

Casey squinted against the bright morning sunlight streaming in through the kitchen window. Seven o'clock had come way earlier than she would have liked, and she'd had to drag herself out of bed to keep Andy from helping himself to whatever he wanted in the apartment. Adding a full load of classes at the art school to her already demanding schedule was taking its toll, but she had no regrets, only an emotional hangover some nights after spending much of the day around Leighton and dark circles under her eyes some mornings, like this one.

A wet towel landed over the back of the chair beside her, making her jump, and she looked up to see Mark ruffling Andy's hair.

"Morning, buddy." He dropped his phone onto the table and opened the refrigerator.

"Can you not?" She whipped the towel from the chair and tossed it into the corner. "It warps the wood."

"Case, these chairs are like a hundred years old and don't even match." He drank from the jug of milk, capped it, and put it away.

She snapped her toast in half and gave the larger piece to Andy. "They're the only ones we have. We need to take care of them. And if we're all going to share the same milk, you need to use a glass."

Mark lifted the table by the corner and toed the makeshift shim back in place before sitting beside her. "Sorry. It's a bad habit I picked up in college. I'll try to remember." He scooted closer and draped his arm around her shoulders. "Look," he pointed out the window, "it's a beautiful day. Right, Andy? Why's your momma all riled up?"

Andy ignored him and took a bite of cereal, most of the milk splashing back into the bowl or onto his bib, only a few Cheerios making it into his mouth.

"Are there blueberries in there? Are you going to give me some?" Mark pretended to try and steal one.

Andy wrapped his arms around his bowl and grinned. "No."

How could she remain irritated when they were so darned cute?

Mark leaned back in his chair, balancing on two legs, and rifled through the cupboard.

One of the benefits of having a small kitchen was having everything in reach.

He pulled out a granola bar. "Want one?"

Casey shook her head and drank her tea.

Mark's chair landed back on all fours with a thump and a creak.

Even the crinkling of his wrapper made Casey sigh. Why was she so on edge today? She didn't know, but it felt like everything was coming to a head. All the emotions she'd been dealing with for weeks suddenly seemed too much, too overwhelming.

He leaned in and bumped her with his shoulder. "Are we going to watch in silence as the handsome little man eats, or do you want to talk about it?"

She didn't answer. He was her closest friend, but how could she explain what she'd been going through? She was confused and frustrated—and pining for her teacher? God, she was a cliché.

Mark shifted even closer. "Okay, here's my final offer. I'll make you my famous fried eggs, if you'll tell me what's bothering you." He flicked her mug. "You can't go all morning on half a piece of toast and tea."

She allowed herself to smile. Eggs sounded good. "Do we have any?"

He leapt up. "Only two, but that'll do. I'll pick some up from the bodega after work." A pan landed on the burner. "Talk, Norford. I don't cook for free. Are you worried about money?"

Casey shrugged. No more so than any other day. "No." She let the warmth of her tea seep into her icy hands.

"School?" The open refrigerator swallowed his voice as he reached in for the eggs and butter.

Casey exhaled loudly. "Sort of." She wanted to add *unfortunately,* but she didn't. "Ever since we've started studying at AV, there's been something going on that I haven't mentioned."

He turned, concern on his face. "What?"

"Okay, not going on. That's the problem." She held her head in her hands.

Andy touched her arm, leaving a wet mark.

Casey smiled and kissed his elbow. What a sweetie. "It's okay, baby. Momma's fine." She watched Mark crack the eggs into the pan. "It's Leighton."

Mark glanced over his shoulder. "What's that mean?"

"I don't know. Maybe I'm imagining it." Second thoughts about sharing crept in, and she dismissed them. She had to get it out, if only to see if Mark thought she was crazy. "It shouldn't be happening, but it's not getting any easier, and it isn't going away."

Mark turned to face her. "Wait. Leighton isn't...You know, being," he stumbled over his words, "inappropriate?"

It took a second for his meaning to register. Then she gasped. "Oh! No! It's not like *that*."

He blew out a breath and turned to the stove. "Okay, then. Case, normally I'm a bright guy, but you're going to have to dumb this down so I can understand. What isn't going away?"

Casey steeled herself. She had to say it. "I *like* her." She cleared her throat. "I'm attracted to her."

He paused, spatula in hand. "Oh." Then he spun around, his eyes wide. "Oh. Yeah, that's not good." He checked the eggs. "You were acting sort of weird on the first day, but I chalked it up to nerves or something. You'd been in awe of Leighton for a long time. Is that the issue? Infatuation?"

"I guess so. I don't know. It's all so confusing." She laid her head in the nest of her folded arms.

"Andy, don't put cereal in your momma's hair."

At Mark's warning, she bolted upright. She didn't have time for a second shower. "Anders Norford, you know better. Are you all done?" She made to take away his bowl, but he resisted, so she gave him another chance to finish eating. He had her so wrapped.

Mark flipped the eggs, then opened the cupboard for a plate. "Continue."

"What I haven't mentioned is that I think Leighton might also be interested in me. But she's done nothing inappropriate." The last part came blurting out.

His eyebrows shot up, plate paused mid-air. "Are you sure? About her interest, I mean?"

"We've had a few moments." And what moments they'd been. She touched the back of her hand and could almost feel Leighton's fingers there while showing her how to do her color chart.

He handed her the plate, moved the salt and pepper in front of her, and plopped into his seat. "Whoops." He leaned back, opened the drawer, and retrieved a fork. "Here."

She cut into her eggs. Runny in the middle and crispy around the edges, her favorite. "Thanks." She stole back the piece of toast Andy hadn't eaten.

Mark folded his arms across his chest. "So, you have a crush on our teacher, and she might have one on you. Only you, Case, only you. What are you going to do about it?"

She scoffed around a bite. "Nothing. Are you nuts?"

He tilted his head the way he did when he was thinking. "Maybe you should get it out in the open, be honest with her. If you think she feels something, too, she's bound to have noticed your interest, and you said it's not going away."

"Are you serious? I'm not jeopardizing my spot at AV by bringing it up." She returned to her breakfast. What a ridiculous idea.

"I don't know. Talking about it might put it in perspective. Maybe the two of you can laugh about it and move on. What do you think, buddy? Is that a good plan?"

Andy grinned. "Buddy."

He probably thought his name was Buddy with how often Mark called him that.

"Right. I'm going to leave my entire future up to the two-year-old." Casey finished her last forkful. "Not happening, but thanks for listening and making me eggs." She wiped the last bite of toast through the yolk remaining on the plate. "I'm glad I have you to talk to. It's been hard keeping it to myself."

He squeezed her shoulder. "No problem, Case. Don't wait so long next time you're crushing on a hot, older woman."

She swatted at him, but he was too fast. She felt better though, more like herself and less like a pressure cooker. She'd assured him she would not tell Leighton what she was feeling, and her reason was sound. She wasn't about to risk losing the opportunity to learn from her. Casey looked at Andy and smiled.

That, and the doors it could open for her, were too important.

Hours later, Casey lounged on the smaller sofa in the studio while she worked on her sketchbook assignment. She looked up to find Leighton standing before her and wasn't able to stop her grin. "Hi." She'd seen little of her outside of class the last few days.

Leighton gave her a warm smile. "Maxine called me from her car to tell me yet again, Andy is adorable. The way she's still gushing over him from yesterday, be glad she didn't take him home with her."

Casey had now done two volunteer shifts in the gallery, both of which Maxine had stayed for and played with Andy. "Some days I wish she would. I'd give anything for a free evening to spend in a hot bath with a glass of wine."

Leighton's smile dimmed. "Single parenting is hard, isn't it?"

"It is. Harder than I thought it would be. But it's so worth it. And he sleeps through the night now, so that's something. Otherwise, I might consider letting Maxine take him." Casey set aside the drawing she'd been working on and stretched.

Leighton laughed as she lowered herself onto the sofa beside her. "Do you have help?"

"Mark's great with him when he's home. And I have someone I trust implicitly for when I'm at the art store and now here. That makes a huge difference."

Leighton nodded. "That's right. You and Mark are roommates." She shifted and her hand brushed Casey's leg, but when her fingers met skin through a large rip in Casey's jeans, she jerked away.

Casey stared at the spot that still tingled. Her heart pounded. Whoa. Leighton had touched her, and not on the hand, but on the tender flesh of her thigh. Had it been intentional? Of course not. But she imagined if it had been and what those velvety fingertips would feel like higher. Arousal flared in her belly, between her legs. God, what was she thinking?

"I heard he enjoyed playing in the gallery. Kids love all that open space." Leighton kept her focus on Casey's sketchbook.

Leighton had reacted like she'd been shocked, and now grasped the offending hand with her other, like she needed to control it. And she was discussing kids like nothing unusual was going on. All Casey wanted to talk about was if Leighton was as lit up as she was right now, but she could play this game, too. She'd told Mark she had no intention of telling Leighton about her attraction, and she'd hold to it. "I think the highlight of Andy's day yesterday was taking off his shoes and sliding around in his socks. He had more fun doing that than playing with anything I brought to keep him busy." Casey recalled his joy and smiled. Good, focus on that, not on Leighton's touch.

"She said he looks just like you." Leighton studied her like she was trying to imagine the resemblance.

Had Maxine volunteered this information, or had Leighton asked? She hoped it was the latter. "Many people say that. It's his complexion and hair, but he has his daddy's eyes." She didn't want to get into a discussion about Andy's father. Time for a change of subject. "Does your daughter like playing in the gallery? I didn't know you were a mom until the black-market episode."

Leighton laughed. "Yes, she loves it. She considers it her personal ballet studio. I've never regretted having those hardwood floors installed. Plus, Kalyssa loves hanging out with Maxine. If she makes a sale, she slips her a couple of dollars and calls it her commission. Kalyssa thinks she's the best thing since butterfly hair clips."

"Does she look like you?" Casey needed to picture the little girl who had inherited half of her genetics from Leighton.

"A little bit. The shape of her face and her eye color. And her hair is the same shade mine used to be when I was her age. You'll meet her soon." With a quick smile, she stood. "How close are you to finishing this week's assignments?" She nodded toward the sketchbook.

"Uh," Casey scrambled to switch gears. "All I have left is the value sphere. I'm almost done."

"Bring it to me when you're finished." Leighton strode away. "I'll be in my office."

Casey studied her until she settled at her desk, then assessed her drawing. She completed it, despite her distracted mind, then scrawled her signature at the bottom and closed the book.

When she approached Leighton's office, she knocked on the glass, though the door stood open. Even this much later, she still felt unhinged from that one, likely inadvertent, touch.

Leighton looked up from her laptop and gestured for the sketchbook. "Come back in ten minutes, and we'll talk."

Talk? About what? Casey left, wary of what to expect when she returned and hoping she'd be able to get herself together by then.

CHAPTER TWELVE

Leighton opened Casey's sketchbook and froze. She considered closing her office door to avoid any interruptions. With trembling fingers, she flipped through it. Her initial response had been justified. Casey hadn't filled the pages with sketches. They contained finished, realized drawings, and they were excellent. Nuanced, gestural, and alive. They leapt off the page.

With relish, she picked up her stack of sticky notes and began writing. No critiques she'd given in the past had been for sketches like these. Students didn't complete ones of this caliber in an hour. Casey had invested considerable time and effort into her assignments, and it showed. The shading was subtle, and the compositions advanced. With the page oblique to the light, she studied the fine-textured surface, but she couldn't find a single instance of the pencil being pressed too hard into the tooth of the paper, a tendency of young artists. Casey might be young, but she was no novice.

Leighton jotted notes and attached a sticky to each page in a place where it wouldn't smudge anything. It was unusual for her to have to try so hard to find suggestions for improvements. How had Casey become so talented? Whether natural or taught, her skills were impressive. Leighton's head always swam when admiring exquisite pieces like these. No, she reminded herself. These were sketches. It wasn't like she'd accessed the Study Room for Drawings and Prints at the Met. It wasn't an Albrecht Dürer before her. Yet Casey's inspired the same sense of awe. She wanted to retrieve *her* sketchbook from her bag and get lost in the sublime feel of dragging graphite or charcoal over paper. Despite having no time for that now, the critique she was about to give excited her in equal measure.

She never gave impromptu criticism. Any other time, she'd notify the student a day or two in advance. Almost without fail, they arrived with bags under their eyes from pulling an all-nighter. Not Casey. She'd completed her assignments early. Still, Leighton shouldn't have set the precedent. All her students needed to be treated as equals, at least on the surface, especially if she harbored a secret interest in one of them. Now she'd have to spring the same on someone else today. She tried to think of who might be caught up. Perhaps Mikala. Leighton's goal wasn't to cause any of them anxiety. If only she'd kept her mouth shut.

Silence hadn't been possible. Casey had looked so sweet and at home on the sofa, curled up and drawing her sphere. She'd drawn Leighton to her. The sketchbook assignments had been an excuse to continue their conversation after her supply of Andy-related topics had expired.

Now she had a second critique to do, so it didn't appear she'd singled out Casey for one-on-one instruction or feedback. She should be using the time to plan next week's lesson. The thought irritated her, but it faded fast. Casey would arrive in a few minutes. Her demeanor softened as she looked forward to their time together. If only Casey didn't have to be her student.

She had little time to brood over the situation because Casey appeared in her doorway minutes later.

"Come in and sit."

Casey sat on the edge of one of the two guest chairs.

Leighton came around to join her and laid the sketchbook on the desk. "We both can see this way." This close, she could smell Casey's perfume, light and fresh. The scent reminded her of spring, of youth, of new beginnings. It brought daffodils to mind. Since it already distracted her, she forced herself to breathe through her mouth.

"These are magnificent, Casey." She flipped to the first page with a bright green sticky note that said *reflected light.* "Your commitment shows."

"Thank you. I enjoy it. I find it relaxing when I'm stressed."

What in Casey's life made her need to use drawing as an outlet? Perhaps it was her job, or Andy, or both. Being a single mom wasn't easy.

"You should be proud. I can see you've put extra effort into them."

Casey appeared pleased by the praise, judging by the corners of her mouth twitching and the faint pinking of her cheeks. She pressed the fingertips of one hand into her thigh, the one whose skin Leighton had touched through her ripped jeans.

Leighton flinched at the memory. After a calming breath, she tapped the page with her index finger. "My only advice here is to watch for reflective light from nearby objects and surfaces. Some of it will bounce off the tabletop onto the underside of your object." She looked at Casey. Her hazel eyes always seemed to absorb the color of her shirt. They leaned toward green today. They reminded her of her mother's favorite emerald earrings she used to wear every Christmas, but this wasn't the time to reminisce. "Just like on the sphere, the value of the vase will be lighter where it curves under."

Casey gave a sheepish nod. "Sorry, I forgot to address it. I knew that."

Leighton was in danger of being mesmerized by Casey's eyes, so she looked away. "Your ellipse is perfect, and your shading is lovely here. You have an eye for values." She turned the page.

When Casey leaned forward to read the notes she'd left, their shoulders touched. Neither moved.

"Your drapery study is sublime." Leighton smoothed the note where she'd written the word *thickness*. "Just remember when you're drawing folds, the heaviness and texture of the material is going to influence the curvature of triangular folds." Leighton turned toward her. "Ingres was so skilled at painting and drawing clothing that historians studied his drawings to determine what fabrics people wore in those times."

"I didn't know that." Casey looked impressed. "I've seen his works at the Met, and it makes sense. They're so elegant and detailed. He depicted the gowns and clothing to perfection."

How strange to think of them gazing at the same paintings at different points in time. Or had they been in the same gallery, mere feet apart, strangers? What if they'd crossed paths without knowing it? The fact they'd met like this, in this hierarchical system, saddened Leighton. Yet if they'd stumbled across one another a few years ago, she'd have been married, and Casey would've been what? Even younger, dating someone else like Andy's father, or a pregnant undergrad. It wouldn't have been an ideal time for either of them, not that the present was any better. Fate dealt them a teasing hand.

Casey, who'd been studying her sketch, returned her to the present. She pointed. "I see it now. The folds are too sharp and make it look like a thin cotton sheet."

Leighton smiled and nodded. She turned the pages, alternating between effusive praise and helpful criticism. Casey seemed eager to receive both. Her maturity showed, like she realized one set of comments made her fly high, while the other told her how much higher she could soar. Casey sat within inches of her and appeared to bask in her attention, like she didn't want the critique to end. Or was Leighton imagining it?

After a few minutes of explaining her notes, Leighton turned to the last page. Before she could discuss the final one, Casey spoke.

"Have lunch with me." The words seemed to fall from her lips, and her eyes shone with eagerness, anticipation, hope, or perhaps all three.

Startled, Leighton searched for words. Afraid her hands might shake, she laid them in her lap. Was she reading too much into the question? She might not have imagined Casey's interest after all. Maybe Stefan was correct. Each morning, a twinge of joy shot through her when Casey arrived. Did Casey feel something similar when she walked into the room? Could Casey also sense that something seemed to exist between them?

She glanced at the clock, noting it would soon be noon. What if Casey was hungry and inviting her to eat with her, nothing more? She might have questions and want to continue their conversation about her sketches, but Leighton didn't believe that to be the case. Casey appeared too invested in her response.

Thoughts flew through her mind. If she agreed, another student might spot them in a nearby café or sandwich shop. Then she'd have to take each of her students to lunch. However, she refused to delude herself into thinking they'd be similar outings. Accepting Casey's invitation would summon trouble. She wanted to go back in time before Casey asked, because once she gave her answer, things would change.

"No." Leighton had been watching her face, the picture of vulnerability. She saw the moment the rejection landed in Casey's clenched jaw and the twitch near her eye. "I can't." On instinct, she squeezed Casey's forearm, then let go. In the quiet, her pulse pounded in her ears.

"Oh." Casey darted her tongue out to lick her bottom lip. "I see."

Leighton turned back to the sketchbook. She pulled the sticky note from the page before Casey's hand caught hers.

"Leave them, please." Casey released her.

Leighton obliged, closed the book, and handed it to her.

Casey stood but didn't leave. "You're sure?"

Leighton brushed eraser crumbs from her pant leg and didn't look up. This was the way it had to be, and she hoped the hollowness in her chest would disappear with time. She nodded. When she found the courage to raise her head, Casey remained standing a few feet away. Leighton drew a deep breath and exhaled. "Close the door, please." She held out her hand for the sketchbook.

Casey gave it to her and pushed the door closed. She grasped the backrest, her fingertips making indentations in the soft leather.

"Sit." Leighton touched the seat. Warmth remained on the chair, and the intimacy of it startled her. When Casey sat, Leighton set the sketchbook on her desk but left it closed. "Do I need to explain why I can't go to lunch with you?"

Casey blushed, not on her cheeks but her neck. It continued under the collar of her shirt.

Leighton chided herself for wondering how far it went.

"Everyone has to eat. It's just lunch." Casey's argument had little weight behind it.

"I don't know that it is." Leighton remained quiet for a moment. "Is it?"

Casey swallowed. "Yes?" Her high-pitched answer came out sounding like a question.

"Yes?" Leighton crossed her legs, angling them toward her because of the nearness of the desk. "Or yes."

Casey's breathing quickened. "It can be." She raised her chin.

"Sure, it *can* be." Leighton folded her hands in her lap to keep them from shaking. "Is that what you want?"

The answer was apparent in Casey's downcast eyes before her whispered no.

"What do you want?" Leighton's voice came out raspy. Why had she asked?

Casey met her gaze and held it. Her chest heaved three breaths before she answered. "I want to get to know you."

Every cell in her body quivered, yet she needed to have this conversation with Casey to set some boundaries, to voice how this could never happen. *Christ.* She needed water. No, a stiff drink. "You'll learn about me, just as I will learn about all my students this year."

Casey shook her head. "No, I'd like to *know* you."

What the... Did she mean in the biblical sense? "I..." Leighton fumbled for words. "I..." She closed her eyes. Yes, she could do this. Just get it out in the open. "I'm your teacher."

"I'm not underage." Her indignation was apparent in her raised chin. "I'm almost twenty-six. I have a college degree and a child. Yes, I'm a student here—"

"You're *my* student." Her tone was icy, but she didn't care. "And I'm the owner of this atelier. I'm not about to risk my business because a student wants to *know* me."

Casey's eyes blazed. "I've read the syllabus and could quote it word for word. We don't receive grades. You critique our projects and assignments. We're supposed to compete against ourselves to become better artists, not against one another. Those are your words, so why would it matter?"

"Because my reputation matters. The atelier doesn't exist in a bubble. Trust me, people frown upon this type of behavior in this day and age." She waved her hand between them. "It's unethical." Her office was soundproof, and they sat with their backs to the glass wall. She breathed a sigh of relief for both as their uncomfortable conversation continued.

"So, if those things you mentioned weren't standing in the way, you'd be interested?"

Leighton swore she saw Casey's eyes transform from green to brown before her. Her throat tightened as she admired the highlights in Casey's brown hair. Would it feel soft between her fingers? She took in Casey's athletic build, her small breasts, and her toned legs. Not to mention her talent, charm, cute sense of humor, and dimples that appeared when she laughed. Plus, she couldn't omit the commendable effort Casey gave to attend classes, work, and raise a toddler from her list of positive attributes. Leighton couldn't help but imagine a what-if scenario. "Yes." The word came out broken.

Casey relaxed, and her body melted into the chair, as though knowing eased her tension. She smiled, but it appeared bittersweet. "Well." She wrapped her arms around her torso.

The air in the room felt heavy. Leighton wanted to open a window, but that was against her rules. Besides, an air filtration system costing what she'd paid guaranteed the air she breathed was clean and safe. Any stale air was a product of her imagination. Her nerves wreaked havoc inside her. Casey always made her a little anxious, even during class. However, she'd said what she needed to say. Now she could file this conversation in the past and forget they'd had to have it.

"You never took your husband's surname, did you?"

"What?" The question startled her.

"Vaughn. It was your name, your maiden name, wasn't it?" Casey ran her hand through her hair.

Where had that come from? "And here I had mistaken quiet for shy." Leighton delivered the sentence under her breath. "Yes. I kept it when we got married. I'm partial to it, and a woman taking the man's name never appealed to me, so I never considered changing it. Plus, the public recognized it as my branding. For years, I'd wanted to name my school Atelier Vaughn. I like the sound of it."

Casey nodded, her eyebrows tight like she mulled it over. "So do I. Why did you get divorced?" She blurted the question like she'd seen her opening and wasn't about to let it pass.

Leighton sighed. It was a personal question, and she had every right to refuse to answer. Maybe one day she'd be able to file those memories away. Yet the desire to share something with Casey won out. "My husband and I didn't get along." She heard how understated it sounded, how simple, like an explanation used to placate young children. Casey was no child, but condensing years of a volatile relationship into a digestible answer would divulge too much of herself. Besides, it wasn't like Casey needed to know the traumatic details.

"I'm sorry."

"I'm not." It was Leighton's turn to raise her chin. "I'm sorry it came to that, but I'm content to be where I am." It was time for her to ask a question. "How long were you and Devin together?"

Casey's eyebrows shot skyward. "How did you know we used to date?"

Leighton tilted her head. "Your retainer."

Casey groaned. "You saw. I'm sorry about that. He could've chosen a better time." She looked at the ceiling. "Not even a year."

"What happened? If I may." Leighton propped her elbow on the desk and rested her chin in her hand.

Casey looked at her feet. "He decided he didn't want a baby, at least with me." She looked up, her expression fierce. "As you can see, I didn't need him."

"Apparently." Leighton stretched her legs, then crossed them the opposite way. It was nice talking to Casey about something other than art. "Do you miss being with him?"

Casey lifted a shoulder and let it fall. "Will you think I'm horrible if I say no?"

Leighton shook her head. How could she ever think that of Casey?

"The majority of the time, I was happy while we dated. He's a nice guy, and he cared about me. I cared about him, too. I still do. We enjoyed one another, but we weren't in love. I was in love with the idea of having a baby more than anything." Casey furrowed her brow. "I'm sorry. I know he's your student, and I didn't intend to imply anything negative about him. We simply wanted different things. Devin isn't a bad guy, and you're welcome to get his side of the story."

She looked so sincere. "That won't be necessary." One of the last things Leighton wanted to do was discuss Casey's love life with her ex-boyfriend.

Casey squirmed, but a smile tugged at the corner of her mouth.

To Leighton's dismay, she imagined placing a soft kiss there. She couldn't be having thoughts like that.

They looked at one another until the silence became awkward.

Leighton cleared her throat. "You handle yourselves like professionals. I don't see your past being a problem." Not only had she seen Casey take care of herself around Devin, but she could sense Casey's reluctance to let problems between them become issues within the walls of the atelier. She was thankful for that. If a problem should arise between two of her students, as their teacher, she'd have to step in.

The harsh reminder of their respective statuses left a dull taste in her mouth.

CHAPTER THIRTEEN

After meeting with Leighton in her office, Casey returned to her easel though her mind was elsewhere. Still, she needed to begin the day's assignment.

Leighton had rejected her invitation. What had she expected? She'd acted on impulse and surprised even herself. If Leighton had agreed, she wasn't sure how she would've paid for lunch. Her credit card would've had to take the hit. Leighton's rejection had been tough to accept, but talking with her afterward had left Casey feeling warm and fuzzy, and she wasn't supposed to feel those things. She was a student, and Leighton was her instructor. Leighton had made that clear.

Besides, what had she envisioned happening? Leighton saying yes and the two of them embarking on a hot, romantic affair with weekend trips to Gymboree? Not that she could afford going there. She and Leighton moved in different economic circles and different, well, everything.

A few minutes later, Mark approached her. He wiped his hands on a paper towel. "I'm starving, Case. Let's get some grub."

"I can't. I'm working on this." Casey taped a piece of paper to her board. Plus, she'd brought a sandwich from home to save money. She didn't mean to take out her rejection by being short with him, but her appetite had disappeared.

"The bust cast study? No one's started that yet. Aren't you hungry?"

Mikala piped up from the next station. "I'm always up for grabbing some food. I need all the calories I can get with Guard training." She patted her toned abdomen.

Mark perked up. He appeared thrilled to find someone to accompany him, let alone someone who'd be willing to eat in the reverent, uncompromising manner he practiced.

"Are you feeling all right? Can I bring you a sandwich?" He nudged Casey with his elbow. Concern darkened his features.

She thanked him and shook her head.

He left with Mikala while debating the superior qualities of a chopped cheese versus a cheesesteak.

Leighton had disappeared, her office light off and the door closed. Casey turned her attention to her assignment, set an alarm on her phone for twenty minutes, and worked on the preliminary sketch for her cast study. She'd chosen a replica marble bust of a Florentine girl from the choices on the shelves.

Once she'd finished the envelope—that's what Leighton had called the straight lines sketched around the figure—the cast drawing would fit within its border. Casey worked sight-size, so when she stood at the masking tape line on her rug, the bust and the drawing would appear identical.

As she focused on straight lines and angles, Stefan wandered over. He munched on a bag of Cool Ranch Doritos without her looking to verify. The scent was unmistakable. Any other time, she'd crave them, but the thought of eating made her stomach ache. She didn't want to think about lunch.

"Want a bit of advice? Hold your pencil up to match the angle you see. Imagine it pointing to the minutes on a clock. See how the line sloping from her ear to her shoulder lands at about the thirty-seven-minute mark?"

She found the suggestion helpful when she tried to replicate it on her paper. "Thanks. I hadn't heard that trick before."

"Leighton and I had an instructor in Florence who taught us that. Back then, everyone could tell time on a real clock." He winked at her, then glanced at Leighton's office. "Have you seen her around? She didn't mention she was going anywhere." He crunched a chip.

The warm corn smell almost made her retch. She hoped he'd search for Leighton somewhere else. "I haven't." At least not since Leighton had told her no, twice. Casey didn't know where she'd gone. Maybe she enjoyed eating lunch alone. She'd made it clear she wasn't interested in sharing a meal with a student, though Casey was certain it was *her* whom Leighton had rejected.

"Hmm. I wonder if she wanted anything set up for the Flemish lesson. Never mind, I'll text her." He retreated to his office.

Casey hoped the unpleasant scent would also leave and refrained from waving her hands to clear the stench from the air. She needed no more reminders about lunch.

At least she'd scored one win this morning. When she'd asked if Leighton would be interested in her if their situation was different, she'd said yes. Imagine that. Leighton Vaughn, interested in *her*. For the remainder of the hour, Casey hid her smile.

Soon, those who'd left to find food began to return.

"We missed you at lunch." Mikala stopped by Casey's station. "I had the most amazing sweet potato fries, but as addicting as they were, I would've shared some with you."

Casey ignored her coy insinuation. Mikala was cute, but she didn't care to flirt with her. She had no interest in starting anything and didn't want to lead her on. They could be friends, sure.

"Did Mark take you to his favorite place?"

"Yeah. I got a chopped cheese." Mikala hovered close. "He's a funny guy."

She glanced at Mark and Devin in the lounge area, laughing at some joke. "Yeah, he's great."

Mikala nodded at her easel. "You work fast. I still need to finish my color charts and my Bargue drawing. I haven't started two of my sketchbook assignments for the week. Cross your fingers Leighton will cut class short, and we'll have more time to get everything done."

Casey doubted Leighton would shorten her class, nor did she want her to. She enjoyed being around her, plus Leighton seemed invested in making the best use of her time with her students. When she wasn't lecturing, she gathered everyone around her for a demonstration. Even when she turned them loose to work on assignments, she circled the room, paying them individual attention, offering suggestions, and asking critical questions.

On cue, Leighton appeared. Casey hadn't seen her return from lunch. She hoped it wouldn't be awkward between them. The rejection stung, but Casey didn't regret asking. Her desire to know Leighton was as strong as ever, and she didn't want to stop trying. She'd achieved the important things in her life by going after them. Perhaps if Leighton got to know her better, she'd change her mind. When Casey factored in her age, her status as a mother, and the evaluation standards of the atelier, she really didn't think getting to know Leighton better was such a big deal.

"Gather round, folks." Leighton motioned for them to join her in the lounge area. She glanced at Casey, then looked away. "Before I start the lecture, I want to bring something to your attention. This winter, the Salmagundi Club will host an exhibition titled *Adoration of the Female Figure*. Their annual classical painting contest is one of the most coveted exhibitions east of the Mississippi. They award monetary prizes for first, second, and third place." She handed a stack of flyers to Phoenix. "The Best of Show winner will receive a six-month, all expenses paid, study abroad opportunity in Florence."

Their reactions might have led an onlooker to think they had a one in ten chance of winning the lottery.

"I encourage all of you to enter. You're welcome to use the painting of a female figure you paint in class, or you're welcome to enter something you do on your own. I can give you a list of live model sessions in the area if you choose the latter."

Six months in Florence. Casey had never been to Europe. Imagine, sketching Michelangelo's *David* or wandering through the halls of the Uffizi Gallery for hours. She took a flyer when the stack passed. It was a long shot, but she'd enter for fun. Why not? Her female figure painting fit the entry guidelines without requiring extra work. It'd thrill her to have her painting accepted into the exhibition.

"One last thing. If you choose to enter, the atelier will cover your entry fee. Please talk to Maxine about it."

Relief flooded Casey at not having to come up with the funds. Erica had never mentioned the atelier covering such fees before. Based on Erica's joyous expression, it was unusual.

Leighton clapped her hands. "Okay, let's begin. Grab your notebooks or laptops. Today we're going to talk about the Flemish Technique. Second-year students, the first part will be a refresher course for you, then I'll work with the four of you on some of the more advanced intricacies and what I'll expect to see in your paintings versus the first-year students'."

A pang of jealousy hit Casey. She wanted to learn what the second-year students would be taught. Maybe she could eavesdrop and incorporate some of what she overheard into her painting. It couldn't hurt to impress Leighton. Plus, she liked when Leighton praised her. In her eyes, Casey was talented and worthy.

Leighton wheeled a large whiteboard to face them. "The Flemish Technique was developed during the seventeenth century's Dutch Golden Age, and artists have used it ever since." She uncapped a marker and wrote *imprimatura* in large letters.

❖

That evening, Casey scraped the leftover paint from her glass palette with a razor blade. She wiped it on a paper towel and cleaned her hands. The darkened sky outside the studio windows and the clock on the wall reminded her how late it'd gotten. She'd missed dinner, but she missed Andy even more. He was growing up so fast, right before her eyes, and she hated being apart from him. At least he'd been excited to stay at Aileen's where he was safe, loved, and asleep.

She turned to Mikala, the only other remaining person. "Will you be finished soon? I didn't realize the time."

"I need about ten minutes, and then we can walk out together." She answered without looking up from where she used her mahl stick to steady her painting hand.

"Sounds good." Casey took a few minutes to tidy her taboret, place her brushes in the freezer, and empty the garbage can at her station. She sealed her used rags in the fireproof container. The atelier wouldn't go up in flames because of spontaneous combustion because of her.

With a few minutes to spare, she studied the painting she'd been working on from a distance, not from a few inches away like when she painted. It was the entire reason Leighton had taken away their stools.

Her values looked good, cohesive. She didn't think she'd over-modeled. However, she needed to soften the edges she wanted to recede into the background. The subtle touches she'd given them were imperceptible from here, the distance someone would view it in a gallery or museum. It wouldn't do. She'd have to rework them tomorrow.

"It's lovely." Mikala startled her.

"Thank you. I only see the things I need to fix."

"We all do with our art." Mikala moved her head like she needed to see past the glare on the canvas. "We're our own worst critics. That's why we need one another to point out when we do something right." She turned to Casey. "But if I had to point out everything you do right, we'd be here all night."

Mikala's outright flirting was getting more difficult to ignore, especially when she ran her hand from Casey's shoulder to her elbow, where she left it. Casey stared at the canvas, not knowing how to respond. Mikala's touch didn't give her shivers or make her heart race like Leighton's had. Even so, she needed to put some distance between them. She bent and grabbed her backpack.

Mikala let go of her arm. "Ready?"

"Yes."

"I'll meet you by the elevator."

Casey picked up a few bits of garbage and threw them away even though Leighton hired a cleaning service to come in once a week. The trash wasn't hers, but that wasn't a reason not to keep the place looking nice.

She shrugged into her jacket as Mikala met her in front of the elevator. The compliment and innuendo echoed in her head. Mikala's flirtations had been increasing over the last few days. Soon, Casey would have to say something.

Mikala caught hold of her elbow. "Hey."

Casey turned, and Mikala stood close. Too close.

She brushed a lock of hair away from Casey's face. "I'm not sure when I'll get another chance." Before Casey comprehended what she'd whispered, Mikala leaned in and kissed her. With her hand on Casey's lower back, she pulled her closer.

Stunned, it took her a moment to react. She broke the kiss and backed away before it went anywhere. "Mikala." It was an awkward situation, and she never knew what to say during times like these. She took a deep breath. "You're a good friend. I like you, but I don't think I feel the same."

Mikala's disappointment loomed in her eyes, but she offered a regretful smile. "I was afraid of that, but I figured this was the time to find out for sure."

"The person who feels the same way for you as you do them, what a lucky person they'll be." Casey smiled to let her know no harm was done.

Mikala laughed, but it sounded rueful. "You always have something nice to say." She slipped an arm around her and called the elevator. "Thank you."

As they waited, the security cameras flashed through Casey's mind. She didn't want to be obvious and see where they were and if they might have caught the encounter. Instead, she crossed her fingers that Leighton had aimed them in another direction. It was late, and nobody should be monitoring them at this hour, anyway. Nobody, meaning Leighton.

They rode down to the first floor in silence, then crossed the reception area.

Despite her lack of interest in Mikala that way, the kiss lingered on Casey's lips. It'd been fine, but it'd stirred nothing in her—nothing but emptiness.

Mikala made sure the atelier's front door latched behind them, and they headed for the train.

Casey's wistful sigh escaped into the cool night air, and a heaviness weighed her down. It'd been so long since she'd been kissed, but the woman who'd kissed her tonight hadn't been the woman she wanted. And the woman she wanted had made it clear she couldn't have her.

CHAPTER FOURTEEN

Leighton stared at the ceiling fan whirling above her bed. Sleep wouldn't come. She regretted the cup of coffee she'd had after dinner. Now her brain spun, and she couldn't stop thinking about Casey. Based on the invitation to lunch and the ensuing conversation, her attraction to Casey was mutual. Until then, she'd worried she was a poor judge when her faculties were so clouded by interest. And desire.

With a sigh, she kicked the light duvet to the side and rolled from her bed. Maybe a glass of water or a spoonful of ice cream would help.

She peeked into Kalyssa's room. From the doorway, Leighton could tell she slept, her hair sweaty on one side. Other than that, she'd moved little.

As Leighton turned toward the kitchen, she skidded to a bare-footed stop in front of the screen showing the feeds from her security cameras. Movement caught her eye, unusual for this late. A glance at the time told her it was almost one thirty. She sat and clicked camera eight into full-screen mode.

Casey and Mikala faced one another. Mikala leaned closer, and acid rose in Leighton's throat. Her eyes remained glued to the screen as Mikala pressed her lips to Casey's. Leighton's stomach lurched. After what seemed like an eternity, they broke apart. Of course, they'd be near one of the few cameras without audio. Smiles spread across their faces, and Leighton's heart dove. Then Mikala wrapped her arm around Casey's shoulders, and they left. Together.

Leighton pinched the bridge of her nose. She shouldn't feel jealousy or possessiveness, or anything related to those feelings. Casey wasn't hers and couldn't be hers. She'd told Casey as much.

She'd always thought she had impeccable timing, but she wished she hadn't walked by at that moment. For all she knew, it wasn't their first kiss. Maybe this was what happened at night in her studio.

If this was what occurred, she should monitor the cameras more. She rubbed her forehead and sighed. No, that wasn't their purpose. Besides, she never wanted to witness anything like that involving Casey again. Her stomach still churned.

Why shouldn't Casey be interested in Mikala? They were both students, free to date or do whatever. It didn't thrill Leighton the intimate moment had happened in her studio, but an objective eye would view it as tame. However, she didn't possess objectivity, not when it concerned Casey. So, it made sense Leighton got what she deserved for pining over a woman she couldn't have. The episode left her feeling in pieces.

They couldn't have a relationship, even a fling. Like she'd told Casey, it was unethical and could put the entire future of her atelier at risk. Unbidden images of Maxine's apoplectic face if she ever found out crossed her mind. Even the imagined depiction was enough to terrify her. Maxine's anger and disappointment would be monumental, and she might distance herself from Leighton's mess. Then Leighton would be motherless *and* without a mother figure. No, she wasn't about to risk losing the only person besides Kalyssa who felt like family, and she wouldn't excise another person from Kalyssa's life.

If falling asleep was difficult before, it'd be near impossible now. Counting sheep would be the smart thing to do. Instead, she wanted to discuss what had happened. If she could share her day with someone and get another perspective, perhaps she could get past it.

She texted Stefan and asked him to call her if he was awake, but she didn't receive a response. In front of her, the screen showed all the security feeds. She pressed the power button, and the monitor went dark. A creepy sensation tickled her neck. What if something happened? Jeffrey could show up, and she wouldn't have as much time to react. Door and window sensors would send notifications to her phone, but she never turned off her cameras. It left her feeling too vulnerable.

She turned on the screen. A car whizzed past the front entrance, its headlights a bright glare in the camera's night vision. All else appeared quiet.

Her phone didn't ring. She paced up and down the hallway, gritting her teeth as she imagined Stefan hugging his pillow and snoring, until she realized the unfairness in her thinking. Sleep was a luxury she'd like to have. Still, she wished she had someone to talk to who could calm her restless state.

CHAPTER FIFTEEN

Casey, like the rest of her class, stood in front of her taboret in the studio, the mid-morning's blue skies reminding her of the sunny day outside, even if the windows faced north. Stefan had asked them to mix the correct proportion of burnt umber and ultramarine blue on their palettes to create a chromatic black. They'd be using it to make the nine values of gray for their grisaille.

"Make enough of each value so that they're ready to go, and you don't have to do this each time you start a painting." Stefan raised his voice so they could hear him as he walked around. "Remember, we squint to see value and open our eyes wide to see color."

He set down a large, but what appeared to be lightweight, box on the model stand in the middle of the ring of stations. "Here are the empty tubes. Once your mixtures are correct, use your palette knife to load the tubes and crimp the ends shut."

"Why are we doing this again?"

Jenna often seemed lost, but Casey liked her. She'd asked to look at Casey's laptop every day the first week until Casey offered to send her a copy of her notes. Now she used a scanner app to send Jenna daily shots of the sketchbook in which she handwrote almost everything. Jenna had confided she couldn't write or type fast enough or sometimes didn't grasp the concepts. Either way, Casey didn't mind sharing. Jenna was a decent artist, but everything seemed to overwhelm her. Plus, her heart didn't seem invested in the instruction the way Casey's and most of the other students' were.

"Good question, Jenna. In the future, or at least for this section of the syllabus, you'll lay out your gray values at the top of your palette to neutralize other colors."

"Should we label the tubes before or after?" Devin scratched his ear with a Sharpie.

Casey made a mental note never to borrow one from him.

"I label each one after I fill it. You should also brush a streak of the color on the outside of the tube as a reminder of that value. I find it more helpful than wondering what that value looks like. And don't forget to tube your chromatic black. You should end up with ten tubes, people."

"Yo, why can't we use ivory black and titanium white to make our grays? It'd be a lot faster." Jaiden flashed Stefan a grin like he might get away using a shortcut with his perfect teeth and boyish charm.

"Does anyone know?" Stefan looked around.

Casey spoke once no one else had. "Because ivory black is a cool color, and depending on the brand you use, the temperature can vary. By mixing our own, we assure it's a neutral black." She congratulated herself, not for her answer, but for sounding confident. It was often an outward appearance she needed to fabricate.

"Very good, Casey. That's right." Stefan gave her taboret a little thump with his fist.

A ding sounded. Leighton strode into the studio and seemed to assess the scene before her. Without as much as a good morning to anyone, she slung her bag from one shoulder to the other.

"Mikala, your halftones should be in the two to three range on the value scale, not four or five. Are you matching them to the Munsell chips?" Without breaking stride, Leighton glared at her.

"N-not yet."

Mikala's stammered words and wide eyes mirrored Casey's surprise at Leighton's tone.

"I can't imagine why you aren't." Leighton glanced over her shoulder as she admonished her. "I assume Stefan hasn't neglected to mention that important step this morning. Why waste your time by taking shortcuts?"

Her tone caused most of the students to stop what they were doing. Even Stefan stared at her. Only Phoenix seemed oblivious to the mood that had darkened the room as he bopped his head to a song only he could hear. Leighton flew past Casey without a glance.

"It's somebody's time of the month." Devin's grumble drew glares from all the women and some guys. He mumbled an apology and resumed mixing paint.

In her office, Leighton flung items from her bag onto her desk, making Casey start with each thump. This wasn't like her. What had caused her sudden change in behavior?

The jovial atmosphere that had existed in the studio had dissipated. On any other day, joy suffused Casey while here, but Leighton's mood had soured it. Casey loved learning and being immersed in art. Here, the people who surrounded her understood the history and the challenge of creation. She fit in for the first time in her life. Now drudgery replaced that buoyant feeling.

She sighed and used her palette knife to smear a small pile of ultramarine blue into the three dots of burnt umber she'd squeezed beside it. The flapping of a pigeon's wings against the glass high above made her glance up. Beside the window, the green indicator light on the camera in the corner caught her attention.

Shit. Her stomach dropped. Leighton was in a mood for a reason. Last night's kiss hadn't gone unnoticed.

CHAPTER SIXTEEN

Not even five minutes after she'd arrived in the studio, Leighton looked up to find Stefan closing her office door with the toe of his red Chuck Taylor's. He placed a mug of steaming coffee in front of her as she rummaged in her drawer for her favorite nibbed pen.

"Parking ticket?" He dropped into one of the leather chairs and sipped his coffee.

"No." She scowled at him.

"Jury duty?" He blew across the surface of his drink and took another sip.

She stared at him now. "No."

He raised an eyebrow. "Yeast infection?"

"No, and that's rude." She didn't bother to suppress her agitation.

"Well, you haven't gotten laid. That much is clear." He pulled an opened package of Skittles from his shirt pocket and shook a few into his mouth before he rolled it up and returned it.

Leighton flipped open her sketchbook. "Aren't you clever?" She wasn't in the mood.

"What's going on with you?" At least he was direct this time.

"Nothing." Her answer came too fast to be convincing.

"Yeah, that's believable." Sarcasm laced his tone. "I'm glad you went into art and not into acting." He propped his feet up on her desk like he dared her to tell him to move them so he could gauge her level of irritability.

Well, she wasn't falling for that. Instead, she eyed the soles of his shoes with enough fury they should've given off tendrils of smoke.

He waited for her to say something, but when the seconds of silence stretched into double digits, he sighed. "This wouldn't have anything to do with Cas—"

"I said it's nothing." What was wrong with her? Who talked to their friend and employee like that? She shook her head and stared at her desk. "I'm sorry. I had an awful night. That's not an excuse to be short with you."

"It's not like you to question my teaching. Go ahead. You can, but you and I both know I'm an excellent instructor. However, I don't need you jumping into the middle of my lesson and undermining me in front of my students. They need to respect both of us." He held his mug to his sternum. "It's also not like you to snap at a student, let alone during a lesson you're not even teaching."

Leighton picked up the second mug and leaned back in her chair. "You're right. I apologize for my rudeness. I shouldn't have interrupted your class." She blew across the top of the hot liquid and took a drink. Even with a splash of oat milk, it burned her tongue, but she didn't care. Her irritation wouldn't die. "She still should've been using her Munsell chips."

"Something tells me this isn't about paint at all, but you don't seem in a chatty mood, so I'll go spend time with my students." He lowered his feet and stood. With one hand on the doorknob, he hesitated. "You can tell me about it, whatever it is. I'm here for you." He waved a hand toward the studio. "I don't think my boss will fire me if I step away from my class for a few minutes."

She chuckled, and it felt foreign. Darkness had plagued her since last night. Until she'd witnessed the kiss, her attraction to Casey had been just that. Then, after hours of nocturnal contemplation, she'd realized what she felt for Casey was more convoluted.

His chair gave a groan as he fell into it. "So, are you going to tell me what's up? Is this why you called me in the middle of the night?" He gave a sheepish grin. "Sorry, I had my phone on do not disturb."

She sank back into her chair. "Yes, but you don't need to apologize. You work enough. I don't need you available twenty-four hours a day."

"Okay." He folded his hands. If they traded chairs, an onlooker might think he was her therapist. In some ways, he was. "However, I assume you were calling me as a friend, not as your co-instructor."

Leighton closed her eyes for a moment. "Yes, I was." She fidgeted. "I saw something on the cameras."

Stefan scooted forward. "Did he break the restraining order? Did you call the police? I should've had my phone on."

She tried to calm him with her palms in the air. "Stefan, Stefan. No, he had nothing to do with it. I saw something happen in the studio."

"Theft?" He paused. "It happens. Art students love supplies, and it's rare for them to be sitting on a bunch of dough. I thought the cameras would be a deterrent."

He could get on a tangent like no one else. She'd forgotten just how much.

"Hey, breathe. No one stole anything." She questioned the accuracy of her statement but continued. "I saw Mikala and Casey kiss."

"Oh." His voice dropped. "Okay. Is that all? Why did you call me? Did you want me to spray them with a garden hose or something?"

"Hilarious." She didn't pretend to laugh, being in no mood for jokes.

He sighed. "Hey, I know that's not something you wanted to see, but it's not that unusual, you know? You've done worse in a vacant studio."

"Hush." Sometimes, she wished he didn't have such an in-depth history on her, but that's what came with friends. It was a package deal. She shrugged. "I just wanted someone to talk to. It upset me, and I know it shouldn't, but it did." Her throat tightened just thinking about it.

He scratched at a bit of dried paint on his jeans. "You're in a rough place, but try to hang in there. I wish I had better advice to offer, but I don't know what to tell you. It's a sticky situation, and I'm sorry things aren't different for you."

Her heart warmed hearing his concern. "Thank you. I don't expect you to have all the answers. Someone to talk to is all I wanted."

He sat forward and squeezed her hand. "I'll change my do not disturb settings on my phone so your calls and texts will get through."

She patted his hand on hers. "You're sweet, but there's no need. I'm overreacting."

He stood. "Give it time, Leighton, give it time. I know it seems dark now, but the light will shine again." He opened the door and had almost closed it behind him.

"Wait."

He poked his head inside.

"Send Mikala in here. I owe her an apology."

Thank goodness she'd hired him. He was invaluable, both as an instructor and friend. Most people would've been fearful to tell her when she was wrong, but not Stefan.

Like it or not, she'd acted without reason, or at least a valid one. Mikala hadn't deserved her tongue-lashing. She'd done nothing wrong, at least not knowingly. It wasn't Mikala's fault Leighton harbored an infatuation with a student and her jealousy had driven her to lash out. Unfortunately, she couldn't explain those things.

Mikala approached her office.

Leighton took a deep breath and waved her inside. She planned to offer her a sincere apology. She didn't have a plan for how to handle Casey.

After speaking to Mikala, whose acceptance of her apology seemed genuine, Leighton needed to switch gears. Her brushes needed to be cleaned and conditioned. She'd been putting it off for too long.

Fifteen minutes of standing at the sink doing a mindless task gave her time to think. She concluded she'd like to be wrong about what she'd witnessed, but in the end, it didn't matter. Whether Casey and Mikala were a thing was their business. She took the clean, wet brushes back to her office to dry on her credenza.

A few minutes later, Casey rapped on Leighton's open door. "Do you have a minute?"

Leighton glanced up from where she reformed the bristles on her favorite long-handled filbert. She was in too fragile of a frame of mind to deal with Casey. "I have one minute. What is it?" Her tone sounded curt, but she couldn't find the will to soften it. From the look on Casey's face she wasn't pleased with her, and Leighton knew she deserved it.

Despite Leighton's irritation and lack of sleep, Casey's eyes enthralled her. Today, they appeared a true hazel. If Leighton were to paint them, she'd use glazes of transparent pigments. Perhaps start with phthalocyanine blue and nickel azo yellow, then add a touch of transparent red iron oxide. Leighton had never known hazel eyes to be so intriguing.

Casey stepped forward. "I want to talk about yesterday."

Leighton interrupted her by raising her hand. "We had a pleasant chat. I enjoy getting to know all my students. Is there anything else?"

Casey turned crimson. "No, I meant last night."

Against her will, Leighton's stomach clenched at the memory. She opened her desk drawer and fumbled for her roll of antacids. "What about it?"

Casey stretched out her arm. "Can I close the door?"

Leighton peeled the wrapper and chewed a chalky tablet. "I don't think that's necessary." She popped another one in her mouth.

"I think it is." Casey inched closer. "But if leaving it open doesn't matter to you, I'll just say what I want about your voyeuristic tendencies right now."

"Shut the door." Leighton hadn't meant to snap at her, but Casey had pissed her off. She needed some distance, so she sat in her executive's chair, which would force Casey to sit across from her. Her desk would form a welcome partition. She didn't need to breathe in Casey's scent or touch her by accident. "I have every right to use those cameras. They're a security feature, and I made everyone aware of them the first day."

Casey didn't sit. Instead, she stood a few feet away. "Regardless, I assume you saw. You wouldn't be so upset if you hadn't been watching. Do you always spy on us?"

Her unwavering voice and hostile eyes took Leighton by surprise. Casey gave her two choices—address the spying allegation or address the reason behind her upset state. She chose a third route.

"Saw what?" Leighton refused to show her hand, and she wouldn't acknowledge Casey's ludicrous accusation. She'd installed the cameras after her separation, not because of voyeuristic tendencies. Motion had caught her eye, nothing else.

"Mikala kissed me in the studio last night, and you must have been watching." She paused. When Leighton neither confirmed nor denied her assumption, she stepped around the corner of the desk. "I also assume that's what's caused your bad mood. Maybe you shouldn't use your cameras to babysit your students, especially when they're adults."

Leighton maintained eye contact, though Casey was breaching her defenses in more ways than one. "Do you always burst into your instructors' offices and comment on their moods? I said I had one minute. Are you finished? I have things to do."

Leighton saw the indignation register on Casey's face as she glanced at the brushes. She moved until a foot separated them. Leighton looked away.

"Did you enjoy watching?" Her voice had become husky.

Leighton couldn't blink. She wasn't sure she remembered how to breathe. If Casey only knew what watching had done to her. It had been the antithesis of enjoyment.

"Did you enjoy seeing her kiss me? Watching her lips on mine?"

The squeak of Casey's hand on the back of her chair happened a split second before the other one landed on the desk. Her warm breath tickled Leighton's neck and made her pulse race.

Would someone glancing in assume they looked at her laptop's screen? Leighton's fingers tightened on the armrests, and she pressed the toes of her shoes against the floor.

"Did you imagine what it—"

"Go back to class. Now." Leighton couldn't do this. She was about to shatter.

With what sounded like a chuckle, Casey straightened. "Class isn't in session. It's open studio time."

"Just leave, please." Leighton couldn't function with her this close.

"Mikala didn't deserve that, you know." Casey set her jaw.

Leighton held her head high. "No, she didn't, and I've apologized to her."

"Oh." Clearly, Casey hadn't been expecting that.

Leighton waved her hand toward the door. "Please."

Casey took a few steps but didn't leave. Instead, she turned. "Nothing happened, if you care. Mikala and I are friends and will remain so." She paused, her hand on the doorknob. "Nothing changes. I still want to know you better." Casey looked at her a moment, then opened the door and left.

Relief flooded through Leighton's body and her trembling limbs. Mikala's kiss had meant nothing. Yes, she cared, more than she'd ever admit to anyone.

More important than that, Casey knew she did. That's why she'd bothered to explain. Well, explained after she'd played with her? Teased her? Dismantled her with a few cheeky questions? Whatever she'd done, Leighton wouldn't have minded more of it in another time and place. Like it or not, that wasn't about to happen with their respective roles.

Perhaps she couldn't control how she felt for Casey, but at least she could manage her demeanor. As for those pesky feelings, she'd bury them. What else could she do? Until whatever existed between them faded, or Casey's desire to know her better waned, she'd have to continue her frostiness for both their sakes if Casey was going to test her like that.

❖

Later that evening, Leighton slid into bed beside Kalyssa and tucked the baby-blue *Frozen* comforter around them. Together, snuggled under images of Elsa and Olaf, Leighton read her the book she'd chosen. Kalyssa scooted closer, nestled against her side to look at the illustrations and words she couldn't quite read herself.

With her mind on autopilot, Leighton turned the pages. She didn't have an awareness of the story, but who could blame her? By the time she'd read the book this many times, she'd memorized it. Guilt hit her. She should be present for Kalyssa, not just in the physical sense but also mentally. As much as she tried, she couldn't as her head swam with the day's events. Casey had conjured feelings in her she hadn't been privy to for some time. She'd give Kalyssa the bedtime reading of her life tomorrow, voices and all.

She kissed Kalyssa and clicked off the lamp. Only the glow of Kalyssa's Pikachu light lit the room.

"Momma?"

"No, darling. We can't read another book. It's time to sleep."

"That's not my question. When do I get to come to the atelier with you?" Kalyssa sat up. Her pronunciation of the French word had improved, but it still made Leighton smile.

Leighton smoothed the hair from her forehead. "Soon, I promise. Do you remember the plastic easel you used last year?"

Kalyssa nodded. "Yes, when I fingerpainted."

"Well, you're a big girl now, so I got you a present, a real easel and brushes. What do you think about that?" The cups and brushes were still plastic, but the easel was wood.

Her eyes grew wide, and she grinned. "Like yours?"

Leighton scooted her down and tucked her in again. "Your easel isn't as big, but yes. Real artists need real easels." She kissed her forehead. "Sweet dreams, my little painter."

She left Kalyssa's bedroom door open an inch and went to the kitchen. She turned on the kettle to make tea. As she waited for the water to heat, she remembered how fierce Casey had been in her office. It'd enchanted Leighton to witness that side of her.

She'd been short with Casey. Her attitude had been intentional, but she needed to balance keeping her distance without harming Casey's feelings. She had no desire to hurt her. Rather, she intended to do what she needed to get them, and the atelier, through the year intact. It was a necessary step to protect her livelihood, but she could also use the safeguarding. Look what had happened the last time she'd opened her heart to someone.

It'd been a roller coaster of a day. She'd had little sleep after replaying what she'd seen on the camera in her mind for the better part of the night. Had Casey not explained what had happened, she'd still be in that sickening state. But Casey had. However, she'd also accused her of being a voyeur. Leighton's indignation soared again. She no longer worried about Mikala kissing Casey. Now she had other feelings to sort through. Casey had no right to judge her for having security cameras.

She'd often heard people say it was better to feel something than nothing at all. Based on the turmoil within her lately, she doubted the veracity of the statement.

The kettle whistled. She'd drink a cup of decaffeinated tea and go to bed. This day needed to end.

CHAPTER SEVENTEEN

Casey arrived early again. She enjoyed being one of the first people in the studio, and it was easier to keep a schedule when juggling school, childcare, and work. When she saw Leighton's dark office, she remembered how livid she'd been yesterday when Leighton had interrupted class. Mikala hadn't deserved to be admonished when the actual issue didn't involve her. Leighton's response had been uncalled for, but at least she'd apologized.

Her own impulsive words in Leighton's office had also been unnecessary. It'd felt like an out-of-body experience, like Casey had watched from a distance. A part of her had liked it. She'd enjoyed seeing Leighton's reactions, like the flush of her chest, her quick breaths, and her white nail beds as she pressed her fingers into the chair's armrests. Never had she imagined she could elicit responses like that from a woman like Leighton.

Regardless, whom Casey kissed was her business, whether or not it was a kiss she wanted. What annoyed her most was how often she'd imagined the moment as Leighton and not Mikala kissing her. She'd fantasized how the evening would end much differently than two women boarding trains to separate destinations.

The coffee had almost finished brewing when Leighton arrived. She also seemed to rise early. They hadn't spoken after Leighton had banished her the day prior.

Leighton didn't head to her office to deposit her bag like she did each morning. On second glance, she wasn't carrying anything, not even a jacket for the chilly air.

Casey offered a meek good morning as Leighton made a beeline for her. Is this what warships saw when an enemy missile rocketed toward them?

Leighton didn't return her greeting. She took the mug from her and set it down.

"Let's go." Her commanding tone left little room for objection.

Yet Casey remained rooted to the spot. She'd just arrived. "Now? Where?"

Leighton's stony face held no answer. "You want to mock my cameras? Fine, I'll show you why I have them." Without waiting for her, she walked to the elevator and pushed the button. It should've opened, but someone must have called it downstairs. Leighton turned to her. "Coming?"

Casey took a few steps. Where was Leighton taking her? She didn't have her jacket, but she wasn't willing to risk asking to get it.

The doors opened to reveal Stefan eating a bagel.

He gave a start, likely surprised to see two people waiting for the elevator at such an early hour. "Whoa. Hi, are you leaving?" His diving eyebrows topped the confused look on his face.

"We'll be back soon." Leighton held the doors open for her. "Casey made coffee."

"Okay, thanks." He glanced between them.

Casey entered the elevator and tried to send him a telepathic message to call the authorities if she didn't return soon. Maybe she shouldn't have pushed Leighton's buttons yesterday, as fun as it'd been. Goose bumps broke out on her arms.

As the doors closed, Leighton pressed a series of buttons. She didn't look at her.

The third floor? Was Leighton taking her to the storage room to give her a tongue-lashing away from curious eyes and ears? She caught the unique scent of Leighton's perfume, and it reminded her of her first day. The disparity of the two situations saddened her.

The doors slid open, and so did Casey's mouth. It wasn't a storage room.

A beautiful loft greeted her. While it maintained the same airiness of the atelier, it'd been outfitted with plush carpeting, hardwood floors, and handsome yet comfortable-looking furniture. The early morning sunshine streamed through tall windows.

Leighton extended her hand and motioned for her to enter.

The faint smell of toast hung in the air. In the corner of an armchair, a doll sat with a blanket tucked around his legs. An island that doubled as a counter with seating for four sat opposite a well-equipped kitchen. The only exception to the clean and straightforward space was the refrigerator, whose front held bright crayon drawings.

A hallway ran the length of the back half of the building, with doors branching off on either side. At the end, a desk held a large screen. The unmistakable gray-scale images of security feeds filled it.

"I have the cameras because my ex-husband isn't a nice man." Leighton made clumsy motions with her hands, uncharacteristic of her usual poised state. "I have a restraining order, but Kalyssa and I live here, and I can't take any chances."

Casey looked around for a shovel. She'd use anything she could to dig a hole large enough to crawl into. Wooden spoons standing upright in a container near the stove looked to be her only option. To say an apology was in order was an understatement.

"Leighton." Casey shook her head and took Leighton's hand. Her skin was as soft as she remembered. "I'm so sorry."

Leighton answered with a gentle squeeze.

"You live here." Casey assimilated the information. Things made sense now, like when Leighton would show up looking fresh out of a shower. Or how she'd choose to take the stairs instead of the elevator with everyone else.

Leighton smiled, but fatigue darkened her fine features, like the weight of the burdens she'd been carrying had become visible. She still looked breathtaking.

"I'm sorry for what I said." Casey wished she could take back her awful comment about Leighton being a voyeur.

More than anything, she wanted to understand what Leighton had been through. What had Leighton endured that merited this kind of security? At the moment, no words sufficed. No bland statements or platitudes would do, and she wasn't sure her invasive questions would be welcome. She contented herself with caressing Leighton's hand with her thumb.

"Now you know why." Leighton shrugged a shoulder.

Casey's irritation melted, and she turned to face her. "You know, when she kissed me, I was more surprised than you."

Leighton looked down, like the memory still bothered her. "Doubtful." She pulled her hand back, but Casey held tight.

"I told her I didn't feel the same way about her."

Leighton's eyes widened as she seemed to catch the slight emphasis Casey had put on the last word.

"I didn't want *her* to kiss me." Casey stepped closer to confide the last part. "Not her." She tucked a lock of hair behind Leighton's ear and traced the line of her elegant jaw. Maybe she'd sketch it later. Casey touched the tiny lines at the corners of Leighton's eyes and heard her shallow breaths. Her own breathing wasn't audible. Leighton left her breathless. She leaned in.

"No." Leighton blinked rapidly.

If Leighton needed reassurance, she'd provide. Casey cupped her face as their breaths mingled. "No, not her."

Leighton stepped away, dropping her hand. "No. We can't. I can't." The last word sounded choked.

Casey stepped back and studied her. Was she shaking? "We're making it more complicated than it needs to be. You're interested in me, and I'm clearly interested in you." She raised her hands, palms up.

Something flared in Leighton's eyes. "It's complicated, more than you seem to understand. Or do you have a plan to allay my funders' fears when they hear I'm seducing my students? Shall I send them to you when everything goes to hell? While you're at it, you can calm Maxine when people call me a predatory lesbian. If she found out…" She didn't finish her sentence, like the thought frightened her.

When Leighton phrased things like that, she had a point, although it was *one* student, and if anyone was tempting someone, it was Casey. Plus, Leighton was bisexual. However, now didn't seem like the time to delve into details.

"You're not seducing me." Casey was certain of this. It'd been her pushing things, and she'd never once not been in control of her choices or felt pressured by Leighton. "I'd tell them you didn't."

Leighton shook her head. "It wouldn't matter because that's not how it'd look. There's little tolerance for this kind of thing in the post-2017 world we live in."

Casey refused to be dejected. There had to be a way for them to explore what existed between them. Couldn't it be their secret? Well, she couldn't keep it from Mark. But if she and Leighton dated, they wouldn't need to announce it on a billboard in Times Square. This wasn't a normal school, and they were adults.

Casey wasn't used to taking no for an answer when striving for things she wanted. She didn't understand why they couldn't figure something out. Sure, she could suggest they wait to date until she graduated, but so much could happen in two years. Leighton could meet someone else between now and then. Or she could simply lose interest. And Casey's experiences had proven things did not remain unchanged. Waiting terrified her.

Nearby, the bells of the Iglesia Ni Cristo church chimed the hour, the ringing foreboding rather than uplifting.

"You have class soon." Leighton's tone dripped with civility.

"Yes, with you." What a way to start the day. Casey wasn't ready. For one thing, she wanted to stay in this beautiful loft and soak in the ambiance of Leighton's sanctuary. She wanted to learn more about her marriage and divorce. She wanted that kiss she'd come so close to getting. Her desire had pushed its way to the forefront and wouldn't be helpful as she tried to pay attention to the lecture. The morning would be tricky as class time forced them to share the same space.

Casey was going to need a minute to collect her thoughts. "I'll take the stairs."

❖

Casey had poured a cup of coffee and eaten half an apple fritter from the pastries Jaiden had brought by the time Leighton entered the studio. Perhaps she'd also needed a moment to regain her composure.

Stefan shot Leighton a questioning look, but she ignored him.

As expected, Leighton continued her lesson on the Flemish Method, and Casey was on the third of the seven steps: the second umber underpainting. She squeezed a dime-sized amount of paint onto her palette, as Leighton addressed them.

"Today we'll be creating the major value contrasts, darkening the darks, and unifying our compositions. Gather around my easel, and I'll demonstrate." She hadn't chatted or made small talk before class, as was her normal style.

Casey didn't push the issue, even when Leighton stopped by her station to check her progress. She finished right before lunch and propped the canvas with the painted side toward the wall so dust wouldn't adhere to it. Mark offered to take her out for warm pretzels before he headed to work, but she declined. Instead, she ate the tuna sandwich she'd brought and flipped through a book in the library. After lunch, with most of the other students tending to different areas of their lives, only Casey and Mikala worked in the studio with their instructors. It seemed a good time to start the Bargue plate she'd chosen, *Leg of Germanicus*.

She'd sharpened her graphite pencil to a two-inch long point, the exact specifications Leighton had shown her, and it lay ready. With one eye closed, she held a long piece of black twine tied to a hexagonal nut at arm's length and used the makeshift plumb line to divide her reference image in half.

"What's that?"

Casey turned. The small voice belonged to a little girl with straight blond hair.

Before Casey could respond, Leighton spoke from her doorway. "Kalyssa, don't bother her."

"I'm not."

"She's not." They answered in unison, which earned Casey a lopsided grin from Kalyssa.

Ah, Kalyssa. Casey took in more detail. She could see Leighton in her features—her high cheek bones and almond-shaped brown eyes—and her periwinkle PAW Patrol T-shirt perfectly matched her Skechers.

Leighton crossed her arms and leaned against the doorframe.

"Is that a ring?" Kalyssa pointed to the end of the string, clearly undaunted by her mother's interruption.

Casey showed her. "It's called a nut."

She giggled and shook her head, making her hair sway. "You can't eat that."

"No, you can't." Casey smiled at her. Leighton watched them with evident interest, making Casey's skin warm and her fingertips tingle.

"What's your name?" Kalyssa fiddled with the nut.

"Casey."

Kalyssa stared at her, wonderment in her expression. "That's my name, too!"

"Really?" Casey squatted to her level. "I thought your name was Kalyssa."

Her head bobbed. "It is. Kalyssa Catherine Vaughn." She pointed toward the lounge. "But Uncle Stefan calls me K.C." She wrote the letters in the air with her index finger.

"Ah, I see."

Kalyssa touched the pencils on Casey's taboret at her eye level. She seemed careful, so Casey didn't discourage her.

"Momma and I have matching last names. The atelier matches my name, too." Atelier came out more like *AT-a-lay.* "I'm the only one at preschool with their mom's name and not their dad's." Kalyssa squeezed her hands into little fists and jumped.

Casey looked at Leighton and smiled.

Leighton sort of shrugged, but amusement shone in her eyes. "Let me know when you've had enough."

Casey chuckled. "We're fine."

Kalyssa picked up the nut Casey had laid on her easel. "Why did you tie this on a string?"

The questions kept coming. "The nut is heavy, so it straightens the string." Casey held it up. "See? I can check if the lines on my drawing match." She stood and showed Kalyssa how to use it.

"It makes you draw it straight?" A dimple appeared between her eyebrows.

"Well, I have to draw them the best I can, but this helps me check." Kalyssa's interest charmed her. Would Andy be so chatty in two years? "Would you like me to make you one?"

Her eyes lit up. "Yes, please."

Casey opened a drawer and dug around for another nut. At the supply closet, she cut a shorter length of string. Her little shadow followed. Casey tied a knot, snipped the excess, and made a loop on the other end. "Here you go."

Kalyssa grinned.

"Do you remember how to use it?" Casey put her hand on the column beside her. "Can you check this for me?"

Kalyssa held the string high in front of her with one eye closed and her nose scrunched. "It's straight." She confirmed it with a serious nod, like Casey had asked her to determine the building's structural integrity.

"Good."

Kalyssa held the plumb line between her and Leighton, who still leaned against the door's frame.

"Momma, you're not straight!"

A loud guffaw emanated from Stefan, who'd been reading a book on the large sofa.

Casey bit her lip and looked at Leighton. A bloom of rose spread across Leighton's cheeks. She didn't seem to find as much humor in Kalyssa's quip as Stefan had. Casey averted her eyes.

"Uncle Stefan, stand up so I can check you." Kalyssa skipped toward the lounge area.

From her easel beside Casey, Mikala snorted.

"I already know the answer, K.C. I'm definitely not straight." He grinned and blew her a kiss before going back to his book with a chuckle.

Leighton shepherded Kalyssa, whose attention was now on trying to shove her little finger through the nut, toward her office. "What do you say to Casey?"

"Thank you."

Casey didn't mind the automatic response. Kalyssa seemed sweet and curious, and Casey liked her.

"You're welcome."

Casey glanced at Leighton. She didn't know whether to credit Leighton's beaming smile and expressive creases at the corners of her eyes to being with her daughter or witnessing them together, but it almost made her forget the tension between them.

Leighton turned Kalyssa toward her office. She mouthed *thank you* and squeezed Casey's forearm.

Her gratitude and warm touch left Casey, once again, wanting more.

CHAPTER EIGHTEEN

S tefan, can you do me a huge favor?" Leighton rushed into the studio's kitchen before realizing Casey was also there. She didn't have time to acknowledge her. "I forgot this is the night I'm supposed to sit on that art history panel at Columbia. Shit! Can Kalyssa stay with you for a few hours?"

He took a pint of ice cream from the freezer. "Sorry, I can't. I'm teaching a live figure drawing class at the Art Students League."

Leighton let out an exasperated sigh.

Casey tore off a sheet of aluminum foil, the metallic rattle reverberating through the kitchen.

Leighton hated Casey bearing witness to her frazzled state, but she didn't have time to concern herself with that now. She'd have to take Kalyssa with her, and she worried about a four-year-old's ability to entertain herself for an entire hour. However, life limited Leighton's babysitting options, and she wasn't hiring a stranger on an app.

"I'd take her with me, but she'd be bored." Stefan took a bite of ice cream. "Plus, tonight's model is well-endowed and doesn't hold still, if you know what I mean." He wiggled his eyebrows.

Casey bit her lip, likely holding back a smile.

Leighton didn't find any of this funny. "No, that's no place for a child. I can't believe I forgot about this fucking panel. I'd try to worm my way out of it, but I promised Maxine I'd do it. She's the moderator."

"She could stay at my place." Casey shrugged like she didn't care either way and rolled her brushes in the foil. "I can watch her."

Leighton hesitated. She was supposed to be keeping her distance from Casey, not having her babysit. Still, what choice did she have?

"Are you sure it's not an imposition?" Her heart rate had already slowed at the possibility of finding a solution.

"Nope." Casey pointed at her chest with her foil-wrapped brushes. "It's just me, Andy, and a pizza tonight."

"You're a lifesaver." Leighton failed to maintain her frosty exterior. Casey's offer saved her, and Kalyssa, who adored younger children, would love meeting Andy.

Stefan leaned against the counter and licked ice cream from his spoon.

Leighton wished he'd go to his office or anywhere other than here. She hadn't told him anything that had happened since the day he'd chastised her for snapping at Mikala and learned about the kiss she'd witnessed. He was bound to have more to say about that, and now there was *this* decision to comment on.

Leighton glanced at the clock. "Does six thirty work for you?"

"Anytime. I'm headed home now." Casey stepped around Stefan to return the foil to the drawer. "I can take her on the train with me, if that helps you." She dropped her brushes in the chest freezer.

Leighton waved off the idea. "I'll drop her on my way. I have time." No one besides her took Kalyssa on the subway. It was too dangerous, too exposed.

"Okay. I'll text you my address. I can get your number from the phone list."

"Great." Leighton hurried to the alcove and pushed open the door to the stairwell. "Thank you. It means a lot." She headed upstairs, wondering how much this would cost her in emotional strain. But for now, what's done was done.

After Leighton finished the panel she wished she hadn't agreed to, she knocked on Casey's apartment door and waited. When Casey opened it, giggles floated out, making Leighton smile. The sight of Casey greeting her might've had something to do with it, too.

Kalyssa and Andy sat on the carpet playing some kind of memory game. Neither looked up at her arrival, but the sparkle in Casey's eyes made up for it.

"She's going easy on him." Casey glanced over her shoulder. "He gets not-so-subtle hints during his turn. He's making a killing and loving it." She stepped aside to allow Leighton to enter.

The simple but clean space was small even by Manhattan standards and the décor and furnishings dated. Leighton had lived in a similar-sized apartment when she'd been in college, and again in Florence, though she'd never had to make do with used furniture. Her mother would never have allowed it. It gave Leighton a sense of missing out on something as she took in the fun, mismatched chairs and colorful throw covering the couch. It pleased Leighton that despite Casey's limited income, she'd made a lovely home for her and Andy.

"So, she behaved?"

"She's been a sweetheart and so good to him."

Leighton scooted around Mark's bicycle to stand beside Casey. Erica had mentioned Mark and Casey roomed together when they'd applied to the atelier, and Casey said Mark helped her with Andy when he could, though Leighton had forgotten about their arrangement in the interim.

Andy took a turn. Kalyssa's focus on the game meant she had yet to register Leighton's presence.

"Hi, baby. Did you have a good time?" Leighton smoothed her hand over Kalyssa's hair.

Kalyssa looked up with a start. "Hi, Momma. This is our fourth game. We had to eat pizza first, then we had ice cream."

"It sounds like Casey was good to you. You'll want to come over all the time." Why had she said that? This was a one-time deal.

Casey touched her elbow. "Have you eaten? Why don't you take off your jacket, and I'll warm some pizza for you."

If she sat, she worried she might not get up again. In the end, her empty stomach made the call. "I haven't, and that sounds wonderful. Are you sure we're not keeping you from something?" Leighton shed her jacket and laid it over the back of a chair.

"Not at all. Can you watch them for a minute?"

"Sure." She sat on the sofa near Kalyssa.

"I have wine and beer. Or milk or water, if you don't want alcohol." Casey held open the refrigerator.

"Beer, please." She didn't want her to have to open a bottle of wine, and after that panel, she could use a drink.

Casey returned with a Corona.

"Thank you." Leighton took a long swig. "You don't know how good that tastes."

Andy won the game to no one's surprise except his. Leighton found the delight on his face contagious. He resembled Casey quite a bit, especially when his dimples appeared.

"Do you want to play something different?" Casey returned the game to its box. "Andy, where are your tracks? Why don't you show Kalyssa your train?"

Andy pushed himself up and went to a shelf where primary-colored baskets held toys and books. He noticed Leighton, and shyness seemed to strike him. He sucked his thumb as he stared at her.

"Andy, this is Leighton. She's Kalyssa's mom." Casey took his thumb from his mouth, but he put it back.

Kalyssa lifted a basket down with a loud groan. "That's heavy." Tracks soon littered the floor. She snapped two of them together. "C'mon, Andy."

Andy squatted beside her, but his eyes remained on Leighton.

Kalyssa elbowed him. "Help me. Let's make a big circle."

Although still wary of Leighton, he used his free hand to pull train cars and a red engine from the basket.

Leighton winked at him as he joined Kalyssa.

Casey brought her a plate with two slices of pizza. "Do you mind eating in here? You're also welcome to use the table. And I brought you a knife and fork in case you need them."

"Thank you." Leighton took the plate. "Here is fine. I'm enjoying watching them." She forwent the utensils and took a large bite.

Casey sat beside her, and when Leighton moaned, Casey laughed. "Isn't it the best? We always order from them. I ate three slices."

Leighton wiped her mouth and looked her up and down. "You didn't."

Casey nodded and blushed.

"Yet you only brought me two."

Her statement made Casey grin.

Leighton's self-imposed mandate to remain frosty around her had failed, at least for now. She needed a moment to relax after the panel, the worn softness of Casey's couch eased the tension in her tired body, and she was hungry. Besides, curt exchanges and avoidance would be inappropriate in front of the children, not to mention rude and ungrateful given the huge favor Casey had done for her this evening. Her mandate could take a night off.

Andy and Kalyssa had almost completed a closed ring of the track when Kalyssa noticed additional lengths. She snapped two sections apart. "Look, we can make it bigger."

Leighton and Casey didn't talk while she ate her second piece. When finished, she sipped her beer. "That was fantastic. Thank you. And what do I owe you for tonight?"

"We're not doing that. You'd never accept payment if the tables were turned, and you know it."

No, she wouldn't. Casey already knew her so well it unnerved her. And she'd injure Casey's pride if she pressed the issue.

"Would you like another slice?" Casey moved to get up.

"No." Leighton stopped her with the press of her fingers to Casey's leg. "We should be going. It's past bedtime." She withdrew her hand. They should leave, but she enjoyed the pleasure of a moment's relaxation. The blush that colored Casey's cheeks whenever Leighton touched her pleased her more.

Andy padded over to her with a book held against his chest.

"Hi." Leighton smiled. Maybe he'd warmed to her.

"He heard you say bedtime." Casey brushed his hair from his forehead.

He pushed the book between them. With a knee on the sofa's edge and a kick for momentum, he heaved his little body onto the couch and flopped on Leighton's lap.

"Oh!" She hadn't expected that.

Andy handed her the book and settled into the crook of her arm. His thumb went into his mouth.

Casey's forehead wrinkled. "Do you want me to take him?"

Leighton shook her head and smiled. "No." His warm body felt good against hers. She missed Kalyssa being this small.

Kalyssa abandoned the train tracks and stood between her legs. "Isn't he so cute, Momma?" She took Andy's face in her hands. "His cheeks are so chubby."

Leighton laughed. "Yes, he's adorable. Your cheeks used to look like that, too, darling."

Andy didn't seem to mind the attention. His features were smooth and delicate. Leighton couldn't see any resemblance to Devin, but sometimes that happened. After all, Kalyssa looked more like her than she did Jeffrey.

"You don't need to read to him. I don't want to hold you hostage." Casey looked worried, but her expression changed to obvious fondness as she watched Andy nestle against Leighton's chest.

"We have to read a bedtime book at some point. It's here or at home, so it might as well be now." It gave Leighton an excuse to stay longer. With always being so busy, be it with Kalyssa or the atelier, she rarely had time to relax, to simply exist. God, how she needed it. She looked at Kalyssa and patted the couch beside her. "Do you want to read with us?"

"Yes." Kalyssa scrambled to sit beside her. She turned to Casey. "We don't have this book at our house."

"You should stay then." Casey smiled at her.

Andy pulled his thumb from his mouth and pointed to it. "Grandma."

"Yes, Grandma gave you that for your birthday." Casey smiled, as though remembering.

"His grandparents must adore him."

Casey shifted on her cushion, breaking eye contact. "He just has a grandma."

A few seconds of silence stretched between them. Only one grandparent? There could be many explanations why, but now wasn't the ideal time to get into it.

"I'm sorry. I didn't know." Leighton pulled Kalyssa against her to make room. "You won't be able to see from there," she said to Casey.

Casey didn't move, and alarms went off inside Leighton. Was she remembering their almost-kiss? The way Leighton had jumped away and told her no? Leighton couldn't blame Casey for being confused. The entire situation confounded her. They needed to figure out a way to exist around one another because the school year had a long way to go.

"Come on, Casey." Kalyssa patted the cushion like Leighton had done.

With a glance at Leighton, Casey moved closer.

Leighton was in trouble if the fluttering in her stomach had any say. Picking up her daughter from a sitter's place shouldn't make her feel like this, like standing at the edge of a tall building and looking down, her knees weak, and fear and exhilaration making every cell tingle.

While she'd soak up the feeling tonight, tomorrow would be different. She'd be back at work, where she was in control.

Leighton angled the book so everyone could see and read the first line.

In the morning, her self-imposed mandate *would* resume.

CHAPTER NINETEEN

No one remained in the studio except Casey. The overhead lights blazed, but the atelier's windows had become black squares hours ago. Today's classes had taken up most of the morning and afternoon. She'd gone home and eaten dinner but had returned, eagerness and stubbornness resulting in her presence.

For most of the night, she'd been working on her wipeout, but she couldn't get it right. Leighton had taught her to look for large masses before beginning to refine, so she'd sculpted the light from the dark, working by subtraction and removing some of the burnt umber with a rag. She rubbed harder or used a bit of odorless mineral spirits to reach the brightest highlights.

Casey referred to the sketches she'd done from the live model that afternoon, but it might as well have been days ago. She couldn't make what she had on canvas resemble the woman's figure.

At the start of class, sweat had broken out on her upper lip when the model disrobed, but soon the arduous task of representing what she saw before her on paper made her forget her discomfort. A few hours later, she regarded the model's curves no differently than the form of any inanimate object.

Now hours later, she deemed her charcoal croquis flat-out inadequate. It didn't give her the information she'd been privileged to access in person. Others might have contented themselves with such a subpar effort, but she was a perfectionist. The result looked flat, inferior, and uninspired.

She slipped and inadvertently wiped paint from an area she'd completed. "Shit." She hurled the wadded-up rag. The twelve-six curveball dropped off the proverbial table and landed a whopping three feet away. Even her petulant throw wouldn't provide her with a sense of gratification, just a painful twinge in her elbow.

With arms folded, she assessed her mediocre effort. This would never get her a spot in the exhibition. The problem was two-fold and always had been. First, she could recognize skill. When viewing a great work, she could describe with ease the aspects that made it so. It might be the unusual composition designed to lead the viewer's eye, a limited color palette that created a sense of harmony, or hard or soft edges that made certain areas advance or recede.

That came easily. The more difficult part involved putting that knowledge into practice. Just because she was familiar with the methods used, creating a great piece of art was a different matter. Much like how musicians might predict a song would become a hit, most didn't have a Grammy on their mantle. Knowing and doing were often the twin rails beneath a train, close, but never meeting.

"Son of a bitch." She picked up her razor blade and slashed the canvas. It sliced through warp and weft with ease. With a sigh, she loosened the wing nut that secured it to her easel, carried the painting to the large waste bin near the workbench, and dropped it in.

About an hour into her second effort on a new canvas, she heard the stairwell door in the quiet, and Leighton came toward her. She'd ignored Casey the last few days, though she'd interacted with other students, even laughing with them at times. Casey didn't want to admit it, but Leighton had acted like she didn't exist.

Now she wore a faded Mets T-shirt, loose sweatpants, and no makeup. Casey didn't want to stare to verify, but it didn't appear she wore a bra. Her beauty couldn't be diminished, even in pajamas with her hair swinging in a ponytail.

Leighton furrowed her brow. "You're here late. Is everything okay?"

Before Casey could answer, Leighton's steps faltered. She veered toward the lounge and peered at the sofa before peeking under the blanket. "Oh, no. Poor boy, this won't do." Leighton laid her hand on Andy's head, but he didn't stir. She looked up. "How long are you planning to stay?"

What she wouldn't give to be her son right now. "I don't know, a couple more hours." Her initial failure protruded from the garbage can a dozen feet away. Casey moved toward them, hoping Leighton wouldn't see her second, pedestrian attempt on her easel. She didn't want to discuss her failed start.

Leighton pulled a key card from her pocket and handed it to her. Then she lifted Andy, blanket and all. "Sweet boy."

In his sleepy state, Andy curled his arms around Leighton's neck and nuzzled against her.

"Shh." Leighton kissed his rosy cheek that bore the imprint of the weave of the sofa's fabric. She looked at Casey. "I'm going to tuck him into a proper bed. Come upstairs when you're finished."

"It won't be too late?" She didn't want to keep Leighton up, but she liked the thought of Andy sleeping in a comfortable place.

Leighton shook her head with a hint of a smile. "No, not at all." She took a few steps and gave her a nod. "Remember, you're destined to be an artist, so do what you do."

As the elevator doors squeezed shut on her son cradled in Leighton's arms, Casey looked at her canvas with a surge of confidence and resumed painting. Ten minutes later, to her surprise, the elevator opened. Leighton carried an armful of things to her station.

"Hi." Her impish grin made her look like she was up to something. She handed Casey an electronic device.

On the screen Andy sucked his thumb, his back pressed against Kalyssa. Both slept.

"You have a baby monitor?"

Leighton shrugged. "I never got around to donating it, so you can see him and hear him if he wakes." She rested her hand on Casey's arm. "But I'll be there, too. I'm not going anywhere."

Casey smiled. "Thanks." She propped it on her taboret.

"This is if you need some caffeine. I know it's a hassle to make an entire pot. I have a Keurig upstairs." She handed Casey a mug.

It was just how she liked it, hot with a splash of milk. Had Leighton guessed, or had she been paying attention?

She enveloped the cup in her hands and inhaled. "Oh, God, yes. Coffee. I want to curl up on the couch, but I need to keep going."

Leighton frowned. "You don't. You know that, right? It's comical how far ahead of everyone else you are. I meant to encourage you with my earlier comment. You're motivated and have lofty expectations, but please don't exhaust yourself."

Casey nodded. Even with her high aspirations, painting something extraordinary enough to enter the exhibition, was a long shot. Still, she'd do her best. What could it hurt?

"Tonight's the only night I plan to paint late. I have to work at the art store the rest of the week." She'd already volunteered in the gallery yesterday. Her first sip of coffee slid down her throat, and she moaned. It's jolt would get her through.

Leighton held one more item. She handed Casey the sweater folded over her arm. "It's drafty in here at night. I use this when I'm working late, so don't worry if you get paint on it."

Why did sharing clothing feel so personal?

Before Casey could take the cardigan, Leighton held it open. "Here."

Casey juggled the coffee cup as she slid her arms into the sleeves. The soft material felt good against her skin. She caught Leighton's scent, either from the sweater or from their proximity.

Leighton adjusted the shoulders and the collar.

They stood so close that Casey had to hold her coffee to the side.

"Buttoned?" Leighton's eyes had darkened.

Buttoned? Casey imagined what that would entail. She wasn't sure she could tolerate Leighton's fingers brushing against her right now even if her nipples had been at risk of frostbite. "No, this is fine."

Leighton still held the front of the cardigan like someone would a jacket with lapels. She let go and trailed her hand down Casey's arm. "Yes, fine. Right." She cleared her throat. "I should go upstairs." She gestured at the monitor. "The kids."

Casey swallowed, and her face felt hot. "Yeah, the kids." Before Leighton escaped, Casey caught her hand and squeezed it. "Thank you."

Leighton looked surprised, but her features softened. "I'll be upstairs." She released Casey's hand after a beat.

About ninety minutes later, despite the flurry of emotions Leighton had stirred in her, Casey had made significant progress. Whether she'd been able to focus knowing Andy slept upstairs or perhaps because Leighton's words had motivated her, she couldn't say. She'd seen Leighton on the baby monitor twice, checking on the children. It didn't appear it'd been necessary. They'd moved little except for Kalyssa throwing her arm over Andy.

Casey stifled a yawn.

As she cleaned up, she tried to envision what would happen when she went upstairs. Leighton's key card in her pocket felt ten times heavier than it should. She wasn't sure what the protocol was in this situation, whether she should grab Andy and go home, or talk and have a drink if Leighton offered. Would she?

Most of the time, Leighton kept her guessing how she'd treat her. Her mercurial nature mystified Casey. One day, her icy demeanor could make the windows frost over, and the next, Leighton would do something like bundle her into a sweater. Not just any sweater either, but *her*s. Casey brought the material to her face and inhaled. She found Leighton's scent comforting and a little arousing. With a sigh, she let the material fall.

Leighton had said no, and she respected that. However, despite Leighton's decree, they seemed to proceed two steps forward and one step back. It confused her and made her want more. Her blood rushed. They couldn't do this. They'd agreed they wouldn't do it. Yet the little dance they continued to do around it left her baffled and frustrated.

Ten minutes later, Casey stood in the elevator. She stared at the panel, unsure if she should text first. No, Leighton was expecting her. She inserted the card and selected the button with the number three. The contraption jerked with a whir of machinery.

When the doors opened into Leighton's living room, a warmth enveloped her. As she stepped inside, Leighton lowered a book to her lap. She sat on one end of the couch in front of a low fire, and its flickering flames danced patterns across the walls. A quilt covered her legs and an almost-empty glass of white wine stood on the end table beside her. She gestured to the other half of the sofa.

"How did it go?" She laid her book down.

Casey flopped beside her with a sigh and rested her head on the sofa's backrest. "It was productive, much better than when Andy was with me. Thank you for taking him."

"Anytime." Leighton shifted to face her. "Would you like some wine? Or something to eat?"

"No, thanks." It seemed like a lot of effort to lift something to her mouth. She wasn't even sure she could get her body off the couch. On her hierarchy of needs, food and wine weren't at the top, anyway. Leighton wouldn't offer what she needed tonight.

Casey stared at the fire and enjoyed its warmth. She should gather Andy and go home. Her tongue stuck to the roof of her mouth, but wine didn't appeal to her. "Water."

Leighton leaned closer. "What?"

"Water." Her speech had become lazy, and she tried not to yawn. Casey looked at Leighton, so beautiful in the warm glow of the firelight. "I could use a glass of water."

Without lifting her head, Casey touched her fingertips to Leighton's neck. Perhaps fatigue made her do it. She hadn't recalled giving her hand the instructions, and everything slowed like she'd become intoxicated. Leighton's skin was as soft as a rose petal, and her pulse raced beneath Casey's fingers. Touching Leighton here, a place so intimate, the conduit through which her life flowed, made Casey's heart beat a wild rhythm. What was she doing?

Leighton closed her eyes.

With her thumb, Casey caressed the divot at the base of Leighton's neck.

Leighton grabbed her hand, her eyelids flying open.

They stared at one another, and Casey held her breath.

Leighton kissed her palm, then placed Casey's hand on the sofa and stood. "Let me get you that water."

Leighton's hoarse voice made it sound like she could use some, too.

As Leighton pressed the glass to the filtered water dispenser on the refrigerator door, she debated whether to invite Casey to stay in her guest room. It was late. She could transfer Andy in there to sleep with her. He should wake beside his mom in a strange place. Yes, she should extend the offer. It was the thoughtful thing to do. If it made Casey uncomfortable, she didn't have to accept.

That said, Casey seemed plenty comfortable. What had she been thinking by touching her like that? Leighton's fingers went to her throat. Yes, she might've let it continue longer than she should've because she'd enjoyed it. She'd never admit how close she'd come to asking Casey for more. No one had touched her like that in some time. But what had motivated Casey to do it after the conversation they'd had? Perhaps the same thing that had inspired her to bring Casey coffee and a sweater. They made a foolish pair. What they wanted stood right before them. They couldn't have it, yet neither had the will to turn away.

Leighton had never understood unfairness as a child, and in the decades since, not much had changed. At thirty-seven years old, she wanted to stomp her foot and scream into the night how life wasn't fair. She wanted Casey, and Casey wanted her. Neither would have what they desired.

Leighton brought Casey the water but set it on the coffee table. Casey's soft snores reminded her of a purring kitten. She retrieved a pillow from the guest room, and with an arm around Casey and one cradling her head, Leighton laid her down. Casey's dark hair fanned across the pale yellow case. Leighton removed her shoes and covered her with the quilt.

Casey hadn't awakened, so Leighton took a precious moment to admire the slant of her cheekbones and her dark lashes against her pale skin. Yes, she wanted her, but she'd also grown fond of her. She brushed Casey's hair from her face. It was just as soft as Andy's, but not as fine. Casey still wore her sweater, and Leighton's heart grew heavy. She cared about her. Not being able to act on those feelings seemed crueler than being forbidden to have sex with someone she desired.

Leighton turned off the fireplace and extinguished the lights.

CHAPTER TWENTY

When Casey rolled over and pulled the blanket to her chin, the unfamiliar quilted texture lured her from her state of semi-consciousness. She surveyed the dark room, recognizing it as Leighton's loft. Bits of the night came rushing back, and so did the fatigue that had come in like a captor and snatched her away. She hadn't been sleeping long.

Casey tossed the quilt aside and swung her legs to the floor. Leighton must have removed her shoes because she almost tripped on them. In stockinged feet, she crept down the hallway toward the glow of Leighton's security monitor. Curiosity piqued her interest, but she'd look at it in a minute. Her priority involved checking on Andy.

The first open door showed a bed with a missing pillow, and its bland walls and decor suggested a guest room. In the next one, a glow emanated from a night light. In a small bed, Andy and Kalyssa slept snuggled beside one another, their limbs sprawled out in all directions.

Andy would be thrilled to see the *Frozen* comforter with its marshmallow-looking snowman grinning up at him come morning. He wore a simple T-shirt and shorts, something Kalyssa had likely outgrown, and his clothing lay folded atop her dresser. Casey should've changed him into something more comfortable before coming to the atelier, but it felt strange taking a child on the train in his pajamas.

He might be wet. Potty training was going well, but kids were prone to accidents when their routines changed. She checked and found he wore a pull-up diaper. Leighton hadn't donated more than the baby monitor it appeared. Casey smiled and pulled the comforter over them. After a kiss on Andy's forehead, she tiptoed out.

It wasn't her business, but she couldn't help but study the screen showing Leighton's security feeds. She determined she'd known of all the cameras in the studio and the galleries, and that Leighton's living space appeared free of electronic eyes. The silence and stillness of the shadows throughout the building gave Casey the creeps, but it would be worse if something *were* moving.

Truth be told, her nighttime expedition had no reason to continue, but after giving the full bath to her left a cursory look, she stood in the doorway of Leighton's bedroom, her curiosity getting the best of her.

As her eyes adjusted to the darkness of the large suite, she saw Leighton, who slept facing away from her. Casey looked at the unoccupied half of the bed. In another life, she'd love to slide in beside her. If she moved from the sofa to the bed for a more comfortable sleep, Leighton probably wouldn't mind, but it didn't feel right. If she slept in Leighton's bed, she wanted to be asked.

Casey returned to the couch, downed half the glass of water Leighton had left her, and went back to sleep.

When she awoke hours later, she heard giggling and loud shushing coming from down the hall. She recognized Andy's exuberant laughter and guessed the not-so-subtle quieting came from Kalyssa. She opened her eyes. Through the window, the rising sun turned the sky into glorious oranges and magentas.

She folded the quilt and went to find them. When she peeked into Kalyssa's room, Casey found Andy, Kalyssa, and Leighton playing on the floor. Leighton wore a robe, her legs tucked to the side, and looked more elegant than any woman had a right to look at daybreak. They built something with large, colorful bricks. Kalyssa sat cross-legged beside Leighton, and Andy stood on her other side. He struggled to separate a yellow brick from a red one.

"Help." He handed them to Leighton, then leaned against her shoulder as she used a fingernail to pop them apart.

"Here you go."

He squatted to exchange the yellow for a green one.

Leighton noticed her. "Good morning. How did you sleep?" Her smile held surprise and something more.

Casey liked whatever it was as she joined them on the floor. "Wonderful. I'm sorry I passed out on you."

Leighton gave her a soft smile. "I'm glad you did. You needed it."

Casey touched Andy's head. "Hi, baby."

He glanced at her, but his attention remained on the toys.

Leighton stood with ease, and how her robe stayed closed astounded Casey.

"I'm going to make breakfast. Who'd like oatmeal?"

"Me!" Kalyssa's answer beat Andy's by a split second.

Leighton looked at Casey and raised an eyebrow.

Casey ran her fingers through her messy hair. "You don't have to cook for us. We should go."

This time, both of Leighton's eyebrows arched, and she gave her a look. "It's oatmeal, Casey, not a gourmet breakfast."

She smiled at Leighton's humor. "Okay, that sounds good. Then we'll get out of your way."

Leighton gave her shoulder a soft squeeze as she passed by. "Don't be ridiculous."

Forty-five minutes later, after they'd eaten oatmeal with warm apples, blonde raisins, brown sugar, and cinnamon, Casey and Andy rode down the elevator. She hoped it wouldn't take too long to get home, shower and change, drop him off, and be back for class. They stepped out of the elevator just as Maxine let herself in the front door.

"Oh!" Maxine looked from her to Andy. "You're here already? I wasn't expecting anyone this early."

"Yeah, we're here early today." Casey didn't give any further explanation. "Have a good morning." She herded Andy out the door so fast, Maxine didn't have an opportunity to ask more questions.

Andy, with his little legs, struggled to keep up, but Casey didn't slow until they'd turned the corner. Leighton's worry about what Maxine would do if a relationship between them came to light echoed in her head. Nothing happened, she told herself. Then she remembered the softness of Leighton's neck under her fingers and the sweet press of Leighton's lips to her palm.

❖

"Good morning, dear." Aileen kissed Casey on the cheek and took Andy from her. "And how's my favorite little boy?"

He threw his arms around her neck and buried his face in her bright red hair. Aileen had never kept the fact she colored her locks a secret. Casey had bought her a box of Clairol's Flaming Desire more than once.

She loved to bake, and her sweet nature and plumpness made her hugs twice as comforting.

Casey set Andy's Minion backpack against the wall.

"We have big plans today." Aileen addressed Andy. "We're going to the park to play on the swings."

Andy lifted his head and grinned a baby-toothed smile.

"I thought you might like that." She kissed him on his temple. "Has he eaten?"

"He had oatmeal, but you know him." Casey chuckled. "He'll eat again if you offer."

"Do you want to help me make pancakes? You can stir everything in the bowl."

At her suggestion, Andy squirmed, and she set him down. He pulled at the sleeves of his jacket.

Aileen touched a finger to her lip and smiled. "I'll take that as a yes."

"Give me a kiss good-bye first." Casey caught him and helped remove his coat.

"Bye-bye." He met her lips with a wet kiss.

Casey planted another one on his forehead before letting him go. "Be good. I love you, little man." She tousled his hair as he took off toward the kitchen. "Thanks, Aileen."

"Have fun today, dear." Aileen hugged her, then held her at arm's length. "Are you getting enough sleep?" She thumbed Casey's cheek below her eye.

Casey nodded. "I've been putting in some extra hours painting, but yes." She didn't mention where she'd slept, and Andy was young enough to have moved on to more exciting things like pancakes. If he mentioned oatmeal, she hoped he wouldn't mention who'd made it for him. Casey didn't need troublesome questions with complicated answers from anyone else. She had plenty of her own.

CHAPTER TWENTY-ONE

Even with the sun shining brightly, the crisp morning air made Leighton shiver, despite her cashmere cardigan. It wasn't her favorite sweater. Casey had worn that one home, and it'd looked so good on her, Leighton didn't care if she ever got it back.

Stefan side-eyed her as he grabbed two folded landscape easels from the stack leaning against the wall outside the front door of the atelier. He loaded them into the back of his beloved red and white Volkswagen van parked at the curb.

Excited about their combined class outing, Leighton followed with the last two as she scanned the street. She didn't recognize any of the vehicles or pedestrians. The day was definitely off to a good start.

Stefan took the easels from her with a grunt. "You seem to be in a better mood."

"Maybe let's not have that conversation here." Leighton glanced at the gallery, where inside, Maxine watched Kalyssa. Hopefully, she hadn't run into Casey earlier.

She didn't know why guilt filled her. Casey and Andy had stayed the night because Andy's bedtime had passed hours before, and Casey couldn't keep her eyes open. It's not like Leighton had found time to extend an offer. She'd found Casey asleep before she could. Casey caressing her neck didn't need to enter the conversation, should one be necessary, nor did her thoughtless kiss on Casey's palm.

"I'm talking about your mood, Vaughn, nothing more." Stefan took the easels from her. "You went from cranky as hell to this." He motioned at her. "Your cheerful humming is driving me nuts."

"I'm not humming." Leighton scoffed. "I don't hum." Was she? She seemed to have an upbeat song stuck in her head.

"Sure, you don't." He scrunched his forehead. "So, you resolved your camera issue?" He all but put air quotes around it.

"Stefan." Her tone held a warning edge, and she glanced at the front door. It was closed, of course. She'd never prop it open, and neither would he. Still, Maxine could walk out at any time.

He glanced at her from where he rearranged things in the van. "I said I wouldn't bring anything up, and I won't. No rule says we can't talk around the issue."

"There's nothing to bring up, and there's no issue." Her curtness belied her response.

He held his hand out for another easel. "You were busy in your office after we talked the other day. Busy, busy, busy."

"My office has glass walls. It's not like it was a secret meeting." She turned so she could watch the entrance.

"Casey didn't look happy." He laughed.

Leighton recalled the conversation. "She's a spitfire, and unhappy doesn't begin to cover it."

"Oh, really?" His eyes gleamed.

Leighton handed him the bag of paper towels and the sunscreen and switched to a whisper. "She was livid and accused me of being a voyeur who watches the cameras for fun or out of boredom. I wasn't about to let her think that, so I explained why I have them. That's why I took her upstairs."

"I can't believe you told her." He stared at her, hands on his hips.

"Not all the details, but yes." Leighton lifted the box of snacks from the sidewalk and handed it to him. "I told her."

"That's a big step." He found room for them on top of the easels. "Still, I wouldn't have guessed she'd get the grand tour. I know how much you cherish your privacy."

She leaned against the open door of the van. "I had to because I wanted her to know." The admittance surprised her. "There was no tour, though. We only went a few feet inside."

He glanced at the third floor of the building. "Did she calm down after she found out you live here?"

"Yes." Leighton recalled how Casey had been calm enough to attempt to kiss her, but she wasn't about to mention that part. When she remembered how Casey had held her hand and caressed her cheek, she felt anything but peaceful.

Was Casey right? Could they have something and keep it quiet? They wouldn't need to shout it from the rooftop. She'd never been a fan of public displays of emotion, certainly not while at work, so she didn't fear slipping up while teaching. When she'd seen Kalyssa with Casey, she couldn't help but imagine what a life with the four of them might be like. Andy had warmed to her, and her protective nature came out when around him. Poor little guy, sleeping on a couch in the studio.

No, it wasn't right. This wasn't how her parents raised her to act. Even if they were gone, she refused to be a disappointment to those who mattered to her, and she wouldn't take advantage of Casey like that, no matter how Casey saw the situation.

She shut the van's door harder than necessary.

"I left a box of maple bars in the kitchen." Stefan gave her an evil grin.

"I don't understand how you do it." She'd need to run sets of stairs if she ate like him. "Let's go inside."

Half an hour later, Stefan had eaten two of the doughnuts by the time Leighton gathered everyone in the studio. Most of them wore jackets since it'd be cool by the water. Casey had arrived last, but she'd run home, taken Andy to daycare, and returned faster than Leighton had expected. She'd planned on texting her directions to meet them there. Now, not having a reason felt like a missed opportunity, despite being pleased to see her.

"Stefan will drive the van with the easels and supplies. He only has room for one of you. The rest of us will meet them down there." Leighton pointed south. "It's a short walk, only half a mile."

Mikala tapped Stefan on the shoulder. "I can help you unload everything." She flexed her biceps.

"That'd be great." He pulled on a black beanie.

"Double-check and make sure you have everything you need." Leighton picked up her pochade box. "We'll be painting en plein air in Gantry Plaza State Park. It offers many choices of subjects. You can paint Manhattan's skyline, the water, architectural elements, bridges, or foliage. Just don't set up too far from the group so Stefan and I can make it around to all of you."

Leighton zipped her jacket. "The assignments you've done so far have been indirect, or painting in layers. Today we'll be painting wet-in-wet, or direct painting. Our goal is to finish it in one session. This is called alla prima, which means *at first attempt*. You'll have to be more purposeful with your brushstrokes. This style isn't as tight, so don't waste time finessing edges and worrying about details in the beginning. Block in your large masses and work from there. And don't be afraid to paint loosely. Realism doesn't mean painting tightly. Remember, the Impressionists were realists."

"This is what you meant by a field trip?" Jenna's scowl announced her opinion on the matter. "I thought we'd be visiting a museum or something."

"You'll be in the field painting. That's why I asked you to wear dark shirts or jackets. If you forgot, like Phoenix here, please borrow a smock, or the glare off your shirt is going to give you fits today." She tossed him one. "Okay, grab your stuff, and let's head out."

Stefan and Mikala left first to find a parking space and begin unloading. The rest headed down, most using the stairs and a few taking the elevator.

Leighton touched Casey's arm as they descended the last flight. "I need to say good-bye to Kalyssa. I'll be right out."

Casey lingered as they entered the gallery. "Mind if I say hi?"

"Not at all. She'd like that."

Behind Kalyssa, Maxine covered her free ear as she tried to hear whoever was on the phone.

"Bye, Mom." Kalyssa ran up and wrapped her arms around Leighton's legs.

Leighton kissed the top of her head. "You can come when you're a little older. Okay, love?"

Kalyssa nodded and flashed Casey a shy smile, punctuating it with a little wave. "Bye, Casey."

"Bye, Kalyssa. Good luck selling paintings to—" She dropped to a knee, lifted Kalyssa's wrist, and smiled. Kalyssa wore the black string, now braided and secured to the nut on her wrist. "I like your bracelet." Casey rose.

"Mom made it for me. I decided I don't care if things are straight or not." Kalyssa's firm tone equaled her expression.

Leighton held back a smile.

"Me either." Casey winked at her. "The smartest people never do."

Casey's whispered words caused Kalyssa to beam. Observing their interaction made Leighton's chest feel strange.

Maxine set down the phone. "Leighton, just so you know, we've been getting multiple hang-up calls the past few days from a blocked number." She flicked a red fingernail at the receiver. "Not that one, though. George couldn't find his wallet. How the man ran corporations is beyond me. Remind me to send his old assistants expensive Christmas gifts."

Leighton couldn't focus on Maxine's ramblings. Was Jeffrey ramping up his stalking? Her knees weakened. There was a reason she never answered the gallery's phone. "Thanks. Keep me updated."

As she and Casey exited the building, she looked around but saw no sign of Jeffrey's SUV parked anywhere, though he could drive something else. She checked the door had latched behind her and touched Casey's elbow. "Would you mind walking with me?"

They headed toward Gantry Plaza. Autumn was in the air, in the way it blew leaves from the few trees along the street and in the cooler temperature. Even as she walked, she remained aware of those around her. The one-hundred feet the restraining order mandated didn't apply to the atelier, but to her and Kalyssa. She didn't think Jeffrey was stupid enough to approach her while sober, but his alcohol abuse made him unpredictable. She didn't know how much he drank or whether he attended Alcoholics Anonymous as the judge had advised.

Casey touched the small of her back. "Is everything okay?"

Leighton nodded. She didn't need to worry Casey, who had enough concerns. "It's fine. Tell me where you are with your entry for the exhibition." She'd asked Casey to walk with her because she wanted to make sure Casey stayed on track to make the deadline.

Casey zipped her jacket to her chin. "It's coming along, and I expect to finish on time."

Leighton glanced at her. "There's only one live model session left. Will that be enough, or should I schedule another?"

"Three hours will be plenty." Casey rubbed her hands together. "But thank you for the offer."

That's what she'd hoped to hear. Casey might not win the opportunity to go to Florence, but she'd be a shoo-in for the exhibition. Leighton had always entered a work in the past, but now it didn't feel right to compete with her students.

"Please allow time for Maxine to photograph it with her professional camera. She'd never say no, but that doesn't mean I want students asking things of her at the last minute."

Casey brushed her hair from her face. "I'd never do that to her."

No, that wasn't her style, and Leighton didn't know why she'd said anything. Besides Casey being talented, hard-working, generous, and caring, thoughtfulness was one of her finest attributes. Leighton admired these qualities in a partner. Everything she wanted seemed to be wrapped in one perfect package, right under her nose and right beyond reach.

CHAPTER TWENTY-TWO

Casey enjoyed walking with Leighton to the waterfront. Field trips always fostered a jubilant atmosphere, whether in kindergarten or higher education, and today felt no different. Even if dating wasn't possible for them, she liked Leighton and enjoyed being in her presence. It gave her a little high. Casey wasn't the type to avoid her simply because she couldn't have her, even if she found their situation frustrating.

They worked for a few hours, stopping only when Stefan brought out drinks and snacks from the van. Most of the students, including Casey, had set up their easels near the water's edge to paint the skyline. Phoenix chose the boats on the East River and Jenna the park itself. Leighton and Stefan picked a central location where they divided their time between their own easels and walking around giving advice.

Leighton stopped beside Jenna, not far from Casey. "Just because you're outside doesn't mean you don't need to assess your painting from a distance. And not once or twice. John Singer Sargent did it so often, he wore a visible path in his carpet."

Casey enjoyed overhearing the advice given in the surrounding conversations.

On the other side of her, Stefan spoke with Mark. "Check your shadow temperature. Remember, warm light, cool shadows." He moved to view her canvas. "Nice job on the realistic gradation in the sky and your use of aerial perspective."

At the end of the four hours, they stood the wet paintings against a railing and held an informal critique. Once they slid the wet paintings into wet panel carriers and loaded them into the van, Leighton addressed the group.

"Before everyone dashes off, I have something for you." She pulled an envelope from her bag. "Phoenix, Mikala, Devin." She handed out checks as she called their names. When only one remained, Leighton looked at them. "Maxine sold a painting yesterday, which is why you're holding a little extra spending money, and Casey was the artist." Leighton handed her the last one with a wide smile. "Congratulations."

Casey accepted it, and goose bumps covered her arms.

The group applauded, and Stefan hooted.

She'd sold her first painting. Someone wanted to own something she'd created.

Mark crushed her in an enthusiastic hug.

When he released her, she looked at the amount and blinked. Could that be correct? She'd have to hold back a percentage for taxes, but her rent worries became less worrisome, at least for the next few months. She looked at Leighton. "Thank you."

Mikala and Stefan climbed into the van, and the rest of the group headed back, their exuberance likely due to the money in their hands.

"You look surprised, yet you painted it. Didn't you have faith it'd sell?" Leighton slung her pochade box over her shoulder.

Its years of paint splatters looked like confetti, or perhaps Casey simply felt celebratory after receiving the good news. "I'm not sure. That part of the process doesn't cross my mind. Instead, I focus on composition, symbolism, drawing, brush strokes, and those kinds of things. I might be the only person who's sold nothing, even someone's sketch, from the gallery yet. My sales techniques need work, I'm afraid."

"Hmm." Leighton gestured the way they'd come, and they followed the group. "You know, Maxine can help you hone those skills. She's excellent at making sales."

"Jenna's great, too, from what I hear. Maybe I should ask her to coach me in exchange for my notes."

Leighton, who'd stopped, wore a frown. "Why is she using yours?"

Casey wished she hadn't mentioned it. She didn't want Leighton to be upset with Jenna. She'd wager that Jenna had never been in trouble in her life.

"Is that not allowed?"

Leighton seemed to consider it. "It's not *not* allowed. I'm surprised, that's all. I didn't know it was happening. Why isn't she taking her own?"

In the sunlight, a handful of silver strands shone in Leighton's hair. The beautiful effect reminded her of a sparkling river running through a field of wheat. Casey wanted to thread her fingers in and find more.

Instead, they resumed walking.

"She takes some, but she gets overwhelmed trying to understand the concepts and can't write fast enough. I use an app to scan what I've written in my sketchbook that day, or I send her the notes I take on my laptop. Mine help her get a clearer picture."

"She should've come to me. I didn't know she was having issues." Leighton's low intonation made her sound offended. "I could've provided her with additional materials or spent more time with her."

"I think she's doing okay now, and I don't mind sharing." Casey shouldn't have mentioned it. "You could always ask her if she needs anything else."

"That's not the point," Leighton snapped, then lowered her voice. Mark and Phoenix walked a dozen feet ahead of them. "The point is, I didn't know one of my students was struggling."

Casey didn't know how to respond, but at least Leighton hadn't told her to stop. Jenna would stress again without her notes, and she didn't want that.

Was Leighton upset she hadn't noticed Jenna's issues because Casey distracted her? She struggled to dismiss thoughts of Leighton every day, and part of Casey hoped she wasn't the only one feeling that way. They'd sparked something in one another but couldn't do anything about it. They had to exist, together but separate, doing nothing that might cause the atelier to combust.

CHAPTER TWENTY-THREE

Some of you looked frightened when I said we'd be doing math today." Leighton turned to her class as they gathered around her, not surprised to find a few grim faces. "Don't worry. It's mostly theoretical." She angled the whiteboard so everyone could see.

"We're going to study the mathematics of Leonardo Pisano Bogollo." She wrote on the board with a dry-erase marker: *0, 1, 1, 2, 3, 5, 8*

She drew a line after the eight. "What's the next number?"

After a beat, a few students called out thirteen.

"Correct." She added it. "Does anyone know what this series is called?" Silence greeted her until Casey spoke.

"It's the Fibonacci Sequence." She appeared reluctant to admit she knew.

"Yes, each number is the sum of the two numbers before it. As I mentioned, Leonardo Bogollo was the mathematician who came up with it. He's better known by his nickname, Fibonacci, which means Son of Bonacci. Tell me, why do we care about these numbers as artists?" She waited. When she didn't receive any responses, she elected to call on the one student she assumed knew the answer. "Casey?"

Casey looked surprised to be put on the spot. "It's the basis for the golden ratio."

Pride swelled inside Leighton as she drew a large rectangle on the board. Of course, Casey had known. She drew a line from the top to its bottom, creating a large square within.

"The width of this square is thirteen, and this one is eight." She drew lines, dividing them more. "So, what's this one?" Leighton tapped the third largest square with her knuckle.

Mikala spoke up this time. "Five."

"Excellent, Mikala. It has to be if the sum of these two squares is thirteen." Leighton labeled the width of the squares in reverse Fibonacci order until the smallest held a number one. Then, without lifting her marker, she drew a curved line through them from largest to smallest. Leighton stepped away and assessed the elegant spiral. When she turned, she saw smiles of recognition. "Does this remind you of anything?" She leaned on the end of the sofa.

"A shell." Jenna looked more interested in this lecture than in any other she'd taught.

"A fractal." Mark drew in his notebook.

"Yes." Leighton scrawled their answers on the board. "We find Fibonacci sequences throughout nature in pinecones, ferns, the seeds in a sunflower, shells, and petal and branch growth. We see it everywhere, which may be the reason it's so appealing to us."

The elevator opened, and Maxine entered but waited near the kitchen.

"However, it's the ratio that's important. If we divide the largest side of our original rectangle by its smaller side, we can round the resulting number to 1.618. This is called Phi." Leighton drew the symbol with a flourish. "If we take any two successive Fibonacci numbers, their ratio is very close to this number. It's called the golden ratio, and Leonardo da Vinci used it when creating his Vitruvian Man." She cut her lecture short and capped her marker. "We'll discuss this more in-depth when we talk about composition later."

As the students returned to their stations, Leighton went to Maxine.

Maxine pointed to Leighton's feet. "Switch shoes with me since we wear the same size. I remember from that time you wanted those ridiculous Brian Atwood Maniac pumps for your birthday."

She still had those shoes, and she disagreed with Maxine's ridiculous label. "Are your heels hurting you?" She sat and pulled off her sneakers.

Maxine slipped from her heels and slid into them. "No, I checked the cameras after getting more hang-up calls. There's a black SUV parked just beyond the line. When I walked out earlier, it pulled away and turned the corner before I could determine who was driving. This time, I'm going to slip out the back door and come around the block."

Leighton pressed a hand to her chest as though it would calm her pounding heart. "No, it's too dangerous."

The shoes looked strange with Maxine's skirt and jacket, but she'd blend in. Women commuted into the city wearing the same every day.

"I have pepper spray in my purse, but I plan to speak with him, nothing more. Can you watch the gallery until I'm back?"

"I'll watch it."

Leighton hadn't noticed Casey standing behind her. "No, I'll do it." She stood and acclimated to the heels. Besides, she needed to watch what happened since she'd be Maxine's backup.

"Okay, I'll keep you company."

Casey's adamance puzzled her, but Leighton didn't want to argue in front of Maxine. "Fine."

They took the elevator to the gallery. Maxine retrieved her purse from her desk drawer. "Don't come outside under any circumstance. Understand?" Maxine's index finger almost touched Leighton's sternum.

"Okay." Although, if he hurt Maxine, she'd probably be out there in a heartbeat wielding a stretcher bar she'd ripped from a frame.

Maxine turned to Casey. "Keep her inside. Sit on her if you have to." She headed for the back exit.

Leighton glimpsed Casey's wide eyes as she wiggled the mouse to wake the security screen. Sit on her? She didn't need Maxine planting additional images in her head of ways Casey's body could press against hers. That's what sleepless nights were for. She sighed and sank into the desk chair.

Casey put a hand on her shoulder. "What's happening? You're scaring me. If he's not a nice man, are you in danger?"

Leighton pointed to a specific camera's feed. "Do you see that SUV?"

Casey leaned closer. Leighton could feel her warmth everywhere, though only their shoulders touched.

"Is that your ex?"

Leighton zoomed in. The glare on the windshield made it difficult to be sure. Behind the vehicle, Maxine came into view. "I think so. He's started calling again. After the divorce, I changed my number so my cell doesn't ring all night, but we have to list the gallery's phone number."

Maxine approached the driver's side and tapped on the glass. She jabbed her index finger at the occupant, confirming it was him. Leighton trembled.

"It's okay." Casey soft voice sounded like she meant it to comfort. Then she wrapped her arm around Leighton's shoulders and pulled her close. Casey must have felt the trembling Leighton couldn't seem to stop. "I'm right here. I won't let anything happen to you."

Leighton was glad she wasn't alone. What would she do if he did something to Maxine? Watch while she waited for the authorities to arrive? Confront him and put herself in danger? She hoped she wouldn't have to decide. Casey's presence calmed her, and the more she focused on the warm arm surrounding her, her trembling subsided.

Maxine's gestures had become two-handed. After a few minutes, she stepped back, and the SUV pulled into traffic.

Leighton exhaled.

Casey rubbed circles between her shoulder blades for a few seconds, then went to the front door. She opened it when Maxine was a few feet away. "Are you all right?" Casey touched her arm.

Maxine shook off her hand and looked at her like she'd turned orange and grew horns. "Of course. Why wouldn't I be?" She tossed her purse on the desk. "He's in for a surprise if he thinks he can loiter around here." Maxine sat in the chair Leighton had vacated and untied the sneakers. "Cigarette butts covered the sidewalk. He'd either been there some time, or he'd been there before."

Leighton swallowed and hoped she'd be able to speak without her voice cracking. "What did he say?"

"The same as always, that he just wants a few minutes to talk to you." She slid her feet into the heels Leighton placed before her. "Only this time, he mentioned Kalyssa, not by name, of course."

Nausea welled within her, and her vision went blurry. She was semi-aware of Casey's touch to her elbow. "What were his exact words?"

"He said, 'I saw my daughter. Don't you think she's old enough to meet her dad?'" Maxine watched her.

Leighton swayed. On top of this, now Casey would have more questions. She'd explain at some point, but not here.

Casey led her to a chair. "Sit. You're shaking."

Leighton hadn't been aware. "Tell me everything." Her voice sounded like rusty iron. "Did he mention where he saw her?"

"No, and I didn't ask. He'd never incriminate himself."

Casey placed Leighton's shoes by her feet.

Maxine shrugged. "The car smelled like cigarettes and bourbon. I couldn't determine if the stench was an open container or coming through his pores. If he hadn't driven off, I'd have called the police for that."

"What else did he say?" Leighton couldn't be bothered with her shoes. She considered calling the preschool, but they would have notified her if something was amiss.

Maxine shrugged. "That if you'd let him explain, he knows you'd understand, and you could put this mess in the past." She trailed her fingers over her keyboard. "There's something else." She glanced at Casey. "You can go back to class now. The fun's over."

Casey straightened. "I'd like to stay if Leighton doesn't mind."

Leighton ignored her. It was easier to pretend she hadn't heard than have Maxine question why she'd allowed Casey to stay. "What else?"

Maxine huffed but continued. "I met with him after the divorce, and we came to an agreement, a monetary one." She avoided eye contact with Leighton by inspecting her manicure. "It was simple. As long as he stays away, he gets a check each month. I told him I don't care how he spends it. Booze, poor investments, women, whatever. If he leaves you and Kalyssa alone, he gets paid. He's the type that needs more incentive than a restraining order. I informed him this was strike one. Not only am I withholding his next payment, but if I see him around here again, I'll withhold three additional checks. The third time, I'll rescind the agreement."

Leighton stared at her. "Since the divorce? How much have you paid him?"

Maxine waved a hand through the air. "That's irrelevant. I consider it a worthwhile investment."

"Why haven't you told me this before now?"

"I wanted to avoid this conversation." Maxine motioned to them. "Now get out of here so I can work, both of you. Don't you have class?"

Leighton didn't point out it was her who'd pulled her from her lecture. It'd been for a good reason.

Jeffrey had seen Kalyssa, and she didn't know when or where. Leighton was so careful, always aware of her surroundings, yet she hadn't noticed him. She put on her shoes. Would this nightmare ever stop?

She and Casey entered the elevator since she didn't have the energy for a flight of stairs. Exhaustion had overtaken her.

Casey caught her hand before she could enter her code.

"What're you doing?" Leighton turned.

Casey licked her lips and kept her voice low. "I know what you said before about keeping this professional, but this changes things. I want you to know I'm here for you. If you need someone to go with you when taking Kalyssa to preschool or ballet, I will. I can accompany you on errands, or I can run them for you. And if there's a night you don't feel safe, I'll stay on your couch. Mark can watch Andy."

Leighton's eyes stung. No one had ever offered to be there for her like this. Maxine watched out for her and Kalyssa, but she had the financial means to do it in a sanitary manner. She couldn't visualize Maxine sleeping on her couch. Stefan was a good friend, but he had a busy social life, always chasing one attractive guy or another. It'd be too much of an imposition for him.

Before Leighton could stop herself, she had Casey in her arms. Her soft warmth dispelled some of her worries, and after a beat, Casey wrapped her arms around her. Leighton needed to end the hug, but it felt too good, like everything she needed in that moment. The sweet scent of her hair and Casey's breasts pressing against hers with each breath made her wonder how long she could draw it out without being inappropriate. For a few seconds, she only wanted to forget everything and enjoy the sensation.

"This was unexpected."

At Casey's soft revelation, Leighton moved back, letting their cheeks brush. They ended up facing one another, holding hands.

"Thanks." Leighton squeezed. "Thank you for being you and for offering your support. Yes, I know I can ask should I need anything, and it means everything to me. I've never had that." Her security system allowed her to feel safe while at work and home. Casey staying the night, even on the couch, would've made her feel other things. Experience told her that. She swallowed, reconsidered what she was about to ask, then went ahead anyway. "You know, you could help me some night you're not working."

"How so?" Casey tilted her head. "If you need groceries or something, I can run to the store for you right now."

Leighton studied their clasped hands. Casey either hadn't noticed, or she didn't mind. "No, I want to get away for a few hours, to escape and forget about all this. Let's drive somewhere, take Kalyssa and Andy, and do something fun. I don't care if it's Chuck. E. Cheese, as long as we're not followed."

Casey lit up. "What about Fun City Play Place? I've wanted to take Andy forever, but he needed to be old enough to enjoy it."

"Is that the place with the tubes?" Leighton had heard of it from a dad at Kalyssa's preschool.

"And laser tag, a toddler play area, bumper cars, and pizza. What's not to like?" Casey grinned. "They'd have a blast, and you can relax."

"What about you?"

Casey's face softened. "What about me? I'd enjoy it, too."

Leighton warmed at her earnest expression. "We'd need to find a car seat for Andy."

"I have one. Aileen uses it to take him places." Casey nodded toward the elevator's panel. "We can discuss details later, but right now, we should get back."

"Yes." Leighton didn't want to let go but let her hands fall anyway.

Casey entered her code, pressed the button, and the elevator moved.

"We should've returned at different times. It's too late now." Leighton sighed.

Casey touched her arm. "We did nothing wrong, Leighton. You shouldn't feel guilty when nothing happened."

Nothing except comfort when she needed it, an offer of kindness, and a hug that left her wanting much, much more.

CHAPTER TWENTY-FOUR

Casey would wager the noise inside Fun City Play Place worked as a form of birth control for many people. Loud music with pulsing bass, squealing tires, raucous children, and a myriad of buzzers and sirens emanating from various games filled the enormous building.

Casey handed Leighton another napkin from the dispenser. It amused her to watch Leighton pat the oil from each pepperoni round before taking a bite of the pizza. "You're not getting the full experience." Casey winked. "All the flavor is in the oil."

Leighton's scowl and clenched jaw made her laugh.

Andy and Kalyssa played on the jungle gym with its maze of slides, bridges, and tubes. Kalyssa allowed Andy to lead but treated him like a hen incubating an egg. Every so often, Casey or Leighton would hear knocking. They'd find the kids waving to them from one of the bubble windows.

"It's not as good as the pizza I had at your place." Leighton dabbed the corner of her mouth with a napkin.

Casey loved how Leighton lifted the slice to take a bite and didn't use a knife and fork. She was otherwise so elegant and well-mannered. Maybe her pizza-eating habits came from being a native New Yorker.

"We can order it again." She hoped Leighton caught the implicit welcome.

"Hmm." Leighton raised her eyebrows and appeared to mull it over. "Do you think we should?"

Leighton must be relaxed because that sounded suspiciously like flirting. "I do." Casey met her gaze and didn't look away. She wasn't sure if they spoke of pizza or something more, but her answer remained the same. When Leighton paused to drink, Casey remembered why they were there. "I know he's an asshole, and Maxine pays him to stay away, but what made you decide to leave your ex? That couldn't have been easy."

Leighton stilled for an instant and her eyes became unfocused, but she quickly regained her composure.

"I'm sorry. You don't have to answer that." Casey brushed stray red pepper flakes from the checkered tabletop. "That was rude of me to ask."

"You'll miss out on opportunities if you apologize before you give someone a chance to answer."

Leighton's intensity made Casey shove her nervous hands beneath her legs.

"He was pleasant and charming at first, and I loved him."

Casey squirmed hearing Leighton talk about being in love, even if it no longer existed.

"He was charming and showered me with attention. At the time, I was an up-and-coming artist. Some critics said I had the potential to be the next great living master." Leighton looked away. "Then I got married."

Knowing what she knew about the result of Leighton's marriage, Casey's chest ached at what was coming.

"Shortly after our honeymoon, he took over our household finances, arranged all our vacation plans, and made almost every other decision in our lives. I never had to worry about anything." She folded her napkin. "At first, I was grateful. It gave me plenty of time to paint. Soon, I learned the problem with giving up control is that it's almost impossible to get back. On top of that, he acted nothing like the man I'd married."

Casey tried to imagine what it'd be like to lose her independence and decision-making ability. She wasn't certain she could give complete control to someone, nor did she want to.

"His poor investments caught up with him. Instead of sharing the problem with me, he tried to drink it away. To compound it, his business losses added fuel to the fire. One glass of scotch at night turned into three or four. When I began asking questions about the low bank balances and high credit card debt, he became violent. I was in denial at first, and didn't want to admit we had a problem. I hid the abuse from those around me, thinking things would get better if we could get past that rough patch. Then I saw that tiny heart beating during my ultrasound."

"Oh, no." Casey wasn't sure she wanted to hear more.

Leighton surveyed the room, and so did she. As compelling as listening to Leighton was, she couldn't let Andy, or Kalyssa for that matter, out of her sight. When she spotted the kids inside the highest tower, she returned her attention to Leighton, who'd also appeared to have been checking on them.

"The angry alcoholic that threatened and raged bore little resemblance to the man I loved." Leighton shook her head, her eyes downcast. "It felt like a nightmare from which I couldn't wake. I had a colossal problem for which I had no answer. My life had evolved into something I didn't recognize. I was intelligent, educated, and respected. I never thought it'd happen to me." She wrung her hands. "I decided I needed a plan."

Casey closed her eyes. "Leighton, I know I asked, but if you don't want to discuss this…"

When she opened them, Leighton looked at her with what appeared to be fondness. "I'm sharing this with you because I trust you."

When Leighton looked at her like that, with eyes that seemed to see into every little corner of her soul, Casey's heart raced.

"Before I could execute my plan, his threats turned to reality one November night." Her eyes glazed over. After a brief pause, she spoke but didn't look at her. "Hours later, after he passed out, I escaped with my black eye, bruises, and my unborn baby." Leighton looked up with fire in her eyes. "He may have hit me, but I couldn't allow him to hit my child."

Leighton's intensity made Casey wary, then again, if someone threatened or hurt Andy, she'd do everything she could to protect him. Her eyes burned with tears as her imagination filled in what must have happened that night.

"With everything I dealt with, I had to withdraw from the spotlight, and I became somewhat private out of necessity. Instead, I focused all my energy on raising Kalyssa and opening the atelier."

Casey caressed Leighton's hand resting on the table. "You're so brave." Anger rose inside her as she imagined Jeffrey hitting Leighton and the terror she must have felt.

Leighton shook her head. "No, I should've left sooner, plan or no plan. He could've injured her inside me or caused me to have a miscarriage." Her nostrils flared. "Yes, I left him, but I was lucky nothing worse happened than what did."

Casey scoffed. "I don't consider bruises and a black eye to be minor."

"No." Leighton pulled her hand away to brush her hair from her face. "He also broke my heart. The bruises have faded, at least the physical ones."

Casey didn't know how to respond to that. "I'm guessing he didn't let you walk away without causing trouble."

Leighton shook her head. "Hours after I escaped, he showed up at Maxine's home in the middle of the night looking for me, but of course, I wasn't there. After I left the hospital, Maxine insisted on putting me up in a hotel. Jeffrey harassed and intimidated George and her doorman until the authorities arrived and arrested him. After he got released, his erratic behavior escalated, and a judge granted me a restraining order." She grimaced. "I still lived in a hotel for another three months while I had renovations made to the loft, and Maxine and I installed as many security features as I could afford. It might seem like a bit much, but I couldn't rely on a piece of paper to protect Kalyssa and me."

"I don't blame you." Casey couldn't believe Leighton had shared all this with her. "Do you feel safe there?"

Leighton rubbed the lower half of her face. "Most of the time. The same day the judge issued the order, Maxine purchased a wheeled measuring device and marked the sidewalks a hundred feet from Atelier Vaughn in all directions. I was so grateful, as I wasn't yet comfortable being outdoors, especially that long."

That saddened her, but Casey almost grinned as she visualized Maxine spray painting the sidewalks. She wished she could've been there to hear the words Maxine had uttered under her breath.

"Together, we adjusted the exterior cameras to cover the area between the school and the markings. If he stepped an inch over the demarcation line, I'd have video proof for the court."

"I'm so glad you had the building." Casey tried to imagine how difficult it would've been if Leighton had nowhere to go.

"The deed for the atelier is in my name, so he hadn't been able to use the property to pay off his debts. My father passed away a few months after my divorce decree. While his death hit hard, I was grateful for his timing. If he'd died while I was married, Jeffrey probably would've received half my inheritance because New York is an equitable distribution state. In the end, I wasn't whole, but I had my baby, my dream, my small inheritance, and my name." Leighton smiled despite the seriousness of the topic. "You know, Maxine told me she asked him to brunch after our separation and tried to pay him to go away. He looked at the agreement her attorney had drawn up and laughed at her. That's when I knew alcohol had diluted his usual logic and love of money. What he wanted was power. Control over the situation. Control over me."

Casey watched her eyes go glassy, and she seemed to withdraw.

Then Leighton shook her head, as though sweeping away memories. "I've often wondered if he regretted it, since Maxine said he would have been better off taking her up on her offer. During the divorce proceedings, I wondered if she'd done something similar because Jeffrey never asked for joint custody. Sure, a lot of things worked against him with domestic violence, stalking, and public intoxication, but he didn't even try for visitations, which surprised me. I've never asked her about it because I'm not sure I want to find out how much my daughter cost. Some things are better left unknown. I received sole custody, and that's what matters." She sighed. "I didn't plan to raise a child alone, but so be it. My needs matters little as long as she's healthy, happy, and safe."

Casey didn't like to hear Leighton dismiss herself with such ease or speak of not being whole. "I love Andy to pieces, but I want more from life besides motherhood, and I hope you do, too, even if Kalyssa is your priority." In Casey's opinion, it wasn't an either/or situation. "You don't see it now, but I hope you do some day."

Leighton blinked a few times in rapid succession and her eyes looked watery. She licked her lips and glanced around like she'd rather focus on anything but Casey. "Yes, I suppose. Someday."

They didn't speak for a minute or two, and Casey absorbed all she'd been told. Leighton also seemed to need the time to compose herself.

"Thank you for sharing that with me." She gave Leighton's hand a quick squeeze. Despite the heaviness of the conversation, she'd enjoyed seeing Leighton smile whenever she spotted the kids.

"I wonder if they want to play on anything else." Leighton strained her neck to see the bumper cars.

Casey took a drink of her soda and shook her head. "I doubt it when they weren't even interested in pizza." She tipped her head to the side. "Why? Do *you* want to go on the bumper cars?"

"Only if I can pretend my ex is driving the other ones."

Casey laughed. "So, I'll be keeping you away from that area. These poor kids would wonder how they wronged you." When she looked up from her pizza, Leighton studied her. "What?"

"Well, if you won't let me drive one, then you'll have to entertain me."

A glimmer in her eye made Casey wonder what she meant.

"Entertain you? That sounds ominous." She squirmed on her seat. "I only know one card trick, I don't have a deck of cards, and I'm terrible at remembering jokes. I used to do a one-handed cartwheel, but I haven't tried in years."

"Tell me about your family." Leighton pushed her plate to the side.

"Oh, you're serious." She'd caught Casey unprepared, and Casey took a moment to consider what to share. "Well, I'm an only child, and my parents live near Rochester. They both work for a religious organization, or rather my mom still does, and my dad is retired."

"Did he take early retirement?" Leighton seemed impressed.

"No, my parents are older." She looked away. "They seemed ancient compared to my friends' parents, and when they'd drop me off somewhere, I'd bolt from the car before anyone could see me with them. On my graduation day, more than one person commented about how nice my grandparents could make it."

Leighton touched her hand. "I'm sorry. That must have been difficult for you."

Casey shrugged. "They loved me, but I wanted parents like my friends had who played with them and took them to do fun stuff. My parents were never there for me because their work always came first. My upbringing is a large part of why I didn't want to wait to have Andy."

"What did they think about your decision?" Leighton leaned her chin on her hand.

Casey scanned the jungle gym until she spotted the kids and gave an uncomfortable laugh. "You don't need to hear that sad story, so let's talk about something else."

Leighton studied her. "I want to know more about you, but if it upsets you, I won't make you talk about it."

Casey appreciated the consideration, since she rarely spoke of her family. She took a deep breath. "I had it all planned. Back then, my parents covered my tuition, as they'd always said they'd do. I'd done my research, talked to people, and knew what it would take. It wasn't like me to decide something that monumental without a strategy. My two part-time jobs would've covered the necessities." She sucked at her straw, desperate to take a moment to regroup.

Leighton swirled the contents of her cup and seemed unhurried as she waited for Casey to continue.

Casey cleared her throat. "They wanted me to work at the same place they did, but I wanted to be an artist. They'd never approved of my carefree, creative side. Art is a worthless enterprise in their eyes, but that wasn't the biggest problem. They're conservative, and when I came out, they acted like I'd committed a felony. My homosexual lifestyle, as they called it, strained our relationship. They wanted me to hide who I was and work for a religious organization when I wanted to be out of the closet and wasn't sure I believed in God." She grimaced. "So, when I told them I planned to have a baby, they cut me off. They severed their financial support and ceased all communication. Disowned me." She twisted the napkin in her hands. "I didn't even get a response when I emailed them photos of Andy when he was born." Casey turned her head and pretended to search for the kids, not wanting to see pity in Leighton's expression.

"Oh, Casey. How could they?" Leighton moved to her side of the table and squeezed her leg. "I'm sorry. I didn't know."

"It's okay." She stared at her mauled napkin. "Well, to be honest, it's not. It's embarrassing to admit your family doesn't want you." Telling Leighton didn't bother her as much as she thought it would. "But that's what happened, and I suppose it was for the best." Casey took a deep breath. "It's amazing what years of guilt and shame did to my self-worth and confidence. Being on my own has allowed me to see myself in a new light."

"Yes, look at you and what you've created." Leighton rubbed her leg and pointed to where Andy waved at them from atop a spiral slide.

Casey smiled. "He's pretty great, isn't he?" So was the warmth on her thigh.

"He's wonderful." Leighton smiled and studied her for a bit too long. "He's a little version of you."

Casey wasn't sure what that meant, but it sounded like a compliment. She couldn't look away.

Andy and Kalyssa shot to the table, out of breath.

"We're thirsty." Kalyssa stood on her tiptoes and reached for her drink.

Leighton handed it to her. "Are you ready for some pizza?"

Kalyssa shook her head, still huffing.

Casey pulled Andy onto her lap. He sucked on his drink's straw as she pulled up his socks. He squirmed until his feet hit the floor.

They tossed their cups on the table.

ALAINA ERDELL

"C'mon, Andy." Kalyssa pulled his hand, and they ran to the jungle gym.

"Where were we?" Leighton smiled at her.

Casey fidgeted. "I was telling you about my family."

"Yes, and even though it was hard for you, I'm glad you told me. I enjoy listening to you."

The way Leighton said it made her stomach do a little flip. Either that or the greasy pizza was coming back to haunt her.

"You mentioned Devin didn't want a baby. May I ask what happened?"

"He couldn't understand why it was important to me, why I wouldn't let it go. He became upset and walked out. After a week, he showed up and said he'd reconsidered, but I didn't want to have a child with someone who needed to be convinced. Besides, it was for the best. We weren't great together, and it wouldn't have worked out. I want Andy to have a wonderful life, a stable one, with consistent people around him whom he loves and who love him back." Casey's conviction on the matter trumped almost everything else.

"That's all we ever want, isn't it?" Leighton removed her hand. "Did you date someone after the two of you broke up? Is that how you came to have Andy?"

Casey laughed. "Dating? What's that? Devin's the last person I dated for any length of time." Although tonight sort of felt like one, if people brought their children with them on dates to play places. "People my age aren't interested in having a baby, or even seeing someone with a child. My generation is waiting until later in life to have kids. I went out with two people after Andy was born, but neither of them were interested in a package deal." She waved at Kalyssa, who beamed at her. "All my friends still spend half their nights going to bars. My life is nothing like theirs. I'm okay with that, though. Perhaps I'm a product of my upbringing, but I've always been an old soul."

"I see." Leighton closed the pizza box.

"What about you?" Casey had wondered for too long.

Leighton frowned. "What about me?"

"You mentioned you had a standing date every week."

"I do." Leighton leaned her head close, put an arm around her, and pointed. "She's the one in the green socks."

Kalyssa chased Andy through the tunnels as he squealed with glee.

"Ah, that's cute." Casey attempted to conceal her relief at the news, but she couldn't contain her smile. It dimmed a bit when Leighton moved away.

Andy tripped and fell, and Casey expected tears, but he popped up with Kalyssa's help and kept going.

"I wanted to have a baby with a partner, but it didn't seem likely, and I wasn't waiting for the stars to align." She faced Leighton. "I don't have any regrets, not with him. Besides, I have an amazing support network, even if they're not my biological family, and his one amazing grandparent more than makes up for not having more."

Leighton said nothing.

Casey leaned against her. "Just ask. I know you're curious."

She shot her a sheepish look. "Who's his father?"

"Mark." Casey watched her reaction. "Mark's his dad. Andy's full name is Anders Marcus Norford."

Leighton's mouth hung open.

"Well, his biological dad. Mark doesn't want children, although he and Andy get along great. He's a supportive friend and roommate, and no, we didn't have sex. That seems to be everyone's second question."

Leighton held up her hand like she didn't need details.

Casey chuckled. "I'd talked about it for some time, and one day he offered. I had to consider it, of course. We discussed our expectations. He didn't mind knowing the child, but he didn't want any long-term responsibility. Don't get me wrong, he adores Andy, but parenting is hard, and some people know it's not for them. His uncle, Erica's dad, is an attorney and helped us with the paperwork to make sure there were no gray areas now or in the future. It's worked out well for us, I'd have to say."

"Mark." Leighton shook her head. "So, Mark likes Zorn."

Casey laughed. "You remember me saying that? Yeah, Anders Zorn is his favorite artist. Erica said Mark used to have a print of his self-portrait on his wall when he was twelve. His mom said he fixated on how Zorn only used red, white, yellow, and black for many of his paintings. No blue. He's a dork, but he gave me the greatest of gifts, and the least I could do was name my child in his honor." She grinned. "Have you been trying to figure out who Andy's dad is since then?"

"No, of course not." Leighton scoffed. "Please, like I'd spend time doing that." She shook her cup, and the ice rattled. "I let Stefan do the sleuthing."

Casey's laughter turned heads. She couldn't recall the last time she'd enjoyed an evening so much her stomach ached. "You've heard me mention Aileen, right? The woman who watches Andy?"

"Mm-hmm. Aileen with the car seat."

Casey nodded. "Yes, she's Andy's grandmother, Aileen Fitzgerald, Mark's mom."

"I had no idea. Andy is a wonderful boy. Your parents have missed out by not welcoming him into their lives. Mine is richer since having met him, since knowing both of you." Leighton placed her hand on Casey's leg again.

This time, the warmth shot somewhere else, so much so Casey couldn't think.

She eased from under Leighton's touch, slipped out of her shoes, and stood before her in stocking feet. "If you'll excuse me, I have some children to chase. One benefit of having Andy while I'm young is being able to play with him." She held out her hand. "Join me?"

Leighton studied her with what looked like amusement. "I think I'd rather watch."

As Casey headed for the tubular opening to the jungle gym, she wondered if Leighton's focus would be on the kids or her. She tied her shirttails in a knot just above her bellybutton, exposing a few inches of skin. Might as well not leave it up to chance.

CHAPTER TWENTY-FIVE

Leighton double-parked in front of Casey's building, knowing she'd never find a spot this late. Andy and Kalyssa had fallen asleep on the drive back.

"Would you mind keeping the car seat?" Casey glanced at Andy. "I'll need to carry him upstairs. I'd ask Mark to help, but he's out tonight."

"I can wake Kalyssa and take it up."

Casey opened her door. "No, you've already driven us home, and you're parked illegally. It's nice of you to offer, but let her sleep. I'll grab it tomorrow."

Leighton considered it. "Then what? You'll have to take it home on the train." She got out of the car.

Casey picked up Andy. "I've done it before."

"No, I'll drop it off. I have an errand in the city, anyway." She didn't, but she couldn't imagine Casey lugging it on the subway. Leighton stepped onto the sidewalk and stopped a few feet from them.

Casey brightened. "That would be amazing."

"Kalyssa loves to ride in the car. When I tell her we're taking something to Andy, she'll be ecstatic."

"Hey, will you text me when you've made it home?" Casey shifted Andy higher. "What time is it now?"

Leighton glanced at the dash through the open door. "It's almost eight thirty." She appreciated Casey's thoughtfulness. The only other time they'd texted had been when Casey had sent her address so Leighton could drop off Kalyssa. Would they text more after this? It might lead to further communications, and she wasn't sure that was a good idea. "Go inside. I'm sure he's heavy."

Casey didn't move. "Was tonight what you needed, to get away and relax?"

"Absolutely." It was a sliver of what she needed. Leighton wanted to touch Casey, hug her good-bye, or press a kiss of thanks to her cheek, but she shouldn't. Plus, Casey held Andy, which would've made any of those options difficult. She didn't need to confuse things further. The line between desire and propriety was already so smudged. Instead, Leighton settled on placing her hand on Andy's back and giving Casey her warmest smile. "Thank you. I'll text you."

When Leighton arrived home some twenty minutes later, she lapped the surrounding blocks a few times and checked out the parked cars and darkened doorways. When it appeared Jeffrey wasn't lurking about, she turned into her spot behind the atelier. With her pepper spray in hand and the safety off, she woke Kalyssa and hurried her inside.

The drive hadn't taken long, and she planned to text Casey after changing Kalyssa into her pajamas and making her brush her teeth. Her daughter had played hard when she didn't request a bedtime story. After Leighton tucked her in and kissed her good night, she retreated to the living room.

She had two missed texts from Casey.

Are you okay?

Google Maps said 18 minutes. Worried

Casey had been watching the time, concerned about her. Leighton texted her, not wanting to prolong her fears.

We made it home safely.

The response came right away.

GOOD. My imagination was doing bad things

Wasn't sure how long to wait before calling the police

Leighton's heart went out to Casey. She hadn't meant to make her worry.

I'm sorry you were concerned. We're fine.

She didn't mention she took a few minutes to put Kalyssa to bed. What seemed important at the time now made her feel guilty. She could've taken a few seconds to text Casey. Why hadn't she? It was intimate, letting someone know when she'd arrived home. Only the most important people in her life asked that of her. Her mom had, and some of her past significant others. Not even Maxine did. Her friends never asked, nor did her students, but she also hadn't socialized with them before. The weight of her suggestion to hang out with Casey felt heavier now. Had it been an innocent escape or something more?

She'd assumed the text conversation was over, but her phone vibrated again.

I'm so glad you're both safe. I wouldn't know what to do if you weren't.

Casey's text seemed laced with meaning, or was she reading too much into it?

Safe and relaxed. I had a good time tonight. Thank you.

A few minutes passed. She hadn't expected Casey to leave it there, but she might still be dealing with Andy if he'd awakened. Bedtime with a small child could be hectic. Even though Casey might not respond again, Leighton didn't move. She didn't turn on the television or get something to drink. She didn't draw a bath or change into something more comfortable. Instead, she stared at her phone like when she'd been twelve years old and the cute boy in band class had asked for her number.

It buzzed, making her jump.

Sweet dreams

Since she was alone, she didn't hide her smile, though a simple text shouldn't create this much elation. They walked a slippery slope, but she couldn't resist. How long could they exist in this state of in-between-ness? Her entire body sagged when she considered the consequences of moving forward or stepping back.

Tonight, however, she'd relish the wonderful evening she'd shared with Casey, at a children's play place no less. It didn't matter where because Casey brightened her world simply by being in it.

Unfortunately, tomorrow they'd resume being teacher and student.

CHAPTER TWENTY-SIX

A week later, Casey studied her framed painting hanging on the wall that greeted incoming gallery patrons. The female figure had turned out better than she'd hoped, considering she'd slashed her first attempt. Upon reflection, her initial piece hadn't been that bad. It'd frustrated her to work from her sketches without the model present, and Andy sleeping in the studio had been distracting. Her impatience and lack of confidence had gotten the best of her, but at least her second attempt had turned out worthy enough for the exhibition.

Maxine photographed it and emailed her a link to a folder of all the shots. Casey chose the one that looked most like the actual colors and values. After a minute or two of touching it up in a photo editing program, she submitted her entry. Maxine had Venmoed her money to cover the fee a week ago.

Stefan framed it for her. He had a knack, and the baroque frame he'd chosen complemented it nicely.

As Casey stood before it, she couldn't believe she'd created the piece. This was how she'd yearned to paint. She probably stood taller with her chest puffed out, if anyone was looking. Her hard work and sacrifice had paid off.

Jenna had printed an artwork label to accompany it. Casey almost choked when she saw the price, even though Maxine had told her the amount she planned to list it beforehand. It was more than the last painting she'd sold. She never imagined her work could garner such sums. Granted, no one had bought it yet, and she didn't need to get ahead of herself. Even if it sold, the buyer would have to wait to receive it should the exhibition accept it.

The front door buzzed. Casey walked to the reception desk and let in Aileen and Andy.

"Hey, little man." She scooped him up and kissed him. "How many books did you get from the library?"

He held up three fingers.

She set him down. "You'll have to choose one to read at bedtime." She looked at Aileen. "Was he good today?"

Aileen unbuttoned her jacket. "He's always a little angel."

Casey rolled her eyes. "I know you say that even when he's a terror. You can be honest with me."

"If we have a problem, we take care of it. There's no need to dwell on it for the rest of the day. Right, love?" Aileen smoothed Andy's hair and opened her bag. "Here are your books."

Andy dropped two on the floor and opened the third.

"Take them over there, please." Casey pointed. "People have to walk here."

He gathered the books and deposited them in the corner where he always played while she volunteered.

Leighton came through the stairwell door. "Oh, hello." She looked between Aileen and Casey. Then she turned her attention to Andy, who zoomed toward her with a book. "Hi, sweetheart!"

Casey's heart swelled at the way Leighton's demeanor brightened when she saw him.

"Did you get a new book?" Leighton hugged him to her leg and took it from him.

He pointed. "Train."

"That looks like a very nice train. I have to go get Kalyssa, but let's read your book later." She handed it to him and turned. "You must be Aileen. I'm Leighton Vaughn."

"Ah, so you're Leighton." Aileen got a sparkle in her eye. "I've heard so much about you. Well, you and Kalyssa."

"Have you?" Leighton looked amused and glanced at Casey.

Damn. She was probably blushing.

Aileen waved her hand. "Not from her. Getting her to tell me about her day is exhausting. Andy talks about 'Leighton this' and 'Kalyssa that' from morning until night."

Leighton folded her arms. "Andy knows my name? He's always so quiet."

Before Casey could answer, Aileen spoke, lowering her voice. "Know it? He's damn near about to wear it out."

"Is that so?" Leighton answered Aileen, but she hadn't looked away from Casey.

Being under Leighton's scrutiny like this gave Casey goose bumps.

"I suppose it's only natural. My daughter is enamored with this one." Leighton jerked a thumb toward Casey. "I made the mistake of putting Kalyssa's easel beside hers." She touched Casey's arm. "She's still wearing the bracelet. I keep waiting for it to fall off, but it hasn't."

"You gave her a bracelet?" The skin around Aileen's eyes crinkled.

"She gave Kalyssa a makeshift plumb line made from a piece of twine and a metal nut, so we had to make it into a bracelet. Heaven forbid we throw away a piece of twine Casey gave her." Leighton rolled her eyes but squeezed Casey's arm.

Maxine rushed in and offered a serene greeting, but her tight facial muscles said otherwise.

"What's wrong?" Leighton's voice went cold.

"I just had a run-in with someone." She glanced between Casey and Aileen.

Leighton ignored her attempt to be discreet. "Jeffrey? Where?"

Her tone made the hair on Casey's arms stand at attention.

"Far enough down the street to avoid breaking the restraining order. I warned him." Maxine folded her scarf over the back of the chair. "I'm going to make a few security enhancements to be safe." She walked around the desk and took Leighton by the shoulders. "You have enough on your mind, so let me worry about this. I've been looking into some options."

"Thank you." Leighton appeared lost in thought.

Casey's stomach lurched at the thought of Jeffrey hanging around. She wondered how Maxine would incorporate more features into the already-secure building. Whatever it was, she hoped it'd keep Leighton and Kalyssa safe.

Maxine turned to Aileen. "Maxine Shipton. I'm Leighton's godmother. And you are?"

"Aileen Fitzgerald, Andy's grandmother and Mark's mom. It's nice to meet you." She shook Maxine's hand.

"The pleasure's mine." Maxine glanced at Andy. "Do you watch him while Casey is here?"

"While she's at school or work." She smiled. "Whatever she needs. I love having him around."

"Well, he's very well-behaved, and I assume both of you are responsible for that." Maxine offered Casey a rare smile. "Excuse me." She hung her coat in the closet and ducked into the restroom.

Leighton came to life. "Aileen, it was so nice to meet you. I hate to run, but my daughter is waiting for me." She shook Aileen's hand, then trailed her fingers down Casey's arm. "I'll be back to get you and Andy."

She stopped at the desk, probably checking the security cameras before she left.

Casey hadn't heard about recent hang-up calls, but that didn't mean they'd stopped. She couldn't imagine living with that kind of stress.

"She's sweet." Aileen took a few steps toward Casey's painting.

"Yes, she's very nice."

"You'll have to fill me in on the security stuff later." Aileen pointed to the artwork label beside the piece. "This is yours?" She stepped closer. "Oh, Casey." Her hand went to her chest. "Honey, it's beautiful."

"Thank you." She'd never been good at receiving compliments.

Aileen turned. "Leighton's coming back to get you?"

Casey studied her shoes. "Yeah. That's why you haven't had the car seat and had to take the train."

"It was no trouble, and Andy loves it." Aileen frowned. "But I don't understand how that involves Leighton."

"We took the kids to a play place last week. Andy fell asleep on the way home, and I couldn't carry him and the car seat upstairs. Leighton was going to drop it off the next day, but we haven't been able to coordinate our schedules." Casey stretched her back in an attempt to appear nonchalant. "She offered to drive us home tonight."

"She's coming into the city just to take you and the car seat home?" Aileen scowled. "At least it's against traffic."

Casey lowered her voice and glanced to make sure Maxine hadn't exited the restroom. "I offered to make her and Kalyssa dinner in exchange. The kids enjoy playing together, and Andy loves when Leighton reads him books. She does voices and stuff."

"Oh, Casey." Aileen's tone spoke volumes.

Casey shivered. Aileen's opinion mattered to her. Yes, she was Andy's grandmother, but they had a special bond, too. "It's not like that." Her whisper didn't sound convincing.

Aileen tugged the sides of her jacket together. "I suppose it's none of my business what it is." She cupped Casey's cheek. "But I care about you and can't bear to see you or Andy hurt." She glanced behind her. "Or Mark."

Mark had walked through the stairwell door as she finished. "Gee, Mom, I see where I rank." He wrapped his long arms around her and squeezed. "You look nice. Sorry, I haven't visited in a while. I've been working on my painting for the exhibition." As usual, he slung his arm over Casey's shoulders.

This time Casey allowed it.

Aileen pointed at Casey's piece. "I see hers, but where's yours?"

He gave her a lopsided smile. "Not finished yet."

"Will it bring in a price like that?" Aileen touched the artwork label. "Because if it does, the railing on the stairs needs to be replaced." She gave him a light backhand to his ribs.

He scoffed. "We can't all be Casey, Mom. Let's hope for something close to that if it sells. If you need it replaced right away, Casey's been covering all the utilities since she sold her painting, so I can help you."

"He has tuition, and I don't, so it's only fair." It felt good to help him for a change.

"No, I'm teasing you. Keep your money. I already had someone fix it last week." Aileen rubbed his arm.

"Are you coming to the exhibition?" Casey wouldn't mind having some family in attendance.

"I wish I could, but I can't." She furrowed her brow. "It's the same night as the library board meeting, and I'm on the agenda to present."

Casey understood. "That's okay. We'll miss having you there, but we'll tell you all about it the next day."

Aileen turned to Andy. "Give Grandma a kiss good-bye."

He did and added a hug before Mark scooped him up.

Aileen hugged Casey and kissed her cheek. "Be careful."

"Thanks for watching him." Casey didn't want to acknowledge the advice in front of Mark.

"Let me know when you get home, Mom." Mark dipped Andy, making him squeal. He waited until Aileen closed the front door behind her. "What was that about?"

"Oh, nothing." It didn't feel good to withhold information, but Casey didn't know how to explain the situation. Everything had gotten so confusing. She didn't like how Aileen had seen through her with ease. The last thing Casey or Leighton needed was others surmising that something was happening between them.

CHAPTER TWENTY-SEVEN

Leighton read books to the children and played with them while Casey made dinner. Wonderful aromas soon filled the apartment. When Casey called them to the table, Leighton arrived last. She might have liked to, but she wasn't about to run toward her as the children had. She still had a shred of self-control left.

"What's this?" She hadn't expected the table to be filled with homemade dishes. So far, pizza had been the extent of the meals they'd shared.

"Chicken enchiladas, but I made them mild, so the kids can eat them." Casey pointed. "That's corn salad and Spanish rice."

"I didn't realize when you said you'd make us dinner that you'd cook. I expected takeout or a frozen pizza. Aren't you full of surprises? It looks delicious." She pulled out Casey's chair.

Casey stuttered her thanks as she sat. At least Leighton had managed not to touch her. Her restraint seemed more fragile each day.

They dished out the food, serving the children first.

She never fed Kalyssa anything spicy, even mild, but Kalyssa asked for seconds of the enchiladas. To Leighton's surprise, she seemed to like them, though Leighton couldn't blame her. They were delicious. Overall, it was a nice dinner, one she didn't have to think about or prepare. The company was nicer.

While tiny versus spacious like hers, and the furnishings likely well-loved by generations, Casey's apartment felt warm and cozy. The word homey had never appealed to Leighton, but that's how it felt, like a home. The comfort she experienced here shook her.

The door banged, and Mark came around the corner. "Oh, Leighton." He stopped short. "Hey, I didn't know you'd be here."

"Hello. How is your painting coming along?" Leighton hadn't thought to ask if Mark was aware Casey had invited her and Kalyssa. Their presence appeared to be a surprise. She wasn't sure how to react, and Casey appeared flummoxed, too.

"Good." He dropped his jacket on the back of the couch and pointed to his room. "I'll be in here if you need me."

"Do you want an enchilada?" Casey rose.

"I'll heat one up later." He shut his door.

Leighton stood and picked up her plate. Kalyssa only had a few bites left. "We should go."

"You don't have to." Casey also picked up dishes and carried them to the sink. "I thought he'd be later. He's just surprised."

Leighton set her plate on the counter. "It's best we head home. Can I help you load the dishwasher?" The olive green appliance reminded her of the one her grandmother had owned.

Casey waved her off. "I can do it."

"You cooked, so at least let me help." She returned to the table and brought Andy's plate and empty cups with her.

Side by side, they cleaned up. Casey stopped to wash Andy's hands and face, and Kalyssa asked her to wash hers. Leighton smiled. They looked so cute, the two children standing before Casey with their shining faces and outstretched hands.

Casey set the leftover corn and rice on the stove.

"You're very good with her. She likes you a lot." Leighton placed cups in the upper rack. "I'm sure you've picked up on that. It wouldn't surprise me if she talks about her new best friend Casey at preschool."

Casey smiled. "I like her. She's my little shadow, at least when I'm in the studio."

"I'm sorry." Leighton dried her hands.

"Don't be." Casey reached in front of her for the dishwasher detergent.

Their bodies touched, and Leighton's breath caught.

Casey closed the dishwasher and placed her hands on the counter's edge.

Leighton threaded the towel through a drawer handle. "Dinner was delicious. Thank you."

Casey didn't turn around. "Mm-hmm."

Leighton moved behind her. She should gather Kalyssa and her things and go. Instead, she ran her fingers through the length of Casey's hair and closed her eyes at Casey's sharp intake of breath. It sifted through her fingers like sand at the beach. Leighton wanted to wrap her arms around her and kiss that soft spot where her neck met her shoulder. She imagined slipping her hands under her shirt as Casey leaned back against her. It'd be so easy to cup her breasts, first over her bra, then under. Leighton's pulse raced at the image, and she settled for resting her hand between Casey's shoulder blades.

Her voice came out raspy. "I don't eat dinner at the homes of my other students."

Casey took a shuddering breath as she leaned into her hand. "I know, Leighton. That doesn't make this any easier."

Leighton swallowed the lump in her throat. "No. I'm sorry about that." She hated it had to be like this and dropped her hand. It was time to leave, even though she would've liked to stay. Mark also lived here though, and she didn't want to make him uncomfortable. Their brief interaction had been strained enough. So, she gathered Kalyssa, and they hugged Andy.

Casey walked them to the door. "Thanks for the car seat and the ride home."

Leighton turned and wrapped her arms around her. Casey smelled amazing, a little like enchiladas, but mostly like her usual, fresh scent. "Good night."

They'd descended a flight when she heard her name. Leighton looked up and stopped Kalyssa with a tug of her hand.

Casey leaned over the railing. "Will you text me when you get home?" She looked so earnest and worried.

Leighton nodded. Again, the request that held unspoken meaning rattled her.

Traffic out of the city slowed her more than it had the previous time she'd been to Casey's. Even so, she and Kalyssa arrived home with no issues and headed inside.

"Pick out your pajamas and brush your teeth. I'll check on you soon." She ushered Kalyssa down the hall to her bedroom.

This time, she texted Casey right away. Instead of receiving one in response, her phone rang. Casey's name appeared on the screen.

Leighton swallowed. She wasn't prepared for this. Calling one another seemed like a step in a direction they shouldn't be taking.

She answered. "Casey."

"I'm sorry."

Casey's quiet voice in her ear disarmed Leighton in ways her texts hadn't. Leighton shouldn't have answered the call. Kalyssa could've needed a bath, or…or…anything would've worked as an excuse. It was too late now, so she cleared her throat. "For what?" Did Casey feel the same when hearing her voice? Leighton cupped the phone with both hands. The way she shook, she was afraid she might drop it. She heard a sound like a swallow.

"I'm sorry that Mark came home and made things awkward, but it wasn't his fault. I thought he'd be out much later."

Kalyssa sang in her room, so Leighton didn't feel the need to rush the conversation. "It wasn't so bad. My presence threw him. Didn't you ever see your elementary teacher in the grocery store? It's strange." She pulled her hair over one shoulder.

"It's not that. This is different." Casey paused. "He might suspect something. I mean, I know we're not doing anything, but he has an idea that…" Casey didn't speak for a few seconds.

"That what?"

"That I'd like to."

"Oh." Leighton fell against the sofa's backrest.

"I'm going to talk to him and explain." Casey sniffed. "He needs to know you've been honorable. I don't want to jeopardize the atelier or your reputation. Before I speak with him, I wanted to let you know."

A shiver ran up Leighton's spine. They'd been playing with fire, and the reality of the situation came crashing down. They couldn't appear to have a secret liaison, even if they weren't. "Yes, that's fine."

"Okay." Only the sound of Casey's breathing came across the line.

Leighton didn't want to end the conversation now that she'd been drawn into it. "I wish it didn't have to be this way."

"I know, but we don't seem to have any other option."

She closed her eyes and tried to imagine Casey in her apartment. It seemed neither of them wanted to sever the connection. Leighton could hear Andy in the background. "I suppose this is the only way."

Casey sighed. "I know."

"Good night, Casey." She needed to help Kalyssa change into her pajamas. It was past bedtime.

"Sweet dreams." It was Casey who ended the call ten long seconds later.

CHAPTER TWENTY-EIGHT

The night of the exhibition had finally arrived. Casey lifted her hair so Mark could zip her. The black dress with spaghetti straps fell to her knees.

Mark stepped back and appraised her. "You look stunning, Case."

Casey viewed her reflection in their shared bathroom's mirror. The result satisfied her. She hoped Leighton would like how she looked. "Thanks, but I just want to get this over with. You look nice in your tux." She adjusted his tie.

"What's the rush? There's an open bar, and you have a handsome man as your date." He brushed his lapels. "I think you need to reevaluate the situation. Let's enjoy tonight." He leaned against the door.

Casey applied some tinted lip color and met his eyes in the mirror. "You're right. I don't know what to expect, and that makes me nervous."

He chuckled. "Well, here's what we know. We both had our paintings accepted because we're awesome. People will exclaim how talented we are and how sexy we look, and they're right. Turn your head like this and pretend to blush as you thank them. Enjoy some free bubbly and view some great art." He brushed his hands together. "Success."

According to him, she needed to act like a 1940s film star. Casey searched for her mascara. "Right."

He remained in the doorway. "Is something else wrong?"

"Regarding what we talked about..." She took a deep breath and looked at his reflection.

He shook his head. "Don't make it weird, and it won't be. I just wasn't expecting to run into her at home. I've been in class with both of you for weeks since then. Why should tonight be any different? You said nothing is going on, and I believe you."

"No, nothing is." It wasn't, despite what she wanted with every cell of her being. Over a year and a half still seemed like a long time to wait for someone. She and Leighton had talked little after she'd told her she'd spoken with Mark and had clarified things. They hadn't texted at all, although she'd wanted to hundreds of times.

"Then do whatever you're doing with your face so we can go. I don't want to miss any of the canapes." He rubbed his stomach and smacked his lips.

She gave him a push that sent him into the hallway. "Then leave me alone so I can finish getting ready."

"Fifth Avenue and Twelfth Street." Casey slid into the cab, and Mark climbed in behind her. The driver pulled into traffic. The heater blew warm air, fortunate for her since her dress exposed most of her legs and her coat covered little. A light covering of snow dusted the streets, but nothing that her heels couldn't handle for the short walk from the cab to the club. She wasn't about to wear boots with her evening wear tonight.

Her painting had been accepted into the exhibition, as had Mark's and Erica's. Stefan planned to be in attendance tonight for them, too. He even hinted he might bring a date. Casey only cared whether Leighton would be there. She'd said she would, but until Casey saw her, she wouldn't be able to relax.

It meant something to Casey to have her painting chosen. To have her art shown alongside professionals was an accomplishment. She was still stunned the judges had picked hers. It'd been a blind jury, so they hadn't known who the artists were, or with whom they might be associated. They'd chosen her work because of her talent. She wasn't often proud of herself. It was a rare moment she considered herself good enough at anything. Tonight, pride filled her, and she wanted to share the moment with Leighton.

Casey almost hadn't, but she'd emailed her parents' joint email address a week ago when she received the news. She'd thought that perhaps now that she could show some success, they'd reconsider their decision. Along with her accomplishment, she'd attached a recent photo of Andy and told them how many words he'd learned and how he loved blueberries, dogs, and trains. She'd received no reply, so she checked the organization's website, but their email address hadn't changed.

The stately Fifth Avenue building that housed the Salmagundi Club glowed in winter's early darkness as light poured from all four floors. With their coats checked and flutes of champagne in hand, Casey and Mark wandered through the galleries, eager to discover where their paintings hung. Laughter and the clicking of women's high-heeled shoes on the honey-colored parquet floors filled the rooms. A pianist played classical music in the parlor.

Casey spotted Leighton across the Hartley Room, and her blood pounded in her ears. Leighton's crimson-colored dress ended mid-calf, and a long slit exposed one leg to her thigh. She'd pulled her hair into a stylish twist, and a sleek sweep accentuated one side of her face. The sleeveless dress draped in folds over her chest and gave a stunning view of her cleavage. She spoke with a balding man.

Casey froze in her awestruck state for so long that Mark faked a cough to get her attention.

"Why don't you go say hello?" He snagged a shrimp from a server's tray. "I should find Erica, although she's bringing Mr. Fancy New Boyfriend tonight and might not want me around."

Casey nodded. Mark headed toward the parlor, and she walked toward Leighton.

Leighton spotted her and concluded her conversation with a smile and a brief touch to the man's elbow. She turned to Casey. "Well." Leighton appraised her.

Her dulcet voice made Casey's blood race through her veins.

"You look lovely." Leighton's eyes gleamed.

Casey's face grew hot as Leighton's gaze traveled to her shoes and up again. She scrambled to find appropriate words to describe the apparition before her. Her mouth went dry. "That dress is gorgeous. You look gorgeous." The bodice gave Casey the best view of Leighton's cleavage she'd had to date. Leighton's breasts appeared larger than she'd believed them to be. Her imagination filled in the details at lightning speed.

"Leighton!" An older gentleman rushed forward and clasped Leighton's hand between his. His silver hair complemented his tuxedo. "I'm sorry to interrupt, but it's so good to see you. I don't think I've had the pleasure of seeing your beautiful face since—"

"The Vigée Le Brun exhibition at the Met." Leighton flashed him a smile before she kissed him on the cheek. "Nice to see you again, Alfred. May I introduce you to Casey Norford?" She took her elbow, pulling Casey beside her. "Her painting is featured in tonight's exhibition. Casey, this is Alfred Harrington. Alfred is involved in private painting conservation and restoration."

"Lovely to meet you, Miss Norford." Alfred kissed her hand in a manner that pointed not only to his age but his upbringing. "May I assume you're Leighton's student?"

"Yes, I'm fortunate to attend Atelier Vaughn."

"She's the most talented student I've had, though I'll deny it if you tell the others." Leighton looked at her in a way that made Casey want to squirm.

"That, my dear, is quite the compliment coming from your instructor." Alfred nodded toward Leighton. "She knows fine art when she sees it. I don't recall a teacher accompanying a student before, and I've been coming to this event for years. She must be quite proud of you."

"She didn't accompany me."

"Oh, we're not together." Leighton turned her head and took a sip of champagne.

Casey hoped their quick corrections hadn't sounded like they hid something. Her discomfort grew because everything reminded Casey of her status as just another one of Leighton's students, despite Leighton's effusive praise regarding her talent. Would that ever change?

After more pleasantries and congratulations, Alfred apologized and disappeared when he spotted another acquaintance.

Once he was out of earshot, Casey exhaled. "I wish you could've accompanied me tonight." She came across sounding wistful and sullen and wished she'd said nothing.

Leighton stiffened. "We're both here, and how we arrived doesn't matter. I'm proud of you and wanted to be here to support you." Leighton touched her arm but withdrew her hand right away.

Casey's shoulders sagged. "Proud of your student. What you mean is you're proud of your student."

"No, that's not what I meant. Don't put words in my mouth." She downed the rest of her champagne. "Besides, this isn't the place for that conversation."

Casey might be Leighton's student, but that shouldn't be what defined her. She saw herself as so much more. An artist, a mother, and a woman. One with hopes, fears, and desires. Would Leighton ever see her that way?

A server passed with a tray of flutes, and they exchanged empties for fresh glasses as a dark-haired woman in a stylish pantsuit approached.

"Well, if it isn't Leighton Vaughn." She greeted her with a kiss on both cheeks.

"Louise, have you moved back or are you visiting?" Leighton looked happy to see her.

"I'm only here for the holidays. Then I head back to Florence."

Leighton used the opening to introduce them when Louise turned to Casey. "Louise, this is Casey Norford. She's a fabulous up-and-coming artist, and she has a painting in the exhibition. Casey, meet Louise D'Angelo. We studied together in Florence. Louise loved the city so much she never left. Now she teaches art history there."

Leighton had introduced her as an artist but not as her student, and Casey didn't know if the omission was intentional.

"It's nice to meet you, Louise. You're so fortunate to live in Italy." Casey couldn't imagine such a rich experience.

Louise provided anecdotes about Florentine life and gave Leighton updates on mutual acquaintances until a chime sounded and the music stopped. A feminine voice tested the sound system.

"Everyone, please make your way to the Skylight Gallery. Our awards ceremony will begin in a few minutes."

The crowd seemed to move en masse, and soon most of the event's attendees gathered in the upstairs. It was standing room only, and artwork adorned the walls surrounding them, or rather, paintings of the female nude did. It was quite the display. No wonder they considered the feminine body the greatest work of art.

Across the room, Casey spotted Mark and Erica. She assumed the handsome man to Erica's left was her boyfriend. Erica gave her a little wave, then grinned and pointed at Casey's painting.

Casey had thought it looked nice in Atelier Vaughn's gallery. Here, it looked impressive enough to hang in a museum. *Had* she painted something decent? It was the most involved painting she'd ever done.

"Does it feel real yet?" Leighton had been watching her.

"Having it hanging here? No." She laughed. "I keep waiting for someone to tell me they made a mistake."

Leighton shook her head. "You need to believe in yourself. Can't you see what you've done?"

Casey had never had an accurate gauge of her abilities. She was a talented artist, but she didn't know the line where good turned to great, or if she'd ever reach that level.

The ceremony was about to begin. Should she stand with Mark and Erica? Would it look strange to remain with Leighton?

The club had erected a small platform stage and podium at one end of the room. A woman tapped the mic and saved Casey from having to decide. "Good evening, and welcome to tonight's exhibition, *Adoration of the Female Figure.*" Conversations died down. "My name is Cordelia Witherson, and as President of the Salmagundi Club, I have the honor of announcing the awards tonight. The last one announced will be the Best of Show, which includes a six-month, all-expenses paid trip to Florence to study some of the world's finest art."

Casey didn't know the artists who took home third, second, then first place. Leighton didn't seem to either by her conservative applause. Casey agreed with two of the three winners. She would've chosen a different third place. Mark's and Erica's paintings were better than the one with the bronze ribbon pinned beside it.

"Now, the moment you've been waiting for. The artist whose painting has received Best of Show and has won six fabulous months in Florence is…" Cordelia stretched her pause with a cat-like smile. "Casey Norford."

Casey saw the woman at the podium and people clapping, but she couldn't hear them. Everyone appeared to be looking around the room.

"That's you, darling."

Leighton's voice broke through her clouded state, and the clapping and hooting startled her.

With a hand on her back, Leighton pushed her toward the stage.

Casey had some memory of making eye contact with Mark and Erica as she accepted her award. She tried to find Leighton in the crowd. Near the back of the room, she spotted Stefan with a red-haired man. He pumped his fist in the air like the Giants had intercepted the ball in the fourth quarter of a tied game. Everything happened so fast, and she'd prepared zero words of thanks. She hadn't believed she had a chance at winning.

Somehow, she remembered to thank her support network and mentioned Mark, Erica, and Aileen. She thanked Stefan, Leighton, and Atelier Vaughn. Then she looked at the heavy award with her name on it. "Finally, I'd like to thank someone who's not here tonight because it's past his bedtime. He gives my life meaning and is my inspiration. My son, Andy."

The knowledge she'd won and would be living in Italy seemed surreal. Florence, for half a year. Only a few weeks of class remained before the semester's end. How strange to think she wouldn't be a student at Atelier Vaughn after that.

When the applause finished, Casey accepted congratulations from dozens of people whose names she'd never remember. Most of the event's attendees had moved to other rooms, but Mark and Erica lingered. They hugged and congratulated her.

Erica pulled her boyfriend closer. "Casey, this is Quentin Cohn."

Casey shook his hand. He seemed pleasant but bored.

"Stefan and his date went in search of alcohol since you looked like you'd be busy for a bit." Mark tugged at his tie.

Casey scanned the room. A crimson dress was hard to miss, especially since people had filtered downstairs. "Where's Leighton?"

"I don't know." Mark's mouth pulled to the side. "I'm trying to remember if I've seen her since your name was called. She might have wandered into another gallery."

That didn't seem like Leighton. Not that she didn't appreciate art, but Casey had won. She'd won Best of Show and the goddamned trip to Italy. Where the hell was Leighton?

She tapped Mark's arm. "I'm going to find her."

"Want help?" The tray headed their way with some sort of fried tidbit on it had already caught his eye.

"No, I'm sure I'll find her." Casey left the gallery but not before swiping one more glass of champagne. After winning, she deserved it. Of course, she'd have preferred to toast her win with Leighton.

She didn't wander through the libraries or the other galleries. Instead, she went straight to the coat check desk. The young man extended his hand for her ticket, but she stopped him.

"Hi, sorry. Did you notice a woman in a red dress leave?"

"Yeah, she was the first person to retrieve her coat, right after the loudest burst of applause. She seemed in a hurry."

"Oh." The room spun a little. Leighton had left.

"Did you need anything else?" He brushed the front of his vest and reached for his phone he'd laid face down.

She considered her options and unzipped her wristlet to find her ticket. "Just my coat, please."

When he'd retrieved it, she tipped him a couple of dollars more than usual since he'd been helpful, and she had every right to be celebratory.

Not only had they deemed her painting the best in the exhibition, but she was going to Florence for six months. Yet Leighton hadn't stayed to celebrate or even congratulate her. She didn't understand why.

CHAPTER TWENTY-NINE

Casey paid her driver, and moonlight glinted off the taxi's rear window as it drove away. Since they hadn't arrived at the club together, she wasn't sure if Leighton had driven, taken a cab, or used a ride-sharing service. So, the presence of Leighton's car in her parking space behind the building wouldn't tell her if Leighton was home. She looked at the third-floor windows. The back end of Leighton's apartment was dark, but light shone from the living room area, a good sign.

She texted Mark during the drive. Without going into detail, she let him know she'd left and would explain later.

As she typed her passcode into the building's front door, it occurred to her that Leighton didn't have a doorbell. She called her phone. Motion-sensitive lights flickered on in the gallery as she stepped inside. The call went to voice mail, just like the one in the cab. She hadn't thought her plan through but had simply headed toward the atelier. Leighton had left, and she wanted to be with her. She'd overlooked the logistics.

Casey hung up and wandered through the gallery. It felt eerie at night. She hoped she'd triggered a security notification, and Leighton would come down. After five minutes, boredom forced her to find another plan. She considered throwing pebbles at one of Leighton's windows, but she didn't know where she was going to find any small rocks. In addition, her arm wasn't strong, her aim wasn't good, the windows were three stories above street level, and this wasn't a Hallmark movie.

She called the elevator and stepped inside. Everyone had a code, even Leighton. She'd used it the night she took Andy upstairs after leaving Casey her card.

Maybe she could guess it. But what if the elevator locked after so many failed attempts, and she got stuck? Surely someone would come by tomorrow, and being trapped one night wouldn't kill her. She hoped the software wasn't finicky and tried the first code she could think of.

One-one-one-one.

She pushed the button for the third floor. A red LED blinked. Nothing. She tried one-two-three-four with no luck. Kalyssa was four, so she tried the few years that might be her birth year. Nope.

Casey tried to think of things that were important to Leighton. What would be a meaningful number to Leighton? Then it hit her. Phi, the divine proportion. She was a goddamned genius! Goose bumps erupted over her skin, and adrenaline coursed through her as she pressed the buttons in rapid succession.

One-six-one-eight.

She stepped back, expecting upward movement, but the elevator remained motionless. The red LED mocked her, and her hope left with her loud sigh.

Then, an idea hit her. In a last-ditch effort that had a fraction-of-a-percentage's chance of working, she entered her own code and selected the button for the third floor.

The elevator moved.

❖

With no other sounds to drown it out, Leighton heard the elevator ascending. She tensed as she set the open bottle of wine on the counter. The only people with access to her apartment were Stefan and Maxine— and Casey, though Casey didn't know it. Stefan wouldn't be showing up tonight, not when the man he'd been crushing on for months had agreed to attend the event with him. And Maxine had likely been in bed for hours. On instinct, she moved toward the knife block, her body rigid.

The doors opened and Casey burst into the apartment, looking as gorgeous as when Leighton had first seen her tonight. She stalked toward her like a lioness who'd spotted a wounded antelope. Without a sideways glance or break in pace, she tossed her coat and small purse on the sofa.

Leighton's breath caught in her chest. "I wondered when you'd try." She let her hand fall from the knife block.

Casey didn't seem to notice as she strode into the kitchen. "You left!" She raised her hands in obvious anger.

Leighton covered her face with her arms to protect herself and shied away. Her hip bumped into the counter's edge. When nothing happened, she peeked out. Her response had been instantaneous and unstoppable, and now heat flooded her cheeks. She wished Casey hadn't witnessed her in such a vulnerable and pathetic state.

Casey stared, eyes wide, lips parted, face pale.

Leighton dropped her hands.

"Leighton." Casey's voice came out a whisper. "Did you think I was going to hit you?"

Leighton looked away, unable to face her. "I...no, not when I have time to think. I...It was instinct." She pressed a palm to her chest and tried to slow her rocketing heart rate.

"I didn't mean to scare you." Casey slumped against the opposite counter and shook her head like she wanted to erase what had happened. "Would you like me to leave?"

"No. I'll be fine in a minute. The fear takes time to overcome, I'm told, if overcoming it occurs at all." Leighton didn't want to get into the details of her therapy.

Casey clenched her fists. "I almost wish he'd step over that line."

The sentiment was sweet, but Leighton didn't want Jeffrey anywhere near Casey, or anyone else she loved. *Loved?* Well, had affection for? Cared for? She'd delve into that later.

Casey sighed, and her features softened. She slowly extended her hand. "Would it be okay if I touched you?"

Leighton nodded and reached out in response.

The simple contact eased her tension. Casey brushed her thumb across Leighton's knuckles.

Leighton tried to slow her breathing for a different reason.

"I'm not him." Casey's tenderness came through in her tone and her gentle look. It wasn't pity, but concern and a lingering bit of anger maybe. Yet her expression held untold affection. "I'd never hurt you."

Leighton averted her gaze. "I know that."

"Good." Casey tucked a lock of Leighton's hair that had fallen from her styled updo back into place. "Can we talk about why you left the exhibition and why you're not answering your phone? I thought I might have to climb a drainpipe in this dress."

Leighton pulled her hand away and crossed her arms. Her actions had been necessary, but now she looked foolish. She also knew Casey would never settle for anything less than an explanation, and when

Leighton considered it, she deserved one. That didn't mean she'd found the courage or knew where to start. "I'm not sure I know how to explain."

"Begin by telling me why you ignored my calls. I know you didn't turn off your phone because you use an app to monitor your security systems and Kalyssa was with someone else tonight."

Leighton debated how to answer and settled on the truth. "I haven't looked at it because I knew you might try to contact me, and I wasn't sure what to say." And her need for a calming drink had been a priority.

"Might? After you disappeared from an event, not to mention one where I accepted the grand prize? The chance I'd want to know what happened to you and whether you were okay was more than *might*." Casey inched closer. "Tell me why you left. Did I do something wrong?"

She hated that Casey blamed herself, but how was she supposed to explain? It would make her too vulnerable, and she wasn't sure she was ready or would ever be.

"What happened after you heard my name called?" Casey's soft voice didn't have the soothing effect it should.

"Casey." Leighton closed her eyes. She needed to stop this like she'd needed to escape from the exhibition. Yet, here she was, cornered in her own kitchen with nowhere to run, being asked questions whose unspoken answers made her hands shake.

Casey stepped closer. Leighton could feel her warmth and smell the champagne she'd been drinking. She opened her eyes to find Casey's held no sparkle, none of their usual glimmer. Something akin to disappointment or hurt made her beautiful features sag, and that tugged at Leighton's heart like few things ever had.

"I deserve an answer. I won something, something huge, and the one person I wanted to celebrate with ran from the building like it was on fire. What happened?"

To be accurate, Leighton didn't run. She'd strode out like the elegant woman she was and hailed the first passing taxi. "I can't." She looked away. Seeing Casey's disappointment in her would break her.

Casey touched her arm. "Please, at least tell me what you felt. I need to know."

Leighton focused on her again. Casey had moved, so close Leighton could tell she must have just wet her plump lower lip. She tried to keep from looking at the smooth skin under the straps of her dress and to ignore the small triangle of birthmarks along her collarbone. Most of all, she struggled to avoid the allure of the dip of cleavage that was almost as tantalizing as the creamy tops of her breasts. If she dragged her forefinger down the center of Casey's chest, she could hook the tip beneath the fabric and—

This was no time for distractions. Casey waited for an answer she deserved.

She rested her hands on Leighton's arms. "What did you feel?"

Could Casey feel her trembling? "I..." Leighton's throat was too dry to swallow. Even if it hadn't been, she didn't think she could force herself to say the words aloud.

Casey handed her the glass of wine, and watched as she raised it to her lips. It coated her throat, though she couldn't taste it. She offered her some, but Casey declined, so she set it on the counter. This time, Casey didn't touch her but remained close. Her eyes bored into her like she had a superpower to read minds, and she'd activated it. Leighton wished it was true. It'd save her the difficulty of saying the words. Unfortunately, she didn't know how to get out of this predicament any other way.

"Something happened at the event." She grasped the edges of the counter behind her as her insides churned.

"What?" Alarm filled Casey's features. "Did he show up?"

"No. It has nothing to do with him." Of course, Casey would leap to that conclusion.

Casey tilted her head. "Then what?"

Leighton fought not to stare at Casey's parted lips and think how she was in the perfect position to be kissed. Now wasn't the time.

At the event, they'd stood across from a large, nineteenth-century pastoral scene framed behind protective glass. Leighton hadn't seen the painting. Instead, she'd been entranced by their reflection. They made a beautiful couple, but that wasn't what struck her most. For the first time, she saw them as equals, a phenomenon that had never happened despite the attraction between them. As much as she'd wished they weren't student and teacher, that was how she'd always regarded Casey, as her student. Tonight that had changed, and she'd seen her as a woman. Then the awards ceremony had taken place, and the announcement of the final award's recipient had shifted her world.

"You want to know what I felt, and I wish I had a simple answer." She looked at Casey, trying to find courage, searching for some guarantee there'd be no judgment, no shame.

"Take your time. I'm in no hurry." Casey covered one of Leighton's hands with hers.

Her determination never seemed to waiver. Inches separated them.

Leighton breathed in and out with deliberation. "First, annoyance."

"Annoyance?" Casey's eyebrows shot up, then curved into a confused frown.

Leighton nodded. "I had three students in attendance whose works had been accepted into the exhibition, and not one of them had placed first, second, or third. Of course, I expected it to be a sweep."

Casey laughed, the merry sound filling the kitchen and sending a pleasant warmth through Leighton. "Go on."

"Then surprise." She became somber. "Your painting is exquisite, absolutely breathtaking. I didn't want to say anything beforehand because I feared my bias colored my ability to view your art objectively. Every one of my students painted the same model, yet none of them looked like yours."

Casey's thank you was almost inaudible, and scarlet patches bloomed on her chest.

"That said, I never expected the judges to award Best of Show to someone unknown. These events are often political, even with a blind jury. It doesn't mean you aren't talented, but as far as the artistic circle in New York goes, you're not a name, or style, that anyone knows." She stroked Casey's cheek. "Yet."

Casey smiled and stood taller.

Her pleasure at Leighton's words and touch buoyed Leighton's courage, and her trembling subsided. "I was standing beside you when they announced the grand prize winner, and I heard your name." Her vision went hazy in remembrance of the excitement, the headiness, the way she feared she might go into cardiac arrest when she realized what it meant. Her heart pounded again at the mere thought.

Casey squeezed her hand. "How did that make you feel?"

Was Casey channeling Leighton's therapist?

"Three things, in this order. I was so proud of you. Not because I'd taught you, but because of what you'd accomplished through the monumental time, effort, and love you poured into that stunning painting." Leighton took a sip of wine for perseverance. "My second thought was to grab you, hold your sweet face, and kiss you."

Casey's eyes bulged, and her grip on Leighton's hand tightened. "Oh."

"I couldn't, especially not there, but I didn't trust myself." A lump rose in Leighton's throat at what she had to say next. "My last thought was that you'd be leaving for Florence soon, and I'd still be here in New York..." She clenched her eyes shut to fight back her tears. "Heartbroken."

Casey squeezed her fingers so hard her knuckles ached.

When Leighton looked at her, Casey's cheeks were wet.

"Heartbroken?" she whispered.

Leighton stared at her a moment, then slowly nodded. "Yes, it will break my heart when you leave. So, I came home. I left because you frighten me. You make me afraid of what I want to do." She never shared her innermost thoughts and emotions like this, not even with her therapist. Casey had a hold on her she couldn't describe, an uncanny way of finding the cracks in Leighton's walls. Yet, she didn't pry them apart with a crowbar but as a tree's roots split a rock, steady and gently over time, until the stone breaks in two.

"You wanted to kiss me?" Of course, Casey hadn't missed that part.

Leighton gave a feeble wave. "The tense is irrelevant."

The glimmer had returned to Casey's eyes. She moved so their thighs touched. "Yes, I'll be leaving for Florence soon, and you know what else that means."

She did. It'd played an enormous role in her running—striding—out of the event.

They were almost at eye level with one another since Leighton had discarded her heels. She shivered as Casey nuzzled her cheek and neck. Her scent invaded Leighton's senses. It was something different, alluring.

"I won't be your student." Casey pressed her lips just beneath Leighton's ear and began gathering the length of Leighton's dress in her hand. The fabric slinked up her legs until Casey grasped a ball of the material.

It had a dizzying effect on Leighton, and she struggled to speak amid the building sensations. "Classes continue—" she sucked in a sharp breath when Casey's fingers brushed her bare thigh, "—for a few more weeks." Desire pooled at her center.

"Yes, not even a month." Casey traced the curve of her ear with the tip of her tongue.

Pleasure pulsed between Leighton's legs, and she whimpered. Was this how generals felt when the battle wasn't over, but they already knew they'd lost? Leighton tried to regain control. "It'd look bad."

Casey pulled back and glanced around. "To whom? Who's going to know? Is Kalyssa here?"

"No, she's staying at a friend's tonight." She could've lied, but she didn't because she'd wanted this for some time. She wanted Casey.

"Mmm." Casey brushed her lips across Leighton's collarbone. "Aileen has Andy until tomorrow, but if you want me to stop," she pressed her leg between Leighton's thighs, "you should tell me now."

Leighton gasped at the sublime pressure, as her vision blurred and her defenses crumbled.

"Or we could return to your three things." Casey's voice grew husky. "The second one, in particular. The one about how you wanted to kiss me." She shifted her thigh.

Leighton moaned. Her long pent-up need for Casey broke loose. She backed her into the kitchen island with a thud, cupped her face, and covered her mouth with hers. She kissed her deeply, thoroughly, with the hunger of a starving animal.

Still, somewhere in the recesses of her mind not awash with pleasure, she knew she should stop. But the self-discipline she'd clung to over the last few months had been exhausted.

Casey's heat made Leighton's hands wander, and her hot, slick mouth held her captive. Leighton dove her hands into her hair and licked the inside of her lower lip, making Casey moan in her mouth. Leighton's core went molten. Their tongues stroked and teased, but it didn't feel like a battle in which a winner needed to claim dominance, not that she wouldn't submit to anything Casey wanted.

She needed Casey, and yes, she'd be heartbroken when she left, but her heart would mend in time. Right? Leighton was no fool. She'd spent a year in Florence and was no stranger to the ways of Italy's beautiful women and men. Casey denying their charms for six months seemed too good to be true. Besides, who was she to expect Casey to enjoy any less of Florence's gorgeous attractions than she had?

She'd done her best to avoid this, but now, Leighton wasn't about to sacrifice the chance to have Casey, to feel her beneath her, to explore parts of her she'd only dreamed about, and to make her come as many times as she could before morning. She wouldn't relinquish this night with her, especially when Casey wore one of the sexiest dresses ever conceived. Had Casey chosen her attire knowing what it'd do to her, how it'd make her blood sizzle? Casey wasn't hers and would likely never be, but Leighton wouldn't deny herself, not now, not with the opportunity to peel this dress off her. If she couldn't have Casey, at least they could have tonight.

Casey still held the lower half of Leighton's gown in one hand. She bit Leighton's bottom lip.

Leighton gasped. It didn't hurt, but it shocked her enough that Casey used the opportunity to flip them. Now the edge of the island dug into Leighton's back, and Casey's leg slotted snugly between her thighs again. Leighton pulled Casey's hips against her, and Casey rewarded her with an appreciative moan.

After fumbling at her back, Casey finally let out an annoyed groan.

"It zips on the side." Leighton threaded her fingers in Casey's hair and lowered her mouth to the hollow of her throat. She kissed and sucked along Casey's neck and collarbone where her perfume was stronger. Leighton's head swam, and a hushed voice of reason whispered a soft warning. She should stop. It wasn't too late. Except that it was. The only thing that could bring this to a crashing halt was if that's what Casey wanted, and that didn't seem likely.

With a quiet curse, Casey lifted Leighton's arm and peered at her side. "What the…"

Leighton used the opportunity to catch her breath. "Would you like me to undo the little hook at the top for you?"

Casey shot her an obstinate look. Then her features softened. "Thanks, but I'm enjoying undressing you. I've imagined it often enough."

Leighton's stomach flipflopped as the material covering her breasts went slack.

Casey tugged at the bodice until she found the bra's clasp. She grazed her fingertips over Leighton's bare skin while brushing her lips along the tops of her shoulders. She took her time.

Was she savoring or teasing? Leighton gave up all pretense she could, or would, and rocked against Casey's thigh. She'd never been like this, needing so much, aching to give in return.

"Yes, like that." Casey pushed back, giving Leighton purchase.

The obvious arousal in Casey's gravelly voice stoked Leighton's, and she quickened her pace.

Casey freed Leighton's breasts, and the cool air stiffened her nipples before Casey claimed them with her warm hands and hot tongue. She caressed and licked them, driving Leighton wild. The sharp draw of one into Casey's mouth made her tighten her fingers in Casey's hair and cry out in pleasure.

Casey moaned and did it again.

A tug on her other nipple inflamed Leighton's desire, and her legs nearly gave out. She pulled Casey to her and kissed her.

"I need to lie down." Her breath came fast. "Bed."

Casey panted just as hard. "The couch is closer." She dragged Leighton to it, shoved her coat and purse to the floor, then turned to her.

A flush covered Casey's face and chest. Her swollen lips looked rosy, and Leighton's fingers had made a mess of her hair. So distracted by the beauty of Casey's wild and wanton appearance, Leighton forgot she wore her own dress around her waist until Casey stepped forward to help her out of it.

In one quick move, she pulled Leighton's strapless bra from her bodice. She slid the dress down, her fingers grazing Leighton's skin as she did, and let it fall to the floor. Leighton's underwear followed, and she trembled at the slow slide of the silky fabric over her legs. With a hand for balance, Casey helped her step out of the pile of material.

Casey licked her bottom lip. "It's a beautiful dress, but this is as gorgeous as I've seen you."

Leighton watched as Casey raked her gaze over her breasts, the nipples standing stiff and erect with the ache for attention, down her stomach, leaving the heat of a caress in its wake, to the triangle of hair at the apex of her legs. Leighton tried to hold back a shiver. Imagining this scenario, as she'd done on many sleepless nights, hadn't included the feelings swirling inside her now with Casey studying her. Instead of nerves or self-consciousness, adoration and fondness swept over her. Yes, she desired Casey something fierce, but the emotions she couldn't get a grasp on seemed so much more powerful. She stepped forward to help her undress, but Casey shook her head.

"That can wait." She dropped onto the sofa and pulled Leighton down to straddle her lap.

Leighton needed the closeness. She kissed her again as she explored the exposed skin of Casey's neck with her fingertips.

Casey trailed her hand up Leighton's leg, stopping at her inner thigh. When Leighton tried to kiss her again, she pulled back. "I enjoy seeing you wanting. I feel like it's always me in this state."

"Then you don't realize what you do to me." Leighton's eyelids grew heavy. All she wanted was to close them and lose herself in Casey. She thrust her hips.

Casey ran her fingers through her patch of curls. "Missing my leg? Should we do something about that?" She cupped her, dipping her fingers into her folds.

Leighton gasped, and her desire bloomed in full. She ground against Casey's hand. At Casey's sly smile, Leighton gripped the hair at Casey's nape, tilted her head back, and kissed the smile right off her face.

She fumbled at the back of Casey's dress. "I want you naked."

Casey leaned forward, pressing their bodies together even more.

Leighton yanked the zipper's pull as she sucked Casey's earlobe. When she'd lowered it as far as she could, she slid her hand inside the bodice and squeezed Casey's breast.

Jesus Christ. She wasn't wearing a bra. Her already-erect nipple tightened more at Leighton's touch.

Casey slumped against the cushions, her lips parted. "That's so good. Keep doing that."

Leighton nuzzled and nipped along her neck and shoulder and pushed the dress down with her free hand so she could get to Casey's other breast. She kneaded it gently, and Casey brought their mouths together again. Leighton's ability to breathe, let alone kiss, left her as Casey drew small circles between her legs with a firmer touch. She groaned.

"Do you like that?" Casey bit the tender spot where Leighton's neck met her shoulder, then soothed it with a swipe of her tongue.

"Yes, but..." She needed all of Casey, to feel her inside her, for Casey to push her over this exquisite but torturous edge. Leighton covered her hand and guided her fingers to her entrance.

She stilled, and Casey entered her slowly, without breaking eye contact. A quiet gasp escaped from Leighton's lips when Casey filled her.

Casey waited, giving her a moment. At Leighton's small nod, she began to move.

God, it'd been ages. She wouldn't last long. After all, she'd been fantasizing about this very moment for months.

Casey took her nipple into her mouth and ran her tongue around it.

"Oh, God." Leighton grasped her shoulders. "Yes, yes." She rocked harder, lifting and allowing herself to fall, taking Casey deeper.

"That's it. Keep going." Casey kissed between her breasts and dug her fingers into the soft flesh of her hip as she helped guide her movements.

While Leighton had feasted on all of Casey's skin she could reach, now she was single-mindedly focused on her own need for release. Her knees ached, and sweat covered her skin, but she rode Casey's fingers with abandon.

Casey moaned softly, her eyes dark with obvious lust as she pushed deeper with each of Leighton's thrusts. "I like you like this." Her voice was low and husky. "Are you ready?" Before Leighton could process the question, Casey curled her fingers and circled Leighton's clit with her thumb.

And that changed everything. What Leighton had craved moments before she now wanted to last, but her orgasm blossomed on the horizon like shades of pink announcing a new dawn. She saw something in Casey's expression. Lust, yes, but something more. Adoration and—no, she couldn't admit it, couldn't acknowledge what was so clearly written across Casey's features. She wouldn't, not when Casey had a transatlantic flight in her near future. Not when she'd be leaving her. Leighton closed her eyes against it.

Casey caressed her side. "I can feel it. Stop fighting it, and let go."

Leighton's core tightened around Casey's fingers.

Casey moaned and reclaimed Leighton's nipple with her mouth, and Leighton surrendered. She let her head fall back and gripped Casey's shoulders. Her body went rigid as the waves of pleasure crested, one after another. She continued to rock as her breaths escaped in small sobs.

Casey stilled but let Leighton take the time she needed.

At length, Leighton collapsed on top of her, her face buried in Casey's neck. She had a faint awareness of Casey's rapid breathing and the pounding of her pulse against her cheek.

Casey kissed her shoulder and smoothed a hand down her back. "You feel so good."

It was Casey who rocked her hips now, slow and lazy. She hadn't removed her fingers from between Leighton's legs, and the small movements made Leighton twitch. Casey brushed back damp strands of her hair.

Leighton hadn't opened her eyes. She focused on enjoying the moment, nothing more.

Casey licked her neck. "Can you do that again?"

"What?" Leighton lifted her head enough to look into the bottomless wells of Casey's eyes.

"One more time? For me?" Casey raised her eyebrows and curled her fingers again into that sensitive place that made Leighton's vision waver.

She gasped. Her answer would've been no a few seconds ago, based on how her first orgasm had wrecked her, but Casey's small movements had somehow flipped the switch on her libido. She moaned, the sound guttural and primal.

"So, that's a yes." Casey turned them and rolled Leighton onto her back, her fingers still inside her.

Leighton shifted, so the armrest supported her head. How could Casey make her want like this, to be had over and again? Utterly helpless to resist, Leighton took what was offered. She bent one leg and rested it against the back of the couch and planted the other foot on the floor, opening herself fully to anything Casey wanted. She briefly wondered if anyone was in the studio below, if she should check the cameras. The way Casey's fingers drove her toward the next orgasm, she doubted she could be quiet.

"Yes, spread your legs for me." She added another finger.

Leighton grabbed the edge of the sofa cushion and jerked her hips upward to take more. "Casey!"

"This." Casey trailed her mouth across Leighton's breasts and ribs. "This is what I've wanted for months." She moved lower, sucking and leaving light kisses along her stomach. Then lower still. She licked from her fingers upward, the stroke firm and deliberate.

Leighton lost all thought.

"Mmm. You taste so good. I'll be gentle."

Leighton wasn't sure gentle was what she wanted.

But Casey was tender in a way that brought tears to Leighton's eyes while still stoking the need that burned inside her. Casey's lips and tongue stirred and soothed in licks and swirls until Leighton begged. For mercy or for more? Casey gave her neither. The closer Leighton got, the softer and sweeter Casey pleasured her, holding her right on the edge.

"Oh, God. Casey, please." Leighton raised up and gathered Casey's hair so she could watch.

Casey gave her a satisfied smile even as her tongue flicked out and made her legs quiver uncontrollably.

"Please." She ran her fingers through Casey's hair. "I need you."

"I know you do, sweetheart."

Leighton fell back, though she continued to watch. She had to ignore the endearment, especially when uttered during sex. She couldn't contemplate what it might mean right now. Casey looked so lovely, so flushed and glowing like she was born to do this.

She drew Leighton into her mouth, sucking gently.

And Leighton came. What Casey gave, she took. She arched into the sofa and drove her heel into the floor as her orgasm shot through her, bright and blinding, then morphed into a rhythmic pulse.

Slowly, the world seemed to right itself, and Casey moved to lie beside her.

"No more, no more." She played with Casey's hair. "At least not if you have any expectations of me returning the favor."

Casey curled against her. "I'm in no hurry." She trailed her fingertips over the swell of Leighton's breast and entwined their legs. "This is nice."

It was indeed. So nice Leighton feared it was a dream from which she'd wake, and in some ways it was. What awakened instead was her need for Casey as she rested her hand where her gown had ridden up her thigh. Leighton plucked at the sexy black dress crumpled around her belly. "Get rid of this."

With a sultry smile, Casey stood and shimmied out of it in a series of movements that had Leighton entranced. Her underwear went with it.

In the dim fluorescent light spilling from the kitchen, Casey looked like one of Prud'hon's masterful sketches in chalk on blue paper. Leighton admired her pert breasts and small pink nipples, her contrapposto stance, and rounded hips. Hips into which Leighton wanted to press her fingers and lips.

She shot off the sofa. "The bedroom. Now." She grabbed Casey by the hand and pulled her into the hall.

As they passed the guest room, she saw Casey glance in. Casey was about to see Leighton had been sleeping with the pillow Casey used the night she and Andy had stayed over. It'd held her scent, though it'd faded, but Leighton still found it comforting.

Leighton didn't bother turning on the lamp. Enough moonlight fell across the bed to make it unnecessary.

Casey touched the pillow and gave Leighton a warm, understanding smile.

Leighton pulled her into her arms and curled her fingers around the back of her neck.

Casey rested her hands on Leighton's hips as though waiting for her to lead.

It occurred to Leighton she didn't know how to do this, how to separate her sexual desire for Casey from the feelings she'd developed. Did she need to? She'd already told Casey her heart would be shattered when she went to Florence. Did it matter if she couldn't conceal all the emotions threatening to overwhelm her?

Tenderly, she brushed Casey's hair from her face and caressed her cheek with her thumb. Then she kissed her, intending to take it slowly and let the passion between them build again, but her desire had ideas of its own, even after two orgasms. The simple, soft press of their breasts against each other's, of Casey's hands caressing her sides, and the sudden heat between them sent her prior intentions spiraling away.

Casey moaned into her mouth.

She'd been waiting long enough. Leighton slid her hands over Casey's back, feeling her muscles and ribs and the way her breaths came shallow and fast.

An urgency existed between them that Leighton had never experienced. With a soft push, she sent Casey backward onto the bed, then lowered herself onto the full length of her. There could be no doubt of her intention now, for either of them. Leighton claimed her with a slow, deep kiss and groaned when Casey wrapped her legs around her hips and pulled her hard against her center.

Leighton paused to catch her breath. She slid her mouth along Casey's supple neck where heat emanated from her skin and her pulse jumped under the surface. As she kissed her way down her torso, Leighton drank in the soft slope of her breasts with their hardened peaks. She licked up and over a nipple, then took it in her mouth. She swirled her tongue around it, unable to get enough, and squeezed the other in her hand. At the press of Casey's hands on her shoulders, she placed quick kisses down her stomach and along her hip.

Casey let her legs fall open.

Leighton had desired Casey for some time, but it didn't stop at the physical nature of their connection. It'd never been quite so simple for her. She found so many aspects of Casey appealing. Maybe her fate had been determined since that morning she'd stepped off the elevator and spotted Casey looking at her painting. Since then, her estimation and admiration of her had grown with each passing day. No, it certainly wasn't just sex. Her feelings for Casey, which had begun as a flicker, had become a full-blown conflagration.

"Do you know how hard it's been to be around you when I'm not able to touch you?" She trailed her fingers up Casey's thigh. "I've often wondered if you could feel me watching you."

The sound of Casey's panting filled the room.

"Your easel in front of my office has been a blessing and a curse. I've spent way too much time enjoying the gorgeous view and neglecting my work." She ran her hands up Casey's thighs until her thumbs brushed through her wet heat.

Casey arched her hips into the touch.

Leighton licked a slow path through her wetness. Casey's scent made her want in ways she didn't know she could. "Do you even know the things I've imagined doing to you?"

Casey whimpered.

Leighton licked her swollen folds and reveled in her divine taste. "Or the places I've imagined doing them?" She pushed her tongue inside her.

Casey gasped. She rested a steady hand on Leighton's head, but her legs trembled.

Leighton replaced her tongue with two fingers. The sweet sound that emanated from Casey made her do it again. Oh, how she wanted to discover just how many sounds she could draw from her. Desire clouded Leighton's thinking. One night would never be enough, yet it had to be. They couldn't continue to have sex until Casey left. Therefore, she'd drag as much pleasure out of this one evening as possible. There was no mistaking the pleasure Casey derived from Leighton's fingers sliding in and out of her slick warmth.

"Yes, again. Just like that." Casey rolled her hips to meet her thrusts. "Leighton." Desire laced her voice. "Leighton, please."

Leighton had an idea of what she wanted, but she had to hear her say it. "Yes?" And as much as she wanted to see her come undone, she wasn't quite ready for this moment to end.

Casey seemed to struggle with the question. She writhed on the bed and grasped at the covers. "Leighton." It came out hoarse.

Leighton kissed where her leg met her body. "Tell me what you want."

Casey blinked several times, then found Leighton, her eyes glassy and pleading.

She was gorgeous—muscles tense, nipples swollen, her neck and chest flushed with evident arousal. Leighton was certain she looked at Casey with too much wonder, too much adoration, too much lo—

No, she wasn't going there.

A sheen of perspiration covered Casey's skin. "Put your mouth on me again. Please."

She'd made her wait long enough. Leighton slipped her tongue through her folds and took her between her lips. She sucked and lapped with gentle strokes until Casey's fingers dug into her shoulder.

"Yes. Oh, God, yes."

Leighton crooked her fingers, and Casey's moans increased. Then she went silent, her entire body tensing. Leighton increased the pressure of her tongue as she stroked her.

"Oh, God, I'm…"

Leighton didn't need the announcement. She already knew, could feel. Casey grabbed Leighton's hand, and her body bowed. She went rigid for a few seconds, then crashed to the bed amidst a chorus of gasps and mumbled words, most of which Leighton couldn't make out.

Leighton nuzzled her skin and pressed random kisses to her thighs.

Casey sighed and stroked Leighton's hair. At length, she urged her upward. "Come here, you amazing woman."

Leighton rested her head on Casey's chest. Tired and sated, she simply enjoyed the softness of the woman beneath her. Something suffused her, like morning sunlight, its warmth flowing over all it touched. Was this happiness? How long had it been since she'd known the sensation? These days, she found herself dealing with all kinds of emotions she hadn't experienced in a while, if ever.

Leighton caressed the edge of Casey's nipple with her thumb. She listened to Casey's heart thumping beneath her ear. It seemed to be racing. Was a heart supposed to beat that fast?

Leighton had no idea. She'd never been well-versed in the workings of her own heart, let alone someone else's. And least of all this woman who could make her feel so many things she didn't understand.

CHAPTER THIRTY

Casey watched the sheer curtains in Leighton's bedroom breathe in and out in the semi-darkness. Leighton had let some of the cool night air in to combat the radiant heat they'd generated during their lovemaking. Considering her stance on open windows, Leighton was breaking all her rules tonight.

Right now, however, there were more pressing matters, like the warm body against her back and Leighton's hand that rested upon her hip. She covered it to keep it there and shifted onto her back. After her last orgasm, she'd said she couldn't take any more, but here she was, already aroused after a restorative nap, turning to Leighton once again.

Something caught her eye, and she blinked a few times. A painting hung across from Leighton's bed. Casey sat up. It was an unfinished vignette of a female nude. In the dim light, she discerned a long gash running from one corner to the other, although someone had repaired it from the back. She knew it was there because she'd slashed it.

Leighton had saved her painting.

Her heart swelled, and she turned to her. Leighton had thrown an arm above her head, her hair disheveled. Casey brushed her lips over her cheekbone, and Leighton pulled her closer, but didn't open her eyes.

Casey placed a kiss on her temple. "You little thief."

Leighton's only response was an amused, upturned corner of her mouth like she'd been expecting it. Casey traced the curve of Leighton's ear with her nose and kissed the corner of her jaw.

"It's not stealing if it's in the garbage." Leighton's voice was heavy with sleep.

Casey had always enjoyed listening to her, but this sultry version was even better, even more arousing. She lowered her mouth to Leighton's breast and kissed it.

Leighton pulled Casey atop her.

"Dumpster diver." Casey grinned against Leighton's cheek and strummed her nipple.

Leighton opened her eyes, and pushed Casey so she straddled her. Her gaze wandered over Casey's breasts. "What do they say? Reduce, reuse, recycle?" The corners of her mouth seemed to twitch with mischief as she rolled Casey's nipple into a hard point. "I care about the environment. What can I say?" She slipped a hand between them.

Casey gasped. Neither spoke for a few moments as Leighton caressed her.

"That's why..." With her pleasure threatening to consume her, Casey struggled to speak. "You saved it?"

"Is that a problem?" Leighton's voice sounded calm though her fingers weren't.

Casey dropped her chin to her chest and her hair fell forward. Her hands remained on Leighton's breasts, but they'd stilled. "No, I just thought..." She struggled to speak under the barrage of wonderful sensations.

"What did you think?" Leighton touched her chin to lift her head.

Leighton's piercing eyes made Casey suddenly feel exposed and more than a bit embarrassed. She looked away. "I just thought..." She rocked back and forth, her body thrumming with anticipation. "I thought, maybe...there was another reason." Her hips moved in erratic, desperate motions, her climax moments away.

"Casey, look at me."

She did. With her hair a mess and her eye makeup smudged, Leighton was still so beautiful. And she was touching her and gazing at her as if she was the only thing that existed in the universe.

Leighton's expression softened into the tenderest of smiles. "Of course, there was another reason."

Casey's orgasm swept through her.

Casey didn't need to turn on the kitchen lights to make coffee. The early morning glow of sunrise washed the room in warm yellows. She pressed the button on the Keurig to heat the water. Based on the empty spaces in the spinning holder beside it, she guessed at Leighton's favorite brew. She chose a Nantucket Blend for herself.

While she waited, she rubbed her bare legs together and danced in place to stay warm. She'd thrown on one of Leighton's Oxford shirts to make her foray into the kitchen.

Leighton had been asleep when she'd awakened. At some point, Leighton had wrapped an arm and leg around her. Something pleasant stirred in Casey at the possessiveness of the embrace. The thought of sleeping alone in Florence popped into her head, and she didn't look forward to it.

They'd been up most of the night, and Casey wasn't sure she'd even managed to doze for multiple hours. Soft kisses sprinkled between whispered conversations kept turning into something more. For hours, they explored unfamiliar terrain and found as much pleasure in the journey as the destination, or at least she had.

Casey pressed a button, and a hiss of steam and gurgle of hot liquid greeted her.

At first, she hadn't wanted to move from the bed. Leighton's warm embrace was too tempting to leave, and being so close, Casey could admire the tiny details of her delicate features. Feathery eyelashes, just a shade lighter than her hair, fluttered now and then. The elegant bones that defined her cheeks and jaw made Casey want to trace them with her finger. Three silver hairs near her temple sprouted like brave weeds in an otherwise immaculate garden. Casey didn't touch her. She held her breath and admired Leighton like she might the most captivating painting in a museum, with quiet reverence. No complaints would come from her if she woke like this every morning.

Life wouldn't be like that, though. Casey didn't know if this was a one-night or umpteen-night stand, but she'd be going to Florence soon, the birthplace of the Renaissance. Who would've imagined that Casey Norford, from a small town no one had heard of, would visit Italy?

She'd walk the ancient cobblestone streets that Leonardo da Vinci, Michelangelo, and Botticelli once walked. Or perhaps she'd rumble over them on a Vespa. Erica had gushed about Via de' Tornabuoni and the window shops of the upscale designer fashion and jewelry boutiques when she returned from her visit last summer. The more affordable stores on the Ponte Vecchio intrigued Casey, despite Erica's tales of it being a hot spot for tourists and pickpockets alike. Shops built on a bridge struck her as unusual, but she hoped to buy inexpensive souvenirs there for the special people in her life. Like Leighton. She swayed at the thought of leaving the person who meant the most to her outside of Andy.

The nutty scent of Leighton's coffee broke her reverie. Casey pressed the brew button on her Nantucket Blend and looked in the refrigerator for milk. Oat milk. So Leighton.

A chime from Leighton's phone where it charged on the kitchen island drew her attention. A notification filled the screen. *Activity Zone 7.*

Casey tensed.

While likely a student had arrived and triggered a motion sensor, the possibility of Leighton's ex-husband gaining entry to the building made her heart race. She loathed how he hovered on the periphery of Leighton's life. Leighton didn't seem to have heard it, so she grabbed the phone and dashed to the bedroom.

Casey rubbed her thigh through the sheet. "Leighton." She shook her a bit. "Leighton, wake up."

Leighton bolted upright. "What's wrong?"

"Probably nothing." Casey handed her the phone. "But you got a notification."

Leighton played a short video. It looked to be of the studio. "It's fine. Phoenix is down there." She flopped against the pillow and pulled Casey to her with a smile. "Good morning."

Casey's heart raced, no longer due to the notification but the naked woman beside her. "Morning." She brushed her lips over Leighton's.

Minutes later, the simple kiss had evolved into something more significant.

"Is this my shirt?" Leighton undid the button between her breasts and tried to pull Casey on top of her.

Casey grinned and pulled away. "I made coffee."

Mischief gleamed in Leighton's eyes. "There's more where that came from. Lose the shirt."

Playful, wise, generous, talented, and gorgeous Leighton. Casey could delay a cup of coffee, but her will wasn't as strong when it came to her.

An idea struck her, and she froze. Why hadn't it occurred to her before? It was the answer to everything, and it got no more romantic. It'd show Leighton the magnitude of her feelings.

Lines formed on Leighton's forehead. "What's going on in that mind of yours?"

Casey's chest heaved with excited breaths. "Come to Florence with me. Think about it. You, Kalyssa, me, and Andy. Wouldn't you like to get away since your ex can't seem to leave you alone? Best of all, you and I don't have to be apart for six months. It's the perfect solution. We'd be together." She brushed Leighton's messy hair from her eyes and gulped air. "Come with me." Her heart tried to break through her chest.

Leighton looked at her with wide eyes, then blinked five or six times. "Casey."

Casey squeezed her hand and grinned.

Leighton shook her head. "No."

❖

Feeling self-conscious now when she hadn't been minutes before, Leighton pulled the sheet over her breasts. How could this be happening after the night they'd shared?

Casey let go of her hand. "No?"

"I can't. Think about it. Surely, you understand." She saw the hurt in Casey's eyes.

"But the stalking seems to be getting worse. Don't you want to get away from here?" Casey tugged the shirt tails over her thighs.

"Does he worry me? Sure, but I'm not going to abandon my life." She surveyed the surrounding walls. "I've built this. It's my dream. I haven't shown what I can do yet, and you want me to walk away in the middle of it." Leighton wished she'd said yes to the coffee, so she'd have something to do with her hands.

Casey stared at her lap. "Not forever. Just six months. It's temporary."

Leighton shook her head and refrained from rolling her eyes. "It's an entire semester. Whom shall I hire to teach my classes?"

Casey buttoned the one Leighton had undone.

Leighton attempted to make eye contact. "How shall I pay my interim instructor? While we're on it, how shall I pay for the flights and six months of lodging?"

"You and Kalyssa could stay with Andy and—"

She scoffed. "Have you seen the size of the rooms in Florence? How do you know they're planning on providing for Andy? Did they even know you had a son before last night? And while we're traipsing through the Uffizi or fucking one another, who will watch the children?" Leighton motioned for Casey to move so she could stand. "I'm sorry this isn't the response you expected to what you surely thought was a grand, romantic gesture."

Wrapped in the sheet, Leighton entered her walk-in closet, then pulled on leggings and a T-shirt. No sound came from the bedroom. She peered around the doorway. Casey still stood in the same spot, holding the tails of the shirt in her hands. "Well, it isn't romantic. It's not fair for you to ask something this monumental of me when you consider the short time we've…" She gestured between them. It wasn't a relationship. They'd had sex. Monday morning would once again see them as teacher and student. *Christ.*

Casey's chin quivered.

At the sight, Leighton's resolve wavered slightly, but she had a dream, too. She handed her a pair of sweats and a sweatshirt. "Take these and get dressed. You should go."

CHAPTER THIRTY-ONE

When Leighton began her Monday morning lecture, Casey wasn't in attendance.

It was bad enough Casey missed her class, but she was absent when Maxine came to congratulate her on her win. Maxine seemed surprised she wasn't there, and Leighton's attempt to make excuses for her only made the situation worse.

After teaching her lesson, and with as much calm as she could muster, she pulled Mark aside. "Do you know where Casey is?"

"She and Andy left before me." He frowned. "I assumed she'd be in class. Do you want me to call her?"

"No, go ahead and work on your assignment. Thanks." Leighton wandered through the studio. Perhaps Casey felt ill and returned home. However, Mark's explanation made her question that scenario. He would've mentioned if Casey had been unwell that morning.

Casey's exuberant invitation echoed in her head. Had she been too harsh with her rejection of the silly idea? She had to admit, under different circumstances, it might have been a *little* romantic. Leighton ran her hand along the top of Casey's taboret.

With a heavy heart, Leighton debated what to do. Casey had yet to be absent or arrive late, and yet this was the day it happened. It couldn't be a coincidence it followed their conversation. Of course, Casey would've taken it hard. She should have realized that.

Even though her annoyance with Casey's unexplained absence reigned supreme among her emotions, she couldn't ignore the nagging feeling that something might be wrong. Her stomach heaved acid at the thought, and she poured her coffee down the sink.

Just before noon, Mark entered her office. "Hey, I texted Case to ask where she was." He extended his phone for her to read.

Casey's response to his question asking about her well-being was a short, cryptic text saying she'd be present for Stefan's class.

Leighton's insides curled into a ball. "Thanks, Mark."

It was bad enough what transpired afterward now colored their first intimate encounter. Plus, they still had weeks to go as teacher and student without their evening together coming to light. She didn't know what Mark knew. He'd accompanied Casey to the event, and not only had she left early, but she hadn't gone home at all. Did he know where Casey had been, and if he did, had he lost all respect for Leighton?

What they'd done stood to be one of the worst decisions Leighton had made. She'd gotten caught up in her happiness for Casey and had allowed herself to indulge in the moment. Why hadn't she waited? They wouldn't be dealing with this drama now. She doubted Casey would've invited her to Florence if they hadn't slept together.

They needed to figure out the situation. Then Casey would go to Florence for six months, which sounded like an eternity. No dimpled smiles, no bubbling laughter, no more lively discussions about art or techniques, no pizza and play dates, no more thrilling touches or comforting hugs, and no more orgasms so fantastic they made her daydream. Perhaps worst of all, no more instances of Casey making Kalyssa's day by giving Leighton's daughter her undivided attention.

Gone. The air left Leighton's lungs at the thought.

Skipping school gave Casey a rare free morning, so she ran a few errands and spent time with Andy before dropping him at Aileen's. Then she treated herself to a coffee and walked through Central Park to sort the jumbled thoughts in her head. She hated to miss Leighton's class, but interacting as student and teacher didn't seem wise right now, and the way Leighton had asked her to leave still stung.

As she walked, Casey considered her options. Her feelings for Leighton were more than a passing attraction. Her interest in her went deeper than pure desire. Casey liked her as a person, enjoyed being with her, respected her, and her protectiveness when it came to Leighton equaled that for Andy. Casey wanted more, and if given the opportunity, she'd spend years learning what made Leighton happy.

However, her fantasy wasn't meant to be. Casey couldn't have what she desired, and she didn't know how things had gone so wrong. Perhaps she'd asked for too much too soon, though complications had plagued their quasi-relationship prior to that. Her parents might be right, for it seemed she made poor decisions at every turn.

Asking Leighton to join her in Florence might not have been the best idea, but she'd been so caught up in her celebratory mood. In the past, she'd always been bold, but in hindsight, many of her decisions could've used more forethought. Despite her best intentions, her courage and strong will often revealed her naivete, like now. The euphoria that had resulted from winning caused her to go too far. The more she considered it, avoiding Leighton's class for the remaining weeks would be for the best. After Leighton's reaction, Casey was sure she regretted sleeping with her.

When she arrived in the studio, she breathed a sigh of relief that Leighton wasn't present. It made things easier. She might not have attended the earlier lecture, but she wanted the notes, and Jenna owed her. Since they had a few minutes before Stefan began teaching, Casey stopped by her station.

"Jen, can I get a copy of your notes from this morning? Whatever you have is fine. I just need an idea of what she taught today." Casey ran a hand through her hair.

Jenna flashed her a bright smile. "Yeah, we missed you. I don't worry as much about my note-taking since Leighton started giving me copies of her lesson plans ahead of time. I find I'm understanding everything so much better and think I can hold my own and keep up with the rest of the class now." She flipped through some papers. "Here's the one for today, and I'll email you my notes."

Casey's jaw went slack. "Leighton's been giving you her lesson plans?"

Jenna nodded. "She offered. I don't know if that's technically what they are, but they outline what she'll be going over each day. She's very thorough, and they've helped a lot."

Was Leighton's preparation to this extent usual? Casey had never witnessed her reference any papers while lecturing. Had she created them specifically for Jenna? Either way, finding a way to make the information accessible to Jenna's learning style had been thoughtful. She recalled how upset Leighton had been when she hadn't been aware Jenna was struggling.

Stefan announced he was starting class, so Casey thanked her and returned to her station.

While she could've let Leighton consume her thoughts, the information she learned today on painting reflected surfaces would be needed to complete her trompe l'oeil. The small, realistic paintings were so lifelike people said they tricked the eye, therefore, it was imperative she learned these techniques.

Casey listened to Stefan talk about the differences between specular and diffuse reflections. While perhaps not as gifted as Leighton, his skills couldn't be discounted. However, while he possessed more than a proficient ability to command the technical aspects, Leighton seemed to imbue her paintings with something otherworldly, something larger than life. Perhaps that's why he'd succeeded in academia, and Leighton had found success as an artist.

"Okay, folks." Stefan erased the whiteboard. "Choose a setup from the still-life objects on the shelves or bring things to use from home."

Casey decided to participate even though the assignment wasn't due for two months, and she wouldn't be here next semester.

At least leaving was the plan. She hadn't emailed her Florence acceptance form yet.

After pouring a cup of coffee, she wandered over to the north side of the room. Students had left most of the protective glass fronts open, and the dark walnut shelves held an unusual array of trinkets resembling collections she'd seen in dusty antique stores in the East Village with Mark on Sunday afternoons. The cabinets overflowed with shells, leather-bound books, feathers, and glass blob top bottles ranging in color from aquamarine to amethyst.

An entire shelf dedicated to metallic objects like silver pitchers and teapots, small oil cans, and mismatched candlesticks reflected light off their shiny surfaces. Another held only white items: vases, milk glass, figurines, eggshells, cue balls, bones, teacups, and candles. Individual Mason jars contained collections of marbles, skeleton keys, buttons, small spoons, and pocket watches. Artists seemed to have an affinity for certain objects. She'd witnessed it many times while scrolling through the Instagram accounts of painters she followed.

Casey touched the smooth surfaces of a copper-and-cream nautilus shell, an Erlenmeyer flask, and an ammonite. She considered an antique globe, a mandolin, and an illustrated deck of playing cards before she selected a vintage folding camera, an hourglass, and a small brass biplane.

The composition of her trompe l'oeil would be completed by a black-and-white photograph of her grandmother as a young woman. The scalloped edges of the snapshot contrasted with the sleek Katharine Hepburn-style slacks her grandmother wore as she stood alongside her Schwinn bicycle. Casey grinned at the prospect of using paint to re-create a photograph.

Lost in thought, she'd neglected to notice Stefan stop beside her. He munched on a red licorice rope. How long had he been there?

"Everything okay?" He pulled off a bite with a snap that made her teeth hurt. "I heard you weren't in class this morning." Three more protruded from his other hand.

"No, but I'm fine." She gave him a pointed look. "I'm here now, aren't I?"

Her tone must have been enough to convince him to quit questioning her. "I just thought I'd ask." He took a step back. "If there's anything I can—"

"There's not, but thanks." Casey gathered her items and took them to her station. Stefan didn't need to get involved in their sticky situation, friends with Leighton or not. The mess they'd created was theirs, and one of them needed to figure out what to do. Her stomach churned from stress and too much caffeine, and her mind whirled as she contemplated possible solutions.

CHAPTER THIRTY-TWO

Casey pushed the loaded utility cart with her clipboard, barcode scanner, and boxes of new inventory down the aisle that housed drawing materials. Before he left, her manager had instructed her to stock the shelves when she didn't have customers, as nights tended to be slow. She began by replenishing the Carbothello colored pencils, checking each one for a sharpened point before she slid it into its labeled slot.

She'd worked at this family-owned art supply store for a few years, making her way up to assistant manager. If she had more time and flexibility, she'd have a managerial role and salary by now. However, she enjoyed quiet nights like this after a day of classes, not that she'd been there a full day or attended Leighton's class. Still, she'd been busy. At least skipping class had allowed her to sort out her thoughts.

As she recalled her walk through the park, she opened a cardboard box. It contained sets of Unison pastels, and she admired the hand-rolled, oblong sticks. They lacked uniformity, and their unique shapes appealed to her. She considered buying them. After all, she'd sold a painting and won an award. Plus, she'd never tried pastels with any true intention. Instead, she shelved the set and told herself she'd consider it.

A bell on the door signaled a customer had entered the store. Casey stepped out of the aisle to offer a greeting, but it caught in the back of her throat. Leighton glanced around until she spotted her. She crossed the distance between them in a few purposeful strides. When Leighton followed her into the aisle, Casey turned to her cart of inventory and resumed working.

"People are questioning why you weren't in class today."

Leighton hadn't bothered with a greeting. Not a good sign.

"People? Or you? I'd think you would've had a pretty good idea why." She scanned pan pastels and placed them on the shelf. While she'd been expecting they'd need to talk at some point, she hadn't expected Leighton to show up at her work, and it unsettled her.

Leighton flipped her hair over her shoulder with a vigorous shake of her head. "You can't skip class."

"I missed one. I attended the afternoon session." For once, the store's lack of customers pleased her. At least no one would overhear their terse conversation.

"You missed *my* class."

The hurt in Leighton's expression and the disappointment in her tone surprised Casey. She'd expected anger.

"Why?" Leighton's voice had grown quiet. "Why weren't you there this morning?"

"The way you reacted," Casey shuffled her feet, her sneakers squeaking on the linoleum floor, "made me believe it wouldn't be long before you regretted what we'd done. Especially after the parameters you established early in the year." She gave a half-hearted shrug. "I simplified things. If I'm not your student, then there's no issue for you." She resumed stocking.

"You think you're doing this for me?" Leighton sighed. "This is your grand plan? Aren't you splitting hairs with your definition of a student? You're still a student in my atelier."

"Yes, but you're not my teacher." Casey sliced open another box, the tearing sound as unpleasant as Leighton's disappointment had been.

Leighton rubbed her temple. "Don't you think we should've discussed this and found a solution together?"

It hadn't occurred to her before, but when Leighton phrased it like that, Casey should've talked with her first. However, the last time she'd seen her, Leighton had handed her clothing and asked her to leave.

Silence descended over them, broken only by the occasional beep of Casey's scanner as she emptied the boxes on her cart.

Leighton picked up a set of Sennelier soft pastels. "These are really nice." She turned it over, then replaced it.

Casey remained quiet but glanced at the clock. How long would she have before a customer walked in? She hadn't said what she needed to say, and she trembled thinking about it. The last thing she needed was an interruption.

Leighton touched Casey's arm. "No, I don't regret it, at least not how you probably think."

Her soft, affectionate tone almost allayed Casey's nervousness.

Leighton withdrew her hand. "Come back to class, and we'll somehow make it work. It's only for a few weeks."

Something had bloomed within her when Leighton said she didn't regret their night together, but her hand shook, making the scanner's laser wobble where it hit the box. What seemed like good news earlier now made her question it, but it meant they'd be together. At least she hoped.

"About that." Casey rested her hand on her cart to stop it from shaking. An awareness hit her that she didn't know Leighton well enough to predict how she'd react. "I emailed the chair of the exhibition, and I declined the opportunity to go to Florence. I'm staying."

❖

"You're what?" The flatness of Leighton's response echoed off the art store's hard floors and walls, making her voice sound foreign even to her ears, which was fine, because Casey sounded strange, too. Surely, she'd imagined Casey say she turned down Florence. Leighton's chest tightened, and she searched for somewhere to sit before she ended up on the grimy floor. There was nothing nearby, so she held onto the shelf for support.

Casey tugged the strings of her apron tighter. Leighton imagined she'd need scissors to get the knot free at the end of her shift.

"I decided not to go."

"Decided not to go?" Leighton pressed her palm to her forehead. She needed to stop echoing everything Casey said, but it was so unbelievable, she couldn't help it. "What in the hell were you thinking?"

Casey blanched. "And what do you suppose I was doing all morning?" She appeared offended as she pushed the cart down the aisle and through the swinging door of the storeroom.

Leighton hesitated, then followed her.

In the back, Casey stood with her hands on her hips, facing away. "I know it's you because I'd know the sound of your walk anywhere. We don't allow customers back here."

Leighton wasn't a customer, and she had no intention of leaving. She turned Casey with a gentle touch to her shoulder. "Now you're worried about breaking rules? You need to contact them again, and tell them you've made a mistake."

Casey's arms fell. "I can't. We emailed back and forth today. The chair wanted to make sure of my decision. They've already awarded it to the person who'd earned the second most points, the first-place winner."

"Oh, no." Leighton covered her mouth with her hand. This time, she found a place to sit on a stack of pallets. "Oh, God."

Casey sat beside her. "I'm sorry you're disappointed, but it's my choice."

Leighton looked at her. "Disappointed for you, yes, but you didn't consider the impact. You made an entire production of wanting to celebrate with me. Don't you realize what people would give for the opportunity? It's a dream come true, yet you've thrown it away."

Casey shot to her feet. "I didn't throw anything away. If you'll recall, attending Atelier Vaughn was my dream, so by going, I'd be throwing *that* away. You brought the exhibition to my attention and encouraged me to enter, while I would've been happy finishing out the school year."

Leighton pressed her palms to her thighs. She needed to remain calm. "Why did you turn it down?"

Casey sat. "When you told me your reasons for not wanting to go, it got me thinking."

Leighton angled her body toward her. They sat so close, she saw the carotid artery pulsing in Casey's neck. She'd had her lips there not so very long ago. Her stomach swooped at the thought she never would again.

"You were right. They weren't aware I had a child because I never mentioned Andy on my entry application. The small room provided wouldn't fit us both, so the additional expense of a suitable arrangement would have been mine." Casey cleared her throat. "I hadn't considered childcare, not only finding someone I trusted who spoke English but also how to pay for it." She picked at her thumbnail. "And when I told Aileen I'd won, the look on her face almost killed me. It hadn't occurred to me I'd be taking her only grandchild away for six months with little warning. She couldn't hide her tears even while insisting I go. I can't do that to her. Frankly, I can't do that to Mark or Andy either. Mark might not want to be a father, but he loves Andy, and Andy loves him. How could I tear the most important people in Andy's life away from him for that amount of time?" She sniffed. "When I looked at it that way, seeing *David* or the Duomo didn't seem that important. Besides, studying abroad won't guarantee I'll become successful. Success has many forms, and if I'm not respecting the people I love, what does it matter anyway?"

They sat without talking, with Casey's ragged breathing the only sound in the room.

Leighton's head spun as she tried to make sense of it all. "I can't believe you're not going." The hollowness of her tone matched the ache in her heart.

Casey made a wounded sound. "Are you that eager to get rid of me?"

Leighton couldn't look at her. "Do you realize what this means? I slept with you because you'd be leaving, because you'd no longer be my student." Leighton pressed her fingers into her forehead as she reconsidered what she'd said. "I mean, I slept with you because I wanted to. I'd wanted to for weeks—no, months—but I allowed myself that pleasure because you'd be leaving. And while I'd miss you something terrible and you might never have been part of my life again, it was an amazing opportunity for you, and I wanted you to have that. The selfish part of me wanted to spend a night with you before I lost you."

Casey took Leighton's hand. "It's okay. It'll be okay. We'll make it work." She sounded like she was convincing herself. "We don't have to tell anyone."

Leighton withdrew her hand. "How do you envision us in that scenario? Sneaking around for another year and a half without getting caught? Mark's a smart guy. I'm sure he already knows. Or did you think we'd be able to keep our hands off one another after having sex and pretend it never happened?" Leighton laughed, but it sounded scornful. "No, Casey, we made a mistake. *I* made a mistake. What I did wasn't right." She stood and paced. Her stomach felt like someone had wrung it like a wet rag.

"What's going to happen?" Casey's voice cracked. "Why is everything going so wrong?"

"Because what I did was wrong." The despondency in her voice surprised Leighton. "I need to tell Maxine and face the consequences. I slept with a student, and I can't hide it."

"That's only going to make things worse." Casey's eyes brimmed with tears.

"We've always been close, but she's been like a second mother to me since my mom died. It feels wrong to keep secrets from her." It was Leighton's turn to sniff. She wished she had a tissue.

A bell dinged, like the one on the door Leighton had entered.

"Jesus Christ. Please, don't leave yet." Casey pushed through the swinging door.

❖

Grateful the green-haired guy knew what brand and colors of spray paint he needed, all Casey had to do was unlock the case, make sure he was eighteen, and ring him up. She returned to the storeroom in less than five minutes. Leighton hadn't moved.

Casey wrung her hands. "Sorry."

"Don't be sorry for doing your job. I shouldn't have bothered you at work, but I didn't know when I'd have the chance to talk to you in person privately if I didn't."

"I understand why you want to tell Maxine." Casey fidgeted from foot to foot. "However, if you tell her, it's going to ruin any chance of us dating or being together." As she said it, she realized she might be off base by assuming what Leighton even wanted.

"Casey."

She hated when Leighton said her name like that, all breathy and pitiful, like she were a child who refused to believe Santa wasn't real. Maybe she felt more for Leighton than Leighton for her. The thought clamped her chest, and she struggled to breathe through the tightness.

"We cannot be together." Leighton pulled her to sit beside her. "Not while you're my student."

Casey could hear her life crashing down around her. There had to be some other way. She bit the inside of her lip and vowed not to cry, even while tears filled her eyes. Strength was her forte, and she'd figure this out. While Leighton sat quietly, likely letting her regain her composure, she tried to brainstorm another option.

"I'm going to quit school." She bobbed her head. It hurt her heart to think about it, but what choice did she have? "It's the only way."

Leighton scoffed. "Stop it."

"No, listen. I've learned a lot, and I can still borrow notes from Mark or Jenna. We need a solution where I'm not your student. This is it."

"I refuse to let you quit." Leighton faced her, arms crossed.

Casey frowned. "Well, if I never go to class, what can you do?"

Leighton's jaw twitched. "Don't be juvenile. You've already given up one incredible opportunity. I won't allow you to give up another. You just said Atelier Vaughn was your dream, and I won't stand in the way of that."

Casey also stood. "I have to. It's our only option."

Leighton stared at her. "No, Casey, it's not. You'll skip no more classes or, God forbid, quit school." She scoffed. "Well, you're free to do what you want, but I won't be in a relationship with you if that's the choice you make. I can't be with someone who throws away talent and opportunity."

Casey tried to swallow. Her life was falling apart, and the harder she tried to gather the pieces, they scattered even more. "What will happen?"

Leighton held up her hands. "I won't know until I have that discussion with Maxine. I imagine I might need to step down as an instructor."

"That's not fair." Casey would shake her head, but she was afraid it might dislodge her unshed tears. "Teaching at your atelier was *your* dream. I don't want to destroy yours any more than you want to stand in the way of mine." She hugged herself to keep the sickening feeling down. "If I'd chosen to go to Florence, we wouldn't be together. Now, because I've chosen to stay, we still can't be. When did it get to be a lose-lose situation?" The stark realization a relationship with Leighton wouldn't happen and she had no available moves left struck her like a rogue wave.

Leighton stepped close and rubbed Casey's upper arms. "We were never in a winning situation, I'm afraid. Sometimes life is unfair."

Casey hated that saying. It was only that way when people were too disinterested or cowardly to find creative ways to make it so.

"Then we agree that attending Atelier Vaughn is your dream, and you will skip no more classes. I expect you to be there tomorrow, even if I might not be your instructor." Leighton straightened.

Casey looked away, hating it had come to this.

Leighton brought her face around with a finger to her chin. "Yes?"

Casey nodded, not trusting herself to speak.

"It's all about brush miles. You need to be in the studio learning, painting, and developing as an artist. I can't stand to see you waste your potential or your scholarship. Deep down, I know you realize what I'm saying is true. If it was just you, you could act with reckless abandon and quit, but you have Andy to think about. And I meant what I said. Nothing will ever happen between us if you throw away the opportunity in front of you. I have no interest being with anyone self-destructive, and that's how I'd view it."

With Leighton's ultimatum, there'd be no point skipping class, and when she returned, things would never be the same. Even Leighton hypothetically referencing being with her couldn't raise her spirits.

Leighton caressed her cheek. "It'll be okay, Casey."

Her voice was so gentle, but instead of being reassuring, for the first time, Casey didn't believe her.

Leighton embraced her, and Casey soaked in the warmth and scent of her. Like this, in Leighton's arms, everything felt right. Why couldn't they stay like this forever?

When Leighton pulled away, Casey wiped her eyes on her apron. The sharp rap of Leighton's shoes as they met the concrete floor echoed off the cinder block walls. A few seconds later, the bell on the door signaled her exit from the store. Casey's heart felt as empty as the sparse storeroom where Leighton had left her.

CHAPTER THIRTY-THREE

As she entered the handsome lobby, Leighton realized she hadn't seen the inside of Maxine's Upper West Side home much in the past few months other than to pick up Kalyssa, or so they could ride together to brunch. She'd been too busy, first with the start of the new year, and then with Casey. The two had consumed most of her attention. More of an effort should have been made on her part. Ignoring loved ones because she'd gotten wrapped up with work or because she'd developed feelings for someone had never been her style. She needed to do better. In more ways than that.

Today Maxine had summoned Leighton. A sense of foreboding overcame her, and her smile was forced as one of the building's white-gloved doormen led her to the elevator. Once upstairs, Alicia, Maxine's longtime housekeeper, greeted her. Maxine stood a short distance behind in the foyer.

"Hello, Leighton. Come in. Let's talk in the library since the solarium is too cold this time of year. Shall Alicia bring you tea or coffee?"

"Just water, please. Thank you, Alicia."

"Nothing for me." Maxine entered the library.

Alicia took her coat, and Leighton followed Maxine into the wood-paneled room. While Maxine was a willing participant in a high-society life dictated by the myriad rules of etiquette, this level of formality didn't normally exist between them. Leighton's mother had been born into money—though nothing close to Maxine and George's level—and Leighton's family had lived that rigid life throughout her youth. When she was old enough to make her own decisions, she dispensed with most of the stress and nonsense that came with that kind of convention. She saw little reason to care about others' expectations or opinions aside from her family.

Until now.

Leighton sat in one of the high-backed chairs. In the past, the library's warmth had always welcomed her. The rich walls and stone fireplace created a relaxed ambiance. Not today. Despite low flames licking at a fake log, a chill hung in the air.

Maxine faced the window. She wore her usual ensemble of skirt, blouse, and jacket. Leighton tried to recall if she'd ever seen her wear anything else. While usually not interested in pandering to the ways of the elite, Leighton had dressed in tailored slacks, heels, and a nice shirt. She'd need all the points she could get with Maxine today.

Apparently, they were waiting for the water before beginning.

A few minutes later, Alicia brought it, served in a cut crystal tumbler with an accompanying pitcher and ceramic coaster, all on a tray.

Why couldn't anything be simple?

Maxine turned. "That'll be all, Alicia. We're not to be disturbed."

"Yes, ma'am." Alicia closed the library door.

Maxine crossed her arms. "Your call surprised me."

Leighton wished Maxine would step away from the window so she could read her expression. The glare from outside silhouetted her, but perhaps that had been her intent.

"Yes, I'm sorry." Sweat formed along her spine.

"It's a little late for that. I never imagined you'd do something like this, but at least you informed me right away. If this had become public knowledge, and you'd kept me in the dark, I'm not sure what my reaction would've been."

Leighton fingered the crystal design. "I know it was wrong, and I'm not sure there's any explanation I can offer you that will make you understand because I'm not sure *I* do." She looked at Maxine. "I may have made a terrible decision, but I won't compound it by hiding it."

Maxine raked her fingernails through the hair at her temple. "I suppose it's reassuring to know you have integrity, even if your ethics are suspect."

The disappointment in her voice cut Leighton to her core. She cared about few people's image of her, but Maxine was one, as close as a blood relative. She'd let her down and didn't know if she'd ever be able to make amends.

"I stayed up much of the night devising a way to keep the atelier in business while keeping its reputation intact. This is what's going to happen."

Maxine curled her red manicured nails over the back of a replica Henry II chair, or at least Leighton believed it to be. The more she considered it, the piece might be authentic.

"As your largest investor, I'll take over the daily operations of the atelier. You'll give up teaching for the rest of this semester, if not longer. I spoke with Stefan this morning. Despite obviously interrupting him with someone, he's willing to teach the rest of your classes this term, and you'll supply him with your lesson plans. We came up with a fair financial arrangement."

"Stefan knows?" Leighton's stomach churned.

"Not specifics, only that you won't be teaching for a while. I assured him you weren't ill or dying." Maxine lowered her head and looked at her over her glasses. "You can fill in the salacious details."

"It's not like that." Leighton glanced at her hand. Great. A tremor.

Maxine's stare pierced through her. "Well, it looks like a teacher seduced a student. Are you trying to convince me of something else?"

Leighton's eyes stung. She didn't know how to explain what she felt for Casey, or how everything had happened, and make Maxine understand. "I felt something for her from the start. I knew it was wrong, and I tried to ignore it, but it grew. Casey volunteered to watch Kalyssa the night of the panel when I couldn't find a sitter. You would've been upset if I backed out."

"Let's not blame this on me." Maxine's tone was colder than the room.

"No, I didn't intend to. This was my doing. When I arrived to pick up Kalyssa from Casey's, she was having the best time." Leighton smiled fondly, remembering. "She and Andy had been playing. Casey had ordered pizza, and I was starving. I stayed and watched them as I ate. Kalyssa adores both of them. I ended up reading the kids a bedtime story." She took a breath before looking at Maxine. "It was everything I've ever wanted in an evening."

Maxine frowned. "You slept with her because you enjoyed a night of playing house together?"

It was more than that. Leighton tried to swallow but couldn't, so she sipped her water. "No, and it didn't happen until the night of the exhibition. We only slept together once." Well, one night. She wouldn't regale Maxine with how many times she'd come and in how many places. This was no time for semantics. Memories of Casey taking her over the back of the sofa and on the kitchen counter invaded her thoughts.

"Why her?" Maxine leaned on the windowsill.

Leighton blinked away the sensual images. "What do you mean?"

"You've shown that Casey gets along well with Kalyssa, and you seem to get along fine with Andy, but that tells me nothing about why you're attracted to her."

Leighton didn't know where to begin. "She's amazing. I've never met anyone so determined. Her worthless family's actions should've handicapped her, but they didn't. I'd say she's destined to survive, but it's more like she's destined to thrive. When she sets her mind on something, there's no stopping her." Leighton could feel Maxine scrutinizing her as she took another sip. "When I look at everything given to me in my life, be it my family or opportunities, and then I look at Casey, it makes me feel I should've accomplished more with what I've been fortunate to have. It's more than that, though. She's a wonderful mom and so good with kids. I do my best with Kalyssa, but Casey makes me want to be a better parent." This time, she made eye contact with Maxine.

"Was she reason enough to throw everything away?" Maxine tapped her nails on the windowsill.

Leighton stared at a nearby bookshelf, not really seeing it. "I didn't consider it like that. After she won, I operated under the assumption she'd no longer be my student because she'd be going to Florence. I got caught up in the moment. Yes, I should've waited until it was official, but..." She looked at Maxine. "I never felt like this with Jeffrey." She held up her hand. "I loved him once, yes. I'm not denying that. But with Casey, it's different, and not because she's a woman. For instance, she already understands me better than Jeffrey ever did. And when I think about how much I care about her, and what she does for me...I can't explain it."

"Humor me and try." Maxine unbuttoned her jacket.

"Whenever we're apart, she's all I think about. When she's around, I forget my fears and worries. Do you know how wonderful and freeing that is? We're a good match, both in terms of our personalities and our art. She pushes me out of my comfort zone, challenges me, and I need that." Leighton crossed her legs, able to relax a fraction just by thinking of her. "Yes, I find her attractive, and her artistic ability is unmatched, as proven by her win at the exhibition. Max, I'm not sure how much more I can teach her. She's so talented, I should offer her a job. Casey already helped Jenna succeed where I failed. It's all these things combined that don't make her seem like an ordinary student."

"First, don't call me Max. I'm not your godmother for the foreseeable future. I'm the atelier's majority financer, and she's your student, regardless of whether it feels that way. So, we need to address that. You and I need to address many things." Maxine crossed the room and retrieved a paper from the desk. "We don't need #MeToo being whispered whenever New Yorkers mention Atelier Vaughn in conversation, so here's what I'm going to do." Maxine laid her hand on the circular rent table. "I scheduled a meeting with the other two investors, and I plan to tell them everything. Whether or not they'll continue to be involved is unknown. I also plan to meet with Casey to get her side of the story." She held up her hand when Leighton tried to speak. "I'll allow no argument here. It's important to establish you didn't coerce her into anything, so I'll meet with her alone."

"I'd never do that." Leighton hadn't sounded so meek in thirty years.

"I believe you." Maxine didn't continue until Leighton raised her head. "It appears you made a very poor decision. I've seen nothing in you to suggest you'd do something so horrific, and I've known you since you were an hour old. This needs to be done to protect you and the atelier. I've hired a stenographer to transcribe the interview, and I'll record the audio with Casey's permission."

"Oh, God." Leighton rubbed her temple.

"In addition, we can't have her viewed as an underprivileged student who needs to preserve her scholarship by keeping her instructor happy in bed. That creates a terrible scenario, so she'll no longer be a recipient of my endowment's funds."

Leighton looked up so fast she hurt her neck. "You can't. Casey needs it, and she's the most deserving person I can think of to attend a place like Atelier Vaughn. She can't afford it otherwise. This will crush her."

"I can, and I will, because you'll be funding her education. Balance due zero, paid in full for the rest of her time here, however long that may be." Maxine left no room for argument.

Leighton nodded. She'd have to find the money, perhaps borrow from Kalyssa's college fund or drum up some commissions. Another reclining nude might be in her future. The painting she'd done over the summer had earned her five figures. It didn't matter how she'd find the additional funds. Casey could remain in school, even if it took

Leighton years to pay off a loan. She'd always known actions had consequences, but facing them was another matter. At least she had a strong stomach.

Maxine laid a piece of paper in front of her. "This is a list of potential investors, or perhaps even benefactors. Some are elderly museum supporters who could use additional ideas of what to do with their vast fortunes upon their deaths. After all, one can only have so many museum wings named after them. Some are new gallery owners looking to make a name for themselves in Manhattan. At the bottom of the list are the names of a few old acquaintances of your mother's and mine. That said, I owe you no favors, so you'll attempt to drum up new funds. Assume your two current investors will bolt after our meetings."

Leighton had never interacted much with them. Maxine handled their investments. Leighton's duties involved signing their thank you cards, sending them complementary prints of her work, and schmoozing and boozing them during the annual holiday party. She breathed a sigh of relief she didn't have to face them.

"Who else knows what happened?" Maxine put a hand on her hip.

Leighton sighed. "I don't know for certain, but Mark is Casey's roommate, and she didn't go home the night of the exhibition, so he might have put two-and-two together."

"Hmm." Maxine tapped her lower lip. "That means I'll need to meet with all the students. You won't enjoy hearing this, but I'll be offering them the choice to leave Atelier Vaughn with the option of a full refund for this year. If they choose to stay, I'll ask them to sign something saying they've never had any issues."

Leighton braced her elbows on the table and held her head in her hands until the room stopped spinning.

"If they feel you've slighted them, we can't have that. Your poor choice may cause a financial setback, and who knows what it will do to your reputation, but that's the price you pay." Maxine folded her arms.

"How long before I can teach again?" Her dream seemed to be slipping out of reach.

"Not this semester, but I'll consider the spring after I inform our investors. We may need to hire an interim instructor." Maxine cleared her throat. "For now, you'll avoid the second floor. If you need something from your office or the studio, Jenna can retrieve it for you. You'll leave the decision-making to me for the rest of the year. I'll run the day-to-day operations with Jenna's help. You may enter the building because it's your home or to assist me in the gallery by hanging the paintings and decorating for the holiday party, but that's it."

Leighton could only nod. Other than Kalyssa, she'd lose almost everything that mattered to her. What would she do with her time? If she'd known the repercussions beforehand, would she have slept with Casey? A chill coursed through her at the shock of not knowing the answer.

Maxine turned to look out the window, and silence fell.

Losses seemed to be piling up in Leighton's life.

That made her recall something else. Since she'd lost so much already, she might as well ask what had bothered her for years. What could it hurt after this? They might even find some common ground in this time of turmoil.

"Maxine?" For a moment, Leighton wasn't sure she'd heard her.

"Hmm?" She didn't turn.

Leighton fingered the button on the cuff of her shirt. "Did you love my mother?"

Maxine's entire body twitched, then her straight, elegant posture returned. "Of course. She was my best friend."

The heavy door preventing George or Alicia from overhearing prompted Leighton to continue. "That's not what I meant." She took a deep breath. "Were you in love with her?"

The only sound came from the ticking grandfather clock in the corner and the crackling fire.

After a few seconds, Maxine turned. "Why are you asking me this?"

"I found a stack of letters when Dad died." Leighton tucked her hair behind her ear.

Maxine sank into a chair beside her. "What kind of letters?"

Her expression led Leighton to believe she already knew which ones.

"Most of them were from the time you and Mom attended Bryn Mawr. I think you wrote to one another over the holidays, or when away." She touched Maxine's hand. "I didn't read them, at least not beyond seeing you were the sender. I still have them if you'd like them."

Maxine opened her mouth, but no words came out. She might have nodded or shaken her head, but Leighton couldn't tell.

"Just let me know, and I'll bring them over." That hadn't been the reason Leighton had brought them up. "Then I found another one."

Maxine paled, her eyes watery, and she pressed her fingers against the edge of the table.

"It was separate from the others. I found it in my father's things, in the special box where he kept his great-grandparent's immigration papers and his father's pocket watch." Leighton let her eyes become unfocused as she recalled the day. "At first, I thought you'd written it to him, but you'd addressed it to Mom, like the others. I wondered why Dad kept that one by itself, so I read it. In it, you encouraged her to marry him. You told her he was a good man and would take care of her, how it was clear he loved her, and she'd have a good life. One part stood out to me. In the letter, you explained how if she didn't have the courage to live a difficult life, you wouldn't hold it against her. You'd always be there, by her side." It was Leighton whose eyes were now filled with tears. "And you were, weren't you? Right until the end."

Maxine squeezed her eyes closed and didn't move or speak for some time. Then she nodded. "We became lovers at college." When she opened her eyes and saw Leighton's face, she dashed her hand in her direction. "Don't look so surprised. It was Bryn Mawr."

Leighton smiled. She'd heard rumors about the all-female college. However, the confirmation of her mother engaging in a same-sex relationship was too much of a revelation for her to wrap her head around, at least right now. From the sound of it, she'd have plenty of time in the coming weeks for that.

"Was she the love of your life?" In a split second, Leighton regretted asking. George was her godfather, and she didn't know how much he knew.

Maxine's eyes flashed. "These are intrusive questions considering George might come home any moment." But before Leighton could apologize, Maxine lowered her voice. "But yes, Deborah was my one, my only love, always and forever."

Leighton had adored her father, and he clearly loved her mother, but the thought of her mother settling for him out of fear was almost too much to contemplate. How long had he known about the letter, and why had he kept it separate? Had he been grateful? Or had he felt as though he'd won a race simply because the first place finisher had been disqualified? It saddened her that she'd never know the answers. "And Mom loved you, too?"

For the first time since Leighton had arrived, Maxine smiled. "Yes, she did, very much." Her eyes held a dreamy look, but it was short-lived.

"But she couldn't bring herself to make a life with me, to face what that kind of existence might look like and the hardships we'd endure, so we lived the life you saw. I'm sure you're wondering, but our relationship was platonic after she made her decision. I'd be quite the hypocrite to condemn your actions if I'd had an affair with a married woman for decades. I lived with enough guilt over the emotional connection we shared."

Leighton hadn't been wondering. Most people didn't want to think about their parents' sex lives. It comforted her to know her mother had been faithful to her father, though. She wasn't sure she could handle knowing her entire childhood had been a sham. "You know, when she was in the hospital, sometimes I'd visit late at night after I'd finished class. I'd find you asleep by her bedside, holding her hand. You, not my father. I remember thinking what a good friend you were to stay with her, even after my father had left. Now I understand there was more to your friendship than met the eye."

The tendons in Maxine's neck stood out like she willed herself to keep her emotions in check. "Yes."

Leighton fiddled with the ring on her index finger. "Does this have anything to do with why I have your middle name and not my mother's?"

"Both your first and middle name have history." Maxine glanced out the window. "I know your mother used to tell you when you asked about its origin that she'd seen the name Leighton somewhere and had liked it. That was partly true. She'd seen it on the return address of the weekly letters my dear grandmother sent me during college. Grandmother was my only family member who saw and accepted the real me. But, Deborah didn't choose the name Leighton, I did. When your mother became pregnant, I struggled with the reality of our decision. After all, it's one thing to tell the woman you love to marry a man. The knowledge of what had to occur for her to get pregnant almost destroyed me. I suppose assuming they'd be celibate was naive of me." Maxine paused and blew her nose. "Your mother had always wanted a baby, and the considerate soul she was, offered to let me name you. She also told me your middle name would always make me smile. Lucky for us, your father had no interest in any of this, or questions would have followed."

"So, she gave me your middle name." Leighton had always assumed it'd been because Maxine was her godmother.

A tear streaked down Maxine's cheek. "Yes, and she was right." She flicked it away and smiled. "It does. By the time Kalyssa was born, the name Catherine belonged to you, but it warmed my old, withered heart when you passed it on to her."

Leighton squeezed her hand. "It belongs to the three of us."

Maxine took a deep breath. "Your father was good to Deborah. She couldn't have chosen a better man, though seeing her with anyone would have been difficult. It was the same for her when I married George." Maxine shrugged. "But it had to be done. You know what they said back then about a single woman the older she got."

Leighton could only imagine.

Maxine frowned and smoothed her skirt. "After encouraging you to marry Jeffrey, I felt terrible about how everything turned out. I never expected that to happen. He seemed like a good man."

"Yes, he fooled us all, so please don't blame yourself. The choice to marry him was mine to make." Leighton gave a hollow laugh. "God, I'm going to get a reputation for making poor decisions."

"It's too soon to be making jokes. That said, you've been happy this year. Even with that fool ex of yours lurking around and calling constantly, you've been in good spirits. I see now that has everything to do with Casey." Maxine tugged her sleeves over her wrists. "I was angry when you called and told me what happened. Disappointed, too. I won't lie and tell you I've gotten over either emotion. However, I know you feel something for her, something more than pure sexual attraction, although I suppose that's there, too. I know you wouldn't have done something like this if you didn't have powerful feelings for her. Perhaps even… Well, I won't say the word, because you need to come to that realization yourself."

It took Leighton a moment. *Love.* While she cared for Casey to such an extent she found herself in unfamiliar territory, was she in love with her?

Maxine hadn't finished. "I know I've been hard on you today, but for good reason. I love you and want happiness for you, but not everyone will be as understanding of your situation as I am. Regardless, we're going to do our best to get you and Atelier Vaughn through this mess. As for the eventual outcome, I can't make any promises."

She didn't even deserve Maxine's help. Her lack of impulse control had caused the problem, and she should face the consequences.

Yet Maxine had always been part of her life. She was the sexagenarian poster girl for a strong, supportive godmother. Her love for Leighton never wavered, and even when Leighton made the mistake of a lifetime, Maxine stood by her. Leighton had her to thank for everything, and not only for her assistance with this. If Maxine hadn't encouraged her mother to marry her father all those years ago, Leighton might not exist.

However, this wasn't the time. The indigo shadows under Maxine's eyes and the fatigue in her features suggested she'd recounted enough about the past for one day.

CHAPTER THIRTY-FOUR

Casey chewed on her fingernail in the back of Maxine's car on the way to the Upper West Side. Rather than meet in the gallery where they wouldn't have privacy, Maxine had sent her driver to pick her up so they could talk. She jiggled her leg but stopped when her snow boots squeaked against the fancy leather upholstery.

Being asked to Maxine's home was just as unnerving as the woman who lived in it. Casey liked her, but Maxine was intimidating at baseline. Her request to discuss what happened sounded more like it might be an interrogation. Casey half expected hundred-watt bare bulbs and to be read her Miranda rights.

It'd been difficult to come to terms with Leighton's decision to tell Maxine. Life would've been easier if she hadn't. Yet Leighton's steadfastness made her proud. Not everyone would choose to do the honorable thing. Casey wasn't sure she had Leighton's integrity. She could learn something from the experience.

Casey showed her identification to the doorman at the front desk before he led her to the elevator. Upstairs, a housekeeper or maid directed Casey to the library. She perused the leather-bound volumes on the shelves as she waited for Maxine. To calm herself, she took slow, purposeful breaths.

The door clicked shut, and she turned. Maxine gestured for her to sit and slid her phone onto the table.

"At first, I planned to hire a stenographer, but I think one less person knowing this story is best. I'll record it, though, with your permission. If you care for Leighton, you'll understand why it needs to be this way."

"I do, and I understand." Casey would do everything she could to help Leighton. It was her fault they were in the predicament they found themselves. Why hadn't she stayed at the exhibition? She jiggled her leg, caught herself, and stopped.

Maxine clicked her screen a few times, then hovered a red nail over her phone. "Once we begin, I'll ask you to agree again for the record."

Casey nodded.

Maxine started the recording, and Casey confirmed her consent.

"As I mentioned on the phone, I want your side of the story." Maxine tapped her nails on the table, then jerked her hand away, like she'd realized the noise might interfere.

Casey fiddled with a hangnail. "I'm not sure where to begin."

With a wave of her hand and an irritated look, Maxine sighed. "Start somewhere. You didn't trip and fall into bed together." She motioned toward the phone. "Pretend that's not there and talk to me. If everything goes according to plan, no one will ever hear this recording. What was said during this conversation will remain between us."

"Okay." Casey steadied herself. "It built slowly over time, from the first day we met."

"*It?*" Maxine arched an eyebrow.

"I don't know what to call it." Casey chose her words. "Our connection, or whatever drew us toward one another."

"And how were you certain Leighton felt the same?"

Despite her discomfort, Casey's guilt over what had happened was so strong she would've answered almost anything. "I could feel it, something between us. The way she looked at me, the way she spoke to me. I watched Kalyssa one night when Leighton was in a bind. When she arrived to pick her up, she looked exhausted, and I offered her something to eat. They stayed for a bit, and she was so good with Andy. I enjoyed the evening. It's not like having sex was a goal we had. Our relationship started as friendship, a mutual admiration, spending time with someone intelligent who had similar likes, and it grew."

Maxine had listened without interruption. "Who made the first move?"

Casey's face heated, and she avoided eye contact. "I did. I accused her of using the cameras to spy on us. That was before she told me about Jeffrey. She took me upstairs to show me she lived there. Letting me into that part of her life felt intimate. She'd shared a piece of herself, one she didn't make available to everyone." Casey swallowed. "I tried to kiss her, but she wouldn't allow it."

"She rejected you?"

If Casey had been blushing before, she was certain her face had turned from pink to crimson. "Yes. I wanted more, not necessarily sex, but to be closer to her, and she kept pushing me away." Casey ran her fingers through her hair. "She was often cold and distant with me."

Maxine's eyebrows shot up. "Really?"

Casey nodded. "I've always been the instigator. Did she tell you I showed up uninvited at her place the night it happened?"

"No, she didn't." Maxine appeared interested, leaning forward and resting her arms on the table.

"Yes, as you heard, I won the Best of Show and the trip to Florence. After the ceremony, I looked for her but was told she left. It hurt that she didn't stay to congratulate me. Out of everyone in my life, Leighton was the one person with whom I wanted to share the experience. I took a cab to the atelier, but she wasn't answering her phone, so I had to hack my way upstairs."

"Hack?" Maxine looked like she'd never heard the word.

"Not hack but figure out a way to get to the third floor. The building is almost impenetrable."

"Yes, I'm aware. I've helped make it that way." Maxine leaned back in her chair. "How did you do it?"

"I tried to get the elevator to work by entering lazy codes people use when they want something easy to remember, even the years I thought Kalyssa might've been born. We'd studied the Fibonacci sequence, and I was certain it'd be the golden ratio, but it wasn't. Nothing worked. I was ready to give up when I tried my code. It allowed me to select the third floor."

Maxine scowled. "It shouldn't have worked. A student's code would only..." Maxine rolled her lips inward. "Oh, Leighton gave you access at some point."

Casey shrugged. "I guess so. We didn't discuss it."

"No, I'm sure you were busy doing other things."

Maxine's sharp retort stung. The least she could do was give her an accurate idea of what happened.

"Not at first. I wanted to know why she left the event."

"Why did she?"

Casey took a deep breath. "She said I scared her."

Maxine scoffed. "You?"

"Yes, or at least made her scared of what she might do because of her feelings for me." Casey remembered how hard it'd been to breathe when Leighton had admitted that to her.

With a sharp exhale, Maxine stood. "You seem quite determined."

Casey straightened. "I am, but I didn't pressure her into what happened. We both wanted it."

"I'm a little relieved that it appears you were doing most of the chasing, and she was doing her best to hold off your advances." Maxine stared out the window. "Not that it makes the result any better."

Maxine's insinuation that the situation might have been different incensed her. Casey wasn't going to let her consider a false version of the story, even for a second. "She didn't seduce me if that's what you're getting at."

Maxine turned. "I think I've heard enough details of your involvement. Let's skip to the part about the consequences of your actions."

Goose bumps covered Casey's skin.

"I'm rescinding your scholarship under the morals clause."

The floorboards beneath Casey tilted, and she squeezed her eyes shut. "Oh, God. No."

"Yes, but wipe that dreadful look off your face." Maxine pushed a box of tissues toward her. "Leighton has paid your tuition in full. We can't have a situation where it might appear you need to perform…let's say, certain duties, to keep your place at Atelier Vaughn."

Casey's head spun. "She had to pay for me?" Could she afford that?

"Yes, and your spot is secure this year. Next year is another story."

So, her time at AV was coming to an end. Casey wanted to weep.

Maxine sat beside her. "I can't believe I'm saying this, but Leighton thinks there's not much more you can learn from her, so you have a part-time teaching position at Atelier Vaughn next fall, if that interests you. You could teach some of the introductory sessions for the new first-year students. Or perhaps take on TA duties. But you wouldn't be instructing any of your contemporaries. That might be uncomfortable for all involved. And I'm sure Leighton will still have a few tricks to share with you during open studio times."

That intrigued her. But no longer a student? And Leighton forced to pay for her spring semester? Casey pressed her hands to her cheeks. "I didn't know it would come to this. We shouldn't have done it."

"No, but you did." Maxine adjusted her glasses and seemed to peer down her nose at her. "I also met with the atelier's two other investors. They've decided to pursue other opportunities."

"Which means they know Leighton slept with a student and want nothing to do with her." Casey wasn't stupid, and hot tears pricked her eyes. "Oh, my God. I've ruined her business, her dream. I never meant for this to happen."

Maxine didn't appear interested in lingering over regrets. "In addition, I've suspended Leighton from teaching."

Casey shot from her seat. "You can't do that. She's an amazing instructor, and even if I made a huge mistake, the other students shouldn't be punished for my actions. I'll quit."

Maxine stopped her with a hand in the air. "Sit down. You're not quitting. Is that understood? Leighton's suspension from teaching is temporary. Stefan will cover her classes for the rest of the semester. What happens come January is still undecided. Right now, Leighton is spending her time garnering investors to replace the two we've lost. If she resumes teaching, we'll likely restructure it so you're not in Leighton's classes this spring."

Casey stared at her. "You're not pulling your support?"

"Leighton is family." Maxine looked offended. "Of course not."

"I'm glad. That would've crushed her." While losing Maxine's investment would have been an enormous blow, the loss of her emotional support would've devastated Leighton the most.

Maxine arranged her hair out of what looked like habit. "In addition, I want you to meet with my attorney."

Casey's stomach clenched. Was she being sued? "Why?"

"I had to devise a way to protect Leighton." Maxine straightened the jewel-studded rings on her left hand.

"I never intended to bring trouble for Leighton or the atelier." She blinked back tears.

Maxine sighed. "I know you have genuine feelings for one another. I also know they won't go away because I'd like them to, so here's what you're going to do. You'll meet with my attorney, and she'll have drafted a legal agreement for you to sign that states your relationship is, and always has been, consensual. You'll give up any rights to sue Leighton or Atelier Vaughn for reasons pertaining to said relationship in perpetuity. Is that clear?"

Casey's relief was almost uncontainable. Tears leaked down her cheeks. "Yes, of course, I'll sign." She pulled a tissue from the box and dabbed her eyes. "Thank you for finding a solution to our mess. I never intended for this to happen."

Maxine folded her hands in her lap.

"Does Leighton know about this?" Casey wiped her nose.

Maxine shook her head. "Not yet. I wanted to have a conversation with you first. Why?"

"Would it be all right if I told her?" Casey hadn't expected being summoned to Maxine's home would transpire into this. It'd been difficult to endure, but it hadn't turned out terrible. She tried to calm her racing heart. Was it wrong to feel relieved? She wanted to run and tell Leighton. Maxine had devised a way forward for them, even if it might be difficult, and Casey wanted to be the one to give Leighton the good news.

"I don't see any harm in that. She won't be around on my orders, but she'll be at the holiday party because it's important for the guests to see her there. You can give her a copy of the agreement that evening. I'll tell my attorney to have it ready for you to sign by then."

Maxine brought her back to Earth with her edict. Holiday party? It wasn't even December yet. Her stomach plummeted. "Not until then?" That meant she wouldn't see Leighton for three weeks.

Maxine clearly saw her dismay. "Thanksgiving is in a few days. Leighton has important things to do, and so do you. You're still a student at Atelier Vaughn, which is what got you two into this mess, and you have projects to finish. It wouldn't hurt the two of you to keep some distance until we can clear up things regarding the investors and the finances." She leaned forward and folded her hands on the table. "Casey, what Leighton did was wrong, even if it was consensual and you were the instigator. We can never condone a teacher sleeping with a student, so you must deal with the consequences."

The ramifications of what they'd done hit her, but just as quickly, so did her resolve to prove her readiness to address the repercussions, and that involved staying away from Leighton. She'd do it. Leighton was worth it.

Maxine sighed. "I've also noticed Leighton, whom I've known her entire life, happier than I've ever seen her. She's met someone who cares for her and Kalyssa. You're bright, determined, and seem to hold your own with her." She pushed her glasses up her nose. "We go forward from here."

Of everything that could've happened during Casey's visit, this was most unexpected. Embarrassment, guilt, and regret for the harm she'd caused Leighton and her business filled her, but so did joy and relief. Maxine had given them a gift.

CHAPTER THIRTY-FIVE

Leighton spotted Stefan leaning over a glass case of pastries in his favorite bakery. He laughed with Kevin, the man he'd taken as his date to the Salmagundi Club. Kevin wore a gray apron with smudges of flour near his waistline. He seemed as pleased with the conversation as Stefan.

"Good morning." She approached the counter.

"Hi, Leighton. Take your pick." Kevin gestured to the baked goods. "Coffee, too. It's on me."

He seemed eager to cater to her needs, probably to impress Stefan.

Stefan leaned over her shoulder and pointed. "I recommend one of those."

She eyed the selection. "A latte and a cherry knish then. Thanks, Kevin."

"Same." Stefan winked at him.

"Please, sit. I'll warm the knishes and bring them to you."

Stefan led her to a table where he had a view of the counter. Leighton glanced between him and Kevin.

"Oh, you have it bad, my friend." She shot him a teasing grin. "I didn't see snickerdoodles in the case. Are you sure?"

Stefan chuckled. "No, and I haven't asked him to make any because everything else is so good." He returned to his blatant appraisal of Kevin.

"Are we still talking about pastries?" She tried to poke his arm, but he was too quick. "Hey, I have some information you'll find interesting."

"Does this have to do with what you told me on the phone?" He leaned his chin on his hand. They'd spoken at length before Thanksgiving.

The reminder of the situation darkened her mood, but she tried to appear unfazed. "Not directly. I've blown your case wide open."

Leighton blew on her nails and rubbed them on her shirtfront. "I know who fathered Casey's child."

Stefan's mouth dropped open, and he clutched a hand to his chest. "No."

"Oh, yes." She made him wait a few seconds. "Mark. I found out a few weeks ago, but I keep forgetting to tell you." She'd had more important things on her mind.

He looked toward the ceiling like he imagined it. "Yeah, I can see the similarities. Both he and Andy have those eyelashes that drive girls wild with jealousy."

She squinted at him. "Do you encounter a lot of wild, eyelash-loving girls in your daily life? Are you spending too much time at Sephora again?"

He pursed his lips. "They carry fantastic moisturizers. How'd you figure out who Andy's father is? And a few weeks? Seriously, Vaughn."

Leighton shrugged. "I asked Casey."

"Hmm." He stared into space. "I never thought of that."

Kevin brought a tray with their order.

"Thanks, Kev." Stefan pulled his warm knish closer.

"If you need anything, I'll be over here."

"Thank you. It looks delicious." She was being honest. When had food last appealed to her? It hadn't been on Thanksgiving. Maxine's chef always prepared fantastic meals, and Leighton was sure this year's was no different, but she hadn't tasted any of it. Maxine always picked at the food on her plate, but George and Kalyssa raved over the dinner.

According to Jenna, Casey had spent Thanksgiving at Mark's mom's house. Aileen's culinary skills had a reputation around the atelier after all the treats she'd sent either with Erica or Mark over the last year and a half. Funny how Leighton had always heard Aileen referred to as Erica's aunt or Mark's mom and never by her given name until Casey revealed who she was. Anyway, she hoped Casey and Andy's Thanksgiving had been better than hers.

"How was your holiday together?" The lava-hot cherry and cheese filling burned her tongue, and she sucked in air. She might need to switch to iced coffee to soothe the pain.

Stefan had taken a daintier bite and blew on it first, showing his status as a seasoned pro in pastry consumption. "Great. He invited me over to his friends' house. They do a Friendsgiving type of deal every year. Kevin made a kale and mushroom stuffing using day-old croissants, and I brought sweet potatoes with marshmallows since they're easy. There were about a dozen of us."

"That sounds nice." It did, except for the marshmallows, which she found disgusting. Still, he'd spent the holiday with the object of his affection, something Leighton couldn't do. That didn't mean she hadn't thought about Casey the entire day.

He yawned. "Yeah, it was. His friends were welcoming."

"Am I supposed to believe you ate mushrooms and kale?" She eyed him.

He gave a little shimmy. "I ate a bite of everything to make him happy."

Leighton chuckled and took a folder from her bag. "Here are the lesson plans for next week. I also emailed them to you."

He pulled it closer but didn't open it. "Thanks, I saw them."

"No questions?"

He shook his head.

She sipped her coffee. "Thanks for covering for me. I'm sorry about the situation I've put you in. And thank you for meeting me here since I'm still not allowed in the studio. This way, I can escape my loft, and we don't have to meet in the gallery with Maxine hovering over us."

Stefan poked his fork toward Kevin. "Do I look like I mind coming here?"

Leighton rolled her eyes. "Your waistline will protest at some point, even if your heart doesn't."

He grinned. "Who said anything about my heart being involved? I might be using him for his body."

Leighton glanced between them. "You should see your face when he's around. I don't doubt it's both."

"You should talk."

His horrified expression told her he'd spoken without thinking.

"Yeah." She didn't know what else to say.

He squeezed her hand. "Hey, I'm sorry."

Leighton shrugged it off. "I'm sorry you're stuck teaching my classes."

"I'm not." Stefan raised a shoulder and let it fall. "The extra money is nice with Christmas around the corner." He ogled Kevin again.

On some level, it pleased Leighton her indiscretions would net Kevin a killer Christmas gift. Someone should get something out of the ordeal since it didn't look like it'd be her or Casey.

"How is she?" The question slipped out before she could stop herself.

Stefan pushed his empty plate aside. "Are you sure you want to know?"

The look she gave him must have been sufficient.

"Her work is terrible, at least by her standards." He picked up a few crumbs with the tip of his finger.

"What do you mean?"

His head snapped up at her sharp response. "Terrible, as in not good. I don't know what's happening with her, but either her head or her heart isn't in it. Jenna is producing better work than Casey right now."

Leighton understood how Casey must feel—empty, robotic, burdened—but there was nothing she could do about it. She'd done her share of moving zombie-like through the long winter days. "Can you help her?" She'd lost her appetite.

"I'm trying, Leighton. I don't like to see her floundering any more than you."

"What should we do?" The atmosphere inside the bakery that had felt warm and inviting when she'd arrived now made her overheated and claustrophobic.

"You're not allowed to do anything, but I'll support her like I do all of them. Right now though, she's lost her artistry with the brush." Stefan shook his head. "If she was an author, she'd have writer's block."

"I hate this." Leighton threw her napkin on the table. "What about her trompe l'oeil? That should've been in her wheelhouse. You mentioned she started it."

He nodded. "Her initial sketch showed promise. She chose some interesting objects and brought in a photo of her grandmother. The composition looked balanced, and she told a story with her items, but she rushed the steps like her mind was elsewhere. She's not thinking and making mistakes she never makes. If painting is making a thousand tiny decisions, she's making the wrong ones half of the time."

"But she seems well?" Leighton hated grilling him for the tiniest detail about Casey, but she had to know like she needed air to breathe. How badly had her decision affected Casey?

"I don't know." He sank lower in his chair. "She looks tired, and I have to remind her to take breaks and eat. I've even offered her my snacks, and you know how I feel about sharing them."

"Do you think she has enough money for food?" Casey was on a tight budget, and Leighton couldn't bear to think of her or Andy going without.

"It's not that. A few days ago, Jaiden brought a tray of banana lumpia his aunties made. There's always food in the kitchen, and it's only going to get worse now that December is here. Or better, in my case." He wiggled his eyebrows but turned serious again. "Casey's uninterested. She's in her head." He waved his hand like he swatted a fly. "Enough about her. Are you eating?"

She huffed. "You just watched me."

"Yeah, a whopping three-quarters of a pastry. You're too thin, and you have raccoon eyes. *You* could use a trip to Sephora."

"I eat." *Most of the time,* she wanted to add. "But I've been painting after Kalyssa goes to bed, so I haven't slept much lately."

He lit up. "You received a commission?"

"No, but it's an important painting."

"How important?" He scratched at his stubble.

She allowed herself to smile. "Perhaps my greatest work yet."

He leaned back. "Leighton Michelangela Vaughn, what aren't you telling me?"

Leighton chuckled, and it felt good. "That's all I'm going to say right now. I don't know what'll happen. It might go nowhere."

"Hilarious. Go nowhere." He laughed. "I wish my paintings had the passport stamps yours do." Stefan muttered something sarcastic that sounded like *five figures* and slapped the table. "Are you going to keep me in the dark?"

She smiled into her coffee. "Indeed. It's the most important piece I've ever done, and I don't want to ruin it by saying too much. Things might not end up the way I hope."

He grabbed her hand and examined her nails. "Did you have a mishap, or are you exploring a new painting style? You have paint everywhere, and you're always so neat."

She yanked her hand away. "It's possible, or maybe I didn't wash my hands well." Truth be told, her entire technique had changed out of necessity. She found it refreshing. It was one of the few things besides Kalyssa that brought her joy these days. Still, she hadn't even allowed Kalyssa into the spare bedroom to see it.

"Did you buy another easel or are you using a tabletop one?" His forehead scrunched, presumably as he considered her easel abandoned in the studio. "Has it been difficult having to paint in your living space?"

It had. She'd had to buy a box fan to put in the window to help with the air exchange. In fact, she'd had to buy a lot of new things. Still, she kept it vague. "I'm making do."

His expression flipped like a light switch. "It's for her, isn't it?"

Leighton couldn't hide her excitement and allowed herself to smile. "So many questions, but yes."

"Your greatest work, huh?"

Leighton studied the dried paint around her nail beds. "It's the most difficult yet inspiring thing I've ever created and the most important piece to which I've ever laid a brush. I'm prouder of this work than anything that came before it."

Stefan raised his eyebrows, like this impressed him. "Does Casey know about it?"

"I'm not allowed to speak with her, remember?" She lifted her mug to hide her quivering lip.

"So, how will you give it to her?"

"I'm not sure I'll ever get the chance." She tried to compose herself as Kevin approached.

"Do either of you need anything?"

After they declined, and Leighton thanked him again, Kevin retreated after what seemed like twenty seconds of making eyes at Stefan. It made Leighton ill, not because she wasn't happy for them, but because she'd been so close to having something similar. It wasn't meant to be, but that didn't diminish how much she missed Casey.

"How are your meetings with investors going?" He seemed hesitant to bring it up.

Usually, she'd welcome changing the subject from whether she'd ever see Casey again, but this topic was almost as depressing.

"Not well. I've met with four potential parties, and I think they caught wind of what happened because they said this isn't the best time for them." She leaned forward. "That's code for they can't trust my judgment."

He looked concerned. "Were those all the ones you had?"

Was he updating his curriculum vitae in his mind? She couldn't lose him, too.

"No, but I had to hit pause because of the holiday. I have a few more, plus I haven't contacted the galleries yet. They might be more willing to overlook my indiscretions to get the publicity, even if their investments might not be as robust." She glanced at her phone. "I should go. Let me know if you end up having questions about the lessons, and thanks for keeping the ship afloat right now."

He stood and hugged her. "You don't have to thank me. Just take care of yourself, will you? I don't enjoy seeing both of you wallowing in despair."

Leighton's chest tightened at hearing him talk about Casey like that.

He held her at arm's length. "Maxine said you'll be around more helping her get ready for the Christmas party."

Leighton narrowed her eyes. "Stop calling it a Christmas party because it's not. It's a seasonal party where all are welcome. And yes, I will."

"Got it." He nodded. "Good."

It *would* be good. With her increased presence in the gallery, she hoped to run into Casey. She disliked hearing about Casey struggling, and Leighton wanted to see for herself. Casey's well-being and happiness were important. Leighton's lack of interest in food or inability to sleep were issues, but it sickened her knowing her actions were having detrimental effects on Casey.

CHAPTER THIRTY-SIX

Leighton dropped an empty box at her feet as Kalyssa bounced into the gallery. Mikala trailed behind her.

"Momma, look at my nails!" Kalyssa did a pirouette, then held out her hands. "Mikala painted them for me."

Leighton assessed the new shade of green.

Kalyssa wiggled her fingers. "Can you see the glitter?"

"I can, and they're beautiful. How nice of her." Leighton kissed the top of her head.

"Yeah." She twirled again.

"How much do I owe you?" Leighton hoped Mikala had Venmo.

Mikala handed her Kalyssa's Hello Kitty backpack. "Nothing. I'm glad I could help in a way that didn't involve decorating this place. That's not my jam. And we had fun."

"Well, thank you."

Kalyssa tugged her sleeve. "We watched *Moana* and ate popcorn. And Mikala's new girlfriend gave me ice cream because I let her sit beside Mikala."

Leighton laughed as Mikala blushed. "It sounds like you had a great time. Preschool can't compete with that." This time, no jealousy flared when hearing about Mikala's latest attraction. She leaned down. "Guess what? You and I are going to change into our new dresses for the party soon."

"Will Andy be there?" Kalyssa flapped her hands.

How much sugar had she had? Leighton tried not to appear flustered in front of Mikala. "I'm not sure."

Kalyssa slumped, her lips in a pout. "Didn't you ask Casey if she's bringing him?"

Leighton should've found a sitter. Kalyssa might be too tired to make it through the party. She couldn't admit to her daughter that Maxine wouldn't allow her to talk to Casey.

Mikala knelt on one knee. "I heard Casey say Andy was coming with his grandma tonight because Casey is still busy upstairs." She stood. "Bye, Miss Kalyssa. Let's do our dance at the party."

She broke into moves Leighton thought she recognized as Beyoncé's. Leighton wasn't sure they were appropriate for a four-year-old, but Kalyssa had a two-minute attention span and the chance she'd remember by tonight was slim.

"Bye." Kalyssa threw her small arms around Mikala's legs. "And I was good and didn't say nothing about all the candy we ate."

Leighton smiled and shook her head at Kalyssa's stage-whispered secret.

Mikala glanced at Leighton with an awkward chuckle as she headed for the door.

Kalyssa appraised the galleries. "It looks nice in here, Mom. Smells like trees."

Leighton smiled. "I'll take that as a compliment." Maxine had asked her to hang live pine boughs. She'd draped the greenery over the doors, windows, and many other surfaces. A few strands of white snowflake lights made the place seem wintery and festive. She still needed to distribute two more boxes of LED candles throughout the gallery. The lights above the paintings, the stringed lights, and the candles would create a wonderful ambiance.

"Ooh, cookies." Kalyssa rushed toward them.

"No." Leighton caught the back of her jacket. "Jaiden's aunties baked them for the party, and you need to eat dinner first." Plus, it sounded like Kalyssa had ingested plenty of sugar already.

"The food people are here." Kalyssa pointed to the entrance.

Giant snowflakes clung to the caterers' black jackets. Leighton showed them where they could set up. They'd served appetizers, a specialty eggnog drink, champagne, and a non-alcoholic punch.

She hadn't seen Casey, and Mikala's information checked. She'd heard Casey was still finishing and framing her piece. Since Leighton couldn't visit the second floor, she might not see her until the party. She pressed a hand to her heart to still the fluttering in her chest.

Maxine blew in, unwinding a gauzy scarf from her hair and shrugging out of her faux fur. She brushed snowflakes from the sleeves before she hung the coat in the closet. "My stylist had the nerve to inform me his last appointment ran long when I saw him out front kissing his boyfriend for ten minutes. I might be over forty, but I'm not blind."

Forty? Three or four presidents had been in office since Maxine's forties.

"At least your hair looks nice."

Maxine ignored the compliment and glanced around. "You made good progress."

"Phoenix and Jaiden helped. The caterers have arrived, and all that's left are the candles."

Maxine peered into the next gallery. "Musicians?"

"Not yet, but it's early." Leighton snapped a battery into a candle.

Maxine glanced at her. "Give yourself time to get dressed. You can't show up like that."

Leighton glanced at her dirty jeans and sap-stained hands. "I planned to change."

Maxine circled a manicured nail close to Leighton's face. "Spend some time on your hair and makeup, too. Those bags under your eyes will scare off potential collectors. You look like a corpse, and you need to look presentable tonight."

Maxine always had a way with words.

Leighton clenched her teeth. "I plan to."

"Hi, munchkin." Maxine touched Kalyssa's back. "Your fingernails look beautiful. Will you fetch me a bottle of water? I'm parched." When Kalyssa scampered off, she returned her attention to Leighton. "Have you seen Casey?"

"What? No, I haven't gone anywhere. I've been right here the entire time." She couldn't have sounded more guilty.

Maxine sighed and glanced at her watch. "I simply asked because I thought she may have finished. What's taking her so long? She needs to go home and get ready. Framing it nicely is important, but hurrying wouldn't hurt. If we display that painting tonight, she'll never see it again."

Casey's painting difficulties must be improving if Maxine was that sure of a sale. The knowledge comforted her, even if Maxine didn't have Stefan's critical eye.

"Mikala said Aileen is bringing Andy tonight." Leighton almost mentioned that Mikala had volunteered the information. "Perhaps Aileen is bringing Casey's clothing, too."

Maxine leafed through the RSVP list. "Maybe, but if Casey doesn't get that painting hung in the next hour, she's going to find me on the second floor, and she doesn't want that."

Leighton's heart went out to Casey. Neither of them needed more of Maxine's wrath these days.

Kalyssa skidded to a stop and produced Maxine's water.

"Thank you, love." Maxine stopped Phoenix as he passed them. "We don't need these tablecloths and chair covers. Could you please take them to the studio?"

"Sure." He grabbed the closest box.

Maxine answered the ringing phone. After saying hello a few times, she hung up. She pressed a series of numbers and shook her head. "Blocked."

"Again?" Leighton shivered. She'd thought the calls had stopped. Had there been a lull, or had Maxine kept quiet about them?

"I can't say for sure." Maxine tossed the list on her desk. "Go get ready, and I'll finish the candles."

Leighton took Kalyssa's hand. "I'll be down as soon as I can."

"Take your time."

They took the stairs since Phoenix was using the elevator to transport the boxes. Midway through Kalyssa's retelling of the ice cream story, Casey entered the stairwell from the second floor.

She stopped short.

"Casey!" Kalyssa flew at her and hugged her like she'd found her long-lost friend. "I haven't seen you in forever."

"Hi, I've missed you." Casey rubbed Kalyssa's back, but she looked at Leighton.

Leighton didn't know what to do. "Hi." She might as well have been fifteen again.

"Come here."

To Leighton's surprise, Casey embraced her.

"I've missed you, too."

"Yes. So much." God, she felt good. Leighton closed her eyes and tried to sear the experience of being held by Casey in her mind. It might be the last time it happened.

Kalyssa piped up. "What time is Andy coming to the party?"

Casey pulled back but didn't let her go. "His grandma is going to bring him around six forty-five."

"Six forty-five." Kalyssa beamed. "I haven't seen Andy in forever."

"He has a new train engine he's been wanting to show you." She looked at Leighton, her hazel eyes aglow. "Will you meet me after the party? I have something for you."

"Me?" Leighton's voice cracked.

"Mm-hmm." Casey appeared calm and collected, though her face looked thinner. Strangely, she didn't seem as affected by their time apart or their chance meeting.

Leighton stepped back. "I'm not sure that's a good idea. Maxine and other important people will be here tonight."

Casey took her hands. "It's all right. Maxine cleared it. May I come to your loft, or shall we meet in the gallery?"

Maxine had okay'd it? Leighton's head spun. "My place is fine." She had something she wanted to show Casey, and she'd been wondering if she'd ever have the chance.

"Tonight then." Casey squeezed her hands.

She nodded, unable to find her voice amid the rush of emotions.

Casey kissed the corner of her mouth. "It's so good to see you, but I have to give Maxine an update on my painting before she has a fit." She smiled and gave them a little wave. "I'll see you tonight."

"Bye, Casey." Kalyssa waved, too.

Leighton watched her descend the stairs. She hadn't spoken to Casey in weeks, and seeing her in good spirits reassured her. Despite not knowing what to expect, she looked forward to this evening's event, or at least whatever came after. Her anticipation soared as she led Kalyssa upstairs to change.

CHAPTER THIRTY-SEVEN

People packed the gallery. Casey didn't know if Maxine had expected so many attendees or if she'd granted entrance to uninvited guests. It didn't seem her style to turn people away. The string quartet's music floated throughout the space, and so did wonderful scents. Aromas like pine, nutmeg, or even the coconut on the crispy shrimp bites filled the air depending on the room. None of these scents could compare to Leighton's when she'd been in Casey's arms in the stairwell.

Casey adjusted her green scarf so her shoulders showed. The dress was the same one she'd worn to the Salmagundi Club exhibition. Her meager savings didn't allow for a new outfit, so she'd accessorized. It looked festive, and remembering the way Leighton had looked at her while wearing it gave her confidence.

She surveyed the largest gallery until she found her. It wasn't difficult. In her ivory gown, Leighton looked like a stunning snow queen in a winter wonderland. She admired how Leighton eschewed the silly rule of not wearing white after Labor Day. If anyone could pull it off, she could, and did. Casey sipped her champagne and watched her. Leighton laughed and touched an older woman on the arm. She hoped Leighton would get an investor or two out of the evening. The atelier could use the funds, and her stomach still roiled when she thought about the consequences of their actions.

Leighton smiled at her. Casey tried to hide hers behind the rim of her glass, but how could she? She hadn't seen Leighton in weeks, and when she did, she looked like that. Giving Leighton the signed agreement stating their relationship was consensual was all she could think about. However, she had to wait until the party ended. Maxine had put the envelope in the top drawer of her desk for safekeeping. Their weeks of torment were almost over.

Casey moved a few feet to keep Andy and Kalyssa in sight. Leighton had been doing the same. Aileen had watched Andy most of the evening, but she'd wanted to view the art. Casey encouraged her and watched both him and Kalyssa. There were too many people to let them out of her sight. She moved closer.

Despite being in a blue dress and white tights, Kalyssa sat on the floor turning the pages of a children's book. Andy's head rested on her shoulder as he looked at the illustrations. Kalyssa couldn't read yet, but it sounded like she made up a story for him. Casey waited until she turned the page.

"Are you two okay?"

"Yeah. My mom keeps asking us that, too." Kalyssa let the book fall closed.

Andy opened it to the page he'd been looking at. "Momma bear and baby bear."

Casey brushed her hand over his head. "Yes. You're both being so good." She left them to their story.

After what seemed like hours later, empty spots dotted the walls where paintings had sold. Caterers and musicians had already carted off their equipment while the students and staff cleaned up the aftermath. They moved tables and chairs back upstairs, took down decorations, and gathered trash and recycling to be taken outside. Maxine sent Leighton to the loft with the checks to lock in her safe. Andy and Kalyssa made a line of dominoes on the floor opposite the elevator.

Casey gathered the LED candles and switched them off. A cold breeze made the hair on her arms rise. A pine bough over the entrance had fallen and prevented the front door from closing, but before she could cross the room to move it, a disheveled man stumbled into the gallery. He steadied himself on the back of a chair and looked around. A bright smear of blood coated the back of his hand.

Nearby, Maxine bagged leftover cookies. Jenna exited the elevator with two rolls of paper towels. From atop the ladder, Phoenix tried to hand Devin an armful of lights, but Devin ignored him, distracted by his phone. No one seemed to notice the intruder except Casey.

And she didn't know what to do.

Devin looked up with alarm in his eyes and yelled, "Emergency alert!"

A few others already had their phones out.

Casey recognized the man clinging to the folding chair clearly helping to keep him upright. Jeffrey. Last month, Maxine had made everyone download a special app with photos of him and a button to send an emergency alert. Unfortunately, Casey's phone was in her jacket across the room because her dress didn't have pockets.

No one seemed to know what to do with Jeffrey already inside the building.

He smiled at her.

How long had she been standing there? She snapped to attention and pushed the elevator's button. Then she scooped up Andy and grabbed Kalyssa by the arm, scattering dominoes everywhere. Kalyssa cried she was hurting her, but Casey didn't have time for an explanation or apology. She cringed to think she might dislocate Kalyssa's shoulder, but worse might happen if she hesitated. The open elevator was halfway between her and Jeffrey, and if he was as intoxicated as he seemed, she had a chance of making it.

"Hey!" He stumbled toward Casey and the children.

Casey hurled herself toward the elevator, dumped the kids on the floor, and entered her code, selecting Leighton's loft. With a few punches to the Close Door button, she jumped out. Her body was the only thing that separated Jeffrey and the closing doors. She trembled but held up her hands.

"Get out of the way."

The alcohol on his breath stung her eyes. She refrained from gagging and tried to conceal her fear. At least she could hear the elevator ascending. Jeffrey had beaten Leighton, bruised her, and could have injured Kalyssa. Casey focused on the emotions those memories conjured within her. It would provide her with plenty of courage.

He'd get to Leighton over her dead body.

❖

As Leighton made her way up the stairs, she ruminated on the success of the evening. Tonight's event had put last year's to shame. Leighton had sold two of her paintings and three of Casey's. A jubilant Maxine had informed her they'd sold twelve works in all.

Pride filled her. Her students had donned their best attire and mixed and mingled with collectors and other art professionals throughout the evening. They represented the atelier well. She caught sight of Casey a few times, but the crowded gallery made it hard to track her, and Leighton had needed to touch base with as many guests as possible while making sure Kalyssa was safe.

A few times, she'd glimpsed Casey talking with someone in front of the painting she'd framed minutes before the event. Casey had chosen the same dress she'd worn to the Salmagundi Club, but she'd added a scarf. It made her look older, elegant, and showed off her gorgeous neck and shoulders. The sight flooded Leighton with memories.

While Leighton had been talking with Kevin, who'd brought delicious shortbread cookies he'd made, Casey passed behind her and touched the small of her back. Leighton almost ended the party on the spot. She turned, but Maxine had pulled Casey into a conversation with a collector who owned two of Leighton's paintings. Unwilling to risk her losing a sale, Leighton didn't interrupt. She'd talk to Casey tonight. Patience had never been her greatest virtue, and she'd bit back a sigh.

After the guests had trickled out, Maxine handed Leighton an envelope with almost six figures' worth of checks to secure in the safe until they could make a deposit. It amazed her people still used them, but payments of any kind pleased her. Later, she'd see how many credit card transactions had gone through.

They'd made money, and a sense of relief washed over her, and not only for what it'd do for her finances. The collectors and New York's art circle as a whole hadn't shunned her like a pariah, as they had every right to do.

Kalyssa and Andy still seemed content, and all the guests had left. Leighton would lock up the checks and be back before Kalyssa noticed she'd gone.

She punched in her code to release the stairwell door and entered the loft. Across the room, Erica and Mikala unstacked the chairs they'd borrowed for the party.

"Thanks for putting those away." Leighton headed for her bedroom and the safe.

Mikala extended her hand. "Here's your access card."

Erica waved her phone and grabbed Mikala's arm. "Emergency Alert. He's here. You got her?" She sprinted toward the stairwell.

"Affirmative." Mikala stepped behind Leighton, trapping her in the hallway.

"Who's here? What's happening? I don't have my phone." She tried to follow Erica, but Mikala held out her well-defined arms. With her closely shaved hair and muscular physique, Leighton bet she intimidated more than a few National Guard members of both sexes.

"It's being taken care of." She wouldn't allow Leighton past her.

"Let me by. My daughter is down there." Leighton didn't want to get into a physical altercation with one of her students, but if Mikala didn't step aside, she would. *He's here* only meant one thing. Jeffrey.

"I can't do that. I have orders." The tendons stood out in Mikala's neck.

Maxine had to be behind this. Of course, she'd assigned the one person to Leighton who understood a directive and could probably protect her best when she'd instituted the app.

Fear seized her. Were Kalyssa, Casey, and Andy in harm's way? Leighton attempted to dart past her, but Mikala subdued her from behind with ease.

"Then let me look at the cameras." She squirmed, trying to break free.

"Go." Mikala released her.

Leighton ran to the monitor and came to a dead stop. She knew that build, that posture, that menacing expression. How had Jeffrey gotten inside?

"No." Leighton choked on the word as she watched him tower over Casey. She scanned the other cameras. Where were the kids? She jerked around when she heard the elevator's arrival.

The doors slid open to produce Kalyssa and a crying Andy. Even though she looked terrified, Kalyssa hugged Andy to her.

"It's okay, darlings. Everything's okay." Leighton opened her arms for them to come to her and hoped her lie sounded convincing. As upset as the children were, she needed to know what was happening with Casey.

Mikala ushered them inside. "The app notified the authorities, so they're on their way. I'll calm the kids down, but you stay there." She pointed her finger at Leighton. "I'm not afraid to tackle you in front of your daughter." She turned to Kalyssa and Andy. "Look how pretty your nail polish looks with your dress. Should we see if we can find any cartoons, Andy?" Her fake cheer made the children relax almost immediately.

Leighton turned and gasped.

Jeffrey's hands were around Casey's throat.

At first, Casey planted both her palms on his chest to fend him off, then they flew to her neck. She pulled at his fingers and tried to break his grip.

"No!" Leighton turned up the audio loud enough to hear, and the noise from the TV helped cover the sound. How was this happening?

"Where is she? She up there?" Jeffrey removed a hand from Casey's throat to jab at the button.

Casey tried to shake her head. Leighton wasn't sure she could speak, anyway. She clawed at Jeffrey's hands as she tried in vain to loosen his grasp. Surely no air could reach her vocal cords.

How was she supposed to watch and do nothing? "For fuck's sake, kick him!" Leighton clenched her hands so hard her nails cut into her palms. Why couldn't she hear sirens? Where were the police? Why wasn't anyone doing anything?

Behind Jeffrey, Maxine had the phone to her ear, her eyes filled with terror. Jenna appeared frozen to the spot. Devin tried to pull him away from Casey, but Jeffrey yanked her with him. When Devin attempted to pry his fingers away, Jeffrey punched him, and he stumbled and landed a few feet away. Crimson liquid flowed onto the floor from his nose.

Casey's eyelids drooped, then closed.

"No!" Leighton hit the desk with her fist. Where was help? Could she get past Mikala?

Jeffrey shook Casey. "Is she upstairs?"

Casey's head fell forward, and her arms dropped to her sides. Jeffrey slammed her into the elevator doors.

"Oh, God." Leighton glanced at Mikala, who hovered in the hall. "Look. I can stop this. If I don't..." She didn't want to say much in front of the kids. The events of the evening had the potential to be seared into their psyches if she wasn't careful. "Stay with them and keep them safe."

Mikala saw the screen and her eyes widened. "Go. I got them. Go!"

Leighton ran for the stairs, thankful Mikala had seen the severity of the situation. "Use the cameras. Don't leave this floor."

She ran into Stefan coming up the stairs.

"You're supposed to stay upstairs. I got the alert while in the studio."

Leighton flew past him. "He's choking her!"

"Who?" His rapid footfalls echoed behind her.

"Casey!"

When Leighton pushed through the first-floor door, sirens screamed outside. She found Mark standing above Jeffrey, who appeared unconscious, blood pouring from his nose. Mark's hands were still balled into fists at his sides, and Leighton had witnessed nothing like the rage on his face in the time she'd known him. Behind him, Casey lay crumpled on the floor, and Maxine and Erica knelt beside her.

Leighton stepped over Jeffrey and rushed to her, pushing Erica aside.

Maxine called Casey's name and shook her shoulder. Leighton kneeled and pressed her fingers to Casey's neck to check for a pulse. It took a few tries, and her blood boiled as she touched the dark red marks in the shape of Jeffrey's fingers. Casey's pulse felt weak, but it was there. Leighton lowered her head and whimpered when she felt Casey's breath on her face.

"Casey. Casey, can you hear me? Darling, please wake up." Leighton repeated the words again and again. She glanced up to see a loose circle of concerned faces, except for Devin, who, even with his bleeding nose, had rolled Jeffrey onto his stomach, twisted one of his arms behind his back, and straddled him. Jeffrey would be subdued when he resumed consciousness.

"Casey, please. Please wake up. I need you. The thought of... I can't...without you." Leighton struggled to finish her sentence. "I can't lose you." She pressed her forehead to Casey's and squeezed her hand.

Casey's bravery left her speechless. The courage she'd showed protecting the children while sacrificing herself stunned Leighton. Her throat constricted and her eyes stung, but she refused to cry, refused to believe this was over. She cupped Casey's face without jostling her. "Please, darling."

Mark touched her shoulder. "Hey, the EMTs are here. Let's give them room to do their job, okay?"

Leighton moved aside for the emergency personnel. She'd hold Casey's hand until someone ordered her to do otherwise.

More emergency vehicles cut their sirens as they came to a halt in front of the building. The EMTs urged everyone back as they attended to the injured.

"How long has she been unconscious?" A wiry woman with short-cropped blond hair addressed Leighton as she kneeled.

"A few minutes. I'm not sure." It felt like hours. Leighton looked to Devin for help.

He shrugged as another EMT assessed his nose.

The woman shined a light in Casey's eyes, took her vitals, and palpated her neck.

Leighton, powerless to hurry things along, wanted to scream. Casey needed a hospital. She needed doctors. Why weren't these people hurrying?

"BP eighty over palp, heart rate one-eighteen, sats eighty-nine percent, GCS thirteen." The EMT held out her hand. "C-collar."

Leighton touched the arm of another EMT tapping on a tablet. "Is she going to be okay?"

He didn't look up. "There's no way to know for sure until we get her to the hospital. The doctors will give you an update as soon as they can."

"She may have an injury to the back of her head. Can you tell them that?"

"Yes, ma'am. They'll do a thorough assessment in the ER."

Stefan squeezed Leighton's shoulder so hard she flinched. He pointed to the entrance.

Phoenix stood in the doorway, looking as pale as Leighton's dress. "Somebody help. I need an EMT." He visibly shook.

A police officer squeezed past him. "Are you injured?" She glanced around the room.

"No, my friend is." Phoenix tugged her back outside.

"Where's Jaiden?"

Stefan's voice was never that high pitched. Leighton glanced around but didn't see him.

"Who sent the alert? Has anyone seen Jaiden?" Stefan turned in a circle. "Where the fuck is Jaiden?" He rushed toward the entrance and almost slammed into the returning officer.

She elbowed Stefan aside and tapped the EMT treating Devin's cut. "Unresponsive male out back. I can't find a pulse. I need your help."

"Hold this to your nose." The EMT pressed gauze into Devin's hand. "Someone will help you in a minute." He grabbed his bag and jumped up.

Stefan followed them, holding on to the door for a little too long, as though his legs might not carry him.

Leighton closed her eyes. Police officers responded to car accidents and violent crimes every day. If the officer hadn't been able to get Jaiden's pulse…

She trembled. For the second time that night, Leighton wished she could be in two places, but she couldn't leave Casey. She *wouldn't* leave Casey. Leighton refused to think how she might lose two people in her life tonight.

Maxine's phone clattered to the floor, but she didn't retrieve it. Instead, she looked at Leighton with wide eyes. "The alert came from Jaiden's phone."

A chill ran through Leighton even though the room was already freezing because of the open door. This couldn't be happening. Was she having a nightmare? As she fingered the stinging half-moons in her palm, acid swirled in her stomach much like the truth did in her head.

"Ma'am, you need to let go of her now."

Leighton was semi-aware of someone unfurling her fingers from Casey's hand. She tried to stand on shaky legs as the EMTs moved Casey onto a stretcher.

Casey looked so small.

Stefan returned, moving like he'd had his spine fused.

Leighton had never seen him so pale.

"They're doing CPR, but..." He shook his head.

She'd been strong up until that point, but it was too much. It was all too much. Leighton's tears dropped onto her dress.

Chapter Thirty-eight

Leighton looked up from Casey's bedside to find Maxine in the doorway. The hospital room didn't have a window, and Leighton didn't know the time. She'd dozed a few times while holding Casey's hand.

"How is she?" Maxine moved to the foot of the bed. Like her, she still wore her party attire.

Leighton shifted her stiff body in the uncomfortable chair and tugged the thin hospital blanket around her. Her dress left her chilled, and the blanket had lost its heat from the warmer hours ago.

"She regained consciousness on the way to the emergency room, and they said she was distraught. Once the doctors saw her, they gave her something to help her rest. Her neurological tests and scans came back fine, thank God." Leighton tucked Casey's blanket around her shoulder and tried to ignore the dark bruises springing up around her neck.

"Thank goodness." Maxine's sharp exhale echoed in the small room.

Leighton was so relieved Casey had awakened. It allayed some of her fears, and hospital personnel had been able to assess her condition better. Plus, if she'd remained unconscious, Leighton wasn't sure Casey would've wanted her family informed, and she would've had to make that decision. It would've taken some research to find them since Casey had listed Mark as her emergency contact on her paperwork for Atelier Vaughn.

"It was an exhausting ordeal, and she's been resting. We've spoken little. Her voice…" Casey sounded like a decades-long, two-packs-a-day smoker, and Leighton prayed her vocal cords would recover. "But the doctor said long-term damage was unlikely if it wasn't apparent in the initial work-up."

"That's good news, and Lord knows we could use some." Maxine set a bag on the end of the bed. "I brought you a change of clothing, a jacket, and some comfortable shoes. There are extras for her so she has something to wear when she's released."

"Thank you." Leighton exchanged it with the bag under the bed that held Casey's dress and shoes. "Could you please take her clothing with you and have it cleaned? I'll ask her if she wants to keep it or not. Seeing it again might be triggering. I know it was for me."

Tonight—or last night, since she had no idea of the time—she'd ruined her dress. The hem had ripped, and grime covered the lower half, but she didn't care. Casey was her primary concern now, though Kalyssa was never far from her mind. "Where are the kids?"

"With Aileen, asleep. She texted me a couple hours ago." Maxine moved a box of tissues and sat in the chair beside her. "I installed Kalyssa's booster seat into Aileen's car. She already had Andy's from bringing him to the party. I offered to take Kalyssa, but she was adamant she wanted to stay with Andy, and I didn't want to upset her further. If she wakes and changes her mind, Aileen has my number."

Leighton squeezed her arm. "That's fine. I trust Aileen. Kalyssa is protective of him, or maybe Aileen mentioned cookies before bed, so don't let her decision get to you."

Maxine straightened. "I'm not."

It'd been an evening wrought with complex emotions, and they needed to go easy on one another. The events had left Leighton raw, and Maxine likely suffered from emotional exhaustion, too.

"Did you watch the recording?" Leighton dreaded asking, but she had to know. She was heartbroken over what had transpired. Never in her worst nightmares would she have imagined the man she'd married would kill one of her students. Her heart went out to Jaiden's family likely grieving in another wing of Mount Sinai.

"Yes." Maxine stared at the foot of the bed and didn't elaborate.

Leighton squeezed her hand. "I'm sorry. I could've retrieved it for the police later. You didn't have to volunteer."

"I wanted to, for Jaiden, and so you didn't have to." She looked at Leighton with tears in her eyes. "He'd just thrown two bags of trash into the dumpster when Jeffrey emerged from the shadows. Jeffrey gestured toward the front of the building, and Jaiden held out his arms like he tried to stop him from heading that way. He shoved Jaiden in the chest. Jaiden stumbled, but regained his balance and pushed him back. Then Jaiden did that football player move." She mimicked the stance.

"The Heisman pose?" Leighton would've bet Maxine's football knowledge to be nonexistent.

"Yes. That's when he sent the alert."

Leighton could feel her shaking. "Are you able to tell me more?"

Maxine pulled a tissue from the box. "He looked up, and Jeffrey hit him. Jaiden's head hit the brick wall, and he landed face-down in the snow and didn't move. Jeffrey flexed his hand for a few seconds, then stumbled to the front of the building." A sob escaped her. "Jaiden never moved again, never picked up his phone glowing under the snow. I watched every second of the recording, including the moment Phoenix found him, the entire time they did CPR, when the medical examiner and crime scene techs did their thing, and when they took his body away. I figured we owed him, for someone to be witness to his heroic death, even if not in real-time."

Leighton let go of Casey's hand to wrap Maxine in a hug. On a normal day, Maxine wouldn't allow anything so demonstrative, but tonight she cried quiet sobs into her neck while Leighton rubbed her back.

"He's a hero. He put everyone's safety before his own. We'll never forget that." Leighton had told Jaiden's father as much when she'd spoken to him on the phone earlier. The police had already broken the news, but she wanted to offer his family her condolences. Part of her blamed herself for what happened, even though she had no control over Jeffrey's actions. Why hadn't she seen his true colors when she'd agreed to marry him? She hoped he'd be behind bars for a long time.

Maxine leaned back and discarded her used tissue for a fresh one. "I think we should return Jaiden's tuition to his family. They may not need it, but they can put it toward his funeral costs."

"I agree. It's the right thing to do." Leighton had been thinking the same. "When everything settles down, I want to reach out to his parents and set up a scholarship in his name. It might be nice to make it available to BIPOC students, if that's something they'd want."

"It's strange to think of someone taking his place next year." Maxine gave her nose the daintiest blow.

Casey stirred. Leighton pressed a hand to her arm, but she didn't wake.

Maxine inhaled. "I've been meaning to speak to you, but it's been so busy. I finished meeting with all the students to give them the opportunity to leave Atelier Vaughn with a full refund after what happened." She gestured between Leighton and Casey.

Leighton's stomach plummeted for the umpteenth time in as many hours.

"Everyone wanted to return, except Jenna."

Leighton covered her mouth. "Oh, no."

Maxine shook her head. "It's not like that. She's never fit in like your other students, and from what I've gathered, her father pressured her to apply. Even I noticed her paintings often left something to be desired. However, she seems to have found her calling in the gallery. Her volunteer hours double anyone else's. She has a natural gift for charming walk-in customers and loyal clients alike." Maxine crossed her legs. "They say that confidence comes from repeated success, and since she's been working in the gallery, hers has blossomed. She leads all students in gallery sales, though none of the paintings sold have been hers."

Leighton had been aware Maxine had taken Jenna under her wing, mentoring her in the intricacies and challenges of running a gallery. They appeared to have an affinity for one another. It wasn't uncommon to find them laughing and chatting over coffee.

"She won't be returning as a student, but I've offered her an internship as my assistant. Perhaps if she continues to show interest and be successful, we can offer her a job." Maxine fluttered her hand. "I'm not getting any younger, and I won't be doing this forever."

Leighton mulled it over. "I like this plan, although I don't enjoy thinking of you not being down there. How long do you think it will be before the atelier is making a profit? We'll have to consider all these changes, although thinking about finances moments after Jaiden's death feels wrong." Still, she'd only gained one additional investor and not a large one at that.

"Sales at the party were more than I expected. The gallery might make a bigger name for itself than the atelier, at least at first. Give it time."

Leighton looked at Casey. "What about her? Let's assume she'll make a full recovery. Do you envision her being a student next year? I'm willing to do whatever it takes to pay her tuition."

Maxine uncrossed and recrossed her legs. "Let's discuss that later."

Leighton's stomach did another nosedive.

"I watched other recordings while I was at the monitor. I wasn't aware of the chronology of events until then. Everything happened so fast." Maxine paused and gestured toward Casey. "She saw him first. In an instant, she picked up the kids and threw them in the elevator. I'm not exaggerating, Leighton. They say people can gain superhuman strength when under duress, and I witnessed it. She kept him at bay until the doors closed and the children were safe."

"Yes, and I'm forever grateful, but why did she put herself in harm's way after that? He couldn't have gotten upstairs without a code. She knew that." Leighton shook her head in bewilderment.

"Oh, my dear, that's not why she held her ground." Maxine touched Leighton's cheek. "She was afraid you'd come downstairs."

All the while, when she'd been so intent on getting to Casey, Casey had been protecting her. What had she ever done to deserve her? She kissed Casey's hand. "You brave, wonderful woman."

Casey's nurse rolled his computer station into the room. "Has she been awake?" He secured the loose tape on her IV.

"Just that one time."

"That's okay. Rest is good for her. Have her use the call button if she needs anything." He looked at a monitor and typed something into his computer before he rolled it out the door.

Maxine opened her purse and took out an unmarked, white envelope. "Please give this to her when she wakes. She'll want it."

Leighton turned it over. It was sealed. "What is it?"

"You'll have to ask her." Maxine busied herself clasping her purse closed.

Leighton set it on the hospital table beside Casey's water and her cold cup of coffee.

"You know, I wasn't honest with you." Maxine fiddled with her rings.

Leighton's mind raced. "When?"

"When we talked about your mother and me. We were never unfaithful to our husbands, but as you know, I stayed late into the night while she was in the hospital. I assumed it was because of her pain medication, but one night, she asked me to kiss her, and I did. After, I asked her why. Deborah had requested nothing like that in all our years of friendship. She said she wanted something beautiful to have when she moved on." Maxine pressed her lips together. "She died the next morning." A tear streaked down her cheek, but she didn't seem to care.

Leighton slipped an arm around her. "She loved you. It makes sense that she'd want to remember the love of her life at the end." It pleased her to know her mother and Maxine had found soulmates, even if their situation had been far from ideal.

Maxine rested her head on her shoulder. They stayed like that for a few minutes. Then Maxine stood.

"Keep holding her hand and give her that envelope. Tell her we're all thinking about her, and neither of you needs to worry about the kids. Aileen and I will take care of them as long as it takes. Be here for her right now." Maxine kissed Leighton's cheek. "I love you." She gently touched Casey's leg, took her purse and the bag, and left.

Leighton's phone had died, and she didn't have a charger with her. In a bit, she'd ask if someone working at the circular desk in the hall had one. Casey's nurse had encouraged her to get something to eat or drink, but she'd declined. She'd eat when Casey ate.

She dozed.

When she woke, fingers combed through her hair. Her head rested on something, an arm. Casey's arm. Leighton raised her head, and Casey smiled at her.

"Hi." Her voice sounded raspy.

Afraid of crying if she spoke, Leighton kissed the back of Casey's hand, turned it over, and kissed her palm.

Casey motioned to the cup of water, and Leighton gave it to her. After a few sips, she licked her lips.

"Are you in pain?" Leighton rubbed the rough hospital blanket over Casey's leg.

Casey squinted, like she took inventory. "Tired mostly." She switched to a whisper. "My throat hurts, and I have a headache, but I think I'm okay." She sipped her water, then handed it to Leighton. "Where's Andy?"

Leighton squeezed her fingers. "Asleep at Aileen's. You don't need to worry about him."

"Was he upset?"

"Only for a minute, but he and Kalyssa are fine, thanks to you. They watched cartoons through most of the activity. Maxine and Aileen took care of getting the kids settled. I needed to be with you." Leighton blinked away her tears. "Maxine would've said if there were any problems. Kalyssa is with him. I'll check on them in the morning, and I can bring them to visit you tomorrow. Mark will want to come, too, I'm sure. I convinced him to go home instead of sleeping on the floor at the foot of your bed."

Casey's eyes glazed over. "When I woke, I thought I'd been dreaming. Then I realized where I was. It really happened, didn't it?" She still looked a bit disoriented.

"It did, sweetheart. How much do you recall?" Leighton caressed her hand as different emotions flickered across Casey's face.

She gingerly touched her throat. "I remember his hands around my neck, and I couldn't breathe. Then nothing until I woke up in the ambulance or maybe when I got here. I'm not sure. It's all sort of fuzzy."

"I'm sure it is." What a nightmare it must have been for Casey in those last few seconds, knowing she was being strangled and not being able to do anything about it.

"What happened? Where's Jeffrey now? What made him stop?" Casey looked at her through narrowed eyes, her beautiful features twisted in confusion.

Leighton hesitated, unsure of how much to tell her. She didn't want to inflict any additional trauma on her while in such a fragile state, but if she were in Casey's position, she'd want to know. "Mark saved your life. I wasn't there. I was still running down the stairs, but Maxine said when Erica got him from the back gallery and he saw Jeffrey choking you, he flew across the room and punched him out. She assured me Jeffrey was unconscious before he hit the floor."

"Mark did that?" Casey appeared to picture it. "I don't think he's ever hit someone before."

"He probably never had a reason to." Leighton knew they were close, best friends since college, close enough for him to give Casey the child she wanted and for her to accept. It surprised her none that Mark hadn't hesitated to step in and save her. Leighton could kiss him for what he'd done, for saving the life of the woman she loved. She just wished she'd been there for it.

And now, she wished she didn't have to tell her the rest, but Casey had a right to know. Jaiden was her friend, too. She took a breath. "Darling, I'm afraid I have something else to tell you." The tip of Leighton's nose stung like it always did before she cried. "The alert? Jaiden sent it to warn us. He was taking out the garbage and Jeffrey punched him. Jaiden hit his head on the bricks and never regained consciousness. They did their best to save him, but he died, darling."

Casey was already crying. "No." She tried to cover her face with her hand.

Leighton set the box of tissues on the bed and gently caressed her arm. "I know he was your friend, and you were both so brave. He tried to protect us, and it cost him his life. You protected the kids and me, and…" She motioned toward the growing rainbow on Casey's neck. "I thought I'd lost you." More tears cascaded as she kissed Casey's fingers.

Casey's eyes held such tenderness. "You did?"

Leighton leaned closer, wanting to be near her, wanting to hold her. "The past few weeks have been torture, yet when I saw his hands around your neck on the camera, they paled in comparison. When you lay unconscious on the floor, everything changed. After experiencing that, I'll never be the same. I saw what life without you looks like, and that's not a life I'm interested in living. I'd known it before, but I'd never felt it as strongly as I did kneeling beside you before the EMTs arrived." She kissed Casey's hand. "I love you."

Something between a joyous laugh and a sob escaped Casey. She opened her arms and Leighton moved into her embrace. Casey kissed her. "I love you, too," she said against her lips. "These past few weeks, I realized just how in love with you I am. I also realized the extent I'd go to show you."

Leighton tamed a lock of Casey's hair. "By protecting the kids?"

"No, the night turned out different from what I'd planned." Casey seemed lost in thought. "I had something I wanted to give you."

Leighton remembered the envelope. "Would it be this, by chance? Maxine brought it and asked me to give it to you."

Casey beamed. Her smile seemed so contradictory to the bruising on her neck. "Yes, I think it is. Open it."

"Me?" Leighton flicked her nail under the flap.

With a warm smile, Casey nodded.

Leighton removed the pages. Whatever it was, it looked official. She recognized the name of the law firm Maxine used. As she read the papers, her vision blurred. When she reached the end, she touched Casey's signature.

"You didn't have to do this." She laid the papers in her lap and blotted her eyes with a tissue.

"I did." Casey rubbed Leighton's arm. "I'd do whatever it takes to be with you."

Leighton cradled Casey's face and kissed her. "The next few years will be difficult, but I can't imagine surviving them without you by my side. Even if the atelier isn't profitable, as long as you're with me, everything will be okay." Her heart might burst.

Casey touched her face. "Shh, we'll figure it out together. It's not insurmountable."

Leighton loved her willfulness. Casey had always possessed determination in spades.

"The agreement was Maxine's idea. She wanted to protect you, but I don't think she's as opposed to the idea of us as she might've once led us to believe." Casey adjusted her IV's tubing.

"No, I don't think she is." Thoughts of Maxine and her mother rushed in. She'd share that story with Casey when the time was right.

"It was her idea, but I had no choice but to sign since you're the only one Andy wants to read him bedtime stories." Casey winked. "What's a mom to do?" She slipped her hand behind Leighton's neck and kissed her again.

It was soft and languid, as if they might not know what the future held, but they had a future together, and they'd figure everything out in time. Nothing needed to be rushed right now.

Someone cleared their throat.

Casey eased away from Leighton to find Mark standing in the doorway.

"Hi."

She waved him closer. "Hey."

Leighton stood. "I thought you went home to sleep."

His tense shrug contradicted his nonchalant posture. "I tried, but I couldn't, not when I didn't know how Casey was doing."

Leighton wrapped him in a hug, then pulled him into the room. "I would have texted to tell you she's awake, but my phone died."

"Yeah, I figured. I tried calling, but it went straight to voice mail." He sat on the end of Casey's bed, turning his attention toward her. "I wanted to see for myself that you're okay."

She gave him two thumbs up, making him laugh.

"Here." Leighton folded the blanket she'd been using. "Take my seat. I need to change into more comfortable clothing and get a fresh coffee. Can I bring you anything?"

"No, thanks." Casey and Mark spoke in unison.

When Leighton had gone, an awkward silence descended on them. Clearly, Leighton had left to give them privacy. Casey was grateful, though she didn't know where to begin.

"You're whispering." Mark touched his neck. "Is it painful?"

"Not really, but they probably gave me something." She coughed, and Mark moved her cup of water closer. She took a sip. "I'm lying here trying to think of the appropriate way to thank you for saving my life, but nothing that comes to mind seems worthy enough."

He squeezed her arm. "You don't have to thank me. I'd do anything for you. You know that."

Emotion swelled in her chest, and she bit back tears. "If I didn't know it before, I certainly do now. And of course I owe you a thank you. So, thank you." She brought his hand to her lips and kissed it. "Not only for my sake, but Andy's, too."

"You would have done the same for me."

She tried to laugh, but it made her throat feel raw. "I would have tried, but let's hope I never have to repay the favor. Or I need to get a gym membership." She studied him, his red eyes and pale skin, and the plain gray sweatshirt whose seams faced outward, as if he'd dressed in a hurry in the dark. "Thanks to you, I'm okay."

He nodded brusquely, eyes downcast. "Yeah. When I saw that asshole's hands on you…"

He didn't finish, but he didn't need to. They'd known each other long enough to finish one another's sentences.

"I can imagine. I suppose you already know about Jaiden." Again, her tears came as the realization she'd never see her friend again hit a second time.

"Yeah. I saw his family for a few minutes before I went home. There must have been forty people down there for him." Mark sniffed. "I spoke to his mom and his girlfriend, then left them to grieve. I couldn't just leave, you know?"

"I can't remember the last thing I said to him, or him to me." She used a tissue to dry the wet trails on her cheeks.

"Come here." Mark took her in his arms. "You will. You've been through a lot."

"I don't even know what time it is or what day it is." She wasn't sure why it mattered, but it did.

Mark released her and pulled out his phone. "Almost four in the morning. Why?"

She placed her hand on her forehead. "I'm not sure. Everything feels foggy and confusing."

"You went through something traumatic. The time or day isn't important. Just rest and recover so we can get you out of here." His rapid blinking made him look even more fatigued.

"Will you go home and sleep now that you know I'm okay?" She took his hand again. "You've been through a lot, too." She noticed the abrasions on the knuckles on his other one for the first time.

He grinned. "Are you worried about me, or do you have more plans for kissing when Leighton gets back?"

Casey considered how to answer honestly. "Yes."

Mark had worried enough about her in one day to last a lifetime, and it showed. Later, she'd tell him what wonderful things had transpired between her and Leighton, but he was right. Time didn't matter right now, and it could wait.

❖

Upon her release from the hospital, Casey accepted Leighton's offer to let her and Andy stay with them while she recuperated, even though the assault had happened in the same building. She'd needed to steel herself before she entered the gallery. However, the episode had exhausted her, and she didn't want to be alone. Besides, her bed and Andy's crib made her bedroom cramped. It's not like Leighton and Kalyssa could stay with them. Leighton's help with Andy would be welcome, too.

Her neck had started to turn a color between yellow ochre and olive green. She wore a turtleneck so she didn't recall the incident every time she looked in the mirror. In addition, they hadn't told the kids what had happened and didn't plan to. She and Leighton believed in preserving childhood innocence as long as possible. If she covered her bruises, it prevented questions she wasn't sure how to answer. It might have been unnecessary, because an open-ended sleepover excited the kids too much for anything else to matter.

Andy and Kalyssa had spent an eventful day with Aileen ice skating and making fudge. Leighton had craved the pizza she'd eaten at Casey's, so while Casey napped, she'd found a location in Queens and called in a delivery order.

An hour later, they gathered around the table and ate. Kalyssa and Andy regaled them with snippets of their ice skating adventure. After,

Leighton allowed the children one piece of fudge each after musing how she'd bet they'd eaten their weight in it earlier in the day. She impressed Casey with how quickly she'd picked up on how life worked at Aileen's. Between the two activities, Kalyssa seemed to have found a kindred spirit in Aileen. Perhaps Leighton had, too. Casey saw her sneak more than a few pieces Aileen had sent home.

After giving Casey strict orders to sit and rest, Leighton cleaned up dinner, washed fudgy fingers and faces, and helped the kids into their pajamas. With the four of them snuggled on the couch, she read Kalyssa and Andy a bedtime story and then tucked them into Kalyssa's bed. She kissed both children, so Casey did, too.

Depending on another person wasn't so bad. It felt nice not to have all the responsibility fall on her.

Leighton lit a fire. They reclined on the couch and enjoyed the quiet. After a while, Casey turned to face her. The random patterns Leighton had been drawing on Casey's hip had moved past distracting. She pressed a kiss to Leighton's collarbone and slid her hands beneath her shirt.

"Casey." Leighton's tone carried a warning.

Casey grazed her skin with her teeth.

Leighton sighed. "Don't you think it's too soon?"

They hadn't had sex since the night of the exhibition. Casey kissed up the incline of her neck. "No. I'm ready, very ready." It was all she'd been thinking about for some time.

Leighton caressed her face. "I don't want to hurt you. You just got out of the hospital."

"You won't." Casey pulled down her collar and fingered where the bruises were the worst. "Avoid this area or just be gentle." She slipped her hands under Leighton's shirt again, higher this time. "Gentle." She caressed her breasts with a touch so light Leighton's nipples tickled her palms, and it made Casey shiver.

Her touch seemed to have a different effect on Leighton, whose breathing caught. Leighton pressed her into the cushions and kissed her. Their mouths met, wild and hungry, and soon their panting eclipsed the sound of the fire. Leighton kissed a path from the corner of Casey's mouth to her jaw, to her ear, then stopped. She pulled back her collar and looked at her neck. With a precision Casey had learned was part of her personality, Leighton appeared to choose which places were fit to kiss. Even when she did, her lips felt like a puff of air or the touch of a butterfly's wing, so featherlight that Casey wasn't sure they'd happened at all.

She moved lower, kneading and kissing Casey's breasts through her shirt. "Take it off."

Leighton gave her room, and Casey pulled it over her head. Leighton's mouth was on her in a flash, and she pushed her hand past the waistband of Casey's yoga pants. She cupped Casey through her underwear and rubbed where the wet fabric clung to her. Then she slipped her hand inside.

Casey pushed Leighton's shirt over her breasts, then shifted their bodies so they faced one another. "I need to touch you, too." She pulled at the strings tying Leighton's sweats. Her hurry was real. Leighton already had two fingers inside her.

"I need a bigger couch."

Her exasperation made Casey laugh.

Leighton stopped and smiled at her. "I love it when you laugh like that, so pure and full of delight." She caressed her cheek. "Hearing it fills me with—I don't know—joy."

"Aren't you sweet?" Casey slid her hand past Leighton's waistband. "We have plenty of laughter in our future, among other things." She dipped her fingers into Leighton's arousal. "I look forward to many things with you."

"Sexual things?" Leighton stroked inside her.

Casey moaned. "Yes, and much more." She liked how they talked a bit during lovemaking. When she'd had sex with people who were silent the entire time, it'd felt impersonal. She'd also learned in their one night together that a few choice words, not even dirty ones, at the right time could have quite the effect on Leighton.

Though at the moment, she was having difficulty stringing words together.

Leighton pressed her palm against her like she was trying to make her come like *she* needed it, like all she wanted was to watch Casey come undone. The thought sent a wave of heat through her. It was working. Even so, Casey needed to touch her. Feeling how much she aroused her and watching Leighton respond were powerful turn-ons.

Leighton slung her leg over Casey's hip, and Casey slipped inside her. Every one of Leighton's thrusts rocked her against the couch. Casey tried to match her pace, but it was useless. Pleasure coiled inside, ready to strike.

"Look at me." Leighton slowed, her strokes purposeful and precise.

She met Leighton's soft gaze, held it as long as she could, and came. For the duration of her orgasm, she floated, just letting it take her. She didn't recall closing them, but when she opened her eyes, Leighton wore the most peaceful and proud expression.

Casey exhaled. "God. Incredible." She rested her forehead against Leighton's neck and pressed a kiss to her hot, damp skin. "Where was I?" She moved her fingers, and Leighton jumped. "Do you want my mouth?" Casey kissed her collarbone.

"No, just like this, so I can see you." Leighton tilted Casey's face so their mouths met. Her tongue was hot and fast, stroking against Casey's with urgency.

Casey did the same with her fingers and used her palm to give Leighton that needed pressure. At this angle, its effectiveness was uncertain, although Leighton surged her hips to meet each thrust. Leighton's request to stay close pleased her. She also needed the intimate connection.

She nudged Leighton's shirt aside and sucked her nipple into her mouth. Leighton moaned, so she moved to the other one. Casey moved up to taste her, to meld their mouths, and together, they found a rhythm.

Casey paused to breathe. "If you don't come soon, I'll have to bend you over the back of this sofa again." She nipped her earlobe.

Leighton came with a small cry against her neck.

"Yes, just like that." She gentled her movements and smiled. A few choice words. She couldn't quite wrap her head around the fact she had that effect on Leighton.

After a few minutes of lazy kisses, Casey turned and pulled Leighton's arm around her. Leighton nuzzled the back of her neck, and a pleasantness enveloped her. She felt safe, cherished, and satisfied. Casey hummed in contentment. "It's hard to beat this."

Leighton kissed her neck. "I agree."

Casey watched the snow falling outside the window. It was almost Christmas. She hadn't asked what plans Leighton had for the holiday. She didn't know whether Leighton was a shop-throughout-the-year type of person or did everything at the last minute. They had much to learn about one another, and she smiled at the welcome thought. "What do you want to do tomorrow?"

Leighton pulled her closer. "Buy a bigger couch."

❖

Casey opened her eyes to the sun streaming through the sheer curtains. After a night of lovemaking, it appeared Leighton had let her sleep. She brushed her teeth, slipped on a turtleneck, and wandered to the kitchen. Kalyssa and Andy ate scrambled eggs and cinnamon raisin toast at the island.

"Good morning." Leighton kissed her. "Hungry?"

She was. Leighton dropped two pieces of bread in the toaster and whisked a couple of eggs.

"Coffee?"

"Sure." Casey moved Andy's hand away from Kalyssa's plate, where he pretended to drive his toast train. "Manners, young man." She kissed his temple.

"I need to run some errands." Leighton poured the eggs into a pan. "I'm going to take the kids with me so you can rest."

"Where are you going?" She'd been through a lot but didn't want Leighton to get in the habit of thinking she was fragile. "I don't think I can rest much more than I already am."

"You rested in the hospital." Kalyssa picked a raisin from her toast. "Mom let us share your pudding while you were snoring."

Andy nodded.

Casey ran her fingers through Kalyssa's hair. "I don't mind sharing with you."

"We'll be back in a couple hours." Leighton glanced at them. "I'll make lunch when we get home."

Casey smiled. "I could get used to this. Where are you going?" Wherever it was, Leighton probably didn't need the kids with her but instead worried about Casey exerting energy watching them.

"You can only know about part of our errands. I'm taking your apartment key and picking up some clothing and toiletries for you and Andy. I've already arranged it with Mark." Leighton buttered the toast.

Andy grinned. "Mark."

Leighton smiled. "Yes, we'll see Mark today."

"You don't have to do that." She didn't want to impose.

"Nonsense," Leighton said, without looking up. "Other than spending time at Aileen's on Christmas Day, what other plans do you have for the holidays?"

"Just that, but I hoped you and Kalyssa could join us. Aileen's expecting you." Casey's stomach growled as Leighton slid the eggs onto her plate.

"That was nice of her to offer, but it won't be too much?" Leighton set the pan in the sink.

"She's planning on it." Casey put on her most serious face. "If you don't, there will be leftovers for days, and I don't like ham that much."

"Since Aileen mentioned eating at two, perhaps we could all go to Maxine's afterward. Her Christmas dinner is usually around seven. She hoped you and Andy could join us."

Casey swallowed a bite of toast. "That would be nice."

"It might be." Leighton arched an eyebrow. "It depends on whether she's also serving ham."

Casey laughed but became thoughtful. "I guess we've made holiday plans for our little ensemble, haven't we?" It was too soon to think of the four of them as a family, but Casey enjoyed the momentary fantasy as she watched the kids eating side by side.

"I suppose we have. Then it's settled. You and Andy can stay here through Christmas or even New Year's." Leighton gave her what looked like a hopeful smile.

"Okay." Casey tried not to grin too wide before taking a bite of egg. "What's your other errand?"

"It's a surprise." Leighton's eyes twinkled.

"I'll be right here resting and waiting then." A sense of weightlessness pervaded her as she finished her breakfast. What she'd said was true. She could get used to this.

❖

When Leighton and the kids returned to the loft less than two hours later, a six-foot-tall Douglas fir accompanied their exuberant faces. The sweet evergreen smell intermingled with the cinnamon-scented candle burning on the mantle.

Casey matched their smiles. She rose from the sofa to keep the tree upright while they removed their winter wear. Andy sat on the floor to tug off his boots, and Kalyssa bent to help him unzip his jacket. Casey might melt if they got any cuter.

"You can relax and watch us." Leighton waved a hand toward the sofa where Casey had been reading.

"Not a chance. I'm not missing out on decorating our first Christmas tree." She froze, aware of the implicit meaning behind her words. Certain her face was flushed, she glanced at her feet.

Leighton came to her, held her face in the tenderest of touches, and pressed their lips together. When she pulled back, her eyes shone with wonder. "Good. Then, what do you say we make some ornaments and decorate our tree?" She brushed their lips together again.

"I'd like that." Casey looked at her sap-covered hand still holding the trunk. "Could we put it in a stand first?"

From where Casey lay with Leighton on the couch, she absorbed the surrounding warmth, not only Leighton, but the children sprawled on the rug in front of the TV where Rudolph and his friends played their reindeer games, and the tree in the corner with its twinkling lights and mixture of store-bought and handmade ornaments. It looked perfect, but how could it be anything else? It was theirs.

Leighton brushed her lips along Casey's cheek and whispered in her ear. "I'm sorry, I know it hasn't been that long, but I'm afraid I'm going to need you after the kids go to bed."

Casey twisted to face her. "Never apologize for wanting sex. I enjoy knowing what you need." She traced Leighton's jaw. "There may be times—far down the road, of course—when I don't have it in me, but I'd be happy to watch you. Or you might persuade me to help you finish. Let's just be truthful about what we need."

Leighton nodded. "You *are* an old soul, aren't you?" She kissed Casey's shoulder. "I have a gift for you, and I can't wait any longer to give it to you."

"Oh, really?" Her throat wasn't as sore as it'd been in the hospital, so she'd attempted a sexy voice.

Leighton swatted her hip. "Not that kind."

"It's not Christmas yet." Casey had always opened gifts on Christmas morning.

"It's homemade and unrelated to the holiday. I've been working on something."

"I heard you've been painting." Rumors about Leighton's mysterious piece had filled the last few weeks. She'd heard theories ranging from a commissioned portrait of the first female vice president to a nude vignette of Banksy. It was times like these she missed Jaiden. No doubt he'd come up with that hilarious rumor.

However, all along, Casey's intuition had told her Leighton painted whatever it was for her. Anticipation made her want to jump up.

"It's a personal gift, one that comes from my heart." Leighton brushed a strand of hair from Casey's forehead. "So, are you ready?"

Casey grinned and nodded.

"Come with me. Get up slowly."

Leighton hadn't stopped fretting about her since the minute they'd left the hospital.

Casey assumed Leighton had hidden the painting in the guest room. The door had been closed since she'd arrived. However, Leighton led her into the kitchen instead. She opened a drawer and withdrew a small white box. It was the length of a remote control, but twice as tall. She handed it to Casey.

Casey forced a smile, though her cheeks quivered. She'd been sure the painting was for her. Unless Leighton had switched to miniatures, her gift was something else. If that was the case, why was Leighton so secretive about the mysterious piece of art?

She stared at the box. It was the wrong size for jewelry. She lifted off the top and looked inside. When she glanced up, Leighton beamed.

Inside were four wooden children's blocks. K, W, S, and O. She tried to decipher it. Was it an acronym? It didn't mean anything to her. Nothing became obvious when she reordered them in her mind. She saw nothing underneath, not even tissue paper. "I don't understand." She looked up.

Leighton seemed to enjoy the moment. "Let me show you." She took it. "Come with me."

Casey followed her down the hallway where she stopped before the guest room door. Leighton opened it a few inches to reach in and turn on the light. A gush of cold air rushed out along with the unmistakable odor of paint. Leighton pushed the door open and stepped aside so Casey could enter.

Leighton had painted the room cerulean blue and sage green. An undulating border circled the room a third of the way up the walls. A twin bed, accompanied by a dresser and desk that matched the headboard, had replaced the previous queen. On the open windowsill, a box fan exchanged the air.

All these items registered with her, but Casey focused on one thing: the border. It wasn't an ordinary one. Leighton hadn't purchased or stenciled it. Where the blue and green met, the sky turned into hills. Along the hills ran train tracks, and along the tracks ran a train almost all the way around the room. Where the border disappeared behind the dresser, the train entered a tunnel on one side and exited on the opposite.

Extraordinary, hand-painted details made it become something spectacular. From the shiny black engine trailing smoke to the many cars carrying cargo like logs, coal, rocks, animals, and toys, Leighton had painted each tiny object with care, humor, and precision. Casey could look at the intricate scene a hundred times and notice something new. It was a work of art. Leighton had sketched the preliminary lines for the caboose, but she hadn't finished it.

Leighton stopped beside the dresser and held the box over the top. When she had Casey's attention, she flipped it and lifted it away to reveal the blocks underneath.

Casey read the letters that now faced her: A-N-D-Y. She shook her head in disbelief. She'd been smiling since seeing the train, but seeing her son's name on the dresser amid this wonderful panorama made her chest tighten. Andy had never had his own room. Casey covered her stinging eyes with her hands when she realized that this was what Leighton had been working on the past few weeks, the most important work she'd ever painted, according to Stefan, and what Leighton had called a gift that came from her heart, one for her and Andy.

Leighton rested her hands on Casey's hips. "It wasn't supposed to make you cry. I hated the guest room, anyway." She pulled her into a hug.

Casey laughed against her chest.

"Will you and Andy move in with us?"

Casey loved how Leighton always included the children, but she hesitated accepting her offer and took a step back. "This is amazing, and I want to…"

Leighton stiffened.

"But I have to think about Mark. It wouldn't feel right leaving him to cover rent or forcing him to find a roommate with little notice."

"But you're not opposed?" Leighton touched her again, a light press of hands on her sides.

Casey couldn't suppress her grin. "No, just the opposite."

Leighton became serious. "You know, Phoenix might be interested in rooming with someone after Jaiden…" She bowed her head.

"He and Mark get along well." Casey lifted Leighton's chin. "I'll talk to Mark tomorrow and suggest it. Phoenix will need some extra support after what happened, and having to face an empty apartment every night doesn't seem the best way for him to move forward. They'd all grown so close. Maybe they could lean on each other."

Leighton's shoulders appeared to relax. "And if they agree?"

"Then, yes. Yes." Casey threw her arms around Leighton's neck and buried her face in her hair. She pulled back far enough to look at her. "Even if they don't want to be roommates, I'll help Mark find someone. I don't want to leave him in the lurch."

"You could always continue paying your half of the rent until he does."

Casey shook her head. "I'll help him find someone whether it's Phoenix or someone else. Who knows, maybe Devin is ready to live on his own and not with his family. Either way, I intend to contribute to our home at least what I'm paying now. I'm not looking for a handout."

Leighton closed her eyes for a moment. "I'd never think that."

"Still, I'd like to help support us." Casey turned in a circle, following the train across all four walls. "This is amazing. *You're* amazing. I can't believe you painted this." She went up on tiptoes to press their lips together. "I love you."

"And I love you." Leighton's eyes looked just as watery as hers.

After a few minutes of soft, slow, meaningful kisses, they parted.

Casey looked around, trying to absorb it all. "Are you going to show Andy?"

"Why don't we show them both? Kalyssa hasn't seen it either." Leighton gave her a pointed look. "Four-year-olds aren't great with secrets, you know."

Leighton pulled the children away from their movie with a promise they could finish it in a few minutes. She led them into the room and stood beside Casey. The kids gravitated to the train.

Andy, who sometimes spoke little or only when necessary, had a hundred different things to point out while he implored them to, "Look, look!" Leighton's efforts had plastered a dimpled grin on his face. He giggled when he noticed the giraffes' heads sticking out of the top of a boxcar and the clown whose bouncy balls had fallen off the train and rolled down the hillside.

"Mom, I didn't know this was in here." Kalyssa took Leighton's hand.

"It was a surprise." Leighton smoothed her hair.

Kalyssa tilted her head. "For Andy?"

"Yes."

"Did you paint it?"

"I did." Leighton dropped to a knee. "Would you like it if we painted something on the walls in your room?"

Kalyssa shuffled her feet. "You painted this for Andy?"

"Yes, I did, but I'll paint something for you. You can help me." Leighton kissed her.

Kalyssa looked at her with the most earnest expression. "If you painted this for Andy, can Casey paint something in my room?"

"I think you should ask her, darling." Leighton smiled at Casey.

Kalyssa turned to her. Casey loved how she raised her eyebrows, just like Leighton. Casey smiled and nodded.

Leighton rubbed her hands together. "Casey should probably live with us if she's going to be doing a lot of painting in your room. Don't you think?"

"And Andy can sleep in here." Kalyssa pointed to the bed.

Casey crouched beside Andy. "Leighton painted this for you, baby."

He put his arm around Leighton and leaned his head on her shoulder. Then he tugged on her hand. She stood and followed him to the end of the train.

He looked at her with his large brown eyes and pointed to the unfinished caboose. "Paint this?"

Leighton ran her fingers through his hair. "Yes, darling. I'll paint that for you, too."

The smile she gave Casey couldn't have contained much more joy.

Leighton's revelation seemed to have gone just as she'd hoped or better, and Casey had to work to contain her elation. While she couldn't compete with Leighton's gift, she expected Leighton to like the present she'd bought. Casey had purchased the Sennelier soft pastel set Leighton had admired at the art store. She'd save it for Christmas morning.

Casey rested her hand on Leighton's back and watched the three people she loved most in the world, happy and thankful she'd been lucky enough to escape harm to share this life with them. She leaned close and whispered into Leighton's ear. "It's the most beautiful painting I've ever seen."

Leighton beamed and cradled her cheek. "Now that's what I call a compliment."

EPILOGUE

Leighton held Andy's hand and admired the exquisite painting while Kalyssa practiced pirouettes on the other side of the room. The life-sized female nude faced three-quarters away. She held a tall rod, and drapery gathered around her feet. From the composition Casey had chosen, Leighton wouldn't have recognized herself as the model if she hadn't known.

A blue ribbon beside the painting announced its first-place status. Leighton had expected the win. While Leighton still painted and garnered success by anyone's standards, Casey had been winning every event she entered for the better part of a year. The magazines that featured her paintings took up half a shelf on their bookcase.

She deserved the recognition. Ever since they'd become a couple and moved in together, Casey's magic with a brush had returned. Apparently, she was one of those artists who needed to be happy to create beautiful things. Her monetary awards had been helpful, too. Casey's winnings and their combined gallery sales had put Atelier Vaughn back in the black.

Andy assessed the painting, his head cocked to the side. "She's not wearing any clothes."

Not that her nudity embarrassed her—she looked damn fine—but Andy didn't need to know she was the model. "No, she's not. Some artists believe the female body is the ultimate form of beauty."

He screwed up his face even more. "Does Momma?" His personality hadn't changed a bit in the three years she'd known him.

"She does, and so do I."

Andy huffed and pulled at the collar of his suit jacket. "This is itchy, Mom."

Leighton looked at the red welt on the back of his neck. "It's the tag, baby. You can take it off. We're almost finished."

Kalyssa spun into Leighton's personal space, her dress swirling around her slender legs as she came to a stop. "Andy, let's go climb the marble steps."

"Don't go too far." Leighton's heart did a little leap as they ran off. They'd formed a relationship somewhere between best friends and brother and sister. It was far more than she could've hoped.

Casey entered the gallery. Leighton never tired of watching her cross a room, especially when she looked so beautiful, her hair blown straight and her makeup subtle yet striking. Beauty aside, Leighton still marveled at her determination, talent, intelligence, kindness, and bravery.

Leighton's failed marriage had convinced her she'd never give her heart to anyone again. Yet there it was, walking toward her. She was so in love she could barely breathe.

"Did you find the restroom all right?" She touched the small of Casey's back.

Casey nodded. "Yes, it just takes me a hot minute to deal with this dress."

They faced her painting. Leighton put an arm around her shoulders, and Casey curled hers around her waist.

Leighton tapped her lower lip. "It's wonderful, you know. The lines of her hips and shoulders lead the viewer through the painting, and the curvature of the drapery brings your eye back around. The softness of your edges over here and the lost edges in this passage—it's stunning." She looked at her. "I once said I worried there was nothing more I could teach you."

Casey chuckled. "I remember."

Leighton narrowed her eyes. "I hate being right all the time."

A crease formed between Casey's brows. "You're not."

Leighton put a hand on her hip. "Do you have a specific instance in mind?"

"I do." Casey lifted her chin.

Leighton lifted Casey's hand. "I was right that you'd want a platinum band and an oval cut so the diamond didn't catch on your clothing." She touched the ring.

Casey's dimples appeared. "Yes, in that singular instance, you were right."

Leighton loved their verbal sparring that never turned out to be serious. "Just tell me the one time I was wrong instead of making me guess."

"Ha! One time." Her eyes sparkled. "Running late didn't allow me to tell you everything about my appointment today."

Leighton flinched. To her dismay, she'd been called for jury duty and couldn't accompany her. "Is everything all right?"

"Yes." Casey pressed Leighton's hand to her stomach. "You thought we're having a girl, but we're not. We're having a boy." She smiled widely, and her eyes shone.

Leighton sucked in a breath. She'd never been so happy to be wrong. Her wife was pregnant with their son. Their other son attended kindergarten, and their daughter spent her time obsessed with ballet and boys, though perhaps not in that order. "A boy." Tears obscured her vision.

"Yes, my love, a boy." Casey kissed her, soft and tame but full of emotion. "We're having a boy. You, me, and our three children. Can you believe it? We'll need to add a fourth floor if our little family keeps growing." Her infectious smile lit the room.

Leighton held her close. "We need to tell Aileen and Maxine, but I want to wait a bit before we send them into new grandma-mode again. Let's celebrate this between us for a few days."

"I'd like that." Casey cupped her cheek before giving her a quick peck. "Now, please take me home so I can change out of this dress and kick off these heels."

Home. The building where they'd met, where they taught what they loved, and where they raised their family. The place where Leighton had almost lost Casey. Instead, they'd built a beautiful life inside, a life Leighton wasn't sure she'd ever have.

Once upon a time, Leighton had believed Casey to be the missing piece that would bring success to her atelier, but how wrong she'd been. Casey had come to mean so much more. She'd been everything Leighton had been missing in her life.

As she took Casey's hand and led her out of the gallery in search of the children, Leighton wondered exactly how *many* bedrooms they could fit on a potential fourth floor.

About the Author

Alaina Erdell lives in Ohio with her partner and their crazy but adorable cats. Prior to writing, she worked as a chef. When she's not focused on writing romances, she enjoys painting, cooking for friends and family, experimenting with molecular gastronomy, reading, kayaking, snorkeling, traveling, and spending time with her beloved nephews.

Books Available from Bold Strokes Books

All Things Beautiful by Alaina Erdell. Casey Norford only planned to learn to paint like her mentor, Leighton Vaughn, not sleep with her. (978-1-63679-479-2)

Appalachian Awakening by Nance Sparks. The more Amber's and Leslie's paths cross, the more this hike of a lifetime begins to look like a love of a lifetime. (978-1-63679-527-0)

Dreamer by Kris Bryant. When life seems to be too good to be true and love is within reach, Sawyer and Macey discover the truth about the town of Ladybug Junction, and the cold light of reality tests the hearts of these dreamers. (978-1-63679-378-8)

Eyes on Her by Eden Darry. When increasingly violent acts of sabotage threaten to derail the opening of her glamping business, Callie Pope is sure her ex, Jules, has something to do with it. But Jules is dead...isn't she? (978-1-63679-214-9)

Head Over Heelflip by Sander Santiago. To secure the biggest prizes at the Colorado Amateur Street Sports Tour, Thomas Jefferson will do almost anything, even marrying his best friend and crush—Arturo "Uno" Ortiz. (978-1-63679-489-1)

Letters from Sarah by Joy Argento. A simple mistake brought them together, but Sarah must release past love to create a future with Lindsey she never dreamed possible. (978-1-63679-509-6)

Lost in the Wild by Kadyan. When their plane crash-lands, Allison and Mike face hunger, cold, a terrifying encounter with a bear, and feelings for each other neither expects. (978-1-63679-545-4)

Not Just Friends by Jordan Meadows. A tragedy leaves Jen struggling to figure out who she is and what is important to her. (978-1-63679-517-1)

Of Auras and Shadows by Jennifer Karter. Eryn and Rina's unexpected love may be exactly what the Community needs to heal the rot that comes not from the fetid Dark Lands that surround the Community but from within. (978-1-63679-541-6)

The Secret Duchess by Jane Walsh. A determined widow defies a duke and falls in love with a fashionable spinster in a fight for her rightful home. (978-1-63679-519-5)

Winter's Spell by Ursula Klein. When former college roommates reunite at a wedding in Provincetown, sparks fly, but can they find true love when evil sirens and trickster mermaids get in the way? (978-1-63679-503-4)

Coasting and Crashing by Ana Hartnett Reichardt. Life comes easy to Emma Wilson until Lake Palmer shows up at Alder University and derails her every plan. (978-1-63679-511-9)

Every Beat of Her Heart by KC Richardson. Piper and Gillian have their own fears about falling in love, but will they be able to overcome those feelings once they learn each other's secrets? (978-1-63679-515-7)

Grave Consequences by Sandra Barret. A decade after necromancy became licensed and legalized, can Tamar and Maddy overcome the lingering prejudice against their kind and their growing attraction to each other to uncover a plot that threatens both their lives? (978-1-63679-467-9)

Haunted by Myth by Barbara Ann Wright. When ghost-hunter Chloe seeks an answer to the current spectral epidemic, all clues point to one very famous face: Helen of Troy, whose motives are more complicated than history suggests and whose charms few can resist. (978-1-63679-461-7)

Invisible by Anna Larner. When medical school dropout Phoebe Frink falls for the shy costume shop assistant Violet Unwin, everything about their love feels certain, but can the same be said about their future? (978-1-63679-469-3)

Like They Do in the Movies by Nan Campbell. Celebrity gossip writer Fran Underhill becomes Chelsea Cartwright's personal assistant with the aim of taking the popular actress down, but neither of them anticipates the clash of their attraction. (978-1-63679-525-6)

Limelight by Gun Brooke. Liberty Bell and Palmer Elliston loathe each other. They clash every week on the hottest new TV show, until Liberty starts to sing and the impossible happens. (978-1-63679-192-0)

Playing with Matches by Georgia Beers. To help save Cori's store and help Liz survive her ex's wedding they strike a deal: a fake relationship, but just for one week. There's no way this will turn into the real deal. (978-1-63679-507-2)

The Memories of Marlie Rose by Morgan Lee Miller. Broadway legend Marlie Rose undergoes a procedure to erase all of her unwanted memories, but as she starts regretting her decision, she discovers that the only person who could help is the love she's trying to forget. (978-1-63679-347-4)

The Murders at Sugar Mill Farm by Ronica Black. A serial killer is on the loose in southern Louisiana and it's up to three women to solve the case while carefully dancing around feelings for each other. (978-1-63679-455-6)

Fire in the Sky by Radclyffe and Julie Cannon. Two women from different worlds have nothing in common and every reason to wish they'd never met—except for the attraction neither can deny. (978-1-63679-573-7)

A Talent Ignited by Suzanne Lenoir. When Evelyne is abducted and Annika believes she has been abandoned, they must risk everything to find each other again. (978-1-63679-483-9)

An Atlas to Forever by Krystina Rivers. Can Atlas, a difficult dog Ellie inherits after the death of her best friend, help the busy hopeless romantic find forever love with commitment-phobic animal behaviorist Hayden Brandt? (978-1-63679-451-8)

Bait and Witch by Clifford Mae Henderson. When Zeddi gets an unexpected inheritance from her client Mags, she discovers that Mags served as high priestess to a dwindling coven of old witches—who are positive that Mags was murdered. Zeddi owes it to her to uncover the truth. (978-1-63679-535-5)

Buried Secrets by Sheri Lewis Wohl. Tuesday and Addie, along with Tuesday's dog, Tripper, struggle to solve a twenty-five-year-old mystery while searching for love and redemption along the way. (978-1-63679-396-2)

Come Find Me in the Midnight Sun by Bailey Bridgewater. In Alaska, disappearing is the easy part. When two men go missing, state trooper Louisa Linebach must solve the case, and when she thinks she's coming close, she's wrong. (978-1-63679-566-9)

Death on the Water by CJ Birch. The Ocean Summit's authorities have ruled a death on board its inaugural cruise as a suicide, but Claire suspects murder and with the help of Assistant Cruise Director Moira, Claire conducts her own investigation. (978-1-63679-497-6)

Living For You by Jenny Frame. Can Sera Debrek face real and personal demons to help save the world from darkness and open her heart to love? (978-1-63679-491-4)

Mississippi River Mischief by Greg Herren. When a politician turns up dead and Scotty's client is the most obvious suspect, Scotty and his friends set out to prove his client's innocence. (978-1-63679-353-5)

Ride with Me by Jenna Jarvis. When Lucy's vacation to find herself becomes Emma's chance to remember herself, they realize that everything they're looking for might already be sitting right next to them—if they're willing to reach for it. (978-1-63679-499-0)

Whiskey and Wine by Kelly and Tana Fireside. Winemaker Tessa Williams and sex toy shop owner Lace Reynolds are both used to taking risks, but will they be willing to put their friendship on the line if it gives them a shot at finding forever love? (978-1-63679-531-7)

Hands of the Morri by Heather K O'Malley. Discovering she is a Lost Sister and growing acquainted with her new body, Asche learns how to be a warrior and commune with the Goddess the Hands serve, the Morri. (978-1-63679-465-5)

I Know About You by Erin Kaste. With her stalker inching closer to the truth, Cary Smith is forced to face the past she's tried desperately to forget. (978-1-63679-513-3)

Mate of Her Own by Elena Abbott. When Heather McKenna finally confronts the family who cursed her, her werewolf is shocked to discover her one true mate, and that's only the beginning. (978-1-63679-481-5)

Pumpkin Spice by Tagan Shepard. For Nicki, new love is making this pumpkin spice season sweeter than expected. (978-1-63679-388-7)

Rivals for Love by Ali Vali. Brooks Boseman's brother Curtis is getting married, and Brooks needs to be at the engagement party. Only she can't possibly go, not with Curtis set to marry the secret love of her youth, Fallon Goodwin. (978-1-63679-384-9)

Sweat Equity by Aurora Rey. When cheesemaker Sy Travino takes a job in rural Vermont and hires contractor Maddie Barrow to rehab a house she buys sight unseen, they both wind up with a lot more than they bargained for. (978-1-63679-487-7)

Taking the Plunge by Amanda Radley. When Regina Avery meets model Grace Holland—the most beautiful woman she's ever seen—she doesn't have a clue how to flirt, date, or hold on to a relationship. But Regina must take the plunge with Grace and hope she manages to swim. (978-1-63679-400-6)

We Met in a Bar by Claire Forsythe. Wealthy nightclub owner Erica turns undercover bartender on a mission to catch a thief where she meets no-strings, no-commitments Charlie, who couldn't be further from Erica's type. Right? (978-1-63679-521-8)

Western Blue by Suzie Clarke. Step back in time to this historic western filled with heroism, loyalty, friendship, and love. The odds are against this unlikely group—but never underestimate women who have nothing to lose. (978-1-63679-095-4)

Windswept by Patricia Evans. The windswept shores of the Scottish Highlands weave magic for two people convinced they'd never fall in love again. (978-1-63679-382-5)